Nica of the New Yorks

SUE PERRY

DEDICATION

For Deborah

CONTENTS

ACKNOWLEDGMENTS

I appreciate everyone who ever liked my writing, and many people who didn't—you've all compelled me to keep going.

Some members of the former group have helped me enormously in the development of Nica of the New Yorks: early reads, wise comments, inquiries (repeated) about when I'd have book 2 ready. I often wondered that myself.

I'd especially like to thank Christina McMullen, Julie Robitaille, Rebecca Stahl, Deborah Schneider, Louise G. White. Ma'Urth is a better Frame for your being in it.

Cover photos and collage by Sue Perry.

0. THUNDER BUILDING A STORM

Tonight marked the end of life as we know it, though few of us understood at the time. Tonight, Maelstrom got free.

The first explosion boomed from the northwest, way behind me, maybe back on the Columbia campus. I didn't remember jumping at the noise, but here I was jogging atop the seats of benches. I was already skittish before the blast startled me—I knew I had no business crossing Central Park alone after sunset, but I needed a run and had persuaded myself I could outpace trouble. I hopped back to the path, sheepish but unobserved—all attention was on the park's perimeters, where glorious fall foliage lined the cobalt horizon. Fall. I'd been in New York more than two months—had moved here to fight Maelstrom—and at the moment, my effort felt pretty much for frigging naught.

Another explosion bleached the sky, this time east of the park. Then north. Then south. Then west. Then west again. People called the blasts simultaneous, but actually they spanned about fifteen minutes. Simultaneous would have been easier to handle.

As I curved back into the city, I heard more echoes of blasts, near and distant, all over the island. With each boom, the air grew further pressurized, as though thunder was building a storm. South of Columbus Circle, the air pulsed in a series of rapid blasts, punctuated with the deep screams of grown men. Suddenly the building's top floor, under reconstruction, was in flames—and from the sounds of it, several workers were caught on the burning floor. I swerved to get out of the way of men, clinging and swinging on the scaffolding, becoming acrobats to reach the ground faster than was safe to move. But of course safe is relative.

By the time the last of them were down, the flames were out. The men began bickering about whose carelessness had caused the explosion—debate that terminated when a construction site across the street exploded in similar flames. I didn't have to see more; already, I could have told them that this was happening at remodeling sites around the city, to free Maelstrom, a being of legendary power and evil who had long been imprisoned.

I knew the exact moment when Maelstrom got free. The air pressure built and built, then with one more explosion, *pffft*, the pressure was gone. I was surprised when my next breath took in oxygen, because the air felt so empty. The explosions had made the ground rumble but now it settled with a groan just below detectible hearing, like the planet had expired.

I resumed running to flee feelings of impotence, failure. Maelstrom 's freedom was inevitable, that's why the allies focused on preparations for the warfare that would follow, as he moved to consolidate power and rule the Frames. We allies couldn't match the military forces of Maelstrom, but we had to prevail. Sure, Maelstrom and his minions, Warty Sebaceous Cysts, had the advantage. But history is full of the vanquishing of big strong bad guys. And not just in my Frame, as it turns out.

My two months working for the allies in New York were not pointless, as they felt at the moment of Maelstrom's escape. They were essential to the long–term goal: Maelstrom might not be contained but he had to be stopped. I gave myself this pep talk but tonight it didn't penetrate. I'd been much more confident about fighting Maelstrom when I was back in Los Angeles last summer, trying to explain the allies and the Frames to Jenn.

1. DON'T INVITE PSYCHOANALYSIS

When your best friend since third grade thinks you're crazy, it gives you pause. I was confident that I was sane, but if I told Jenn how I'd spent my summer while she was away, she'd be crazy not to think I was. Crazy.

Correction. Not *if* I told her, *when* I told her. Jenn had been back in Los Angeles for two weeks and every day that I avoided telling her about my case, she got more distant. I had to tell her the truth, but whoever said honesty was the best policy didn't have to explain detective work in other dimensions or sentient lawn chairs.

I confess, my experiences sounded crazy to me, too, now that I was cut off, back in my own Frame, awaiting word about what my next move should be. I was already fighting fear that the word would never come—that my engagement in the Frames was over. I didn't need to add *maybe I'm nuts* to my list of things to never think about.

Jenn and I were having a last night together before she left town again, on another quest to improve her health through spiritual retreat. Two years ago, Jenn was diagnosed with multiple sclerosis, and the doctors have been surprised at how rapidly hers has progressed. Never surprise your doctors.

She was draped across the futon in my office, her back to me at my desk. She was in the middle of a daily ritual: install a free phone app, try it, decree "Loser," delete it. Meanwhile, I watched the skylight for clouds that held messages, and checked internet travel deals to see if any resonated. Nope. None of the deals made me think *yes, that is where I'm supposed to go next, to fight Maelstrom and reconnect with Anya and Annyl.*

When I closed the travel web site, Jenn didn't look up from her phone. "Loser," she murmured and made a few clicks.

If I had any interest in women, Jenn would be my main event. I love her luminescent skin and her eyes that are green enough to be cat–worthy. She has a well–formed opinion for every occasion. Also, she can out–curse a rapper.

But she hadn't cursed all evening, not even a measly *damn*. That's how uncomfortable I'd made her with my refusal to tell her about my detective work. I couldn't let her leave town with our friendship in this state.

She looked up again. "What's with the snort?"

"I was picturing you in a t–shirt that says 'Some of my best friends are crazy', one of those lame shirts with an arrow pointing to me."

She lowered her phone, I shut my laptop.

I started before I could change my mind. "As you know, while you were at your latest retreat, I became a private detective and, amazingly, I got clients. I was busy the whole time you were gone."

"I'm happy for you. You've been searching for a new direction. Do you think this is it?" Formal and polite. Not good.

"Yes, I believe it is." I withheld my doubts about when/if/whether my case would resume. "I haven't been comfortable talking about my work and as I've been all too aware, that makes you unhappy."

Jenn tapped fingers against lips in a fake yawn. *Get on with it.*

"Everything I'm about to tell you is confidential." This got full attention, as I knew it would. "My information will sound bogus and I can't prove it right now but I will—at some point." She frowned, perhaps reacting to my uncertainty. But she also curled her feet under her. Listening.

"My clients are other beings—people, maybe, humanoids, definitely. Never mind about that, it's a detail. My clients are named Anya and Anwyl, and they're not from this world. I wish you could meet them. She is—she's like a living sunrise. He is—scary, but in a good way."

"They're not from this world. Your clients are aliens."

"Not like spaceships and death rays. They're from another Frame, which as near as I can figure is another dimension. It turns out there are Frames all around us in all directions, with all kinds of life, all living simultaneously."

"Fascinating! How do we go to a new Frame? I want to see one."

I tilted my chair to look out the skylight. "I don't know how to go by myself. My clients would take me. We would walk through a tunnel between Frames called a Connector. Or they would just take my hand and bring me with them. They are beings of great power so they can do that."

"What's going on in all those other Frames? Magic? Space colonies?"

"Just—beings, living their lives. About half the beings know they're in Frames, the others are like us, in Neutral Frames. Neutrals don't know about other Frames, with a few exceptions."

"You're one of the exceptions. And now I am, too. We're special."

I could hardly begrudge her sarcasm. "Some of the Frames look like ours, but they're not like ours. And stuff can turn out to be alive. This building, for example, is sentient. Her name is Henrietta and she held the door shut one time when it was dangerous for me to enter."

"Someone else might think the door was stuck. I didn't know you had a cat."

I followed Jenn's gaze and saw the reason for her *non—sequitur.* Dizzy, the building's formerly stray cat, strolled in from my waiting room. "That's Dizzy. She lives here when she's in this Frame. I haven't seen her for days. She's probably been Traveling in other Frames."

Jenn made a noise like I cut her off on the freeway. "I'm not laughing."

"I'm not kidding. That cat saved my life once in another Frame."

Jenn sliced a finger across her throat. No more about the cat.

Maybe I should have stopped. But then Jenn was certain to conclude I had made up a ridiculous story to exclude her from my case. "Another thing about the Frames is that the Watts Towers are sentient. Anyway, the two tallest ones are. They're sentient and animate—they move around. They talk. They have rad powers, actually. One of them disappeared, though, on an espionage mission, and we think he's hurt."

"He disappeared? Nobody noticed that a ten—story tower disappeared?"

"The Neutral version of him didn't disappear in our Frame. Beings like the Watts Towers, who are not animate and sentient in every Frame, have different versions of themselves in different Frames. I'm not clear on how that works."

"Interesting that your favorite folk art sculpture would be so powerful and special. And a spy, too."

Talking about the Frames had energized me, but this snagged my balloon on a power line. "Of course you don't believe me yet, it would be weird if you just accepted all this. I'll skip a lot of the details, they'd take longer than we've got."

"You mean there's more? Can we order pizza first?"

She made the call, then I went out to fetch our pies from the pizza joint across the street. Dizzy walked ahead of me down the hall. I squeezed my eyes a couple times to clear them. Too much time on the internet, my vision was blurry. The threadbare paisley rug was bleeding into Dizzy's gray and white fur.

Correction. I could see the rug through the cat. Dizzy was becoming transparent. The cat did a gradual fade out and right before she vanished, flicked her tail. I felt honored—never before had Dizzy allowed me to see her change Frames. But why couldn't she do that in front of Jenn? That would have cut through Jenn's disbelief. Not for the first time, I had to wonder how much conversation the cat understood.

Every meal is Christmas morning for Jenn. While she compared pizza slices, I resumed my spiel, occasionally waving my slice of jalapeño with green olives.

"My clients, Anya and Anwyl, introduced me to the Frames. They have a prophecy that says I could help them. They're leading an effort to save the Frames."

"From evil, I assume." Jenn crammed pizza into her mouth but I caught the snicker and was grateful for its modesty. Situation reversed, I'd be at the guffaw stage. She chewed, she swallowed, her tone got serious. "Just a few months ago, you were feeling lost and pointless after Ick died. Now here you are with a new career and a job to save the universe."

Jenn knew, better than anybody, how rough it had been after the death of my fourth husband—she pulled me out of that tailspin. But still. "Thank you, Dr. Shrink. Please don't psychoanalyze me."

"Don't invite psychoanalysis."

She ate pizza. I played with my food.

Jenn broke first. "I'm sorry," she said, "tell me the rest."

"The rest won't be easier to believe. There's this super evil being named Maelstrom, who's in prison, but wants to rule the universe like he did once before. We—Anya, Anwyl, the Watts Towers, all the allies including me—have to stop him."

"He can rule the universe from prison?"

"His henchmen are working to free him. There are three henchmen, they're called Warty Sebaceous Cysts, and they act like morons but they're cunning and cruel." Thinking about the Cysts iced my heart. They acted goofy while they orchestrated genocide, then hunted and murdered witnesses; while they ransacked my thoughts, then told their flying chainsaws to finish me off. I'd be dead if it weren't for a sentient volcano, who –

"Did you say 'warty sebaceous cysts'? Like the lumps on Sadie's stomach?" Sadie was Jenn's dear departed mutt.

"That's not the real name, that's just as close as I can get to saying it—a lot of the names are in languages I can't pronounce."

"Of course they are. Languages of other Frames."

"Someday I'll be able to prove this to you. But I can't right now, because we took Warty Sebaceous Cysts to court and we lost. The court is a special tribunal called the Framekeeps. The Framekeeps forbade Anya and Anwyl from associating with me because I'm a Neutral. But they said 'stay away from Nica of Los Angeles' so that gives us a loophole. I'm going to move, and then I won't be Nica of Los Angeles, I'll be Nica of Somewhere Else, and I can get back on the case."

"You're moving! Where? When?"

I dropped into a chair, refused to slump. "I don't know. Anya said 'you will know' but I don't—yet. I'm. Expecting to get that information. Any time now."

Jenn folded her plate and wiped her hands. Her staccato movements told me her attitude was unchanged. What had I expected? Not to be believed, certainly, but that she would see my sincerity, see that I believed, and wonder.

Jenn pulled her hair at right angles to her ears, her gesture of utmost frustration. Her hair was garnet underneath, burgundy where the sun kissed it. People think she dyes her hair because the colors are so rich. But there is nothing artificial about Jenn. "I thought you were going to talk straight." Her voice lost decibels. "I didn't know you were moving." She held out her pizza debris for me to dispose of. "Are you writing a screenplay, bitch? I know I make fun of wanna–bes but I wouldn't make fun of you. Hardly at all. You know that, right?"

"Of course I know that. I did tell you straight, and I –"

"I need to talk about something else."

And so we did, and although hearing about the Frames annoyed her, our friendship was back on track, thanks to the prospect of separation for an unknown length of time.

I considered driving her out to meet Hernandez, who had shared many of my Frames adventures. But he was in such a funk lately, I wasn't sure how that meeting would go.

Maybe he'd act like a veteran with delayed P.T.S.D. Maybe that's what he was. Maybe all those tours in war zones had finally nailed him. Maybe the signs were there already: educated, skilled man working as a custodian, after all. Which made me feel disloyal to Hernandez.

Another explanation for my summer adventures was psychotic break. Which made me feel disloyal to myself.

No. Things happened like I said. That had to be the reality. I'm not a masochist. I wouldn't hallucinate the Frames then exclude myself from them.

2. NEW YORK FOOL

When I first detected that New York was my relocation destination, I ignored the evidence. I love New York but I've been there often. I wanted unknown and exotic. *Nica of Shanghai* sounded about right. But no one consulted me. Instead, my travel services emailed alerts about fabulously low airfares one way to New York. Every day there's a deal going somewhere, I sniffed. When I stopped for coffee, the sound system blasted Laura Nyro—*New York Tendaberry*. I hadn't heard that for decades. Leaving the coffee joint, I took a short cut through a parking lot and every car had a New York license plate. This was all before lunch. Come afternoon, the homeless guy who asked for change had a Brooklyn accent; public radio launched a series on vintage jazz, live from the Blue Note; and the top news story was the bomb scare near Wall Street.

When I went to toss trash in the dumpster behind my building, the cinderblock wall grabbed my attention. Hummingbirds are my favorite bird and someone had spray–painted two giant lime green hummers in confrontation mode: beaks down, chests arched, wings back. I once had a yard with a faux honeysuckle and the hummers spent all day around it—seconds eating and hours confronting others who tried to eat. This drawing captured the essence, which had to be awfully hard to do with spray paint. Was this graffiti new? Surely I would have noticed it before. Then I discovered the lime green writing that gleamed atop older, basic black graffiti. I dropped my garbage bag, moved closer. The inscription smeared when I touched it. NEW YORK FOOL the blocky graffiti shouted. Tagger's signature or talking to me?

I needed to find Hernandez. He was the only Neutral who'd shared the Frames with me and we'd spent many hours speculating about where I would be called to go next. Hernandez was due to start his custodial shift in my building, so I jogged to the parking garage to intercept him.

"It's New York," I yelled as Hernandez pulled his battered red pickup into a parking space.

"How long before you leave?" He slammed the truck door then patted it apologetically. He had not yet adjusted to the revelation that his truck was sentient.

"A week at most, I figure."

"No time to waste." He unlocked the custodial closet without looking at me. His daughters recently left for Spain to live with their mother, and people leaving him was an issue. In fact, from the moment his girls took off, he kept himself crazy busy, with a second custodial gig and hours of daily driving around southern California, doing reconnaissance for Anya and Anwyl.

I trailed after Hernandez as he pushed the custodial cart into the elevator. He set to work as though I weren't there. I'm not into forcing friends to talk with me, so we did the *adieu* thing and I went to find the Henrietta's building manager.

The building manager gets a gleam in his eye around me, because he has been led to believe that I'm doing police work and he lo—o—oves police work. I informed him that my case would take me to New York for an unknown stretch of time. I paid four months rent in advance and—jackpot!—he offered to set me up with a rental in the owner's property in Manhattan.

I wanted to tell Hernandez but his truck was gone—he must have cut his shift short. I looked for Dizzy, but hadn't seen her since the night she vanished in the hall. I felt so disconnected from my life in L.A., I might as well already be gone.

What with my scrambling to get out of town and his overbooked schedule, I didn't see Hernandez again before I headed for New York. Our last contact was an empty text exchange.

:: At airport, boarding soon. Keep me posted on yr recon work.

:: Safe flight! Will do.

With that, I added Hernandez to the growing list of loved ones I didn't know when I would see again.

3. ONLY CROSS AT RED LIGHTS

I couldn't remember the last time I'd felt lonely, but I spent the first couple weeks in New York fighting a creeping nostalgia. Everything reminded me of something. Somebody. The absent and the dead. And I was irritable, as irritable as my second father–in–law's bowel syndrome. Here I *was*, already—*moved*, already—but nothing had changed. I was still excluded from all things Framesian. For all I knew, Maelstrom and the Cysts might be vanquished by now, without my involvement.

When I wasn't sulking, I did believe that Anya and Anwyl would fetch me when it was time. I was unsure what to do with myself until then. I had developed confidence in my private eye abilities—I rarely turned to fictional detectives for advice nowadays. I could open up shop as a private detective, but hadn't decided how to attract clients and hated to leave a case unfinished if—correction, when— Anya and Anwyl appeared.

My new abode was on the Upper West Side, just shy of Columbia University, in an as–is brownstone with a name etched over the front stoop: *The Julian*. Call it lovingly unrestored. The Julian had decayed with dignity intact. The front stairs, jagged with missing concrete chunks, rose to a magnificent lead crystal door that shimmered softly, day or night. The inner foyer was scuffed by so many feet that the parquet grain was plaid. Two lean mahogany staircases led to five stories of narrow apartments on separate, locked halls. Mine was second floor, west half. In the main room, floor to ceiling windows gave plenty of light to examine the peeling pastiche of wallpapers. I loved my apartment from the moment I stepped inside, sharing space with so many generations of tenants.

And I loved roaming outside. At night, I killed hours and energy on zigzag walks during which I thought of nothing but the color of the next traffic light. My initial rule was *keep moving* so I crossed streets going whichever direction was green. Then Manhattan's pedestrian anarchy overtook me: lights don't matter. You cross the street if there is a lull in traffic, or if you suspect that oncoming driver is a wimp who will brake for you. With this realization, my rule became *only cross at red lights*. To follow that rule I had to pay attention, whatever the hour, which made brooding impossible.

Each day, to become familiar with my new stomping ground, I rode a different subway line to its farthest terminus, then tracked back by a combination of walking and station–hopping. The regime gave me purpose; and reason to spend time on the subway.

I glanced out today's train window and an express train with film–strip windows flashed by. The train paced mine briefly and in each window was a still life of unknown souls, then the windows shot ahead—and down! Did that train go down or did my train go up? How many levels were there in this underground universe?

Was it any wonder I loved the subway? It was as close to Frame Travel as I would get for now.

On one day's exploration, I passed a bookstore and my first impulse was to run. In other Frames, I'd witnessed books as mercenary soldiers who flew upside down, shedding razor–edged text that cut through anything—or anyone.

This was my first bookstore visit since discovering the violent lives of books in other Frames, and I was relieved that being surrounded by books felt every bit as cozy, restorative, and enticing as it ever had. Books could not be inherently evil, their natures must have somehow been twisted. So far, this was the only way that my Frame seemed superior to other Frames: here, we appreciated the true nature of books.

The bookstore clerk flirted, "I bet you're a California girl. You've got a real even tan."

"Okay," I said and escaped to the back aisles. I was overdue to dye my hair.

I knew, because encounters like this were on the rise. My natural hair shade is beach bunny blonde. That—coupled with my skin's tendency to tan after the briefest sun exposure—is the bane of my existence. Yes, I would be a better person—stronger, healthier, *yada yada*—if I accepted my looks. But I barely made it to sweet 16 before I grew terminally sick of guys hitting on me because they suffered from blonde fetish. And so I dye my hair. When I was a teen, I went for a mottled print that suggested leopard skin. I have also enjoyed nuclear yellow hair, which makes me feel like a *Marvel* heroine. Nowadays I'm mostly a chestnut brunette, which keeps moron encounters to a minimum.

The bookstore had a display of best sellers, including *Lose Twenty Pounds of Worry in Twenty Days*. Self–help hogwash that would never have come into my life, had Jenn not bought me a copy. In another Frame, a copy of *Lose Twenty Pounds* had died at my inadvertent command. As a memorial, I would buy a copy of *Lose Twenty Pounds*.

The clerk lost his flirty smile when I set my purchase on the counter. With a sucked–a–lemon look, he rang me up quickly. Interesting that *Lose Twenty Pounds* could be a bestseller yet sound a dork alert. Maybe I should carry a copy at all times—think of the blonde trouble that would avoid.

I was kidding but within a block I felt an urge—a necessity—to return to the bookstore. I fought the feeling for another block then went back and bought the stock of *Lose Twenty Pounds*—four more hardcovers, two paperbacks. It made no sense but I had to. Maybe this was a sign from beyond my Frame.

4. I'M YOUR MUSICIAN

Or maybe it was a pointless whim. I spent the next several days interpreting all manner of pointless whims as messages from other Frames. Meanwhile, I traversed a different subway line each day, which helped me calculate how long I'd been waiting here for Anya and Anwyl to reconnect.

On my eleventh day, I just missed a train at Columbus Circle station. *Next train arrives in 9 minutes*, the message board assured me.

The train and its racket receded and that was when I heard it. Him. The slide guitarist, set up at the far end of the platform. He looked like a retired biker, with a shaved head and an anarchist's beard and thick coarse worn garments suitable for long trips on rough roads. He played a blues that was as beautiful as it was mournful. It took me back to the unparalleled glorious sunset on the day that Ick died.

Next train in 4 minutes. Next train in 10 minutes. Next train in 13 minutes. It was impossible for me to leave that music. The longer I listened, the deeper it reached. It dragged my yearning and frustration to the surface, then shouldered them with me, then took them from me in a gentle catharsis.

I sat on a bench, close enough to read the script in cracked lime green paint on the open guitar case: *Kelly Joe.* I only had a twenty–dollar bill so I dropped it in the case. If I'd only had a fifty I would have dropped that in. "I thank you for your kindness," Kelly Joe murmured without looking up from his strings. I bet he needed to concentrate. I play a lot of instruments a little bit, which was enough to recognize how difficult that passage was. He made it look as effortless as a pelican skimming waves.

While he played, one leg tapped an erratic beat. He didn't sing but he hummed in a resonant baritone. Intricate drawings covered his forearms—tattoos that seemed to animate as he played.

The next two days, I chose subway lines that went through Columbus Circle station and was thrilled to find him playing in the same spot. The day after that, he wasn't there and I spent most of the day checking back for him, in vain. I found him on the following day and I stayed for hours.

I wasn't the only one who spent excess time in Columbus Circle station to hear to him play. Among the regulars was a young woman, Manhattan trim and savvy, who listened with tears flooding her cheeks. To give her privacy, I watched Kelly Joe's hands glide over the frets. I was frustrated at my powers of observation, or lack thereof, because his tattoos looked different than I remembered them. Today there were totem animals that I hadn't noticed before. When I looked up, I must have frowned and the young woman must have thought the frown was for her. She shoved the heels of her hands across her face to dry her tears.

I reached a hand toward her, yanked it back. Not cool to touch a stranger. "Sometimes crying is all we can do," I said. Which set her to bawling again. A train came, she moved to board it. "See you tomorrow," I called, and when she braced herself to clutch a pole in the packed train car, she showed just a hint of smile.

Right when I said 'See you', Kelly Joe's music paused then shifted melodies. As the train pulled that teary face away, the music spread through my bloodstream, changed my pulse. By the time the train disappeared into the tunnel, I relived every leave–taking that ever mattered to me. They no longer made me sad. I felt their inevitability, sensed our lives flowing in currents now parallel, now merged, now divergent.

I moved closer to Kelly Joe. As always, the grace and strength in his hands entranced me. I wanted him to never stop playing.

I grabbed his wrist and stopped him. "Hey!" I said. Among his forearm tattoos was a lime green hummingbird in confrontation mode. No way had I missed this tattoo previously. It had not been on his arm until now. "What the hell! What is this?"

He got very still but did not pull away. He murmured, "My messages," which, I later learned, is what he calls his tattoos. He means messages *to*, not *from*, him.

He looked up from his frets. I saw his eyes and dropped his wrist. "Who are you?" I whispered. His eyes were a deep shifting blend of grays and blues like unpolished silver. Like Anya's eyes. They looked at me, into me, beyond me. He gathered the change people had tossed in his case, packed his guitar, and stood.

"I'm your musician," he replied. "Tomorrow your lessons begin. Have an enlightened evening, Nica."

A train arrived and commuters flowed around Kelly Joe, the only one not in a hurry. He tucked his earnings into the clenched hands of an old man, sleeping or passed out below the escalator. Then the rush–hour crowd absorbed them.

5. TATTOO ON MY HEART

On that same day, I met the cat, Leon. Stray cats are a fixture back home in Los Angeles and in many cities I've visited, but I'd never seen one in New York. Or maybe I did but mistook it for a smaller–than–average rat. The cat sat on the stoop of my building. He was an orange tabby with long fur or short dreads. He looked like he had rolled in glue. I sat at the other end of the steps, hoping to make friends with him. As soon as I sat, he jumped down to the sidewalk. He was small for a pony but the largest cat I had ever seen, and a graceful jumper, floating from the stoop to the sidewalk with a ripple of spine. Below me, he rolled on the cement. His fur was so matted that when he rose, his coat had sprouted cigarette butts.

His thinking was equally unkempt. When a big dog went by on its evening walk, the cat held his ground. However, when I stepped to the door—away from him—the cat fled.

Inside my apartment, I allowed myself one comprehensive recollection of my encounter with Kelly Joe, my musician. At last things were moving in a promising direction! However, with nothing but time on my hands, it was too easy to wander too far inside my own head, so after the single recollection I washed my face at the bathroom sink. I stared into the mirror, pondering which subway route to—gak! A face appeared behind my shoulder in the mirror.

Outside the bathroom window, the unkempt cat clung to the fire escape railing in a balancing act better suited to a bird.

All that evening, the cat wouldn't come inside and he wouldn't go away. He was on the stoop when I went out to get some dinner, across the street from the pharmacy as I shopped, and back at the window when I prepped for bed. My bathroom window has bars so I was comfortable keeping it open that night as an invitation to him.

By morning, the cat was perched on my chair. I shut the window and corralled him in the bathroom, where he pinged like a tennis ball on the space station. I stayed with him until he accepted or forgot he was trapped, and meanwhile read all seven languages' instructions for the hair clippers I bought at the pharmacy. While he watched, I clipped myself first, converting tresses to dense velvety fuzz. I hadn't had a clip for years and the liberation was immediate. I petted my head and sighed.

"It feels great, you'll be glad you did it. Think of the savings in furballs!" I held him in the sink and he didn't resist near as much as I expected. He so needed to be touched, he didn't care what I did to him. I'd known times like that and perhaps he felt my sympathy.

After I clipped the cat, I opened the window. He shot out like horizontal lightning, but then stopped on the fire escape and watched me bag his nasty clumps of fur. I went out for breakfast brew and by the time I returned, he was asleep across the back of my couch.

Without fur, he was nothing but bones. And scars, which looked like knife cuts. Across his skull was a jagged homemade tattoo that said *Leo*, with an o like a diamond. It was probably his name—he had the long nose, hint of crossed eyes, and lion markings if you squinted while drunk, which his mutilator probably had been. But in case *Leo* was his mutilator, I dubbed the cat *Leon*. "Why did you let anybody do that to you, Leon? What are you, part dog?" I knew the answer. He was too sweet to fight. A terrible trait for a street cat, whatever your size. I scritched his head and he broke into a purr that rumbled the dishes and made me nostalgic for earthquakes, confirming my homesickness.

From that instant, I had a *Leon* tattoo on my heart. He kept falling over while I petted him, because he would lean into my hand with such gusto that he lost balance. I hadn't laughed like this in weeks. Hell, this was the longest I'd spent with another being in weeks. Lesson there. I moved to New York because I was so eager to be part of something special with Anya and Anwyl; instead, here I was, cut off and alone.

Could I trust Leon? Monk and Miles, the Watts Towers, once told me that it was okay to love Dizzy, but that I shouldn't trust her because cats have only their own side. What were the odds that two cats in a row would have a side that aligned with us, the allies, against Warty Sebaceous Cysts and Maelstrom? If Leon was trustworthy did that increase the chances that Dizzy wasn't? Did you ever notice that male cats seem less bright than female cats? Maybe it's because they are more easy–going, which means –

Nica! Focus! I was late getting out the door for today's subway line. Although I was reassured to catch myself digressing. First time in ages. I really hadn't been myself lately.

Self–knowledge gained. I liked being alone when in my city of birth with loved ones nearish–by. Being alone across the continent made for a whole other shebang, and only felt okay now that I knew Kelly Joe and Leon. Momentarily this made me feel weak, but needing loved ones nearish wasn't a trait that I could change, so I acknowledged it and moved along.

6. A PLACE OF GREAT POWER

My plan was to take the number 7 train under the East River into Queens. I got to Grand Central then kept walking. I didn't like using either mega–station, Times Square or Grand Central. Going inside was like entering scenes from before I was born.

"Good morning, Nica." I recognized Kelly Joe's baritone and spun around. He was right behind me.

"Hey." I suffered a sudden loss of conviction. Maybe he wasn't a tutor from the Frames, maybe he was some weird street busker that I had just made a date with. Except how did he know my name or where to find me? Well, if he were a weird enough street busker he could.

I got a grip. After all, I wore Anya's lanyard across my torso, hidden under my clothes. The lanyard signaled me when I was in danger and it never let out a peep around Kelly Joe, although it had been driving me nuts since I arrived in New York, with prickling warnings of no consequence. Just this morning, it gave a jolt of pain because I was about to step in a puddle.

Kelly Joe stood motionless while I worked through all this. We were close to Grand Central so the sidewalks were crowded and people flowed around us. He studied my head.

"I cut my hair off," I acknowledged.

"You did. It suits you both ways."

I wanted to know a lot more about him. He didn't talk or act like a Frame Traveler. Except for playing music of unearthly soul. And, p.s., having tattoos that changed.

"We should get started. Anya gave me a list of ways you need to be trained," he said.

Anya. Hearing her name come out of someone else's mouth. If hope is a brain scan, mine just spiked after a lengthy flatline.

"An –"

He rested a finger on his lips. "We won't mention her again," he said.

Which left me with so many questions I had a logjam between brain and mouth. Why not? Was she in danger? Were we? From the Framekeeps? From Warty Sebaceous Cysts? How did he know Anya, anyway? To passersby it may have seemed like I was sharing my guppy impersonation. I hoped Kelly Joe wasn't someone who put much stock in first impressions.

"It's a fine morning for a walk," he noted.

I shut my mouth and joined him heading east, across Lexington Avenue and away from Grand Central. It was indeed a fine morning for a walk. Sun warmed the air but did not yet bake the sidewalks. Commuters had commuted, so traffic noise was no longer continuous. All around us, pedestrians whistled for taxis, placed orders at food stands, barked instructions into cell phones. Hell–bent bicyclists swerved at the last minute and yelled like a collision would be your fault. It must be Kelly Joe's presence that made my sensations so acute.

Or it was just New York. Dirty loud crowded vibrant alive. On the streets there, I was isolated and part of a whole. I could not comprehend the variety of lives around me but felt they were people much like me.

Kelly Joe held out his hand. "Will you take my hand? I want to show you where you are."

I wanted to push his sleeve up to check his forearm tattoos—did they change all the time? were they changing right now?—but figured I should wait until I knew him at least six minutes. I took his hand instead. His skin was cool and dry despite the humidity, his grip was casually strong, and his clasp distracted me. Those long thin musician's fingers. I stopped thinking about ways to play them when I could no longer hear myself think.

New York is always loud but this was to loud like a supernova is to a cigarette ember. I searched for the source, but the noise came from all directions. This wasn't the New York I knew. Around us, the buildings looked familiar but all signs of people had vanished and vehicles seemed to be grazing on the asphalt, as I had seen them do in Miles and Monk's Frame, Next Vast. This was not my Frame. My musician was a Frame Traveler, powerful enough to take me with him when he shifted Frames.

I was so excited I felt shy. I tried to sound cool and collected, but I stripped my throat yelling above the hubbub, "Did we Travel to Next Vast?"

Kelly Joe leaned close to reply. "Thereabouts." His voice remained soft yet I heard him, or felt the words. With his cool breath on my ear lobe, I wished he'd say more. Instead, he gripped my hand tighter and we Traveled to another Frame where it was quieter, although still much louder than home.

Here the streets were under water and each block's sidewalk bobbed like a dock. Our steps intensified the bobbing and made buildings bump each other. Which was impossible! I had a slew of questions but he touched a finger to his lips.

I sensed rather than heard him say, "When I have questions, I observe more closely until I have answers." Then he chuckled.

"What are you laughing about?" I yelled. *Me*, the answer had to be.

"Anwyl said I'd need time for questions."

"He knows me!" I looked around, taking it all in, grinning. At last I was Traveling again.

As we approached the East River, a disturbing noise grew, like someone cackled while gargling. With each cackling episode, I grew more uneasy.

"That's just the river," Kelly Joe assured me. "Pay it no mind and it will ignore you, as most predators do."

"Okay but why does —" I cut myself off, challenged to prove I could walk one block without questions. "It sure is loud here."

"And in all the New Yorks," he nodded. He Traveled us back to the first Frame we'd visited, the loudest of them all. The noise was like a thousand mix tapes, played simultaneously, backwards. I tried to pick out individual sounds but the harder I tried, the more I got lost in the rush of noise.

"I hear everything but nothing," I complained.

"Soften your attention," he instructed. "Take your focus away from what interests you."

I couldn't get it. He began to hum. I tuned into his baritone and gradually the background noises sharpened and separated. They were voices. Hundreds of voices, near and far. Yet I saw no beings in this Frame.

Eventually, over many visits, I pieced together the situation, no thanks to Kelly Joe, who seemed more willing than Anwyl to tell me stuff, yet—like Anwyl—rarely told me things I could understand.

New York is a place of great power, with a persistent presence through many Frames. Of course it has sentient structures, as all cities do. What is different about New York is that the land itself transmits so much power that it imparts a little bit of sentience to *every* structure, from the Waldorf Astoria to the pretzel cart across the street. The sentience derives from the construction materials, the wood and metal and glass and rock, much of which comes from sentient beings. Every structure is a mixture of sensibilities that, in places of power, becomes a personality. Usually the sensibilities add together and create a modest intellect, occasionally they conflict and induce schizophrenia. Each personality persists through all the New Yorks, that is, all the Frames where the land imparts power. The land's power is strongest in the Frame where we walked now, (whose name sounds to me like) Frivolous Bedlam. The land's power weakens with distance from Frivolous Bedlam and in those Frames, fewer buildings have sentience so the noise level diminishes. In the New Yorks, a quiet Frame is one that is far from the source of power. Or it's a Neutral Frame. Neutrals can't hear the buildings because of filters that shield Neutrals from awareness of other Frames.

As my own Frame teaches, sentience guarantees neither intelligence nor wisdom, and as Kelly Joe and I walked in Frivolous Bedlam, most of the chatter around us was simply that: buildings gossiped, discussed the weather, complained about leaks and creaks, told jokes. The truly sentient structures—the beings like Henrietta, my home in Los Angeles—were quiet. They only speak when they have something to say.

"That one shaved herself and then a cat," I heard a voice, followed by titters.

I stopped walking. "Hey, they're talking about me!"

"As they do, as they will." Kelly Joe murmured.

"How do these buildings know or care? They didn't see me shave the cat. I don't live anywhere near here."

"Few Neutrals are Travelers nowadays. The buildings like to keep an eye out."

I stumbled. Struggling to keep up with the pace of information, I'd stepped in a pothole.

All too soon, Kelly Joe brought us back to my Neutral Frame, where a typical Manhattan work day suddenly seemed silent.

"Thank you for taking me to other Frames! I've missed Traveling. So much! Even though Traveling used to make me feel like crap. How come that didn't feel bad? One time when Anya held my hand and we jumped off a roof, Traveling didn't hurt then, either. Was it because you held my hand? Why is that less bad? The worst was the time Anwyl took a bunch of us to far Frames really fast, to escape Warty Sebaceous Cysts. Is going to far Frames the hardest?" Ahhh. I hadn't had a good babble in weeks. Kelly Joe stood, fidget free, as patient as a broken clock. "You're welcome to answer any of those," I concluded.

"When I take your hand, you Travel on my energy and I share your journey. You'll feel less pain as you Travel more."

"What if –" I plugged my question spigot.

Kelly Joe's finger was back to his lips. "It's time that you learned to Travel on your own."

That left me speechless.

7. A DEEPER MODE

Cut to unknown hours later. "So your instructions are, relax and don't think about it while concentrating with every molecule of my being. In your Frame, do you have the concept 'mixed message'? Wait, don't count that as one of the questions I'm hardly ever allowed to ask, rhetorical shouldn't count."

"This is my Frame, too," was all Kelly Joe said.

"Sorry, failure makes me testy."

"Success will come."

"It really doesn't help that you're so calm and reasonable."

He watched a traffic light change. "Would you like to take a break?"

"No way. Not now." And I strode up Second Avenue as though the next Frame had a head start.

My feet advanced, left right left right. The only thing on my mind was stepping into a new Frame. Walking into a new Frame was all I thought about and that pallet the delivery guy just dropped with a thud that chattered my teeth which reminded me I might need to find a dentist —

Crap.

I stomped back to my teacher. Kelly Joe met my gaze, face unreadable. His expressions were on par with Monk's sentences. If you thought you got the meaning, that only proved you didn't.

He took out a harmonica from a jeans pocket that had a white worn strip where the harp lived. Much as I loved listening to his music, I needed to get this right. I strode forward. The only thing on my mind was stepping into a new Frame. Right left rightleftrightleft.

Kelly Joe strolled behind me. He bent bluesy notes, all keening, yearning, and sighs. The music distracted me, but with it I tuned out other distractions. Left right left right left right. I heard the music as I pulled away from it. And then —

— something clicked, my thinking shifted to a deeper mode, no longer influenced by my thoughts, which were pollen in the winds of daily life. Now I had to strain to hear the harmonica because it was so loud here, so many voices chattering at once. I stumbled with a sudden vertigo, like I dropped sideways in an elevator. At the same time, I thought I might barf.

The stumble converted to a victory leap. This combination of sensations was what I felt when I changed Frames in the past! I jumped up and down while shouting, "I did it! I did it!" By the time I had leaped back to Kelly Joe and clasped his biceps in an awkward hug, whatever had clicked in, clicked out again and I was back in my Frame. I continued to whoop my success.

New York is a good place to act like—or be—an idiot. I could have run down the block with a roman candle in each fist and armadillos looping around my wrists—and the only sign that any pedestrian noticed would be the minimalist change in direction to avoid collision with my circus.

I stopped on a mental dime. "Wait. Was that me or you who did that?" If I needed his music to change Frames, what had I accomplished on my own?

"Compare this experience with our earlier walk."

"This time I felt woozy and nauseous! That was awesome!"

"Yes, that's the proof that you found your way. My music showed you how to focus. Soon you won't need help."

I took off west without him or his harp. I tried changing Frames another dozen times, succeeded maybe twice. I grew ever more dizzy and nauseous. Fortunately, we returned to our home Frame within a short dash of a trashcan and soon I was no longer nauseous. Unfortunately, that was because I vomited a considerable volume into the trashcan.

Barfing is wrong. I so hate it. Go ahead, call me *emetophobic*, you won't be the first. My first and third husband, Ben Taggart, learned the medical term so he could tease me about my phobia in two languages. Whatever you call my concern, over the years it has been a deterrent to all manner of bad behavior. Shows how much I love Frame Travel; I'm willing to *emeto* for it.

Kelly Joe extracted a neckerchief and water bottle from his denim jacket. He dampened the cloth and gently wiped my face, then encouraged me to empty the bottle down my stinging throat.

"Thanks, you'd make a good dad, Kelly Joe." I returned his empty water bottle.

"Those are words never spoken," he said, with an un–positive expression I didn't know him well enough to define.

We got to Columbus Circle subway station and he stopped at entrance.

"You'll want to go home. A visitor left you a message."

"How do you know?"

"The way that all information spreads in the New Yorks."

"The buildings in Frivolous Bedlam!" Was that a chuckle? "Did you just laugh at me? How was I funny?"

"Your accent is unique when you say..." he thought his words were inflected differently but they still sounded exactly like "...Frivolous Bedlam."

Damn. I'd never get those names right. But I slammed the door on frustration—at least I had some new Frames to mispronounce now!

"I need to hear you play a couple songs before I go home. I've had a rough day."

"Have you?"

"Amazing but exhausting and don't forget I barfed."

"Then come along." For a moment, I thought he might smile.

That afternoon, his music was giddy and fun. It sent me flying to the moon on homemade wings and dancing a jig around Saturn's rings. A pair of kids seemed to inspire the difference. The girl, maybe four, and the boy, maybe three, bounced in place as kids do when they must move but can't go far.

The platform was packed, a train delayed. Typically, this generates bad tempers, and usually, when a late train arrives, the crowd presses *en masse* into the cars. Today, many lingered to keep listening. Now there is a testament—Kelly Joe's music kept New Yorkers from pushing forward.

I slid back on a bench, ignoring the way one pants leg stuck on something. Glad I wasn't wearing shorts. A train pulled in; a train pulled out. I closed my eyes to let the music penetrate more deeply. Could music be addictive?

A gulp and a sniffle. On the other end of the bench, someone was crying. It was the same young woman who cried here yesterday. Her eyes said she recognized me, too. She turned her head away.

"Did you come to this station every day before he played here?" I tried to break the ice, waited a New York hour for her to respond, closed my eyes again.

"Ye–es," her voice cracked, "it's my commute."

"Did you stop at all since yesterday? Crying, I mean."

"I don't remember." She stared at the cavity left by the most recent train.

"You remind me of me after my fourth husband died." She reacted to the *fourth*. "It takes me a while to get things right."

"Didn't you have hair yesterday?"

I snorted. How to answer her underlying question. Why had I buzzed my head? The blonde thing hadn't genuinely bothered me for ages. Starting new? Solidarity with Leon? Behind the gentrification, it's still Travis Bickle's Manhattan? My companion shared my hair color. Maybe blonde was her crowning glory. If I ever got to know her better, I could ask her. Her question held a splash of concern. When you're twenty, you buzz your head and people figure *style*. Let a couple decades elapse and a new guess arises, *chemo*.

She waited—polite, patient, bemused. I rubbed my silky scalp. "Long story."

"My brother cut his hair like that. He allowed me to rub his head but no one else could." She stormed up again. Even dry, her eyes would be the watery blue that goes best with blondes. My brown irises had let me skip that stereotype.

"I'm sorry you feel so miserable. Let me know if a private detective could help."

She reacted with surprised thoughtfulness. "Maybe—I—that might—I—never thought of that. But I couldn't afford that."

"I've got a floating pay scale, goes down with need, up if you're an ass. May I?" I tore a piece from the paper grocery bag that stuck out from her tote. On brown paper the shape of South America, I printed my address and cell number. "I just moved here," I added, as though I planned to get business cards made. Ben and I made business cards once. *Sheridan and Taggart, Marauders at Large*.

"S.T.A.T.Ic.? Your last name is an acronym?"

"Sheridan Taggart Ambrose Taggart Ickovic."

"I see," she said. And maybe she did.

A train pulled in. The kids and their adult boarded and Kelly Joe broke his own spell with a waterfall of minor chords. He does that sometimes, releasing us back to our lives.

"Thank you for your offer." My bench companion slipped my address scrap into her tote. She caught the train and I headed for the exit. It was barely three miles. I would walk home.

I passed Kelly Joe humming into his fret board. "See you soon," I said. He nodded in rhythm or reply.

I would have stayed longer, had I known how few times he would play there.

8. AGAIN? ALREADY?

As I approached the front stoop of the Julian, Leon the feline cockroach scurried down the stairs and away. Had I spooked him? Unlocking the building's front door, I remembered that Kelly Joe had mentioned a visitor. I'd put it out of my thoughts because I feared disappointment about my visitor's identity—which shows you my lonesome state of mind.

I opened the locked door at the end of my hall and spied a piece of paper between my door and its jamb, wedged there by someone who got past two locked doors.

Skeeny, read the blocky letters on the outside of the page. I shrieked. Ben Taggart, my first and third ex–husband, had been here—*Skeeny* was his latest nickname for me. Kelly Joe had been right when he told me to go home. Why hadn't I listened to him? Following instructions has never been my thing but sometimes I do see its value.

Inside my apartment, the cat food dish was empty and the water bowl was dry. Leon had been inside today. In fact, he had beat me inside now and perched on the kitchen windowsill. I replenished his supplies and he listened intently to the sound of food morsels settling in the bowl but he kept staring out the window. Whatev, kitty.

I opened Ben's note and found joy peace hope in just two words: *It's me*. Ben was alive and nearby and sober enough to find me.

Celebration is more fun with a partner. Leon wouldn't come to me so I went to him. When I reached to scratch his jaw, I got a view of the alley. Someone sitting on the fire escape. I ran to pull my shoes on. Leon jumped down in his sinuous way and trotted to his food.

Outside, I made lots of noise as I stumble–raced up the alley to the fire escape. Note to self, it doesn't save time when you skip tying your laces. I leaped to grab the first rung of the fire escape and hoisted myself up, which one does while practicing expletives.

Ben sat sleepy–eyed and grinning at my arrival. "When'd you get a cat?" he greeted me.

I flopped next to him on the landing. From here I enjoyed a vista: a glimpse of empty space above the Hudson River. "Yesterday. When'd you get to New York?"

"Same. Yesterday."

"How's life as a Ken?" Ben had assumed a new identity, *Ken Harris*, and fled Los Angeles to duck harassment by the dirty cops who I called Mathead and Scabman.

"I'm going by Kenneth now. You wouldn't believe how many people made Barbie jokes."

"Yeah. I would."

"You're the cynic, you would know." He put me in a toy headlock and gave my scalp a light nougie. "The return of fuzzhead, I see."

The headlock position made the world spin. Whoa. The Frame Travel plus barfing had me woozy unto delirious. "Want to come inside for some water?"

"Don't make any special fuss for me."

"I'm big time dehydrated and need to guzzle a gallon or else." In fact, I was going to pass out soon. That's how things are for me. I ignore the little warning signs and that gives me stamina then *kaboom* and I'm flattened.

I made it to the front stoop, then stumbled. Twice. Ben put an arm around my waist. "You must need a lot of water."

When Ben entered my apartment, Leon fled to the bathroom doorway and watched as Ben sat me on the couch, delivered me a coffee mug of water, then tossed me a beat–up flip–top. "Hernandez says call him. Number 3 on speed dial." Ben went to forage in the kitchen. "I'm hungry. You?"

"More water would be good."

"Make the call, he's been stressing." Ben opened cupboards, surveyed my sparse supplies, filled my saucepan with water in *lieu* of a pitcher. He brought it to me just as Leon was braving the journey from bathroom to couch. Startled, Leon's claws made cartoon skedaddling noises on the beat–up wood floor.

By then, I had figured out how to make a call on the antique phone, so greeted Hernandez with a laugh.

"Nica, it's good to have your laugh back in my head," Hernandez said.

"You sound tense. What's the latest? Your girls enjoying Spain?"

"I believe they are. They were homesick at first but they've stopped calling so much."

"Sounds like a good sign." I joined him in a sigh. "Did you change your cell? I don't recognize this number."

"I have a separate phone for Ben's calls. And that's a good thing because those cops came to my house. They're asking questions at the Henrietta, too."

"Mathead and Scabman? Crap. What pests. What did they want?"

"Said they were looking for Ben –"

"Again? Already?" I thought I'd convinced their captain that Mathead and Scabman should stop pursuing Ben. And me.

"Patti helped do some digging." By *Patti*, he meant Detective Patti Henson, his new *amour*. We all met this summer on a child abuse case. "Detective Fitzpatrick is no longer with the L.A.P.D." Detective Fitzpatrick was Mathead. "And as for Detective Moriarty –"

"No way? That's Scabman's real name?" He couldn't be further from Sherlock Holmes' arch nemesis.

"It is. He's on indefinite medical leave after a fifty–one–fifty."

If I could whistle, here would have been a great time for it. In California, 5150 is a forced hospitalization because someone is a threat to himself or others. "Guess I'm not the only one who got the creeps when he was nearby. I know I don't have to tell you to watch your back."

"That's a given. You find any bad construction out there?" With this, Hernandez referenced the reconnaissance work that we had done for Anya and Anwyl around southern California. Back home last summer, we'd uncovered evidence that Warty Sebaceous Cysts controlled a southern California restoration and remodeling firm, Digby Construction. Digby projects would somehow contribute to freeing Maelstrom.

"I didn't think to look. We know Digby is only in So–Cal."

"No reason to assume Digby is the only construction company involved."

"Damn. You're right, of course." I felt as clever as Wiley Coyote. "I'll start checking."

"I've got intel that might help you." While Hernandez caught me up on his investigations, Ben delivered a plate of sliced fruit, crackers, and cheese, then ate most of it. He removed one of my shoes. *Jackpot, foot massage!* Wrong. Ben dangled the lace at Leon.

My phone conversation ended shortly after I asked Hernandez how things were going with Patti. "Some things to work through," was all he would say.

Ben discovered the Murphy bed and lowered it until it hit the desk.

I gestured toward the kitchenette. "You have to move the desk in there. I usually just sleep on the couch." Always take the option that requires less housework. Daily chores are a toothache in the mouth of life.

"That sounds like you, Neeks—I'm sorry! It slipped out!"

Neeks. I jerked when I heard Ben's old nickname. Warty Sebaceous Cysts had stolen it from my thoughts, and ruined it—hearing *Neeks* reminded me of Warty Sebaceous Cysts, so strongly that I had begged Ben never to use it again and he switched to calling me *Skeeny.*

But the nickname was only ruined if I allowed it to be. To hell with the Cysts. (Which was much easier to say when they were nowhere near.)

"Go ahead and use 'Neeks' again."

"Okay!" Ben did a cheerleading rah thing and flopped onto the Murphy bed's liberated mattress. "Not bad," he rated the comfort level. He pulled a plate of food in front of him, patted the space beyond it. I joined him on the mattress, and as I spread spicy chutney on the Brie, Ben murmured, "Don't react." Leon hovered on the farthest corner of the bed. Ben tossed a pinch of cheese and Leon's purr reverberated through the mattress.

Sometimes there's nothing better than a little family time—that special warmth that comes from being with people who will never hurt you on purpose.

"I assume Hernandez told you that Mathead is out of L.A.P.D. but still looking for you."

"Yeah. And You. Maybe she was after you all along. She's connected with the incident at my apartment, right?"

The incident. The day Warty Sebaceous Cysts killed Ben's houseguest then obliterated Ben's conscious memory of the events, leaving only terror behind.

Ben knew I had explanations I wasn't sharing but he didn't grill me. He trusted me to tell him when the time was right. No signs of Ben the hustler king today. Just my Benny, open unto exposed, trusting unto at risk, friendly unto a high point of anyone's day.

"This recovery's going well for you," I stated the obvious.

"Just took a three–month chip." But it wasn't the time sober—although every minute that Ben didn't use heroin added other minutes to his life. Something had clicked. He seemed to be embracing, not disdaining, this sobriety.

Ben stared behind me. "New York has a book shortage?" He was looking at the built–in bookshelf, empty save for my copies of *Lose Twenty Pounds of Worry in Twenty Days.*

"Long story."

"Always is." He smiled like he was remembering some of them, rolled on his back, wiggled his fingers. Leon stared with feline skepticism. "If Leon had eyebrows, one of them would be raised." After one more futile finger wiggle, Ben sat up. "I never had a worry problem."

"I noticed."

"You know what I've had?" His seriousness surprised me. "A dreams problem. I have so many that they tangle and turn into schemes. I'm working on taking them one at a time."

Which felt like my first discovery of Leon's scars. I sat up and the room twirled from residual effects of Travel or my surging complex of emotions. I grabbed my shoes, only one of which had a lace.

Ben grinned at the mismatched shoes. "Nica indecisive? Is this a first?"

"It's an experiment. Come on—I want you to hear this musician I discovered in the subway."

Kelly Joe had not happened into my life accidentally, but I couldn't explain that to Ben. When and how would I explain the Frames to Ben? He needed to know. Deserved explanation.

Ben grabbed me in a bear hug. "Neeks! Come back!"

He never tells me to focus. I appreciate that.

9. TELL ME ABOUT THE BRAINWASHING

"Nica?"

When a voice you don't recognize says your name, it can take a while to hear it. In this case, it took the seconds required to pass two front stoops and to ponder Leon. When Ben and I left my apartment, Leon was inside, but now the cat had appeared at the corner ahead of us, which meant he left the apartment by the fire escape, went up the alley and rounded the corner. He did this every time I left the apartment and whichever way I headed, he showed up at that corner. Maybe my step varied when I intended to turn east rather than west and he detected the difference. Leon watched us for a moment then did his cockroach scurry down some basement steps.

"Nica?"

Behind us was the young woman from the subway, the one who sobbed while Kelly Joe played. "Hello," she nodded to Ben. "My name is Lilah Strongfellow."

"Good to see you again, Lilah. This is my brother, Ben." I always introduce Ben as my sibling, it's a much closer fit to our relationship than *first and third ex-spouse*. "I'm taking him to hear Kelly Joe play. Want to come along?"

"The musician wasn't there earlier. I've checked twice today. Every time I hear that music, I am so drawn to hear it again." Lilah matched our rapid strides and raised us one. After a few steps, I was straining to keep up with her.

Lilah said, "About your offer to help. Thank you. I could use some."

"I'm gonna take off," Ben announced. He gave Lilah a flash–o'–sun smile, squeezed my far shoulder in a sideways hug, and veered across the street and away. How much of my life had I spent watching Ben veer away from some plan of mine?

Lilah said, "I'm sorry to intrude."

"Not at all. Brothers come and go." Not to mention addicts, recovered or no.

"Brothers." She lost a battle against tears.

"You didn't wait for the music."

Even without the tear tracks on her cheeks, her smile would have been sad. "I don't know how to stop crying, these days." We walked a while.

"Ever since –" I prompted.

"I have a brother, too. We're twins. He's the reason I need help. Someone is brainwashing him."

"Hold up." I sat her at a café table and clutched a chair to hide my dizziness. Today's Travel was still affecting me. "Let's stop and chat for a bit. What can I get you?"

When our drinks and I got back to the sidewalk table, Lilah was checking her makeup in a mirror decorated like a rose. What would it be like to be a girlie girl? Sitting beside one was as close as I would ever get. "What's your brother's name?" I asked.

"His name is Sam."

I had her type his work and home addresses into my phone.

"'Sam' is short for 'Samuel'?"

"No. 'Sam' is short for 'Samson'." She watched me put the names together and sighed. "And 'Lilah' is short for 'Delilah'. Yes, our parents named us Samson and Delilah Strongfellow. They were good parents otherwise."

"Your word is what I'm taking for that. Tell me about the brainwashing." I opened my note–taking app.

"Everything went wrong after Sam met some people at a bar in Brooklyn. He's been on a search for new career paths so he talks with people about what they do. He's always been friendly. Long story short, he met some people and they invited him to a meeting. They claimed to belong to a group dedicated to improving the world while having fun. It sounded like a social club with a do–good orientation." She frowned at her *latte*.

"Sounded like—but wasn't?"

"Every time he came back from one of their meetings, he was more angry— at things that previously amused him. He began to take everything personally. If an old man walked slowly, the man must want to make Sam late. My brother developed an us–versus–them attitude."

"Where does this social club meet?"

She pointed to my phone screen. "That second address is where the club used to meet. The club moved or shut down about the same time that Sam quit his job and stopped living at the first address."

"Does he have a new job? Perhaps he moved in with a new girlfriend?"

This got the tears moving. "I don't know. He stopped confiding in me." She took a long sip, then slid the saucer away like it was the *latte* that made her cry. "He closed his bank accounts. However, his cell phone is still in use in all five boroughs."

"You may be a better sleuth than I am." I didn't ask how she got that information but doubted her method was legal. "Sam has been snowed into joining a cult, is that your guess?"

"That's what I need you to find out. The police don't care unless there's a corpse. Here is all the information I've been able to assemble." From her tote she removed an accordion folder. She watched me paw through the photocopied phone receipts, confidential personnel files, handwritten notes, and photographs— of Sam, of buildings. She asked, "How much do you charge?"

"Two hundred a day plus reimbursement for expenses." Lilah did some arithmetic in her head then nodded. I could have charged more but I get by, thanks to small inheritances that cover my basics. I didn't need to gouge somebody who had to do math before she could accept my fee. Anyway, I liked Lilah. "If that rate becomes a problem we can renegotiate."

"Thank you so much. I am so lucky I ran into you."

If Jenn were here, she would say there are no accidents, no luck. I can't decide whether knowing about the Frames makes me more—or even less—a believer in Fate. But it felt significant that Lilah was also a regular, listening to Kelly Joe play. Like I was meant to help her.

We resumed our pilgrimage to Columbus Circle and I said, "I have one stipulation before I take your case. You can't look for Sam. This has to be my case, not ours. I work alone. You okay with that?" I resisted adding a *shweethaht*. I don't know why I went mid–century hard–boiled, but my gut told me that if I let Lilah stay involved, she'd step all over any tracks there might be.

Lilah stopped walking. "But I have to—"

I pretended I was Kelly Joe or a statue and waited without saying more.

"Very well. I accept your condition." She resumed walking without looking to see if I followed.

"You mentioned the police. Have you filed a missing persons report?"

"I did but they were able to contact Sam so by their definition, he's not missing." After every couple syllables, she checked to see how I was taking this news. "I should have told you that sooner, I know."

"I get why you didn't. Any idea what Sam told the cops?"

She shook her head.

Columbus Circle subway station was devoid of musicians. The subway platform felt bereft. A train approached and I got ready to board it.

"I'll stay here for a bit," Lilah said.

My train left Lilah on the platform and I felt a version of survivor's guilt. I knew I would see Kelly Joe again—he had a training list from Anya and no one wants to disappoint Anya. Lilah had no such certainty.

10. FLANNEL SHEETS ON A WINTER NIGHT

I intended to take the subway to Brooklyn to check out the former location of Sam Strongfellow's social club. That required two transfers and I botched them—I went the wrong direction on the damn M train then undercompensated and wound up back where I started. By that time I needed sky, so I fled the subway and detoured west to catch sunset on the Hudson River.

I became aware of a baritone hum behind me, reviewed recent memories and discovered the sound had followed me for about a block. I turned and let Kelly Joe catch up.

A bus went by and for the bizillionth time, Anya's lanyard prickled a mild warning. About what, I didn't know and had ceased to care. The lanyard gave me so many alerts these days that the warnings were meaningless. I had to ignore them so as not to be driven mad by them.

I wore the lanyard stretched bandolier style across my shoulder and torso. Every day I wore it under my clothes, because Anya said it was important for me to do so. Anya also said she would teach me the lanyard's uses, but complications ensued and I remained untaught.

I bunched up the shoulder of my top to show Kelly Joe the lanyard underneath. I assumed he would recognize what it was. "Can this be part of my training? It's driving me nuts."

He put a quick hand on my shoulder and covered it. "That equipment can only help if no one knows you have it. Any being with power can override it. Who else knows you have this?"

"Only—A and A," I put my finger to my lips the way he had done when he stopped me from saying Anya's name, "and the healers. And maybe Shastina. And now you."

"Let no one else know."

"Got it. Okay." I felt foolish but I was used to that.

The Hudson glittered in the setting sun and birds fluttered in a sidewalk tree, preparing for nightfall. There is more nature in a city than most people notice. Kelly Joe noticed. "The current has shifted—do you see how the fresh ripples intersect the fading ones?"

"Thank you, I do see that—now. Is this river crazy, too?" I couldn't enjoy the view if I knew the Hudson was cackling somewhere, even if I happened to stand in a Frame where I couldn't hear it.

"No. This river's ailments are physical. You may be surprised to learn, as I was, that what we Neutrals do to the rivers in this Frame affects their essence in other Frames."

That almost qualified as a personal anecdote. Kelly Joe was much more open tonight. I would later come to understand that he is more open on the days when he doesn't play music. He withdraws after he plays.

"You mean Neutral pollution made the East River crazy? Wow. I wonder if we'd stop if we knew."

"I have few answers and that's not one of them," he said. "What do you know about your—this?" He touched my shoulder where the lanyard was.

"I know what little I've been told and what I've experienced. It reduced pain when I had a bad injury. It's supposed to warn me when I'm in danger but since I moved here I can't take it seriously. It warns me about everything—even truck exhaust. It warns me all day and I can't figure out what it thinks the danger is, most of the time."

"You need to calibrate your equipment so it understands what danger means to you."

We strolled along the wide sidewalk by the river and he casually looked one way and the other. I wondered if he chose this route to maximize distance from other pedestrians.

During my weeks alone in New York, I was a Teflon ghost, untouchable, unseeable. Kelly Joe had restored the Frames to me—and a sense of looming danger. I could feel it, closing in.

"Has there been a threat? Are we in danger?"

"If not now, then soon. Let's start calibrating your equipment. To do that, remember a time you were in danger and imagine getting a warning from your equipment when that warning would have helped you the most. Yes, go ahead and do that now."

I remembered the being that looked like a human cobra. He dragged me into another Frame and blasted my shoulder with an energy that left it scarred. If I hadn't escaped his interrogation, he would have killed me. I imagined the lanyard jolting me with lightning warnings the instant I first saw him. The lanyard jolts started in my imagination but turned real. "Ow," was how I let Kelly Joe know I had followed his instructions. No one can be eloquent all the time.

"Good. Now, one more."

I remembered laying defenseless on the volcano Shastina, feet uphill, too weak to stand, surrounded by Warty Sebaceous Cysts and their Entourage, the creepy manufactured beings who act out the Cysts' disturbing impulses. The Cysts ransacked my thoughts, then turned me over to their flying chainsaws and clockwork dogs. As before, the jolts started in my imagination but turned real. I rubbed my chest where the lanyard crossed it and told Kelly Joe, "Double ow."

"Now look around you and feel the freshness of the evening. Does your equipment cause you pain about this?"

"None whatsoever."

"As it should be. Your equipment learns from your past to watch your future. You'll feel fewer small warnings even after just two calibrations. Repeat the procedure every day, but calibrate gradually, with only one danger each day. Accept some small warnings and be glad for them. They bring your attention to the now."

"Okay, got it. I think. But there's a flaw in the system. Those warnings I just imagined? If I got them back when I needed them, I wouldn't have done anything differently. I would have made the same choices."

His laugh was like flannel sheets on a winter night. "No equipment can repair poor judgment."

"Does everyone have equipment like this? Do you?"

"I do not. My fate is known."

I didn't like the sound of that. There's a line between acceptance and resignation and he was on the wrong side. That's one of my issues with fate. Why keep trying if there's an inevitable?

"There is no fate," I proclaimed with the assurance of a high school debater.

"Do you reject your prophecy?"

My prophecy. The prophecy that brought Anya and Anwyl to me. Although how they decided the prophecy was about me, I still don't know. *In the blackest of days, a seer, a walker, and a Neutral will lead the foes of darkness.* Anya is a seer, Anwyl is a Framewalker, which makes yours truly the Neutral.

"Of course not! I so want the prophecy to be true. It validates—everything. Whatever the hell it means—it's so vague, it's more a Rorschach test than a prediction."

He stared where the sun had been. "Is it power or importance that appeals to you?"

"Neither. I want –" What did I want? Why had I come here, chasing the chance of meeting Anya and Anwyl again? Kelly Joe waited while I thought it through. "I want to make a difference."

"It's good to make a difference." He stared into the blackness where the river was. Someday, maybe I could ask him about it. That sadness in him. And something else I couldn't name. Yet.

It was odd, having a conversation with Kelly Joe, but I could get used to it. Maybe I could capitalize on his mood and get answers to a few of the questions that littered my head.

"How do you change your tattoos so often? Doesn't it make your skin sore?"

His chuckle suggested warm molasses. "I don't change my messages. Sometimes they change."

"Messages. They tell you things?"

"From time to time."

"May I see them?"

He slid his sleeves up over his elbows and folded his arms. I unpocketed my phone. This was a job for flashlight app!

Tonight the tatts were stark as prison graffiti, all black and gray. The lime green hummingbird was gone.

"Was the hummingbird a message to me?"

"I don't know." He started to hum.

"Don't you wonder about your messages?"

Eventually, he said softly, "I no longer wonder."

The way his voice sounded, my question session had expired. "The hummingbird had to be for me. It made me stop and talk to you." I moved my phone flashlight up and down his arm. No sign that previous tattoos had ever been there. Encircling his left wrist was a simple but intricate pattern like a Celtic knot. It reminded me of the Connector map, which shows the routes between Frames.

"I want a tattoo like that." I held my light on his wrist.

"No. No, you don't." He pulled his sleeves down and resumed walking.

"Does it hurt to get inked there?"

"The memories can."

I pretended to be cooperative and let it go. "What else is on the agenda for tonight?"

"Only one way to find that out, Nica. Come along now."

11. NEGATIVE POWER

At night, Frivolous Bedlam is festive. The buildings have their lights on and flash them when they laugh. Taxis and buses rev in the mechanical equivalent of drum circles. Electric awnings and escalators rattle and glide, adding syncopation. If possible, night is noisier than day there.

"You'll want to be comfortable in Frivolous Bedlam," Kelly Joe explained our excursion. "The buildings will watch out for you and they know all that happens in the New Yorks."

I unfocused my attention and listened to the buildings gabbing.

"They used cheap stucco on my cornices. Won't last a decade."

"Neutrals."

"Wait until they pull your carpets up, that won't be fun."

"How refreshing to have new carpets!"

"Stop looking on the bright side. You're annoying."

"There's the one who shaved a cat."

"Just call me Cat Shaver," I waved in the direction the words had come from. The closest buildings spun their revolving entry doors and spread the name down the blocks, until a joke distracted them.

"Knock–knock," one building called.

"Who's there?!" other buildings shouted.

"Who isn't?" the first building yelled.

This joke was a huge hit—block after block, the buildings repeated it. Meanwhile, they continued other conversations.

Kelly Joe sauntered evenly but my pace and direction were erratic. I'd speed up, slow down, detour, trying to catch everything the buildings said, but that was impossible.

He stopped in an intersection. "Excuse my interruption," he called without raising his voice. The adjoining blocks grew quiet, attentive. "Has Cat Shaver had visitors at her home on Ma'Urth?"

My Frame was called Ma'Urth. Good to know.

A murmur rose then diminished as buildings passed the question northwest, toward Julian. Kelly Joe resumed his stroll. The murmur rose again as the answer came back, "She has not but the cat has."

"Thank you kindly," Kelly Joe replied, then leaned in to my ear. "Sometimes you can get information from the buildings when you ask them for it." Later that night, I came to appreciate the *sometimes*.

An internal flashbulb popped. I had set out to investigate Sam Strongfellow's social club in Brooklyn. If I visited the location in Frivolous Bedlam, I could actually talk to the building!

I tugged Kelly Joe's jacket sleeve and yelled in his ear, "Can we detour? I need to investigate a case and maybe the buildings can help."

He looked at me like we'd never met and stopped walking. He stood still, as he does, and I fidgeted, as I do. Eventually, he replied, "Perhaps they can. In any case, you'll get practice finding your way around Frivolous Bedlam, and that's important." I understood why I needed practice. The streets were the same and yet often unrecognizable with the buildings so lively.

As we walked, I described the case. When I mentioned that my client was one of his regular listeners at Columbus Circle, he rubbed his arms absently as though his tattoos ached. This strengthened my sense that helping Lilah was something I had to do.

Based on Lilah's annotated photo, the social club meeting room was above a Chinese restaurant in the second floor of a building on Keap Street, just south of Williamsburg. In Bedlam, the building had buck–teeth delivery doors that protruded differing amounts over the sidewalk and rattled when the building tittered at knock–knock jokes.

The stairs to the second floor had an entry gate. Unlocked. The second floor meeting room was a single open space with nothing in the room, but it didn't feel vacant. This is typical of rooms in Frivolous Bedlam. The buildings don't use their rooms yet the rooms remain perpetually clean and comfortable, the essence of shelter.

I circled the perimeter of the meeting room and opened each window, which let in the distinctive odor of Frivolous Bedlam, a smell of overworked electronics and fresh–cut timber. I tried to imagine the equivalent room and view on Ma'Urth.

Kelly Joe had a hand against a wall and stood as though listening.

"Anything I should know?" I touched the wall, knowing I wouldn't sense what he was sensing.

"This room has held negative power, but not in this Frame. Negative power is blocked from Frivolous Bedlam."

Downstairs and outside, I stepped into the middle of the intersection and yelled to the buildings, self–conscious about the differences between our species. "Folks. Um. Structures. A word, please." The ceaseless chatter continued. I screamed, "I need information about this building on Ma'Urth. The Frame where I shaved the cat."

Only Kelly Joe listened to me.

"Cat Shaver speaks of Ma'Urth." He said it like I hadn't just said it. He got his voice to go everywhere without raising it. The wall of chatter broke and many nearby buildings paused their gabbing.

I took over, or tried to. "Neutrals came to that room, up there—um." Could the buildings see me point? Did they refer to their innards as rooms? "The Neutrals met every day." Did the buildings know what meetings were? Did they recognize days here—did they have a sense of time passing? I sympathized with the centipede who became unable to walk because he obsessed with the motion of his feet. "Now those Neutrals are gone. I need to find them. Do you know where they went? Those Neutrals?"

"No, don't. Not only," replied the buck–toothed building with the meeting room.

"Don't what? What do you mean by 'not only'?"

"Not! Only?" The building across the way picked it up and changed it.

"Not, on–ly." Another building picked it up.

"Naught tone lee!"

The words circled the block as the buildings played with the sounds, distorting a response that was inscrutable to start with. The buildings laughed then got bored or forgot about us and resumed their chatter.

I looked to Kelly Joe. "Well, that was helpful."

"Their answers may make a different sense later. Their memories are different than ours, as are their words. You'll want to return another day and ask again." He extended his hand. "You'll need rest soon. We'd best get you home."

This time I agreed with him.

12. A WEE BIT OF RESENTMENT

After all that time in Bedlam, when we got back home my ears buzzed like they were on tour with Spinal Tap. "So my Frame is named Ma'Urth –" I began. People in line at a Halal food truck glanced at me. I must be speaking louder than I realized.

Kelly Joe's lips moved but I heard nothing. I gestured that my hearing was wonked. He gave a slow twirl to his fingers, suggesting patience. Did he really know me so little?

New York is a different city on mute. If anything, it felt more crowded, although by this time of evening the streets were less packed. I got jostled repeatedly because my ears missed the cues that somebody was about to collide. The taxi headlights all seemed to be on bright—I guess my eyes were trying to compensate for my failed ears.

By the time we reached my neighborhood, my ears were functioning again. Kelly Joe stopped walking at the subway stairs a block from the Julian, and I heard his parting words, "Have a restful evening. You learned well and made progress today." He touched my arm and was down the stairs to the trains.

Looking down the stairs made me stumble. He was right, I needed rest.

At my corner, Leon sprinted up from a basement and paced me, five feet away but I could hear his purr. "Hey buddy, good to see you! Did Ben show up again?" Leon trotted past the Julian and around the corner. "See you inside."

Outside my apartment door was a sight that made me whoop. It was late enough that this might have disturbed someone, were it not for the downstairs neighbor, who was hosting a hell–raiser of a party. After the emptiness of the Henrietta back in Los Angeles, it was refreshing to live with other tenants. I rarely saw anyone but I heard them all the time. Fortunately, noise helps me concentrate and sleep.

What made me whoop were two shipping boxes, to N.Y. me from L.A. me. When I dropped the boxes at Amtrak they were cubes; now they were abstract, but the repair tape had kept most of the contents inside.

I dragged the boxes to a place of honor in my main room, for they held the important worldly possessions of Nica S.T.A.T.Ic., the stuff I wouldn't leave behind but couldn't fit in my carry–on.

Leon perched on the chair and watched me unpack. One box was boring: warm clothes and boots. The other box held my special stash. Coffee maker. Books and mementos of loved ones. And speakers! I set them up and blasted my most New York music on shuffle, alternating mid–century jazz with protest folk with CBGB house bands. Last unpacked was a cheap aluminum lawn chair. It once belonged to my friend and gardening mentor, Jay, an early victim of Warty Sebaceous Cysts' scheme to free Maelstrom. Back home, when I sat in the chair I witnessed Jay's bloody death—from the chair's point of view. The chair was sentient.

I had been reluctant to sit in the chair after it shared its memories of Jay's death, but I couldn't leave it behind when I left L.A. So here it was. I unfolded the lightweight frame and stared at the webbed seat, wondering what else the chair knew. I flopped on the couch and stared at the chair. I imagined taking the two steps to go sit in the chair but I stayed on the couch.

When I woke up, the windows glowed with dawn and mine was the only music in the building. Oops. I silenced my speakers.

I went out to buy fancy coffee beans to commemorate the arrival of my caffeine–dispensing equipment. When I returned, Leon stood on the sidewalk, gazing up at Ben, who sat on my stoop, texting. Ben had a latest generation iPhone as well as the antique flip phone for calls from Hernandez. I knew better than to wonder how he paid for phone service.

Upstairs, I deposited the coffee beans and replenished Leon's food and water levels. The cat was recouping months of food deficit every day.

"Are you missing L.A. that much, Neeks?" Ben sat in the lawn chair before I could stop him.

I forced myself to resume breathing. If the chair imparted visions to Ben, he was too busy texting to notice. I had to smile. Nobody could lounge more thoroughly than Ben.

He tapped the chair arms. "You should put this out on the fire escape. You could watch the sunsets."

"Wouldn't somebody take it?"

"Not if I stop them. Be right back," and he was out the door before I could warn him that I needed to leave soon.

I marched over to the lawn chair. Knowing that Ben would be right back allowed me to grow a pair. I lowered my rear onto the webbed seat. No power surges. No death gargles. Just a surprisingly comfortable seat. I really did want to put it out on the fire escape. I unlatched the bathroom window bars, hoisted the chair out to the fire escape.

I was deciding the best spot for the chair when Ben came up the alley. "More in the corner there by the stairs." I slid the chair to the corner he indicated. The instant I touched the chair's frame, I knew this was the best spot. Ben handed me a bag from the pharmacy, fished a black coil from it. The coil was a bike lock, which he looped around the chair's leg and the fire escape rail. Anyone who wanted the chair enough to cut the bike lock should go ahead and take it.

"New York is weird, it takes forever to find a grocery store but there's a pharmacy on every—are you? You're checking for a receipt." Ben sounded resigned.

I pulled my hand out of the bag. "Still a habit." Habits like that get cemented when you're a first–time bride and your groom turns out to be a shoplifting junkie. But of course *shoplifting junkie* is redundant. And yes, I may still harbor a wee bit of resentment. I get rid of it then it crops up again. Mental crabgrass. "Thanks for the lock, that was a good idea. I need to go out and do detective stuff now, want to come with?"

We left Leon curled on the chair on the fire escape. I looked forward to finding out why the chair wanted to be outside in that spot.

I went to check out the social club building on Ma'Urth and Ben tagged along. Here on Ma'Urth, the building was decrepit. The first floor Chinese restaurant was padlocked and below its door stretched a rat that was not freshly deceased. As in Frivolous Bedlam, the second floor meeting space was one large empty room. Here, the meeting room smelled like rancid fries. No sign of the social club remained in the room, nor any indication of where I might find Sam Strongfellow.

As Ben and I exited the building after our look–see, something whizzed past our heads, splattered behind us, sprayed liquid that stung. I grabbed Ben's arm and he grabbed mine. At our feet steamed an empty Styrofoam cup. Someone had thrown hot coffee at us.

On the sidewalk stood a ruined woman with yellowed hair that looked broken not cut. Her skin drooped in elephant sags. "You people. Told you get out means stay out."

"By 'you people' do you refer to the social club that used to meet upstairs?"

"Social club? Kidding me?" She spat in my direction.

Ben interrupted me to speak to the woman like an old friend. "This neighborhood's bringing back memories. Good times! Does Joe the First still hang here?"

At the mention of Joe the First, the woman's hostility dropped a hundred notches. I had a flash into Ben's world. Joe the First would be a dealer, the ruined woman was an addict not pursuing recovery. Still, she could trust a fellow addict— even a sober one—in a way she wouldn't trust me. I appreciated Ben's help with my investigation, if not the reminder that his past could have dumped him here.

While the woman appraised us, I made a show of taking notes. "Not really a social club... Do you happen to know where the group went?"

"Not far enough," the ruined woman growled.

"How long ago did they leave?"

"Not soon enough," she sneered, then added warmly, to Ben, "They moved along. Use'ta get a lot of mail and now nothin'."

I raised a hand in thanks or surrender and headed for the corner. That last might be useful information – had the club forwarded mail somewhere else?

"Tell them, waiting for them. We are!" The ruined woman's ominous wave included a group of five souls, clustered behind a beat–up loading dock across the street. To my semi–trained eye, they looked like addicts who had just scored.

"They're fresh," Ben confirmed my suspicion. "They won't hear your questions."

After we rounded the corner, Ben slapped a rhythm on a dumpster. "Okay if I ditch you? I need to catch a meeting."

"Of course. Thanks for helping with that woman."

He was already across the street. To go to the subway station. Or. To circle back to score from those—did I really just think that? And had he really stared at those junkies as much as it seemed?

What had the social club done to earn such hatred from that woman?

My brooding cut itself short: Kelly Joe walked up the street toward me.

13. WHEN WE WERE STILL SAFE

I greeted Kelly Joe with a smile as wide as the Sahara, and added Egypt when I saw that he carried his guitar on his back. But he wasn't here for music. He slipped his guitar case onto my back and said, "Traveling with objects takes a special concentration." He adjusted the straps with tenderness which I pretended was for me, not his guitar.

Special concentration is not how I would describe the effort. *Crippling, brain–eating energy suck* was closer. But I got the hang of it. Eventually.

When Kelly Joe shouldered his guitar case again, the sun was a couple hours lower in the sky. "Well done, Nica. Be proud of your progress."

But we weren't done. He reached a finger to the bottom branch of a nondescript street tree. A ladybug walked onto his finger. He touched his finger to my shoulder and the ladybug climbed aboard. "All beings can Travel by walking through Connectors. Only beings of power can Travel as we have done today."

"Does that mean I'm a being of power?"

"It just might."

I curtailed my victory dance, mindful of the ladybug on my shoulder.

"It takes special skill to share your power so that another being can Travel with you. That is what you'll learn next and you'll start with this one." Kelly Joe gestured to the ladybug.

"How will we keep it on my shoulder?"

"It will stay. You have affinity with them. Take your guest to Frivolous Bedlam."

"How do you know that I have affinity with ladybugs?"

"Someone told me."

I touched finger to lips—our symbol for Anya—and he nodded. I noted, "Ladybugs do always seem to be around."

"That's an honor few receive." He resumed walking, stopped when I didn't follow.

"I had no idea."

"Now you know."

"Now I do." I propped my butt against a bike rack.

"Are you stalling?" Kelly Joe asked.

"Kinda, yeah. I want all the training I can get and thought I had endurance. But. Could we sit for a bit?"

"Our time is short. Better exhausted than untrained."

"Are you leaving soon?" Kelly Joe looked puzzled so I explained. "You said, 'our time is short'. 'Our', meaning you and me?"

"By 'our' I mean all who live in the free Frames."

No more stalling. I sucked it up and knuckled down and gave it all I had.

From then on, every training session was more brutal than the last and had an urgency that fed my growing sense of dread. Ironic, because someday I'd look back with nostalgia at this time when we were still safe.

I've got enough of the athlete gene to enjoy getting pushed, but not over cliffs. Still, I practiced and I repeated until I learned the subtleties of Frame Travel. Traveling to the same Frame as Kelly Joe without holding hands. Changing Frames while stationary. Changing Frames while in a moving object—bus, subway train, bicycle. Defensive Travel. How to resist Travel if being forced.

I got enough practice with Frame Travel to become a professional barfer, but it took more and more to trigger the *emeto* reflex. I really was getting used to Travel, trip by trip. No matter how much I practiced, though, I failed to transport any being larger than a ladybug.

On the second Tuesday of that week, Kelly Joe answered a couple questions.

"What happens if I Travel to a space that is occupied?" I wondered.

"You will be repelled and Travel to the closest available space."

"What do I do if someone notices me vanish or appear?" I inquired.

"You nod to greet your fellow Traveler. No Neutral will notice someone Traveling."

The days merged and blurred. I marked the passage of time by the emptying of Leon's food bowl. Each day, I'd scout construction sites until Kelly Joe appeared. I'd train then I'd limp home, and on the last block Leon would flank me. I'd cringe to find Ben in the sentient lawn chair. But the chair conveyed no messages. Apparently, it enjoyed being outside with a hint of river view. Each evening, Ben fixed a snacky dinner while I went on the internet to try to identify the construction companies behind suspect building sites. The building ownerships were an opaque web of LLCs Incs LLPs Ltds DBAs. I didn't have enough experience with that world to know whether this was odd but I couldn't identify a single owner.

Coming home one evening, I ran into Lilah at Columbus Circle subway station. She jumped up from the bench like she had sat there longer than she wanted me to know. "You haven't phoned. Does that mean nothing is new with your investigation into Sam's disappearance?"

"I've talked to every tenant and building manager near the social club meeting room and his apartment. I've talked to the mail carriers. I've talked to his old firm. Sam and the social club attracted no attention. No collection notices, no police visits, no forwarding addresses. They weren't friendly but they weren't rude. No one remembered seeing Sam with a girlfriend but frankly no one remembered seeing Sam." I didn't mention the junkies who hated the social club. That would trigger questions I couldn't answer. Although I suspected that held the key to the case—the discrepancy between their view and that of allegedly polite society. "I did warn you that results could be slow or disappointing."

"Yes, you did." Her voice had the *it's not your fault you'll never get this* of my ninth grade math tutor. The train arrived and she sat far from me. We stopped talking.

I don't know why Ben's leaving surprised me. He has a history of moves, sudden and frequent. That night, he was washing dishes while I did knee flexes and punches.

He broke a dish and he cursed. I stopped punching. When Ben is in a decent state of mind, anything smaller than an atomic bomb detonation counts as spilt milk. Now he slammed broken pieces of plate into the trash.

"I don't care about dishes," I reminded him.

He nodded, trashed the remaining fragments gently, kept nodding while he dried his hands and fished the ancient flip phone out of his pocket. He tossed it onto the couch.

"I don't call Hernandez until tomorrow."

"I know. I won't be here then. New York isn't good for me. I have lots of memories of other times here and they're all about using. That's not supposed to matter but. Everywhere I go. It matters."

At some level I had known this.

We went for an extra long walk that night, cracking extra–funny jokes and sharing extra–bizarro sights. We concluded with an extra–long hug.

He rubbed my scalp fuzz for good luck. "You gonna let your hair grow out again?"

"Undecided."

"What about Leon, will he stay shaved?"

"No, he'll need fur come winter. I'm hoping he'll learn to groom himself before then."

"My advice is to give him lessons before the fur grows too long. Avoid extra fur on your tongue."

"Lame."

"Thanks. See ya, Neeks."

"See ya, Benny."

He took off to the west and I watched him disappear. He must have turned at some point because he isn't the type to walk into a river.

When I got home, I wasn't alone because I had Leon and the lawn chair on the fire escape. I lowered myself into the chair and Leon curled at my feet, the way he did when Ben sat in the chair. It was too dark to see my vista above the river but I could enjoy the edges of the alley, which glowed with city light. I re–lived all the jokes and soul–searching Ben and I had exchanged on this fire escape, staring at the same sliver of view. My recollections were far more detailed than usual—the chair was sharing its memories.

"Thank you," I whispered. I squeezed its aluminum arms and went inside to get some sleep.

14. I KNEW THAT FLASH MOB

The next day was devoid of Kelly Joe. At some point, I stopped wandering the streets just in case he would show up and I went home. By now, I had seen dozens of construction sites with workers who could be from other Frames, but I had yet to figure out the ownership of any of those construction companies. That afternoon, I spent hours on the phone and internet, using all my illegal charms— cajolery, threats, misdirection—to get past the smokescreens of LLCs Incs LLPs Ltds DBAs. City departments and construction unions proved to be no use. Then I realized. Hotels are phobic about disgruntled guests.

I called ten hotels under renovation, with roughly the same line each time. "I've been a guest so many times but this visit could be my last. Those workers on that scaffolding outside! They were so rude. I'm shaking again thinking about what they said to me." Half the hotels met my request for a number I could call to complain to the contractor. The contractors all worked in different companies, but when I checked them on line, in the maze of owners and partners and dummy corporations, one name recurred. Lantana Ltd. I checked my other suspect construction sites. Every single site was involved in some way with Lantana Ltd. Bingo and *eureka*.

I called Hernandez. "Lantana Limited is Warty Sebaceous Cysts' construction company in New York." I ran down the evidence.

"Where else does Lantana operate?

"I don't know, I called you as soon as I got the name."

We put our phones on speaker and did internet searches together. We found lots of Lantana Ltd. projects in New York's five boroughs, plus Hoboken and Newark, New Jersey, but nowhere else on the eastern seaboard. Which made me wonder, "Are Digby and Lantana the only players or does every big city have its own troublemaker?"

"We don't have the personnel to answer that question. I'll let Anya and Anwyl know about Lantana."

"You're in touch with them?" *It was my sixth birthday and nobody remembered.*

"The last few days they've been here with some—guests—men and women, from what I can tell. I show them Digby sites, then I leave and they stay. I don't know what they're doing but I drive by the site the next day and work is shut down. No cops, no attention, but the construction stops and so far it stays stopped."

"I wish they would tell us what is happening! Next time you see them, tell them where I went."

"They know you're in New York."

"Hunh." After we hung up, I went for an extra run to improve my attitude. Running always helps. By the time I was on cool–down, I was no longer a six–year–old with a forgotten birthday. I was a high schooler without an invite to the cool party.

After my run, my block felt empty and dark, yet it was neither. I got my key out and was ready to open the Julian's front door well before I reached the front stoop. No Leon had materialized to slink alongside me. A large and immediate worry knot twisted my gut. Where was he? Was he okay? I forced my steps to maintain a normal pace.

Unlock the front door, take the stairs, unlock the door to my hall, unlock the door to my apartment. I was relieved to be home, where everything was per usual. Leon slept on the lawn chair on the fire escape, twitching with dreams. I exhaled so loudly I was surprised I didn't wake him. Now I felt silly for my concern. Focus on the Cysts' construction companies must have spooked me.

A skipped dinner—that was my problem. And Ben's absence at dinnertime. Fine, I would eat now and I didn't need Ben to enjoy my meal. In fact, I didn't need dinner food, which was lucky because I was out of dinner–like foods. In fact, I was well nigh out of food. I sliced my last banana into my last half–bowl of granola and curled on the couch to savor every bite. After I finished, I grabbed my shoes. I had time to make a quick grocery trip before bed.

That was when Leon's shrieks started. I ran to the kitchen window, saw him still asleep on the lawn chair. *Dreaming of a cat fight*, I figured—but the shrieks intensified. When they got to *trapped in a garbage truck* I headed for the bathroom window. When they reached *attacked by coyotes* I climbed out on the fire escape. Amazingly, the cat remained deeply asleep while screeching like a banshee in a torture chamber. Experience told me that if I touched the cat during bad dreams he could claw me unintentionally. But Leon's dream distress was unbearable.

I knelt beside the chair and blanketed him against my arms and chest. He awoke with the world's tiniest mew. As soon as my arms touched the chair, I was swept with the urge to get both of us inside pronto. But I could leave the chair outside. As I stood with my armful of groggy cat, the lanyard began to stab with warning pain. Ever since Kelly Joe had taught me how to calibrate it, I had felt nothing from it. Until now.

Out past the alley, street sounds had changed. At first, it sounded like a parade or an impromptu rave. People laughed and cheered, portable speakers blasted electronic dance music.

I locked the bathroom window behind us and set Leon on the couch. Outside, the party sounds grew closer. I went to my front window but couldn't bring myself to reveal my presence by moving the blinds. I slipped out to the hall. My apartment door locks automatically when it shuts, so I drew the deadbolt to keep it open behind me. I felt pretty safe in the hall with its locked door to the stairs. The street sounds were now more festive than a lynch mob.

The hall window looked toward the intersection, where traffic was stopped in all directions. It seemed that a flash mob was dancing its way up my street. It had stopped to dance in the intersection, but moved along as drivers honked. The flash mob swung its portable speakers and danced along my block, coming closer with each step. There were about 50 of them, all with silky platinum hair. Correction.

There were about 100 of them: as many footsteps also came from the other direction, headed my way. By now, the footsteps sounded more like marching than dancing.

I ran to the other hall window and peeked between the curtains. The flash mobs converged outside the Julian, where they did a routine. A hundred left knees lunged and two hundred arms grabbed air with fingers like hooks. Spectators cheered the impressive coordination. By the time a hundred necks bent, heads tilted to gaze at this very window, I was reacting to my brain's *scram* command. I gave a *mew* even tinier than Leon's and sprinted to get behind my deadbolt.

I knew that flash mob. Outside my building was a giant economy size collection of Warty Sebaceous Cysts' Entourage. They seemed to accompany the Cysts everywhere. Did that mean the Cysts were outside too?

I sat behind my locked doors and window bars, listening as hard as I could. After the music stopped and spectator applause dwindled, how many pairs of boots retreated and dissolved into city noise? Did all 100 pairs depart?

Long after the boots retreated, my lanyard jolted me. The street–facing wall of my apartment shook and there were shouts and crashes downstairs. And smashes. And more yelling. And eventually pounding that sounded like hammering.

Leon and I stayed inside, away from windows, with all lights on. Leon didn't sleep for a long while, which was unusual for him. In a companionable way, he watched me pace and circle the room. My heart played drums with every little noise outside. But *fight or flight* gets old. Eventually, Leon went into the kitchen for a snack and reason told me that if he was comfortable enough to eat we must be okay. Belatedly, I noticed that the lanyard had stopped prickling. I continued to pace but I didn't move as fast.

By the wee hours I wanted music; however, I also wanted to hear every last noise. I played music through my phone's speaker and continued to patrol my apartment. I needed to get my *fuck you* back, so I turned to Eminem. His cyclone emotions gradually smoothed me and by the time dawn tinted my windows, I was on the couch with Leon draped across my feet and we were listening to Gershwin. I contemplated ways to thank the cat and the lawn chair. Without Leon's noisy bad dreams, probably chair–induced, I would have stepped outside just as the Entourage closed in from both directions.

15. SHOULD EVERY QUESTION HAVE AN ANSWER?

It was a bright and sleepless night but as soon as the sun came up, I did manage to doze. I awoke to honey bees in a bag, a buzz which came from Leon's megapurr as he gazed out the kitchen window. Kelly Joe slept on the lawn chair on my fire escape.

Asleep, he had a profound air of placelessness, like musicians who live on the road. How many Frames did he grace with his music? He slept with the slightest hint of smile. Did the chair know his dreams? Would the chair dish? Imagining such an invasion of privacy made me sheepish as well as nosy.

I opened the bathroom window and unlocked the bars.

Kelly Joe woke instantly. "Good morning. Eight Seventeen Keap Street asked to speak with you. I'll be out front." That was the Brooklyn address where Sam Strongfellow's social club previously held meetings.

When I went downstairs, I discovered the cause of last night's shouting, smashing, and hammering. Someone(s) had smashed the Julian's shimmering antique glass door. This morning, the front door was two–by–fours laced with rebar and cinched with an industrial–strength deadbolt. No doubt other tenants appreciated the deadbolt. I appreciated living in a sentient building. The Entourage had tried to enter the Julian, and the building had kept them out.

With a Sigh of Ages, I joined Kelly Joe on the stoop. "Last night was a weird one."

"So it was and more to come. Your fear was justified but now let it go. You'll rise to every occasion."

His confidence made me feel safe again. "Did you expect them to show up? Is that why you've been pushing my training?"

"We've been warned to expect many things." Kelly Joe touched finger to lips, which meant Anya had told him.

We took the subway downtown, headed southeast to Keap Street in Frivolous Bedlam. I was able to Travel without a hitch in conversation. I was learning! Some of the more difficult kinds of Travel were definitely not second nature yet, and I didn't like imagining an encounter with the Cysts or Entourage. *Say, guys, could you stop menacing me for a sec? I need to concentrate to get away from you.* Would my current understanding be considered third nature? First nature? Or would –

I could no longer hear myself think. We'd arrived in Frivolous Bedlam.

Among the usual chatter, I heard the occasional *Cat Shaver* as the buildings sent word to Keap Street that I was on my way.

"If the buildings talk about me, doesn't that make it easy for Warty Sebaceous Cysts to find me?" I must have voiced this fear because Kelly Joe answered me.

"No one can visit Frivolous Bedlam without invitation and evil is not invited here. Warty Sebaceous Cysts would need control of all the Free Frames before they could enter Frivolous Bedlam."

"Our side had got some powerful resources."

"So long as our cause remains just, we'll stay aligned with Frivolous Bedlam."

"How could our cause not be just when we're fighting the Cysts."

It was rhetorical but he replied, with a dark voice I didn't understand. "Justice and evil aren't opposites."

"Can you give me a fr'instance?"

Metal scraped the asphalt behind us. A flock of food carts trailed us. "Aw!" said the front cart when I turned around. "We wanted to surprise you."

"I'm very surprised," I assured them, and they pirouetted with huzzahs.

"Hey, musician, play with us!" On this block, the buildings fluttered their first floor doors and windows as Kelly Joe passed, and he tapped their walls to match whatever rhythm the building created. Every time he matched a rhythm, the buildings cheered.

After a block of this, he swigged from his water bottle—building play was physical—and responded to me. "Should every question have an answer?"

"Maybe not. But my questions should."

"In other words, every question should be answered."

I stopped walking. Cart brakes scraped behind me. "Are you teasing me?"

"I just might be." And Kelly Joe hummed a bit as he led me forward.

Damn, I loved this man. And I wanted more than this occasional glimpse of him under the shells of teacher, musician, wanderer.

Behind us, food carts tossed my name back and forth like the playground game, Red Ro—ver Red Ro—ver. Cat Sha—ver Cat Sha—ver.

"How am I able to talk to these buildings and carts? Is English a universal language?"

"Speakers and listeners don't need the same language." Which launched an explanation that lasted two blocks of walking. The basic answer is that we have abilities we don't use in our home Frame. As we do more and better Travel, we develop a kind of fitness that unlocks new abilities. The first and most basic is the Traveler's ability to understand speech by other Travelers.

And here we were in Brooklyn, outside the social club's former meeting place. "Hello again, Eight Seventeen Keap Street!" This time, I would talk with an assumption of being understood. "It's me, Cat Shaver. I understand you have some information for me about where that social club moved to."

The building replied, "This just in. In protest over the increase in violence associated with street gang activity, residents will walk King Avenue tonight, as part of the 'Take Back Our Streets' campaign." The voice changed from newscaster modulation to the tense whisper of a frightened child, "I see dead people." Then it took on the jangly positivism of a commercial. "Make your lawn greener and save yourself some green." The newscaster came back. "Authorities released the identity of a third American fighting with the Jihadists." Next the voice matched the nasal sarcasm of Robin Williams. "So you're going to a cemetery with your toothbrush. How Egyptian." Then the voice imitated a tinny newsreel. Someone yelled into a loudspeaker in German and a crowd roared approval. The someone might have been Hitler. Finally, the metal delivery doors wiggled and the building blew a giant raspberry, issuing a sustained *pffffft* that made me wonder why I'd hurried to get here.

I crowbarred my mind to stay ajar. The building had asked me to come here. It wanted to help. This collage of gibberish must mean something. But all I could understand was that somebody in some Frame watched a lot of TV and the building remembered it all. For the splittest of seconds, I distracted myself wondering how the building would have answered in the age of radio.

Eight Seventeen Keap Street kept repeating the snippets in different orders. I looked at Kelly Joe with the confidence of a rookie sent back to the minors. I had not a clue, and the next repeat of the seemingly random snippets made me want to tell Irene goodnight.

It was the strangest feeling. When the building shuffled the phrases one more time, I understood.

16. THOSE LEFT BEHIND

Bronx cheer. Dead people. Lawn food.

"Woodlawn Cemetery!"

Eight Seventeen Keap Street snapped its awnings, slammed its windows, and issued a couple more raspberries—aka Bronx cheers—which its neighbors picked up for fun. "Well played, Cat Shaver!" the building behind us said, and I got the feeling they could have just told me the damn name.

"The social club moved to Woodlawn Cemetery?" I asked. The buildings ignored me, making elaborate noises based on the Bronx cheer.

Kelly Joe didn't have to shrug to give me a shrug.

I had my answer and it made no sense. I'd never been to Woodlawn Cemetery but I had seen it from the subway station that bears its name, at the end of the number 4 subway line in the Bronx. Famous people are buried there, so Woodlawn Cemetery has many visitors. Did it have meeting rooms for a social club? Or had the social club joined in a suicide pact? If they had killed themselves, surely that would have made the news—oh. Heh, maybe it had. I hadn't caught the news in weeks.

Kelly Joe pushed up a sleeve of his denim jacket. "This came today." Among his messages was a new tattoo with pale gray ink: weathered tombstones climbing a grassy hill.

"Guess you're coming with me to Woodlawn Cemetery!" I could hear the relief in my voice. Now that the Entourage had appeared, it seemed like a hiatus had ended and I needed to find Sam Strongfellow and give Lilah closure while I still had time to do so. But now that the Entourage had appeared, I liked how safe I felt around Kelly Joe.

He led me down to a subway track. "We'll have to finish our Travel in Ma'Urth but we can start from here. Frame Travel to cemeteries is blocked in respect for the Neutral dead."

The buildings began to play with the word *cemetery* as though it were new to them.

"Do cemeteries only exist in Neutral Frames? What do they do with their dead in other Frames?"

"That's a topic for another time."

It was as close to a rebuke as I'd ever heard from him. My questions seemed to upset him although I couldn't ask why. I couldn't speak. Frame Travel on a speeding train is like threading yourself through a needle during a toboggan run. I kept my chin tucked and my jaw clamped to lessen the sensation of whiplash.

Back on Ma'Urth, we exited the train at Woodlawn station and discovered that just outside the cemetery gate was a small construction site. On this late afternoon, it must be past quitting time—the chain link fence surrounding the site was locked and the site was empty. Nonetheless we stopped. I reacted to the sign: Lantana Ltd. Kelly Joe sensed something inside the site. He circled the fencing then said, "Our enemies are bold."

"Good afternoon!" The cemetery gate guard was a pink–skinned fellow whose Woodlawn khaki stretched tight across a stomach as round as a trash can. "We close in 50 minutes, but I can push that to an hour so long's I don't have to hunt you down on the grounds."

"Much appreciated," Kelly Joe nodded.

Woodlawn Cemetery was huge. Big enough to have a seat on city council, if its residents could still vote. It was perfect walking weather, the sky packed with clouds fluffy enough to decorate a pre–school. I hadn't noticed a cloud overhead since I got to Manhattan. With so many tall buildings, it kinks the neck to look at the sky. I was happy to see these clouds, although I couldn't muster my previous innocent love, now that I knew to be cautious around them. Clouds can be messengers—and spies.

Kelly Joe's gaze moved from cloud to cloud as though he were looking for someone he knew.

"You never seem to worry about eavesdropping clouds," I noted as we climbed a grassy knoll.

"Here, we'll speak with care. In the city, clouds don't hear much. Most words reverberate among the buildings and the flow of the rivers distorts the rest."

We wandered at a fast clip to maximize our hour before closing time. Woodlawn was acres of grass, trees, hills—a lovely peaceful resting place. But within half a mile, I needed out. The tombstone inscriptions oppressed me with the longings of those left behind. Woodlawn would be a nice place to be dead, if the living stopped clinging. But I wouldn't judge. Some of us get more practice letting go than others do.

"Might as well get out of here. I can't figure out why that building sent us here. Let's go back to Bedlam. I need to talk to Eight Seventeen Keap Street some more."

"I'd let the experience sit overnight, but whenever you want to return to Frivolous Bedlam, go on ahead. From now on, you may Travel there on your own. It's safe for you to make that trip." Kelly Joe's delivery was syncopated, matching our steps as we descended a steep hill.

"Wow!" I was allowed to Travel solo! *Nica S.T.A.T.Ic., Frame Traveler.*

"Only the trip between Ma'Urth and Frivolous Bedlam, mind."

"Just for now, right? Someday I'll be able to go to other Frames on my own?"

"Someday soon."

Nica S.T.A.T.Ic., Detective of the Frames.

We were a couple turns from the cemetery exit when the wind picked up and delivered a new cluster of clouds overhead. The air became as still as the moments between lightning and thunder. I stopped; and touched Kelly Joe's arm to confirm he had stopped, too. I couldn't look at him because I was staring at the clouds, from which a familiar voice emanated, a bass voice that blanketed the landscape and rattled the tombstones.

"Go, cloud, and take this message to all who love my brother."

I loved the brother and I loved the being behind that voice. It was Monk, the Watts Tower with a knack for speaking inscrutably. He radiated the deep calm of a zen master, until his brother Miles vanished. I couldn't tell from Monk's voice whether this message about Miles would be good or terrible. Every muscle in my body tensed.

"Go cloud, and carry my message," Monk repeated, sounding puzzled. "Cloud, why do you linger?" It was like listening to the start of a recording, *Is this thing on?*

A voice that sounded like Monk but with less vibrato repeated everything he'd just said: that is, the cloud repeated Monk's words, so Monk could review his message. There was nothing to review. Monk had failed to give the cloud a message to convey.

The air vibrated with the static buzz of Monk's laugh. "Thank you, cloud, for waiting. Joy makes clumsy news! Here is my message: Miles is home and his injuries will heal."

(He didn't say *Miles*, and actually his name isn't *Monk*. Those are the nicknames I gave them because I can't say their names, which are 17 syllables and all consonants.)

Miles was alive and safe. I dropped to the ground and pressed my face in the grass. I'll always love the odor of lawn chemicals because they remind me of that moment.

The wind picked up again and the clouds scuttled away.

Kelly Joe's eyes glistened and he mumbled, "Praise and thanks, praise and thanks." I leaped up and hugged him. He grew a shadow smile when I used his shoulders to launch my next leap higher. We had found nothing at Woodlawn but hearing Monk's message made the trip priceless.

When Kelly Joe and I got back to the cemetery gate, the guard leaned out of his kiosk to say, "Right on time, 'preciate that."

I fished out my photo of Samson Strongfellow. "Nica S.T.A.T.1c. I'm a private detective and I'm looking for this man. I have reports he's been here at Woodlawn Cemetery. I know you see many people but –"

"That –" The guard was in the act of taking the photo when he recognized the face and withdrew his hand. The photo fell and he muttered apology but I was the one who picked it up.

"Why're you looking for that—him?" And why would you serve pond scum for dinner?

"So you've seen him?"

"Too often! I gave him warnings and a citation. I promised jail if I saw him again."

"No kidding! What did he do?"

"He harassed the guests—shouted insults! Crazy things. White supremacist, blow–up–your–enemies things. He yelled at everybody, even a little girl the size of an angel. 'Course he made her cry. As far as I could tell, he hates everybody."

"Was he alone?"

"'Course not—cowards never attack alone. He was the ringleader but the others'd egg him on. I hope you don't find him near here."

"Thank you for your time and your candor."

He had to slam the gate to align the lock or get rid of his anger toward Sam.

At some point during my conversation, Kelly Joe had wandered off. I found him at the construction site. "Did you hear all that?"

"I did." He nudged his head in the direction of the subway platform. "You go ahead, I'll catch up."

"Okay." The force of will it took to not ask why, what, wherefore. In the Silence Olympics, I got the gold.

The so—called subway was elevated here and the train tracks were upstairs. This gave me a good vantage to watch the construction site. I couldn't see Kelly Joe and then I could. Here he came, strolling and humming, with smoke tendrils rising from inside the site fence. By the time Kelly Joe was on the stairs, flames flared like a Christmas tree ignition. As we stepped aboard the train, the platform shook with an explosion from inside the construction site.

"Staging a work slowdown?"

"Thereabouts."

17. THE BASIC STATE OF BEING

On the train back into town, Kelly Joe slid his sleeves above his elbows and studied his messages. The tombstone tattoo was gone, that skin tanned with no evidence of ever having been inked. "When the tattoo disappears, does that mean what was supposed to happen, did happen?"

"Time will tell."

"Please don't advocate patience around me, it stresses me out."

He chuckled and lowered his sleeves. "Change is underway," is all he would say. He repeated that when we walked into my apartment, and added, "Best you stay in Frivolous Bedlam. Take a few minutes to gather things you'll need. You should be safe to return here, briefly, to change clothes or make a phone call. But don't leave Julian. Go outdoors in Frivolous Bedlam, not Ma'Urth."

Things were finally happening! My relief trumped my fear. "What kind of danger am I in? Is it the Entourage? That's what I call them. That team of identical guys who are mental appendages of Warty Sebaceous Cysts who were outside last night."

"That's an amusing name for the mind eaters but they're not amusing."

Mind eaters. The Entourage were officially called mind eaters. TMI. Names are important to attitude. Ludicrous is easier to withstand. Maybe we should start calling Maelstrom *Clamface*. "Are they after me? Is that why I need to stay away from Ma'Urth?"

"No knowledge, no worry." Kelly Joe said, like it was a saying.

"Not with me. I've got an apocalyptic imagination. The truth will be more tame."

"No. No it won't be."

For once, I stopped asking questions.

It didn't take long to move me. While I schlepped small everyday items from Ma'Urth to Bedlam, Kelly Joe fetched furniture from who–knows–where. Maybe there was a discount furniture Frame. Or maybe, in some unsuspecting Frame, tonight Logram and Mametto would look at each other in confusion: "What happened to our couch?"

I made a final stroll through my apartment on Ma'Urth. I guess I had everything I needed for now—Leon. Snoozing on the lawn chair on the fire escape. Should I take the cat? The chair? My hand brushed the chair and I got a feeling I should leave the chair where it was. But the chair had no advice about whether to take Leon.

Kelly Joe appeared at the bathroom window. "It's time to go," he announced. I petted Leon with advance nostalgia, and he added, "He'll be safer without you."

"Safer but not safe? Can I bring Leon with me to Bedlam?"

"Cats can't be brought, they bring themselves or they don't come."

Another move. My apartment in Bedlam seemed even more alien once it was furnished like its counterpart on Ma'Urth. Of course, I was barely accustomed to any of the New Yorks, and I had never felt settled back in Los Angeles when I lived illegally in my office at the Henrietta. So it had been a long time since any home had felt like home. But here I was and Kelly Joe had found me a couch that looked downright comfy. I flopped hard on the couch to test its springs.

Kelly Joe seemed to mistake my flop for frustration. "You want to understand what's going on. What I can say is that a shift in focus is underway. We need to keep you out of sight during the transition."

"Thanks for that. I was afraid your reasons might be obscure. Don't worry, I'll just sit here and tell myself jokes. How many Neutrals does it take to change a light bulb in a Frame that has no lamps?"

"You only need to sit if you choose."

And then he was gone, and I was here.

I chose not to sit.

My first day alone in Frivolous Bedlam was magical and reminded me for the umpteenth time that I should never resist the unexpected. I wandered and roamed, eavesdropping on building conversations more tangled than soap opera plots, more scattershot than a convention of comedians. I went inside buildings, too. I've always loved the possibilities in an empty room—although I needed another way to describe Bedlam interiors. *Empty* has negative connotations and these rooms had none, just fresh open respites. Outside was where the action was, and outside at all hours, food carts frolicked and motor scooters goofed off with bicycles. In Bedlam, *playful* is the basic state of being.

I finished my wandering at dusk. None of the buildings had their lights on yet and Julian's front door glittered with the day's last sunlight. The antique glass was especially beautiful because here it was untouched by the Entourage's attack. As it reflected the sunset, it filled me with hope about our cause.

I wanted to introduce myself to my building but wasn't sure how. Julian didn't chatter, which meant he had true sentience like Henrietta. I knocked on his front door. "Julian, it's me, Nica. Cat Shaver."

"Good evening. Do you prefer Nica or Cat Shaver?" His voice was a sophisticated tenor that warbled like he gargled with marbles.

"I'm good either way. Surprise me."

"I do not know you well enough to know what you might find surprising. I will call you Cat Shaver for now, to remind myself of your reputation, which amuses me."

"You must find your occupants funny."

"Quite often, but Henrietta was right that you are especially entertaining."

His manner was so appreciative I couldn't take offense. "How do you talk to Henrietta when she is so far away?"

"Where there is ground we connect," he said, like it was an adage.

"Tell her *hello* next time you speak."

"From your mouth to her door."

I went inside and after I entered my apartment, I heard Julian's voice, muffled. I opened the door and leaned into the hall. Now I could hear him clearly. "Henrietta sends her regards."

"Wow! You heard back that fast?" He had just conversed with a building thousands of miles away. It took the shared—sentience buildings longer to send a message across the street.

"I did. She inquires as to whether you plan to shave the creature known as Dizzy?"

"No way, I value all my fingers."

He laughed like the creak of grandma's rocking chair.

I left my apartment door open and opened all my windows, too, to let some chatter in.

It was mighty silent inside.

End of Day 1. Here I was. Staring down boredom. Already. I needed input. I Traveled back to my apartment on Ma'Urth, grabbed an apple, opened my laptop then shut it. Kelly Joe hadn't said I could stick around long enough to amuse myself on the internet. I grabbed my books plus a copy of *Lose Twenty Pounds of Worry in Twenty Days*. Leon had come inside to eat. I petted him for a few, then returned to Bedlam, where I read for maybe an hour, went home again for a mineral water. Leon met me in the hall. I sat to pet him for a few, then went back to Bedlam.

It became a cycle. I returned to Ma'Urth every couple hours, until I realized how predictable my visits were. So this would have to be my last stop home for a while. I'd leave as soon as I finished petting Leon. On second thought, I'd leave now: Leon stopped purring and tensed, just before someone out in the hall rattled the doorknob. Someone in my locked hall area.

I got the hell back to Bedlam and this time I vowed to stay there.

Being in a new place, it's hard to get a start with sleep, and Bedlam was far less familiar than any hotel room. I went for a long run to boost my chance of slumber. Very late at night, Bedlam was a bit quieter and considerably less bright. The streets had a warm dark glow like aging holiday lights. Most of the food carts were parked in clusters and seemed to be resting.

It was nearly dawn before I tried stretching out on my Bedlam couch. Maybe I should close my eyes. Damn. All those trips home and I'd still forgotten my pillow. I repositioned so that the armrest of the couch was behind my neck. I inhaled. I squirmed. I exhaled. Maybe I should do some calisthenics.

Leon walked out of the bathroom, purring of course, and lounged across my feet. I loved that vibration through my—wait. Leon was on my feet. Which were in Bedlam. Had I somehow brought Leon with me on my last trip from Ma'Urth? Had I started my Frame shift while petting him? Leon was considerably larger than a ladybug so it seems like I should have noticed.

Kelly Joe had implied that it wasn't good for Leon to be here. I scooped him up. Leon doesn't mind being held but he won't collapse against me, he stands on me. Weird, but workable. I returned us to Ma'Urth with Leon standing on my chest and hurried him out to the fire escape. It was creepy to be outside on Ma'Urth. The alley air was thick as though the Entourage were about to converge. I petted Leon until he curled on the lawn chair, then stumbled inside and sank to the couch. I was indeed getting stronger—I had been able to Travel with Leon and hadn't collapsed until minutes later.

I was safe inside Julian yet felt exposed. Being home on Ma'Urth felt like I was sunburned and naked. As soon as I could, I grabbed my pillow and Traveled to safety.

Back in Frivolous Bedlam, I flopped on my couch. Damn, I'd meant to check my clock at home. I had no sense of time's passage here. But I wouldn't go back just now. Maybe I should read. I let my volume of Yeats open to my favorite page, then Leon walked in from the bathroom. This time there was no way I could have had a role in his arrival.

"Holy *frijoles*, Leon, you're a Traveler."

Still no sleep. I went out for another run and Leon came with me. In Bedlam, he displayed no fear outdoors. He lost the cockroach slink and trotted beside me, tail in the air. Now we were Cat Shaver and Cat, which brought us sporadic attention. A building would take time away from its knock–knock and slam–slam jokes to announce, "Cat Shaver, Cat is here."

"He sure is! Right here! Thanks!"

It had to be a game, because they kept doing it. In a related game, the buildings said, "Cat, Cat is here."

"Thanks is thanks," I would reply. Or, "Here is right here!" The way delivery doors clattered, I got the sense I wasn't playing the game right, but couldn't guess what they wanted me to say instead. No matter. Another block and they forgot about us again.

When I was tired enough that I could have slept standing up, I led us back to my apartment. *En route* to the couch, Leon arched, puffed, and hissed at the center cushion, where a gray and white feline sat.

"Dizzy! How did you—never mind." Even if the cat could tell me how she had come from Los Angeles to find me in Bedlam, I wouldn't know whether to believe her. I loved the cat, but Anwyl hated her and Anya feared her. What did they know that I didn't?

As my confusion roiled, the cats circled each other, crying like demon babies. I hate cat fights but you can't separate cats who are in fight mode, you'll trip the Attack switch and get shredded. But water can distract them!

Dizzy lunged, mongoose quick, at Leon's throat. I yelled, ran to the sink, poured water in the nearest bowl and hurled it in their direction. I soaked the couch and missed the cats, now a shifting mass of orange white gray fur as they fought.

Correction. As they play–fought. I should have realized theirs was a fight game; cats don't attack as a first resort; they've always just done their nails.

I love watching cats pretend to battle—the drama, the pomp, the underhanded tricks—so I sat on the dry side of the couch and got an exceptional show. Dizzy led every maneuver, no two alike, and seemed to be testing Leon. She had ruthless cunning but he had evasive enormousness. Two viable solutions to the vulnerable plight of the street cat.

From one moment to the next, it was over. Dizzy caught up on her grooming and Leon on his purring. I briefly fretted about which or whether cats could be trusted, but it didn't matter. I wouldn't chase them out—assuming I could. I loved them, and Ben had long ago trained me that love could be irrelevant to trust.

Oops, I'd left the kitchen tap running water—hey. I had running water in Frivolous Bedlam. I checked the toilet and sure enough, it flushed.

I stretched out on the couch. Maybe I'd read. But the problem with keeping only my favorite books was that I had every one more or less memorized. Except for *Lose Twenty Pounds of Worry in Twenty Days.* "Nobody needs to know," I instructed the cats, and opened the self–help drivel. It wasn't as bad as I expected, but when you start that low, the limbo contest is already over.

I was learning about loneliness these days and tonight's lesson was that time passes more quickly with friends. Dawn approached to the sound of pages turning and cats thunking the floor during play fights. At some point, I did fall asleep. When I woke up, the cats were gone and the books were in the air, flapping slow circles around me.

18. I TRUST YOUR INSTINCTS

I stayed calm, like a zombie at the DMV. The last time I'd seen books flying, they had rained text that pulverized flesh. There was nothing menacing about this group, though. If I had not witnessed books murdering innocents, I would have been enchanted by this vision of flying books, so I forced a smile until it became genuine. Anyway, if these books had wanted to hurt me I'd already be sliced thinner than prosciutto.

Lose Twenty Pounds of Worry in Twenty Days adjusted its flap rate to hover above me. The other books copied its moves, some more gracefully than others. My woodcut–illustrated edition of *Summer* couldn't get the hovering right, would advance too far then have to circle and try again.

"Good morning." I sat up, which startled *Summer*, who shed a brief rain of text and collided with *Madame Bovary*.

Lose Twenty Pounds dipped in what looked like a formal bow, and at his barking command the other books tried to follow suit. Although they seemed to acknowledge him as a leader, they were not so much a squadron as they were flying puppies, so the bows devolved to mid–air collisions, all of which released more rains of text.

Lose Twenty Pounds squeaked harshly and the other books settled onto the kitchenette counter. *Lose Twenty Pounds* shed a few syllables of text along the edge of the couch, slicing away fabric to reveal wooden frame. He shot over my head, squeaked several times, flapped over to the table and shed text that peeled a curl of glass from a bowl. I didn't understand his language but the meaning was clear. Text was dangerous and you had to control yours at all times. As the other books learned control, the hardwood floor became pocked with a thousand cuts from impaled text. Gradually, the text dissolved and the floor's cuts healed. The damage to the couch remained.

"Go ahead and practice on the couch, it's already trashed." I retreated to the farthest corner of my main room, away from couch guts that bulged through the sliced fabric. *Lose Twenty Pounds* dipped a bow but continued training in the kitchen, slicing strips of tile from the counters. As I watched, I understood why he'd ignored me. Furniture, once sliced, stayed damaged; but the building's injuries healed themselves—like time–lapse photography that played just outside my view no matter how hard I stared.

Each time text hit the floor or tile, from outside my apartment came a noise from Julian. The building seemed to feel each letter's impact. However, his reactions were more suggestive of intense massage than injury. I had to conclude that *Lose Twenty Pounds* knew what he was doing.

I watched my books circle and wished for a way to talk with them. There was much I wanted to know. Were they aware when they were immobile in a Neutral Frame like Ma'Urth? How did they feel about their actions as mercenary soldiers? Did books have regrets? Would that depend on which book it was? Did every copy of *Lose Twenty Pounds* have the same personality? My questions smothered me like deployed airbags. I envisioned a book rescue, with rains of text that popped the airbags. Which gave me an idea about how to get some answers from them.

Lose Twenty Pounds hovered and the other books perched on the edge of the tile counter between kitchenette and main room, dust jackets extended. They raised and lowered their spines at squeaks from *Lose Twenty Pounds*. They were doing exercises or stretches.

"'S'cuse me. I want to talk to you. With you, I mean." *Lose Twenty Pounds* pivoted toward me, his pages rippling and his cover low, a stance I've come to know as relaxed. He squawked and the other books ascended.

"If you understand my words, dip once to mean yes." I used my hand to show what I meant. *Lose Twenty Pounds* dipped, then the other books dipped but *Summer* took an unintentional dive. I reached to retrieve *Summer* from the floor but *Lose Twenty Pounds* squawked and blocked my motion. After a long moment, *Summer* rose without my help, in a wobbly arc with covers flapping out of sync.

I waved my fingers back and forth. "This motion means no." *Lose Twenty Pounds* made an abrupt side–to–side shake. The others managed a one–sided hiccup.

"Can you read?"

Dip. *Yes.*

"Can you spell?"

Dip. *Yes.*

"Does it hurt you when you shed text?"

Shake. *No.*

"Can you choose which text to release?" *Selected Letters of Raymond Chandler* shot forward from the pack and dropped three letters on the trashed arm of the couch. The tiny letters strobed my vision as they descended. Y–E–S.

Excited books whizzed everywhere while *Lose Twenty Pounds* squawked what sounded like warnings. As I later learned, he spoke Refrencian, the limited, militaristic language that Librarians use when recruiting books to join the military, then squad leaders use to command those mercenary soldiers. *Lose Twenty Pounds'* warnings became prophecies when excited books crashed and collided. Soon my books littered the floor, spines bellowing as they panted.

While I pondered whether to pick them up or leave them be, Leon and Dizzy were suddenly among them, picking their way through the splayed covers. Leon seemed puzzled and curious about the books but as he moved to sniff one, Dizzy jumped him and held the ruff of his neck in her teeth, which immobilized him. "They're okay, Dizzy, these books are friends." I stooped to reach for the closest, splayed book, mindful of the sharp page edges but confident that *To Kill A Mockingbird* would never hurt anyone.

My limited field of vision filled with work boots and denim legs. Kelly Joe stood in my hall, taking in the panting volumes, the minute letters that bristled on the couch arm, Dizzy's hold on Leon, my calm. "Good morning," he concluded.

"I'm glad you're here. I've got some questions for you."

"You're Nica," he agreed. "I have a few minutes for answers."

"I think these books are safe—friendly. That's possible, right?"

"I believe it is, but on Ma'Urth we have a bond with books." He tilted his head this way and that to read all the titles.

"They're not inherently vicious! I'm so glad you see that!"

"Many would say we're blindered about books."

"Oh."

Lose Twenty Pounds sank to the counter. Kelly Joe tilted his head to read the back blurb and looked up as if it weren't the worst drivel he'd ever read. "I trust your instincts and you should, too."

I couldn't decide which felt greater, my musician's validation of my books, or the respect in his voice.

One by one, as the books stopped panting, they flew from floor to counter with less noisy flapping than previously. I got the impression they wanted to listen. I didn't want the books to hear anything discouraging, so moved on to my next set of questions.

"Anya and Anwyl—and Miles, and Monk—why don't they like cats?"

The cats on the couch showed no reaction. Leon was curled like a cooked shrimp; next to him, Dizzy cleaned her butt. Preposterous candidates for world domination. Anya and Anwyl didn't like to talk in front of Dizzy, but I figured she either understood nothing, or everything, and either way there was no point trying to disguise the conversation.

"Mistrust of cats is an attitude you'll find around the Frames, but again, on Ma'Urth we have a different perspective—though some say cats have tainted our judgment, and mock us by calling our Frame 'Cat–Urth'."

I scoffed to hear this but the mockers had a point. I let cats get away with stuff that no one else dared try around me. "Should we be concerned about these cats?"

"I save mistrust for misdeed." He flipped through *Lose Twenty Pounds* with a two–handed skim that kept fingers in the margins, away from the bone–slicing text and page edges. His hands and jaw were scraped and bruised.

"Were you in a fight?"

"Of a sort. Is this a good book?"

Lose Twenty Pounds grew still and I sensed my answer mattered to the book. Mattered a lot. The poor book couldn't help it that someone filled his pages with pablum and baloney. I drew on my debate team experience to non–answer: "I've barely started reading it but so far I'm surprised by the degree to which I like it. I bought several copies, in fact. But I don't know why I felt compelled to do that."

"You'll understand when it's time to know."

"Do you understand?"

"Surely not." He closed the book. "Today it's safe for you to go home to Ma'Urth and you'll want to do so." Then, as suddenly as he had appeared, he walked out of Frame.

I got ready to go.

"I don't know whether to take you back or leave you here," I told my books. *Lose Twenty Pounds* twisted left–right then up–down. *No, don't take us back. Yes, leave us here.* He squawked and hovered on the kitchenette side of the counter, until I went in the kitchenette to see why he hovered there. *The Blue-Eyed Shan* was stuck between pipes under the sink. As I extricated the book, its dust cover ripped. Behind me, *Lose Twenty Pounds* squawked and shed text on the tile. t–a–k–e–t–h–i–s–o–n–e–to–h–e–a–l.

The other books returned to their flying practice; the cats resumed play–fighting; and outside my open window, buildings were in hysterics. It must have been a good joke—even Julian murmured amusement. I wanted to stay and hang out; on Ma'Urth I'd once again be cut off from the Frames; but Kelly Joe had given me an order, however much he'd presented it like a suggestion.

I took a moment to wonder whether I was now comfortable in two Frames or no Frame.

19. OUR TIME ARRIVES

Within the first minute back in my apartment on Ma'Urth, I whacked my shin against the decorative table in the second floor hall, then smashed my toe into the kitchenette counter in my apartment, which delivered two reminders: I could slow down; and I was not yet familiar with my Manhattan abode. I pressed ice against the knot on my shin and limped like Quasimodo to check all my locks.

Today it's safe was the way Kelly Joe had described my return to Ma'Urth. Today.

I briefly dated a guy who was a disaster junkie. His version of foreplay was to practice fleeing. We'd get out in a hurry—from my apartment, his condo, our favorite dinner joint. For the first time, I could use what I learned from him. I closed my eyes and moved around my apartment until my muscle memory knew every turn and obstacle. Then I did the same in the hall outside my door.

As I zipped along the hall, backwards, I heard the stomping of the Entourage flash mob outside and even though I knew I imagined them and Julian would protect me, I spooked myself. I spun, faster than a politician's story, and my eyes popped open. Before my vision focused, I collided with someone in my locked hall, someone who pinned my arms to break my momentum.

When I recall that moment, I'm never sure whether it was adrenalin or the lanyard that blasted lightning through my extremities, but the jolts were so powerful that if my arms hadn't been pinned I might have become airborne.

My cheek pressed against a tunic of finely woven gray cloth. I inhaled the fresh wild scent of a forest after a flash flood.

"Well met, Nica of the New Yorks," Anwyl drawled above my scalp.

"Finally! You're finally here!" I mumbled into the cloth.

"With absence, an hour turns to night," Anya's glorious lilt filled the hall. Hearing her voice overwhelmed me. At some deep level I had feared I would never see either of them again. But here they were, filling the hall with their threat and promise. I shoved my face into Anwyl's tunic to hide my tears and realized that he still held me. On more than one occasion, he had supported me, but this was more embrace than brace. Wowza! My temperature spiked in all the right places.

Anya touched my arm and Anwyl released his hold. There's nothing more peace–inducing than sharing a smile with Anya. She hooked my arm in hers and pivoted us toward the staircase to the lobby. Anwyl loped downstairs ahead of us. He was a wolf on the move, looking for the hunt. At the Julian's front door he checked outside before he held the door for us to exit.

Kelly Joe sat at the bottom of the stoop outside and hummed into his harmonica, bending mournful notes as though thinking aloud. When Anwyl spotted Kelly Joe, he barked a noise that, from more easy–going lips, could be construed as a laugh. As my musician stood, Anwyl leaped the remaining steps and grabbed Kelly Joe, which carried them to the sidewalk. Their hug was a quick clasp of forearms. Anwyl stared into Kelly Joe's eyes then released his grip with twin slaps of affection and concern.

Kelly Joe took one of Anya's hands in both of his and bowed his head briefly. Genuflection on a midday Manhattan street wasn't the incognito we were going for.

"Our time arrives," she greeted him.

"Their time departs," he replied in a ritualized sing–song. Now it was their turn to exchange an eye–gaze.

She reached up to touch fingers to his forehead. "Be at peace, my brother," she whispered.

"When I have earned peace." His tone was rolling thunder.

My take–home messages were a jumble. Kelly Joe mattered to Anya and Anwyl and both seemed concerned about him. I'd often sensed his underlying sorrow but now I sensed self–hatred, too.

For the rest of the day, a small but relentless part of my mind plotted schemes to get one of them to dish about what all this meant. The rest of me was consumed by excitement and exhaustion. Anya, Anwyl, and Kelly Joe. To be with all three of them was amazing.

We headed east like we had a destination. Kelly Joe redirected their attention to me. "Nica's a dedicated student. She learned 'most all you needed her to learn and then a little more."

"I expected no other outcome," Anya smiled.

Anwyl focused on the *half empty*. "Almost all is not all. What skill does she yet lack?"

"I can only Travel with ladybugs."

"Ladybugs?" Anya asked Kelly Joe.

"*Coccinellidae*," he explained.

Of course. Now they understood. Anya's voice was warm enough to thaw Pluto. "This affinity serves you well. When first we met, you had one such being with you." She held my arm like reunited sisters.

Anwyl had the newsworthy response, though. He spoke kindly, proving that oxymorons can come true. *Anwyl kind.* "I shared your struggle when I learned to Travel. Transport of a living being requires more energy than we believe we have. Adjust your belief and the skill will follow. On the morrow you must practice. But before this day loses its sheen, show us the structures you have identified as altered by Warty Sebaceous Cysts."

It was disorienting to have Anwyl speak to me as though my brain had all its lobes, but I adapted to the novelty and savored it throughout the afternoon as we visited Lantana construction sites. More than half the sites showed signs of recent damage, mostly fire.

"Have you been this busy or do you have friends who help you?" I asked Kelly Joe.

In honor of Anya and Anwyl's arrival he gave an obscure answer. "Yes indeed."

The last construction site we visited was the one outside Woodlawn Cemetery. The site was gone, with scorched pavement as a reminder of Kelly Joe's arson job. Parked on the pavement were a pair of food trucks. Anya touched them in a way that told me the trucks were sentient and she was saying hello.

Anwyl held a hand on the aluminum siding of Alonzo's Biscuits, then reported to us, "As the sun sets, disturbance will rise in there." He nodded toward the cemetery and led us through the gate.

The guard at the gate kiosk called, "We close at sunset. In twenty minutes, I lock this gate." Today the guard was a snip of a girl who didn't seem to care when none of us responded. My companions continued into the cemetery to a three—branch fork in the road. They each took a separate branch.

"I'll catch up," I said and returned to the gate kiosk. Would this gate guard also get angry to see a photo of Sam Strongfellow?

The gate guard was reading about celebrities and tugging fingers through the unruly black frizz that capped her head. Her nails were long, square, and white as a Goth's belly skin. In the twilight they glowed like, well, tombstones.

"Hi, again. The guy who works this gate. What's his name again?"

"The one who died, you mean?"

"Died? I just talked to him."

"He dropped dead on his shift. They only noticed his body after they put out the fire."

"There was a fire?"

"Mm hmm, at the construction site. They said he had a stroke. He was always yelling at everybody. That's not healthy."

"There've been problems with some cemetery visitors. Maybe he yelled to keep them in line?"

"Those guys. They're just kids. Although for kids they were scary."

"'Kids', huh? You're what, 18 next birthday, Rosie?" She looked surprised then touched her name badge. Yup. That's how I knew.

"A kid can call a kid a kid."

I laughed. "A kid can do whatever she wants."

"Truth!" We bumped knuckles to seal our agreement.

"I'd like to talk to those other kids. Any idea how to find them?"

"Yes."

I waited earnestly.

"Count two then turn around but not like I told you," she whispered.

"OK, thanks, wish me luck finding it," I said loudly while heading onto the grounds. Coming down the north fork of the road were a quartet of *twenty—something* men, walking abreast to fill the road.

The quartet stayed four abreast, making me step onto the grass to pass them. All four stared. One of them said, "Typical New York white bitch," which set the other three to muttering, although they were the ones with the local accents and the pale skin.

Rosie was right. They were scary. I returned to the road once I got past them and I made sure not to quicken my pace even when I heard them pause behind me. Speeding up was a *chase me I'm prey* choice.

The loudmouth said over the muttering, "Leave her for now, man." Four sets of boots stomped toward the gate, paused. The gate buzzed and the boots continued out of the cemetery.

I resumed breathing and assumed that distant *click* was Rosie, locking herself into the guard kiosk.

It wasn't over. Here came four more guys, again spanning the road, again with a swagger that said they were looking for trouble. Some of these guys felt like out–of–Framers. Where were Anwyl and Anya and Kelly Joe?

I turned a curve in the road and I spotted yet another four, coming from behind a mausoleum with pink and black stone. They appeared suddenly—they weren't there and then they were. As though they had arrived by walking a Connector from another Frame.

I focused on the immediate threat, the four in the road ahead of me. Three looked to the fourth, who sneered, "She's a jogger, the rich ones have time to stay fit," which got the others angry at me. Seriously. The four coming from the mausoleum were close enough now that I could hear one say to the others, "Anyone who dresses like that is a tease." It was as if each group had a hatred coach.

The lanyard was not helpful. It blasted me with pain that made it hard to stay as alert as I needed to stay. "I know, already, stop jolting me!" I yelled at the lanyard, which made the closer group pause, all too briefly.

I was almost as mad as I was frightened, and I calculated my escape while I strode toward them like I hadn't heard their taunts. *I'm not prey, jerkwads, I'm not prey.* I cupped my hands to shout over their shoulders, "Hey, guys, wait up!" Big guy with a stick right behind you. Which could become true, if my companions could only hear me.

My plan was to run like hell and get lost in the lengthening shadows. *I'm not a jogger, toad, I'm a runner.* As soon as I got past the ones blocking the road, I would sprint across the grass away from the Connector. They wouldn't expect it, which could buy me a few seconds of lead.

And if wishes were spaceships, I'd get beamed up.

The four from the mausoleum caught up to the group blocking the road. Now they stretched eight across—and the flanks kept moving, as though to get behind me. "Look at her," somebody sneered, prompting his hatred coach for more reasons to loathe me.

The promise of mayhem filled the air like Africanized bees. I searched their faces for hints of humanity, common ground, loopholes. I found the clenched jaws of fanatics. I was stunned to recognize one of the hatred coaches.

"Sam Strongfellow?! Lilah has been looking everywhere for you!"

This disrupted their attack. Seven of the eight had never heard those names before, and none of us were expecting me to react with indignation.

"Lilah," Sam repeated blankly.

The others shuffled.

I hate bullies. They put me in a blind white rage, ever since the time in middle school that bullies broke the arm of my friend, Tommy Dinatello, and he had to drop out of his bike race. I got suspended, along with the bullies, for my counterattack. *Violence is always wrong* or some nonsense like that.

"Your sister, dumbass! She's worrying about you while you're harassing people in a fucking cemetery!" And I shoved him, and we weren't expecting that either, and I got lucky, and he lost his balance. He didn't fall, though, he stumbled. And as he straightened and the eight tightened their circle and my rage cooled, a scramble of thoughts congealed to a single concept. *I'm doomed.*

Faint as a liar's conscience came mournful twists of blues harmonica. The guys on the flanks shouted and leaped at me. Correction, they launched sideways and fell on their sides. While the four on the ground moaned, the four who were still standing spun to face their attackers. Yes, they had been attacked. My cavalry had arrived.

Even being on the same side, my cohorts frightened me. Anya called commands like thunderclaps. Anwyl used one arm to pin both of Sam's arms, and with the other hand, held a wicked blade at Sam's throat. Kelly Joe put a boot on one of the fallen and shoved him prone, while beckoning the three who were still standing to come closer.

"We can take them. There're only four and two of them are girls," a rank-and-file bully yelled.

A hate coach told him to shut up.

With a boot on the arm of a bully, Kelly Joe resumed playing harmonica, and with each note the eight showed less conviction. The four on the ground stopped writhing. The three who were on their feet—and not in Anwyl's grip—milled around. Anya stepped out of the failing light and linked her elbow with mine. "It is fortunate that some of you recognize your opponents," she announced to the group. "We wish to avoid loss of life, even the lives of (and she said a name that sounded like) Lobotomists."

(No matter how hard I listened the name still sounded liked) "Lobotomists," Anwyl spoke with contempt. "To call theirs lives, you bestow favor unearned."

This got seven of them riled up, until a guttural syllable issued from Sam. He couldn't speak words, he'd stab himself on Anwyl's blade.

"Your point is well honed," Anya said to Anwyl, as though discussing gardening over tea.

Kelly Joe pocketed his harmonica. "When you're ready to listen, we'll explain—one time—how you might keep living," he told my harassers.

They grew so still that crickets resumed chirping around us. I guess I had some PTSD going because I didn't fidget much while we waited. The sun slid under a bank of clouds and suddenly the scene turned golden, like Rembrandt had painted a rumble. The sun slid more and the light dimmed fast.

Adding to my shock was my companions' matter-of-factness. We had entered a new phase, one Anya had warned me would come. *Diplomacy will give way to battle.*

Crickets chirped. Anya spoke into the darkness. "Your choices are two. You may retrace your journey by Connector and return to your beginning point, or we will send you beyond the Far Frames." Go back, or die. The only choices. Fact, not threat.

20. THE FIRST TO DIE

They chose life. Kelly Joe and Anwyl escorted them back to the mausoleum beside the Connector, disappeared for a time, then reappeared without them, bearing an acrid fragrance like sage in a wildfire, which I came to know as the scent when a Connector is destroyed.

"I thought Connectors didn't come through cemeteries out of respect," I said as we headed to the exit. The bars of the gate sliced black shadows across cars on the street outside.

"This Connector was a rogue passage, newly formed," Anwyl answered.

"Those clowns built a Connector?"

"No. Only a being of great power can make a Connector."

"The Cysts," I yelled, because I wanted to whisper. My voice echoed among the tombstones. I wished the crickets would chirp again.

"Working together, Warty Sebaceous Cysts have grown sufficiently powerful," Anya agreed.

My companions were quiet walkers. Only my shoes scuffled on the asphalt as we entered the straightaway before the gate.

"What good does it do to return them to the Frame they came from? Can't they Travel back?"

"And surely they will, but not at the time or route they chose," Kelly Joe said. "Lobotomists can only Travel by Connector."

"Death will join the allies but not for the non," Anya added.

I stumbled over the implication. Death or exile were the only choices for those guys. Did that mean that Sam was lost to Lilah?

At the gate, Rosie was locked in her kiosk, watching without blinking, talking into a handheld radio. I pantomimed that all was well. A buzzer bleated, meaning she unlocked the gate. We pushed out of the cemetery and headed for the elevated train station across the street. Anwyl and Anya walked a few paces ahead, debating what that rogue Connector might indicate about the Cysts' plans.

"What the hell is a Lobotomist?" I asked Kelly Joe.

His warm chuckle pissed me off. It was his isn't–that–a–funny–way–to–say–it reaction. "Which part did I say wrong?" I demanded.

He swallowed his chuckle. "Here now, say it after me. Lob–"

"Lob–"

"–otoh–"

"–otoh–," I repeated carefully.

Maybe that noise really was a cough like he pretended. "–mist."

"–mist," I said pessimistically. "Lob–otoh–mist. Lob–otoh–mist. Bleeding hell. Let it out so you don't choke." He didn't chuckle this time, he hooted and ha'arred. Nothing was funnier than my pronunciation. "I say it exactly like you do. Lob–otoh–mist."

He doubled over. I'd never seen him give in to a laugh before.

Call me sadist. "Lob–otoh–mist. Lob–otoh–mist."

Anya and Anwyl turned, saw Kelly Joe bent over with me draped across his back, trying to pull his fists from his ears while I cackled, "Lob–otoh–mist." I was laughing, too. There is no pleasure quite like laughing with a sad person.

"We're getting ready to fight the Cysts," I assured them. Anya smiled, Anwyl removed a Metro card from his tunic. Which set me howling. In fact, no matter how dire our situation, it makes me smile when Anwyl enters a subway turnstile like any John Doe. Although I've never seen him add money to his Metro card. Hmm.

The subway platform was crowded. Apparently a train had failed to arrive. Anwyl and Anya got separated from us by a clump of tweeners carrying backpacks that seemed to be empty. No grown–up can understand the fads of the young.

Laughing had released tension from my encounter with Sam and the seven mental dwarfs, but I dreaded telling Lilah what happened to her twin. Not that I understood it.

I followed Kelly Joe to the railing. "What does it mean? The L word."

He stared across the street and into the cemetery, which was dark except for lights that lined the roads and an occasional swank mausoleum. "A Lobotomist is a being that sacrifices free will in exchange for something it wants, usually money or celebrity or sex. Lobotomists have a craving that makes them willing to do anything. In the war, Lobotomists will be the first to die."

Poor Lilah. And poor detective who had to report to Lilah. "Can the Lobotomizing be reversed?"

"Sometimes it can, if a stronger craving arises. Or if the manager dies. Lobotomists have a manager that controls the group's thinking."

"Are these things always around? No one has mentioned them before."

"You'll only see them in wartime. They want tending that's not worthwhile, except during war. As fighters they're relentless, but it takes time to train them. The ones tonight were trainees. Warty Sebaceous Cysts are surely training thousands." He unpocketed his harmonica while he talked but put it away again, unplayed.

"We need to stop them before they get trained."

"Only one way to stop the Lobotomists. Stop the manager. The manager's identity will be hidden, but it will be someone close to Warty Sebaceous Cysts, someone they trust to build an army." He said this last to himself, as though trying to solve a riddle, while he threaded us toward Anya and Anwyl through a crowd that was all silhouettes in the light of an approaching train.

"You talk like war is certain. Won't the fighting peter out when we stop Maelstrom from escaping?"

"War is coming. Maelstrom will be free," Anya interrupted.

The train arrived with the screech of a thousand vultures. WTF. Why were we trying if we knew we would fail? "I thought we were trying to keep Maelstrom in prison."

How could it be a fact that Maelstrom would get free? I shook my head to deny that prospect. Then Anya took my hand and my hopelessness morphed to resolve as she said, "We must stop Maelstrom. It is up to us, not his prison, to stop him."

Anwyl added, "Or all shall perish in the attempt." Mr. Bright Side.

Our train jerked into motion and I clutched a strap to stay in balance. Anwyl stood next to me as though glued in place. Clearly, a big change was a–comin', because he volunteered information. "Since last we met, Anya has worked to fulfill her vow to overthrow the Framekeeps." He sounded proud, and no wonder.

The Framekeeps are a tribunal of thirteen beings. They uphold laws and hear petitions. Last summer when we were in Los Angeles, Anya and Anwyl petitioned the Framekeeps to punish Warty Sebaceous Cysts for genocide. Had the Cysts been found guilty, they'd be back in prison, at least. The Cysts had just finished a long prison term—the most recent of many—so maybe their sentence would have been worse than prison; maybe they would have been trapped in a collapsed Frame. Warty Sebaceous Cysts were indeed guilty of the genocide, but Anya and Anwyl lost their petition, because Warty Sebaceous Cysts secretly controlled a majority of the Framekeeps. Sure, after the hearing, Anya vowed to overthrow the Framekeeps. But the Framekeeps seemed so powerful.

Anwyl's voice was rich with admiration. "Anya has rallied support yet maintained secrecy and these things are not easily done."

"I had no idea Anya was doing that," I said. I had no idea because I had been excluded from the Frames and nobody ever explained much to me, anyway. I didn't add that—I didn't want to remind Anwyl that he had never confided in me before.

He gripped the rail as though it were a traitor's neck. "Anya visited the Frame of each traitor among the Framekeeps, met with those loyal to the free Frames, and selected a replacement for each traitor. One Frame yet remains to enlist. We go there now. Come." He reached a hand out— like Kelly Joe used to do—to help me Travel.

"I can Travel on my own now. You start, I'll keep up."

"As you wish." Anwyl retracted his hand.

Across the train car, Kelly Joe and Anya changed Frames with us. I matched the Frame shifts easily and held my smile, although it went *rigor* on me as my wooziness and urge to barf escalated. Still, it was easier to Travel in sync with a group rather than a single other being.

We reached a Frame where we were the only ones in the subway car and took seats facing Anya and Kelly Joe. "Your teacher has taught you well," Anwyl said to me but spoke to Kelly Joe.

"She is a Traveler of the Frames now," Anya agreed, with a smile that made me feel like a double rainbow.

The light strobed as our train came out of a tunnel. We shifted Frames one more time and my heartbeat did a drum solo. This must be the home Frame of the being who had kidnapped me. My kidnapper had looked like a human Cobra and he had a dozen close relations in this subway car, all between me and the door. But nobody menaced or noticed me, so my heart finished its solo.

Around us were Cobra people with leathery skin and long necks that disappeared into flat jowls. In addition, on the train were improbably gorgeous male models, sculpted for *come hither*, plus a few jaunty grandmas whose eyes shone with experience and acceptance. With each train stop, our subway car grew more crowded and the pecking order more clear. The models would leap to stand whenever a Cobra person needed a seat, and everybody—including my companions—gave their seats to grandmas.

On subsequent visits to this Frame, called Expletive Deleted, I learned there are three principal races. The Cobras are privileged and run things. The male models are an underclass, maintained for breeding, unskilled labor, and abuse. The grannies are revered spiritual leaders whose existence protects the male models from worse treatment, because every once in a while a model unpredictably transforms into one of the grannies.

We changed Frames again as we took the stairs to the street and left the subway at Bleecker Street. The streets pulsed with building noise.

A sidewalk pretzel cart swiveled as we passed. "Hey, you're Cat Shaver!"

"I am."

The cart swiveled to yell behind, "It is her and she talked to me." Soon we were trailed by a fresh juice wagon, a toffee nuts cart, and several identical pretzel carts who may have been related. "Cat Shaver, would you put a bite in one of my pretzels? Please?"

I turned in surprise. The first cart squealed its brakes then dipped in a little bow to confirm I had heard right. I, Nica, was at a loss for words.

Anya smiled and Anwyl prompted, "Your popularity aids our cause."

Okay, here goes. I grabbed a pretzel, left a tooth impression for future archeologists to puzzle over, and dangled the bitten pretzel from the spokes of the cart's metal shade umbrella. This provoked *huzzahs* and spins from the food carts. Damn, I should run for office in the food carts' district.

"Well done, Nica of—the New Yorks." A dimly familiar voice gave sly emphasis to my new affiliation. The owner of the voice clasped arms with Anya. It was Hari!–Ya, the Cobra woman I had last heard speak when she served as a Framekeep at our hearing against Warty Sebaceous Cysts. "All is ready for your—action," she told Anya and Anwyl. "We will talk in here." She led us into an urban park between buildings, which had brickwork, fountain, benches, and no greenery. In the park, the volume of building chatter was lower, but the fountain water crashed like Niagara Falls.

I tried to keep up with the conversation via lip–reading as my companions finalized details for a visit to the Framekeeps, which was set to happen the next day. For my benefit, they summarized what would happen tomorrow. We all had a part in the plan.

I enthused, "That is such a dope plan. Can't we start now?" It was a rhetorical question, unless the answer had been yes.

21. THE FUTILITY OF MY REQUEST

The plan required several final steps and we spent the evening making them. Rather, the others did. I got left in Frivolous Bedlam. I couldn't get anyone to tell me why I was in/out–of/in danger. But danger there seemed to be. When I made a visit to my apartment on Ma'Urth, the lanyard washed new–toothache pains through my body. It was like a weather forecast. Storm brewing. I would leave at the lanyard's first flash of lightning—I didn't want to test the limits of Julian's ability to protect me.

I had returned to Ma'Urth to call Lilah and persuade her to stop seeking Sam. I practiced a few run–throughs of vague evasive messages that I could leave without faltering. *I ran into Sam briefly. He's where he wants to be.* Lilah would read between the lines and sense the evasion, but whatever negative she inferred would be better than the truth: *Give up on your twin, he's a zombie for the Cysts because he traded his humanity for his vices.*

No such luck as voicemail. She picked up on first ring. "Do you have news?"

"I ran into Sam. It's like you said, he's really hooked in with that club. But he seemed healthy and making his own choices and when I mentioned you were looking for him, he got pissed." I didn't add that his only emotions fell on the angry to hate–filled continuum.

"Did you tell him I need to speak with him?"

"He knows that you want to. I recommend that you –"

"What are your next steps?"

I sighed. "I plan to talk to the leaders of the club."

"Good, I like that. Where did you run into Sam?"

"I won't tell you that. The more involved you stay, the harder it is for –"

"You have no idea what harder is." She hung up on me and I was okay with that.

I realized two things. I couldn't stop Lilah from searching for her brother—I hoped he stayed out of Frame; that might protect her from finding him. And I did want to talk to the social club leaders—they might be the Lobotomist managers.

I grabbed a quick snack and got ready to Travel back to Bedlam. My plainwrap phone buzzed. I'd forgotten this was a night for Hernandez to call.

"Anwyl there?" he greeted me.

"A and A have stepped out. They're crossing t's and dotting i's for a big day tomorrow. I don't expect to see either of them before then."

"Framekeeps tomorrow?"

"Why are you so much better informed than I am?" My words were garbled—I shoveled yogurt into my mouth while we talked.

"Tell Anwyl the main five are taken care of. He'll know." Hernandez sounded pumped.

"Has he got you committing illegal acts? Don't answer that. How are you, anyway? How is L.A.? I miss everything about L.A. I love everything about being here, though, and I'll miss it when I leave. Am I confused or enlightened?"

"What's your thinking on that?" he asked in a way that said he wasn't listening.

"Have—ow!" I stubbed my toe. It was getting dark but I was reluctant to turn on a light, because the lanyard's pain was sharpening. "I've got to go soon."

Which freed his hyenas. "Patti's ex– called her and she was just going to see what he wanted and then she just needed to finish her thoughts with him. Finish her thoughts."

"She can't go back to him. He hit her. I didn't know cops could be that stupid about people."

The silence grew. I pictured Hernandez hunched at his table in a house that was empty of daughters, squeezing a beer bottle until it caved and shattered from the inside.

"Why are you still out there on the left coast? Everyone is here now."

"Been wondering that myself. Have fun tomorrow."

"And how!"

I considered phoning that moron, Patti, but the last person you can save somebody from is herself. And the lanyard pain was jolting now. I shoved snacks into my backpack and was zipping up to depart when Hernandez' phone buzzed again.

"Yo anew," I answered.

"Neekster." I dropped my backpack and fruit scattered. The voice hit me like a penny. A penny from the top of the Empire State Building: a two–syllable sledge hammer. It was Ben and he was high.

"Oh, Benny," and I started to bawl.

"Wh's wrong?"

"Just some stuff, not worth explaining." But he knew that I knew. If he was high, he'd be hating himself for this relapse and my negative feelings would help neither of us. That's the problem with knowing someone so long and so well. You get stuck being truthful whatever your intent.

Because life can always get more complicated, the lanyard's warnings escalated to stabbing pains. But whatever wicked this way came, I couldn't hang up on Ben just now.

"S'rry. I thought." Amazingly few syllables to transmit so much frustration and disgust.

Suddenly this was the most important conversation of my life. "Benny, I need you to do something."

"Wha'?"

"Go to a meeting. As soon as we hang up."

Electrons flowed through my phone. I considered the futility of my request. What happened to Ben was up to Ben, not me. I checked the screen to see if the call got dropped. No, we were still connected. I rubbed my chest where it was numb from the lanyard's shooting pains.

"Good advice. Oops." And the call dropped.

I knew from too much experience that I dare not let my worries rampage. They can demolish me without changing Ben's situation an iota. So I put him out of my mind, in much the same way that you might cease to think about swallowing a handful of rocks. That leaden discomfort persists under all else. I've had those rocks in my gut for years.

From the fire escape came animal howls that would have inspired the term *caterwaul* if it didn't already exist. The lanyard seared my skin. I scooped my backpack from the floor and got out before I met the reason for those wails.

I knew when I arrived in Bedlam because the lanyard stopped hurting. I collapsed on my couch, grateful for the absence of pain and danger—to me, anyway. One of those wails had sounded like Dizzy's voice. If I went back to Ma'Urth, could I help Dizzy? Doubtful. Did she need help? No clue. Maybe Julian knew what had happened out on his fire escape on Ma'Urth. I headed for the hall outside my door to ask him. Before I got there, Dizzy and Leon slunk in from the bathroom.

Dizzy's fur was so puffed she looked like a fur balloon; Leon was puffed, too, but his shaved coat made him fuzzy as an Impressionist sketch. Leon had a fresh cut on one ear—any deeper and it would have split his ear. I took him to the kitchen sink and he let me mess with him long enough to clean the cut and staunch the bleeding. Then he did his cockroach thing and by the time I got back to the couch he and Dizzy were playfighting, ferocious as nurf balls. Watching them made me laugh, which made breathing possible once more.

If only somebody—cats, lanyard—could tell me what had almost? just? happened back on Ma'Urth. What the hell had been on the fire escape? Did the *whatever* injure Leon, or did the cat hurt himself in his haste to get away? What about the lawn chair? Was it in danger out on the fire escape? Could a visitor from the Frames sense that the chair was sentient?

There was way too much I didn't know.

22. BOOKS DON'T MEAN BAD

When I'm stressed, indoors oppresses me. I left the cats to their playfighting and headed for the streets. As soon as I opened Julian's front door and put a toe on the front step, the buildings called hearty greetings to Cat Shaver. I waved and *hiya*'d my way west.

"Hey! Cat Shaver! Slam—slam!" a building called, sing—song.

"Who's there?" I played along.

"That's just what I was wondering!" the building shrieked and other buildings snapped their awnings or slammed their doors. Food carts pirouetted and popped wheelies. I could spot the two truly sentient buildings on the block because they remained silent. Thinking deeper thoughts, no doubt, and waiting for meaningful conversation; but sometimes the sentient buildings do seem like their cement hardened too fast.

It was quiet on the promenade by the Hudson River, which regularly emitted a vibrating throb like the last ring of a Chinese gong. Was the river chanting?

How could a river be sentient? Where was the sentience? It couldn't be in the water because the water flowed away. Did the river think differently when it rained? Did all sentience require thinking? How peaceful to have thought—free existence. All my wondering about the river gave me an egg scrambler of a headache. That plus the effort to not worry about Ben.

To escape my thoughts I concentrated on the all—around. The setting sun left a familiar glint on the water—was there only one sun for all the Frames? Damn, thinking again. The river's chants matched the rippling of currents that expanded to the banks, retreated, expanded downstream. The chants deepened as daylight waned.

Listening to the river took me three blocks without thinking. That had to be a record. But—

Something had changed. The building voices repeated my name and no longer sounded carefree. Per Kelly Joe, danger was unlikely but not impossible here in Frivolous Bedlam. "Hey, it's me, Cat Shaver. Anything new? Anything I should know?"

The chatter hit me like a burst water main. Every building for blocks replied. They were afraid. I had brought danger to them. They knew I hadn't done it on purpose but I had created a problem that I needed to solve, pronto.

Up the street came my explanation. Suspended in the dusk air were shadows that gleamed rhythmically, bright then dark, bright then dark, like flapping meat cleavers. My books were flying toward me, light catching their dust jackets, and they didn't look Pixar like they had in my apartment yesterday. *Lose Twenty Pounds* must have kept drilling them because their movements were now precise and identical. They flew the way books flew as mercenary soldiers, which reminded me that even a few books could cause enormous destruction. It might set a bad precedent, however, if I screamed and ran.

The buildings murmured in fearful tones.

"Books! To me!" I remembered this command from some movie battle and I pretended I was that movie's commander, which minimized my desire to whimper. The book squadron accelerated toward me. Oh goody. "And. Shelve yourselves. I mean. Land. Halt."

Summer dropped like a dove hit by buckshot, pages still open. The others made short adept landings like jets on an aircraft carrier, covers closing as they touched down. *Lose Twenty Pounds* rose to hover before me and I could feel the books' attention: they wanted my reaction to their demonstration.

"Wow! Amazing progress for one day of training! Well done! Let me take you home." I began to pick up the parked books, first blowing on *Summer*'s scraped pages—although there was little street dirt here. When I hefted the stack, *Lose Twenty Pounds* landed on the top. "Well done!"

These were a lot of books to lug for blocks but it was worth the backache when the buildings began goofing around again. My eyes filled with tears. For the buildings' naïve cheer. For the books' fierce loyalty. If I had it to do over, I would never have brought so much as a bookmark to Frivolous Bedlam. But that isn't how things went down.

I adjusted my load of books so that I wasn't hunched over, so that I could shoulder the extra responsibility. It was up to me to make these books safe outside Neutral Frames—where they were fine because they were immobile—and, dammit, I would figure out how.

The sidewalk and streets were rough because the books had shed text, which cut and sliced the pavement. Did my books still lack full control, or did books always shed text? "Hey, my bad, I forgot to tell you all that you need to stay inside, no books allowed outside here." *Lose Twenty Pounds* gave an abrupt shift on the top of the stack. "You didn't know, I didn't tell you. Not a problem this time, it just can't happen again."

Lose Twenty Pounds tilted up as though eyeing a large flying shadow, blacker than the darkening evening. The other books tilted, also, but not at the same time and not in the same direction. It became a moment worth a million YouTube hits. I lost my grip on the stack of books and first one book slid, then another did. With every attempt to correct my balance, I created a bigger instability. Books popped out of my arms in all directions as thought their jackets were greased. I'd shove one back in the stack and that would pop another out the other side. Finally they were in heaps on the pavement and I was alongside them, gasping.

The shadow that had spooked *Lose Twenty Pounds* was a pelican, the first I'd seen in Bedlam, and surprisingly far inland from the river. It was a huge bird with a scarred beak. It circled a few times as I gathered the strewn books. The buildings chattered to the pelican, sending thanks skyward, along with mixed messages. One offered assurances that the pelican could return to the river because Cat Shaver had the books under control now. Another begged the pelican to stay because books were still present.

Nerves being high, a dispute broke out between buildings for each viewpoint.

"You're overreacting. Calm down," a building snapped.

"They're books. Books bring bad."

"Books. Bring. Bad." Somebody repeated then somebody else did, too. The debate took on the cadence of—what else—a knock–knock joke.

"Books don't mean bad."

"Says who?"

"Halls. Halls of Shared Knowledge."

"No ledge? No ledge who?"

"Who don't mind books!"

Nearby buildings slammed doors and rattled awnings: well played! Apparently the buildings had returned to normal.

I stretched my aching arms to grip my books, and with my chin pressed into the top of the stack, I trudged home.

A shout greeted me from Julian's front stoop. I'd know that pissed–off voice anywhere but was surprised to hear it now and here. And bellowing. Anwyl was often angry but usually controlled.

Anya appeared in the doorway behind him. Dizzy and Leon also emerged. The cats undulated around Anya's legs and pranced down Julian's front stoop, just as Anwyl sprang down to the sidewalk and grabbed the books away from me.

"Does one betrayal not suffice? How many foes does this embrace hold?"

Anya shushed him and he actually shouted at her, "*Two* cats and now these. Faugh." He clamped meathook hands to the ends of my stack of books and hurled the books inside. They clattered and yelped in Julian's foyer.

"I can explain," I assured Anywl and Anya, curious to hear what I might say.

Anya spoke to Anwyl in a voice that could cut diamonds. "Her way is not yours to shape. No one can walk another's path."

He swallowed his many replies. Next to me, Dizzy began a feverish butt–grooming session. Anwyl growled; as always, the cat seemed to infuriate him. When Anwyl glared at Leon, I stepped to intercept the look and pet Leon. The cat scurried up the block. He seemed more spooked by me than by Anwyl.

In the foyer, the books squeaked and shrilled. I pushed between Anwyl and Dizzy and went inside. About half the books were airborne, the others dragged themselves into takeoff positions. A part of me wanted to soothe the books and check for damage; the rest of me wanted to get them back to Ma'Urth where they would be immobile. It felt like sheer luck that I had kept them in control so far. All of me hoped they weren't hurt. "Help each other upstairs and shelve yourselves," I ordered the books. "Remain shelved until I say otherwise."

"Books in Frivolous Bedlam!" Anwyl's fury entered the building ahead of him.

Anya posed a question, which shut him up for some time. "See you not that Nica has become their tamer, the one who shapes order from disruption?"

The way she said this, it sounded like she was quoting prophecy. I looked at Anya and she nodded, which filled me with hope. Maybe I was making good decisions. Maybe I could handle the books.

Dizzy and Leon strolled upstairs. Dizzy veered and brushed Anwyl's leg as she passed.

Anwyl's gaze moved from Dizzy to the retreating books to Leon's shaved fur to my shaved hair. "Then the dark times are now and truly upon us," he recited with enough irony to sink the Bismarck.

I was pissed at Anwyl for hurting my books and even testy with Anya because she'd allowed that without reprimand. "You recite those prophecy things like they're clear but they could be about anyone and anything. I can't believe you listen to them."

"The prophecies are guidelines that provide aid in times of calamity. They describe how the side of right succeeded in the past. You may question them but never doubt yourself, Cat Shaver." Anya giggled. "The prophecies make no mention of that." She ascended the stairs, saying over her shoulder, "Let us prepare for the morrow."

Anwyl stomped up the stairs, which made me pissed at him for still being pissed at me. He stopped and turned. When I met his gaze, I shivered. He looked at me with desire so intense it made lust seem *blasé*. For a moment I flashed on this fulfilling a prophecy, too, but discarded the insight as too weird. My weirdness threshold was different back then.

"Have you a chill?" he murmured.

"Not hardly." I clutched the bannister, insanely conscious of him.

"Welcome home, Nica," Julian's voice made me start. "I trust you will enjoy a restful night before the demands of the morning."

"Thanks, Julian," I said, and patted his wall.

"And is that Anwyl, son of Reyn, on my stairs?"

"Well met, Julian," Anwyl replied. He turned and continued upstairs.

I took a moment then followed.

The rest of the visit was all business and they didn't stay long. They made sure I knew when to take action during the Framekeeps hearing. I knew; and I couldn't wait. I'd nursed a grudge against the Framekeeps and this was payback sublime: I would provide the distraction that set the coup in motion.

23. YOUR STEPS MUST BE YOUR OWN

The morning was bright as a new switchblade when Kelly Joe and I headed for the Framekeeps' hearing, where we would meet Anwyl, Anya, and our co–conspirators. The thirteen Framekeeps each provide a meeting venue and the Framekeeps rotate their hearings. This meeting was in Hari!–Ya's Frame, Expletive Deleted.

Even at dawn and in other Frames, the Brookyln Bridge was crowded with tourists. In one Frame, humanoids crawled up the cables to the top of the gothic turrets, a route restricted to maintenance crews at home on Ma'Urth. That view must be amazing! Maybe if all went well today I could persuade Kelly Joe to check it out on our way back.

Kelly Joe and I walked five miles: east across the Brooklyn Bridge from Manhattan toward Brooklyn, then north, then west on the Williamsburg Bridge, back toward Manhattan. Only by this circuitous route could we reach our destination. Kelly Joe made the Frame shifts while I held his hand. Our journey required precision, because our target was a government and commercial district that spans the air between the Brooklyn and Williamsburg Bridges and exists in only one Frame. However, it has semblance of existence in adjoining Frames, and if you enter a building where it is a semblance, you fall through the floor. It's a long bad fall into the psychotic East River.

Kelly Joe narrated his Frame–changing and I listened as hard as I could—if the day's activities went south, co–conspirators might have to hightail it out of Frame separately, so I needed to know the route. But making those subtle transitions solo, pursued by Framekeep guards? I tightened my grip on Kelly Joe's hand. We couldn't get separated. No matter what.

As we Travelled from Frame to Frame, although the scene otherwise changed, the Brooklyn and Williamsburg Bridges looked identical to the bridges at home on Ma'Urth. I had to let Kelly Joe concentrate so my questions piled up like baggage on a jammed carousel. Why did some structures and landforms persist from Frame to Frame, while others changed? Was there a record of what was in every Frame—what changed and what didn't? That would be a handy Traveler's guide!

In most Frames we visited, the Williamsburg Bridge was encaged in gridded steel safety walls, just like on Ma'Urth, but there was a shocking difference. At home, the steel protects pedestrians and cyclists by confining them inside the bridge span. In other Frames, humanoids used bouldering moves to advance sideways along the outside of the cage, rock climbing over oblivion. *That* I would not ask Kelly Joe to try on the way back.

On the Williamsburg Bridge, I kept hearing voices I couldn't locate. They sounded like Dustin Hoffman with a mouthful of Jujubes, and came from the middle of the bridge, near the J line train tracks. Aha. Whenever two trains passed each other, they spoke.

Bread 'n'. Butter.

Cat. Dog.

Outta Sight. Outta Mind.

Kelly Joe released my hand. "We've arrived." He talked close to my ear to be heard about the East River, which here was more frenzied but less threatening. For the first time, I felt sorry for it. Did it ever know a moment's peace?

Kelly Joe positioned himself beneath the erector–set bridge pillars and looked up. Above us, glossy green clouds loafed in sharp yellow air. He shifted his alignment then looked toward the Brooklyn Bridge, which cast its stolid antique silhouette to our south. The skyline looked funny—it was missing the bridge that stands between the Brooklyn and Williamsburg Bridges on Ma'Urth, the homely stepsister of the bridge family, the Manhattan Bridge.

The protective steel cage around the Williamsburg Bridge was gone and there were no side railings. No government district stretched to the Brooklyn Bridge. Yet when Kelly Joe resumed walking, he headed straight for the edge of the Williamsburg Bridge, into the light gusting breeze. He turned back, saw my *abort* look, raised a hand like Mother Teresa with a leper. "The buildings of our destination are in a Frame all their own. Just off this ledge is a short Connector to them." He reached out his hand for me. "The first step will be the hardest."

"It's the second step that will really suck."

As he chuckled, he pulled out his harmonica and bent a few notes. It soothed me enough that I stopped inching backward.

"Any chance you could hypnotize me with that thing?"

"Your steps must be your own."

"Free will is overrated. I'm not convincing my feet."

"We're running late so I'm going on. No one will fault you if you wait here. But don't change Frames without me."

He stepped off the edge and he disappeared. I re–ran the moment in my head and confirmed he hadn't plummeted down—he had simply vanished.

"Wait for me!" I stepped forward quickly, before my thoughts could catch up with my action, then gasped a laugh. A tattooed forearm and hand had materialized and groped for me, fingers wiggling like Groucho Marx's eyebrows. I reached for my musician's hand and walked off the edge.

24. A CONVENTION OF MIDDLE–SCHOOL PRINCIPALS

The Connector was short and narrow. Narrow. Kelly Joe hadn't mentioned that. It barely fit the two of us, abreast. Good thing he knew where to step; better thing I hadn't veered when I followed him off the edge.

In five steps we were in the government district. Kelly Joe hurried us along the edge of the district, past pillars that towered above the streets. The pillars were a dark dense stone, gnarled and layered as though growing. A film of water slid along each pillar and—impossibly—across, making a thin sheet of water in the air between each pillar.

Our destination was a monumental stone box, a warehouse to the gods. Pink and black granite gargoyles lurked in the shadows under its protruding eaves. The gargoyles looked still but not carved and I felt their eyes on me.

Kelly Joe donned a low–slung hat that hid his eyes. I pulled my sweatshirt hood up and forward to hide my face. Show time.

The building's carved granite door was so heavy it took both Kelly Joe's hands to open it. Inside, a long hall funneled us to the arched entry of the meeting room. Lining the walls, hovering on black shiny books, were squat fleshy cupid guards in saffron swaddling clothes- babies with cold stares and erect postures. Their books were edged with dark stains that might have been dried blood. Scattered through the meeting room were other guards of many species, all wearing the Framekeeps emblem, a colorful faceted geometry like an exploded, wire–mesh Rubik's cube. The guards held themselves with the special self–confidence of trained and sanctioned killers. There were no soldier books inside the meeting room, but of course the dozen in the hall were enough to destroy everyone and everything here.

I was glad to shove such thoughts deeper and fill my head with inanities, in case my thoughts leaked to someone who could read them. *What would I cook for dinner tonight? I'd have to go shopping first.* Underneath I must still be tallying guards and weapons against us, though, because each step was harder to take. By the time I reached a seat, I was shuffling through wet concrete.

The meeting room was packed and the hearing was already in session. We found the last open seats, in back. Twenty rows of audience separated us from the thirteen Framekeeps, who sat at their woven glass table, facing us. Between the Framekeeps and the audience sat today's supplicants and the Framekeep assistants.

The Framekeeps were in different places at the table today and one of the humanoids sat in the center wearing the pearl gray leader's robe. The tall flowering cactus, leader at the last hearing, wore a magenta robe and sat at one end. The cactus stared at Kelly Joe and me. I hoped the cactus was on our side—the cactus had led the other hearing fairly and seemed like a cool guy. Gal. Cactus.

I'd had a good impression of a few other Framekeeps, too, but despite the exotic variation among species, overall the Framekeeps were like a convention of middle–school principals. I hoped our new batch would be less pompous and authoritarian.

If we delivered a new batch of Framekeeps. At the other hearing I had attended, I hadn't seen nearly as many armed guards. Today, the guards outnumbered our allies several times over, and ... *maybe we'd go out to dinner tonight, then I could skip grocery shopping.*

It became easier to still my real thoughts because the proceedings provided mental Novocain. I struggled to pay attention, although everyone else in the audience seemed to follow intently.

Perhaps the rest of the audience was dead. Let's be polite and call the proceedings ponderous. When the current case concluded, the reactions were so bloodless that I couldn't tell which side had won. Holy mother of Mergatroyd, now it was time for procedural *yada–yada* that required Framekeeps to read stretches of legalese from their tablets. I emitted a strangled whimper and Kelly Joe showed me his finger touching his lips.

While the Framekeeps droned, I developed a boredom scale and assigned life events to it. Let it run 1 to 100, 1 being stimulated–to–the–limit–of–sensation and 100 being catatonic; assume I had not yet experienced 1 or 100. With that assumption, in the teens were Frame Travel, my adventures with Anya and Anwyl, cracking jokes with Ick, sex, and my early marauding days with Ben. This hearing fell somewhere in the 80s, rivaling high school, Catechism class, and my dentist's waiting room. Developing my boredom scale got me through the rest of the *yada–yada* and I had fun imagining the possibilities that could rank as numero 1, my least boring experience.

Then the Framekeep assistants announced the next case pending before the exalted Framekeeps. With a rustle, a creak, and an epidemic of whispers did boredom flee that day.

25. TANTAMOUNT TO TREASON

Anya and Anwyl entered the meeting room, followed by nine beings of nine species. The cherub guards flew in from the hall and zigzagged overhead, books tilted sharply, ready to shed text. For a moment the scene was like a silent movie—guards seemed to jump position in light that flickered. The flickering light came from a being that resembled a 3D television set with a loose connection.

When the last two allies entered the meeting room, for a few seconds I could see nothing because my eyes were thick with tears. Monk! And Miles! I hadn't realized the room was tall enough to fit the Watts Towers. Miles showed signs of recent rough treatment. He had many sections of fresh steel and concrete, as yet undecorated. He translated unevenly with a dip to the side—a kind of limp. For the briefest of moments I distracted myself wondering how the Watts Towers had gotten from Los Angeles to New York. I shoved my knuckles across my eyes to clear the tears and musings. I noted with satisfaction that the cherub guards' books reared back whenever the guards flew toward the Towers. The Towers had an ability to incinerate books that came too near.

The central Framekeep paused her recitation about the new case and waited as the newcomers found places to stand by the walls. The audience turned to look at the cause of interruption and whispering spread.

"In the matter of-of land use adjustment in the Frame Marzipan, statute seven point th–three, and I quote, 'whereas land–landowner...'" The central Framekeep developed a stutter because she kept looking at the newcomers and losing her place. Perhaps she noticed that nine of these late arrivals were the same species as nine of the current Framekeeps, including her.

The case proceeded. Kelly Joe slipped from his seat and went to stand beside Monk. Anwyl joined them for a whispered conference and I got the impression they were weighing alternative strategies. Had they expected this many armed guards? Did they know the room would be crowded with spectators? Did they think the Framekeeps would step down without a fight? Were they comfortable with civilian casualties?

Meanwhile, the Framekeep assistants read all law relevant to the current case, then the central Framekeep intoned, "Those with comments, step to the center aisle and await my recognition to speak." No one moved. The pause turned to dead space. If it were a red light, I would have run it. Still no one moved.

"Have none of you concerns?" From her position near one end of the Framekeep table, Hari!–Ya sounded frustrated with the spectators. "This is your sole opportunity to comment." Today, her long red hair floated around her as though she were underwater.

"I hold a concern," said a voice like rain on bells. Anya glided to front and center.

Some Framekeeps looked startled to hear that voice, the others reacted when she shook her hair loose from the shawl that had shielded her head. The central Framekeep cast a quick glance at Anya's nine companions of nine species, frowned like her seat had sprouted thorns, and typed something on her tablet. Perhaps responding to a typed command, cupid guards on black shiny books flew in to hover above the space that separated spectators from Framekeeps.

Anya angled so that she could address Framekeeps and audience together. "To be a Keeper of the Frames is a great honor. Framekeeps uphold the tenets of our free Frames. We are grateful for your service, your sacrifices, and your wisdom. However, article one, section three point six of the Constitution of the free Frames states," and from here she recited a long paragraph about impartiality and the rights of citizens to replace Framekeeps who put personal considerations before the good of the free Frames. When Anya spoke legalese it wasn't *yada–yada*, it was affirmation of the protective nurturing power of law.

Two of the Framekeeps must be Constitutional scholars, because as soon as she said 'article one', they jumped to stand, back–to–back, as though expecting attack. For the others, awareness dawned only as Anya concluded,

"...'irrespective of motives, when a Framekeep rules according to personal interests, those rulings are void and that Framekeep must resign. Resistance to this article is tantamount to treason.'"

Now all the Framekeeps reacted. Some typed rapidly on their tablets, others studied the audience. The two gorillas who managed the dolphin's water tank stepped forward to stand between the tank and Anya. Hari!–Ya remained still, wearing a smile that sputtered like a damp campfire.

Dozens of cupid guards on black shiny books swarmed into the room. They surrounded the Framekeeps and assistants; they clumped at every door. The air was so thick with them that they blocked the light. Around me the audience sat frozen in twilight, maybe hoping that with stillness came invisibility. Meanwhile, humanoid guards packed the front of the room.

Anya didn't raise her voice and her tone remained enchanting but it penetrated the commotion. "At hearing the last, Framekeeps ruled in favor of Warty Sebaceous Cysts, and they have become Framekeep masters."

Amid audience gasps, the dolphin pronounced, "The imagination and resentment of a losing claimant have fashioned this absurd accusation." It made me sad to count a dolphin among my foes.

Anya continued, "By section ninety–seven part three of the Framekeep charter, as a citizen of the free Frames I exercise my right to fairness and demand that all thirteen Framekeeps cease official duties immediately and resign."

The central humanoid shrilled, "You have no proof and you must know we will fight any such accusation."

"Arrest them as a precaution while we investigate their accusation," the dolphin advised.

Anya replied, "By section two–two–five, part c, i through iii, 'when the rulings of the entire body are in question, every and each member shall step down until a special hearing repudiates the charges'." She paced her small open area. At each turn, she added a law quote.

"'By section seventeen, part nine–j, 'A Framekeep accused of wrongdoing shall be tried by peers'.

"Section seventeen, part nine–k, 'No Framekeep can hold office while under accusation'.

"Section eighteen, part a, 'A majority of citizens present at the proceedings will vote to appoint temporary Framekeeps.'"

"Then let us step down and complete this preposterous hearing immediately," said a tiny fluttery creature. There was no replacement member of this species present today, so this Framekeeper must be on our side.

"By section nineteen part q, 'the hearing to resolve charges must not interfere with the business of the Frames'." Anya replied.

Anwyl stepped away from Kelly Joe and Monk. "The business of the Frames is to prepare for war with Warty Sebaceous Cysts, a war you guaranteed when you ruled in their favor, at their behest." He gave a hand chop of a gesture that cut off discourse and perhaps the heads of any who sought to argue.

"I, for one, will not step down. You make outrageous claims with no proof," buzzed the 3D TV with poor reception. Its words came with sparks from a shorted circuit.

Anya replied agreeably, "We are not the sole citizens of the free Frames who hold concern."

That was my cue. I walked straight and tall up the aisle to stand beside Anya and I tried to mimic the confidence of my co–conspirators but I didn't see reason for confidence, even with the astounding battle skills of the allies. There were nearly as many guards as spectators. There was enough text in those soldier books to reduce us to atoms.

I yanked my hood back, hoping the Framekeeps would remember me despite my new hairdo or lack thereof. I was rewarded with noises of shock and anger. Cool. They recognized me. While I spoke, more guards poured from the back room. By the time I was done, there were three guards for every spectator.

"Hi again. It's Nica, formerly of Los Angeles. We met at your last hearing. You may recall that I was a witness in the case against Warty Sebaceous Cysts, who tried on more than one occasion to steal my thoughts. Last time we met, you treated me like a dirt clod because I am a Neutral. You banished me from the free Frames without even letting me say goodbye. This has distressed me and interferes with my sleep and relationships. Because lawsuits across Frames are not an option, after you step down, please consider stopping by to offer your personal apology." It didn't have the ringing pronouncement of Anya's speech, but it occupied the time until she gave me the cue to stop.

"Thank you, Nica, no one considered the impact on you." She raised her arms. "Framekeeps. Your time has concluded. Step away from the table."

Several Framekeeps sat down, making the bank of guards behind them more visible.

"Refusal to cooperate will not change the outcome," Anya said warmly.

"In what section and part is that written?" The taunt came from the construction crane, whose enunciation was crisp and staccato.

"Your replacements will write that section," Kelly Joe heckled.

The dolphin floated upside down in his tank as though on vacation. His casual stance was negated by the fury in his voice. "Are you blind as well as foolhardy? See you not how gravely we outnumber you?"

I'd been wondering along the same lines.

Anwyl demonstrated what real cool looked like. "Count again," he suggested, and his hand sliced the air above his head.

26. ALL IN FAVOR?

With Anwyl's gesture, most of the guards raised their guns and angled their books—to threaten the remaining guards, the Framekeep assistants, and the thirteen Framekeeps. Anwyl pushed forward to stand behind Anya and the cherub guards dipped their books in salute.

Now I got it. We weren't worried about the tons of guards because Anwyl had recruited the guards to join our coup.

I wasn't the only one getting it. The un—recruited guards who suddenly had weapons trained on them finished their double–takes and their looks of disbelief congealed to disgust while their eyes darted as though searching for opportunity to resist. Finding none, the un—recruited guards dismounted their books and bound them with woven metal straps, which our guards hung from their belts.

Most of the spectators must also be co—conspirators. They followed Kelly Joe's lead to surround and herd the few remaining audience members away from the doors. Meanwhile, yet more guards with guns ushered the Framekeeps and their assistants into the center of the room.

It got noisy and then it got silent.

Anya led three of the Framekeeps back to the woven glass Framekeeps table, saying, "You shall not be replaced. We honor you for upholding truth, even as those around you succumbed to corruption. We are grateful for your service to the free Frames. Please be seated." As the three took seats at the Framekeeps table, Anya continued, "Now, to replace the traitors. I nominate Serj, son of Djok, to serve as Framekeep."

"All in favor?" Miles called. *Ayes* erupted and a 3D TV moved from the allies to the woven glass table. And so the coup proceeded. Anya nominated, *ayes* confirmed. Soon only one seat remained open at the Framekeeps table, the position previously held by Hari!–Ya—who glared at Anya with a look that I would have interpreted as vengeful, had I not known otherwise.

Hari!–Ya gathered her robes to return to the table. Anwyl shook his head and guards blocked Hari!–Ya's path. She drew back, more haughty than the Red Queen, and glared at Anya. "You brought no others of my kind with you here today, because in Expletive Deleted you could find no traitor who would do your bidding. Thus I have no replacement and the seat remains mine. Be forewarned, I will oppose you from the Framekeeps table, while my people shall oppose you outside this room."

Anya replied gently, "Section one, part seven f. 'The composition of the Framekeep roster shall comprise the thirteen principal families of sentient, animate and ambulatory beings.' However,—section one, part eight—'one or two positions may be occupied by exalted seers or Framewalkers, who may be of any species."

Anwyl called to the room at large, as though it had just occurred to him, "To occupy the seat that remains open, I nominate Anya, an exalted seer, daughter of Niav of the first lands."

Ayes and whoops filled the room. Anya moved to the center of the Framekeeps table, then held up her hands for silence, which came immediately.

Hari!–Ya filled the silence with bitterness. "You will want to be far from this Frame when word of your treachery spreads to my fellows." She stalked to the end of the room, stopped when the guards blocked her exit, remained staring at the door as though none of us existed.

It was a great scene, and a convincing one, I hoped. The Cobra people were firm supporters of Warty Sebaceous Cysts. Only by looking like Anya's enemy did Hari!–Ya have a chance of surviving as Anya's accomplice.

"Former Framekeeps," Anya addressed the deposed. "We know who you serve, be it by choice or duress. You shall receive a hearing and due punishment, but not this day. More urgent matters press us than retribution for your misdeeds. Make no mistake, retribution shall come. For the non, you may maintain your freedom if you return to your Frames immediately."

Kelly Joe stepped out from the back wall and spoke with the sidestep swagger of a rapper. "Call it your freedom or call it a head start."

With wails, groans, and vows of revenge, the former Framekeeps, their assistants, and the scant few spectators who were not co–conspirators were evicted from the meeting hall with an escort of guards. Based on the individual vibes, two of the deposed Framekeeps should be on suicide watch, three would hide in shame, and the other four would be off to join the Cysts as soon as the escort released them.

The door closed behind them and Anwyl called, "Silence for our leader." Monk, Miles, Kelly Joe, the spectators, and the guards all turned to the Framekeeps table, where Anya sat down and addressed us. "Today, together, we have struck a necessary blow for the free Frames. Now our work begins, with this deed that marks for persecution and extinction, those among us who were not already so marked by our foes."

No one flinched, at least not on the outside. "The morrow shall not come too soon," a spectator called, which sounded like Framespeak for *bring it on.*

Anya smiled a blessing. "Leave this place with all due haste and hope. We thirteen shall follow as quick as we can." She wanted to meet privately with the Framekeeps.

Anwyl instructed the guards, "My cadre shall remain with our Keepers. You others, escort these allies out of this Frame where ambush is most likely. But prepare for ambush in any Frame and all days while our enemies run large."

As the spectators departed, Anya called the Framekeeps session to order and began by briefing them, "Soon Maelstrom will be free and Warty Sebaceous Cysts prepare for his war. Already they train Lobotomists."

"This we expect from them," a humanoid Framekeep sighed.

"Yes, our foes are familiar to us. Let us ensure this is the final time we fight them," Anya agreed. "Also know that the mind hunters of Warty Sebaceous Cysts have grown to thousands."

"This is dire news," the same Framekeep whispered.

Holy crap. Thousands of Entourage? I groped for a chair, abandoned by my adrenaline. Our victory over the Framekeeps felt as secure as a paper boat in the cyclone of Cyst activity. Before I could sit, Kelly Joe was beside me. He tilted his head toward the exit. I followed him out and as he held the door for us he said softly, "The fear will pass."

"I'm feeling pretty small right now." My normal tones echoed like a shout. Outside the meeting hall, the government complex was silent; deserted.

"We grow to fit the need. Someone's been asking after you." Kelly Joe nodded across the street. The complex was not completely deserted! Across the street were two wonderful exceptions.

Monk and Miles. I ran to climb aboard the Watts Towers, looking for good handholds. Monk's girders, welded at sharp angles, were covered in cement that was dense with broken pottery shards, making him easy to climb. Miles had circular struts and was even easier to climb, usually; today, however, his struts lacked hand–holds because his slick fresh cement remained undecorated. This top part of his structure had seen the worst damage.

My run slowed as I registered something. The Watts Towers are nearly a hundred feet tall but I was at eye level with the top of each Tower. They stood off the edge of the complex, behind the water that flowed sideways like a fence. They must be standing in the East River. Water coursed up their sides when they stood still, shot back down when they shifted positions—which they did repeatedly, as though the river was a fly that would *shoo* when they moved.

I squatted at the edge with both arms extended to touch one, then the other. "Miles. Monk. I've missed you so much."

"The heart reaches across the Frames," Monk said. I grinned. How wonderful to be barely–understanding him again!

"Yeah, but it's always nice to touch—not just reach for—the ones you love."

"Agreed," Monk said.

I touched one of Miles' repaired struts. "When you started to crumble. I was afraid you were dead."

"Nuts to that."

"What happened to you? Were you a prisoner? How did you get hurt?"

"The more lips keep zipped, the safer we stay," Miles replied.

"Did the healers help you?"

"I wouldn't be here without them."

When I needed the healers, I lay in dirt and the healers—a community of earthworms—undulated below me. How. Wow. To heal Miles.

"That's a lot of healers." I said.

"It was surely a sight to see," Kelly Joe agreed.

The air buzzed with the static charge that developed when the Towers laughed. When the charge faded, it emphasized the silence that saturated the streets of the complex.

"It's not safe for us here, is it? The Framekeeps overthrow was supposed to be a victory, but now we're in danger."

"The illusion of safety is our enemy's friend," Monk said. I took that to mean that we were in danger here all along.

The river shrieked. I startled and fell out of my squat onto my knees. "Don't worry, I'll get over feeling scared."

"Fear has us all shittin' bricks from time to time," Miles said.

"Bricks make good weapons," Monk noted.

I snorted.

"They were more powerful than we were the last time and we stopped them then," Miles said.

"All tomorrows are possible," Monk added.

The river shrieked and moaned. The water that flowed sideways took on the sheen of spoiled milk.

"It's time we go," Kelly Joe said.

"We will see you, Nica, when it is our time again to see you," Monk said, with what sounded like sadness. I understood. They couldn't stay with us. The allies had to oppose the Cysts on many fronts and that meant we would often work separately.

"Give us a climb," Miles said in farewell.

I had to climb off the platform over the void above the East River. Sometimes I'm brave and anyway the Towers wouldn't let me fall. Nor would Kelly Joe. I held my breath and pushed through the water then exhaled with a shout, clinging to Miles. I scrambled from girder to girder, then Monk tilted and I climbed onto him and hugged him for a while. To return me to Kelly Joe's side, Monk somehow rose up and tilted over the street so that I could jump down.

And then we split up. The Towers translated north. Kelly Joe and I headed east. Anya and Anwyl remained south, in the meeting hall. Hernandez was way out west. We had the compass covered. We had this. For the first time since entering the Framekeeps meeting hall, I shed my worry. Worry and fear. They never help. In fact, they eat my courage and thin my resolve. I know this, I've lived this. Yet sometimes I have to slip deep into them in order to regain my balance.

Kelly Joe and I retraced our steps through the district of suspended buildings at an even quicker pace than we had arrived. Every Cobra person we passed had a smug hostile look, as though they wished us ill and knew the wish would come true. The river's cackles grew louder and echoed under the streets.

I put it on my anti–bucket list: never again visit Expletive Deleted.

27. SCUFFED BY THE STEPS OF THE WICKED

On the Williamsburg Bridge, the trains spread the news. *Bread 'n' butter. Framekeep ouster.* They moved faster than they had before. The coup had given the day a freefall acceleration.

Step step step step. As soon as we reached the Brooklyn Bridge approach, Kelly Joe could start Traveling us the hell outta this Frame. I spotted the Bridge arches—we were almost there.

I stopped. A short couple blocks inland was the building on Keap Street that, on Ma'Urth, had housed the Lobotomist meeting room where Sam Strongfellow got indoctrinated. That building might have information that led us to the Lobotomist managers, the only way to stop the Lobotomists.

"Keap Street," I said and my musician nodded. "Maybe outside Frivolous Bedlam that building can tell us things about the Lobotomists."

As Kelly Joe considered, he rubbed the arms of his denim jacket, or the tattoos beneath. A pair of Cobra women passed us with a sneer and a hiss. Kelly Joe extended a hand to me. "We'll need to be ready to Travel away and we can't stay for long. Word of the coup is spreading."

I accepted his terms by taking his hand.

I caught myself hoping we'd run into Sam. As awful as my last encounter with him had been, the way he'd responded to Lilah's name told me he wasn't all vile. Perhaps the process of becoming a Lobotomist was reversible.

When we got to Keap Street, Kelly Joe stopped and frowned. "From this neighborhood, we can Travel to no other Frame." Expletive Deleted turns out to be full of deadends like that. Which can become traps.

Here in Expletive Deleted, the building that housed the Lobotomist meeting room had shattered windows, crumbling steps, and pocked sidewalks where someone had pogoed with a jackhammer. Building chatter was subdued; the buildings sounded tired.

"No grannies around here," I noted.

"I feel no peace here," Kelly Joe agreed.

Inside the second floor meeting room, something flickered behind the broken window glass. The flicker repeated, brighter for longer. We hurried into the dark splintered hole that was the building entrance and up to the second floor. The stair railing glistened like stomach bile.

The big meeting room was empty save for a pair of male models, sitting on the floor, setting little bits of something on fire, like runaways burning family photos.

"Your kind can't come in here," one of them warned. Like all male models, he had a voice like a personal fitness trainer, firm and upbeat.

"Whatever that kind is," the other sneered, displaying the Lobotomist M.O. Hate everyone who isn't like you.

"Did I miss the meeting today?"

"You weren't invited," the more hostile one said.

"Indirectly I was. In meetings at home on Ma'Urth they told us to branch out, get to know some—others." I had to speak carefully. The Lobotomists were enough like a cult to use special jargon, which I didn't know.

More Hostile resumed the burning of bits.

Less Hostile sounded envious. "We're supposed to go to Ma'Urth but we're not ready yet."

"Really? You seem pretty ready to me."

My new friend, Less Hostile, confided, "I'm going to be ready by the time the managers visit."

"Good for you! That is a worthy goal. How long have you got until they show up?"

"They will be at our acceptance ceremony, eight rotations from now."

"Nice!" Too eager.

More Hostile stopped burning bits to study me. Time to go.

"Maybe we'll see you later." Kelly Joe and I strolled out. Behind us, More Hostile gave Less Hostile grief for talking to us.

As we hustled toward the waterfront and the Brooklyn Bridge, the streets were empty of all but foreboding. Kelly Joe added to the gloom, "You'll want to avoid Lobotomists. You maybe might deceive other trainees but pod handlers will read your thoughts."

"Copy that. So a handler is a supervisor that's lower than a manager?"

A nod. He was focused on Traveling us away from Expletive Deleted. We were halfway across the Brooklyn Bridge when Kelly Joe turned to me, which suggested that he was done concentrating on tricky Frame changes.

At last I could ask the question that had been pestering me. "Lobotomist recruiting occurs in the same building in multiple Frames. And that building feels creepy. It doesn't gab like the goofy buildings, but it lacks the uppity attitude of the truly sentient buildings. Can a building be bad?"

"Not in my experience but we're all small in the Frames." Another one of those sayings, by his tone. He called to the air, "What do you think, Spanner? Can a building be bad?"

"There is no precedent." A voice as rich as the low tones on a trombone enveloped us, a voice that infused the pavement below our feet.

This is why I love Traveling. Brooklyn Bridge was speaking to us, and if that wasn't wonder enough, its voice was aurally translucent—whenever it spoke, I heard other, distant, voices, which cut off whenever Brooklyn Bridge stopped talking. Eventually I would learn that a bridge carries the voices of the land, water, and beings that touch it at the moment it speaks.

Brooklyn Bridge continued, musingly, "However, lack of precedent does not equate with absence of possibility, as we know."

"No fact is better known. Spanner, this is Nica of the New Yorks. Guide her feet as you would my own."

"I welcome the return of that gait. Nica, you crossed me at an exercise pace, a fortnight past."

Wow. Brooklyn Bridge recognized my feet after a single run, two weeks before. This made me go all fangirl but Kelly Joe took it as routine so I mimicked his man–of–the–Frames demeanor. "Yup, I was here. I tried to run but mostly I jogged in place waiting for an opening. The crowds are crazy on you."

"In most Frames of my awareness this holds true."

"May I ask you a personal question?"

"You have piqued my interest. What do you seek to learn?"

"Are you sentient in all Frames?"

"No being can answer that question about itself. Where I lack sentience, I lack awareness that a Frame exists around me."

"Thinking about that is going to cause me some headaches later." I groped for another question. I didn't want the Bridge to stop talking. The wash of underlying voices made me feel wonderfully connected, in much the way that Kelly Joe's music did. "Are you animate in any Frame?" I bet watching Brooklyn Bridge walk would be even better than seeing Monk and Miles translate.

"No, my duty is to span these waters, persistent through the Frames." The Bridge's pride swelled the concrete and had me walking taller.

Suddenly I did something I hadn't done for years—a spontaneous handstand. When I was a kid, I'd get so enthused I'd get destructive, in a bull–meets–china–shop way. My dad taught me to do handstands to expend energy safely. I hand–walked a few steps on the Bridge then sank to my shins. Our recent Frame shifts had messed with my balance. I reoriented quickly but continued to kneel, massaged by Brooklyn Bridge's rolling laugh, which was like a train in a mile–long tunnel.

"Nica is animate in all Frames," Kelly Joe told the Bridge by way of teasing me.

"Whether on fingers or toes, it is a pleasure to support pure steps such as hers. Particularly now, when I am scuffed by the steps of the wicked."

"Those will grow," Kelly Joe sympathized as we resumed walking.

"In numbers and in wickedness. Yes, Anya and Anwyl have warned much the same."

The feet we'd seen on our Frame shifts today, feet clawed and gnarly, swaddled in cloth, fortified in armored boots. You can't spot wicked steps by staring at feet. You can make yourself paranoid as a ferret. I reassured myself by telling Brooklyn Bridge, "With you on our side, I feel much better about stopping those wicked steps."

"I am on no side and all sides. It is my duty to support all who pass over me."

"Oh."

"However, to whom I impart information is at my discretion." And if a bridge could wink, this one was doing so now.

Kelly Joe reached for my hand while saying to the Bridge, "Thank you, Spanner, for another safe passage. We'll be –"

The Bridge interrupted, "Excuse me. Hold a moment. Anya and Anwyl have stepped onto my other terminus."

"Should we wait for them?" Kelly Joe stopped walking.

After a time the Bridge reported, "No. They will meet you at Nica's abode in Frivolous Bedlam. Nica, with your next step you will depart my domain. I enjoy your pace and look forward to its resumption here. Meantime, safe strides to you both."

"Hope to talk again soon!" I replied, but wasn't sure if the Bridge could still hear me. Or maybe it did reply and I couldn't hear. The world was too noisy. We were back in Frivolous Bedlam.

I turned for a final look at the solid gothic spires of the Bridge. "Why didn't we talk to the Williamsburg Bridge? Can't we trust it?"

"I couldn't say. I've never been in a Frame where it's sentient."

"Really? So it's just a structure then, like the Manhattan Bridge."

"The Manhattan Bridge is not just a structure."

The Frames were always more complicated than my understanding. "Oh. I. Assumed that it was just a structure because it doesn't persist. It was missing from most of the Frames we visited today."

"Such was not always the case. In the last battle for the free Frames, we nearly lost that spanner. Warty Sebaceous Cysts destroyed it in most Frames. As the Manhattan Bridge heals, it re–emerges here and there. But never mind about bridges." He waited for me to look at him. "We need to conclude your training. You may be called upon to transport beings."

"Yeah, I've got a ways to go with that." A woman passed us, dragging a tiny leashed dog. The dog bared its ludicrous little teeth at me. I gave the dog a thumb's up and told Kelly Joe, "Bet I could Travel with that dog." It was a safe bet to impress my teacher. Leon was bigger and I'd transported him.

"The time for gradual training is behind us." He held out his hand. "You'll transport me."

I could have laughed but it wouldn't have made him kidding.

"You're stronger than you believe." He held my gaze.

With the confidence of a dyslexic at a spelling bee, I took his hand.

He explained as we went. I would succeed when I learned to tap energy reserves I thought I lacked. It was like crossing the finish line at a marathon, then having someone tell you *oops this isn't the end, go another mile* and somehow you muster what it takes to move again, and after that mile someone says *Leon got hit by a car, hurry!*

After my nine billionth attempt to transport Kelly Joe, I lost count of my tries. My will to succeed was bolstered by my thought that the most likely use of this ability would be to transport an ally who was too injured to Travel alone. Eventually, I found the right combination of self–trickery, stamina, and stubbornness and I delivered Kelly Joe to Ma'Urth, where I collapsed on a sidewalk in the Bowery. Next to my face was a maggoty pile of chili fries. Turns out that major gross–outs boost energy. I thanked the fries, got to my feet, and returned us to Frivolous Bedlam.

Kelly Joe's praise, the pavement scraping my cheek, his arms sliding beneath me. He carried me somewhere and when I came to, my field of vision was filled with torturers.

28. YOUR NATURE IS NOT A FLAW

Maybe not torturers, *per se*, but they showed no mercy. Anwyl, Anya, Kelly Joe peered at me upside down and sideways as I dangled off my couch, whimpering. Transporting Kelly Joe from Bedlam to Ma'Urth to Bedlam had done me in. I was too weak to barf. I was a candle spluttering in the gutter. I was garbage washed up on shore. I was –

Anwyl bumped my leg with his boot. "Arise, we have much to accomplish."

"I'm dying," I informed them.

Kelly Joe dragged me vertical. "You're not." It must have been Anwyl's influence, Kelly Joe was usually sympathetic.

Anya touched my cheek like the rain that ends the drought. "You distracted the Framekeeps well today."

"I loved it when they recognized me. I liked being their ill wind." This made Anwyl chuckle. I propped myself against my wall. "I thought we would kick back and celebrate getting rid of the bad Framekeeps. But nobody even paused to blink."

Anya nodded. "Our actions today signal that we will stand between our foes and their desires. Conflict will escalate from this moment forward."

Kelly Joe added, "Each of us must be ready to use our powers at any moment."

I slid down the wall to rest a minute on the couch arm. I was too weak to feel dizzy.

"I've taught you long and you've learned well," Kelly Joe continued. "Now, Anya and Anwyl will see what you know and what they need to teach you."

"You mean they're here to give me a final exam?"

"It does not hurt to think it so," Anya said.

But Anwyl overrode her with, "It will be with our enemies that you face your real tests."

No one had to say more. They wanted to make sure an encounter with our enemies wouldn't be my truly final exam.

I got myself to stand without props and they tested what I knew about Frame Travel, then tweaked my performance and tested me again. I showed all of us how much I had learned, and then learned some more.

The effort left me a trifle worn and I concluded in my starting position, upside down and sideways on the couch, head lolled over the edge of a seat cushion. They looked funny, tilted. As they finished praising me for my great work and progress, I smiled and a little drool ran up my cheek.

Suddenly I sat up, re–energized. Anya was dishing out vague dangerous assignments. Kelly Joe would lead unspecified raids with allies unnamed. Anwyl would consult with anonymous military experts to pinpoint the significance of certain recent events. Anya was off to unidentified Frames to convince others to join our cause.

"Take no unnecessary chances." Anwyl gave Kelly Joe this order with a farewell embrace. I resolved anew to understand Kelly Joe's self–destructive bent.

But first things first. "What about me? What's my assignment?"

Anwyl and Anya exchanged a glance, then Anya said, "It will benefit our cause if you can locate additional compromised construction sites."

"So it's safe for me to go back to Ma'Urth now?"

"Yes, your return poses no problem for us." Weird way for Anwyl to put it, but I didn't ask for clarification. He was all gruff impatience today.

"Why can't I help any of you?" The prospect of being on my own again made me feel lonelier than a carrot on a stick.

Anwyl said, "In this phase of our campaign, surprise begets success."

"Your thoughts are easily read," Anya added gently.

"Wait, have I been holed up in Frivolous Bedlam to protect me or to keep my leaky brain uninformed?"

"Your isolation met both those needs."

I felt a special sort of exhaustion. Today had seemed like a new beginning as part of the team, but now here I was facing *solo* again, and because of a personal defect. "What's the point of all this training if you're ditching me?"

"We can't know when our paths will intersect next but we can be sure they will," Kelly Joe said as I glared at each in turn.

Fine. I yanked the strings from the violin I'd been playing. I would be on my own and I would find ways to make myself useful. Anyway, "Somebody could teach me how to hide my thoughts."

Anwyl and Anya exchanged a look that was even less scrutable than usual.

"Your nature is not a flaw," Anya's words were softer than her fingers on my arm in farewell, "and will do great service to our cause. We shall next meet in days yet darker..."

"...lightened only by our union," Kelly Joe finished the saying.

"We must away," Anwyl braced Kelly Joe's shoulders then he and Anya were gone.

Kelly Joe gave me a grizzly bear's hug and then my musician was gone, too, leaving me alone with my leaky thoughts.

I reassured myself that they would have left me in Los Angeles if I was never going to be part of the action. I glared at the ceiling. At some point Leon and Dizzy joined me, vibrating me with their purring and grooming, respectively. It was nice to not be alone.

"Books, to me."

My collection rose from the built–in shelf and circled overhead. During a sharp turn that must have required extra concentration, *Summer* shed text, which whizzed past my nose. *Lose Twenty Pounds* squawked at *Summer* until I interrupted. "Don't rag on her, it was an accident. You're all improving. It's just a matter of practice. But maybe widen your circle so you're not directly overhead. After I rest a little more I'm taking us home, so this will be your last chance to practice flying for a while." I mostly trusted *Lose Twenty Pounds* to stay inside my apartment in

Frivolous Bedlam if that was my order. But he was so gung ho to train the others, I could imagine him reinterpreting my command if I was absent for long.

The books followed orders from *Lose Twenty Pounds* to refine their loops and quick–drop landings. I had adopted Kelly Joe's unshakeable supportive tone with my books. Acting like Kelly Joe made him feel less absent. True, he had just left, but he was off on dangerous missions and who the hell knew when I'd seen him next.

All the allies had dangerous missions. I could lose any of them. Nearly losing Miles was just the beginning. The only way I could function, facing so much dread and uncertainty, was to make myself too busy to examine the possibilities, and to take action that genuinely contributed to the cause. Sure, cataloguing Cyst construction projects was important but I could do more. I had to. We all needed to push full bore. For them and for me, I needed missions of my own and I had some ideas about what I might do. Hadn't had a chance to talk about those ideas with fearless leaders but maybe that was just as well. What they didn't know, they couldn't forbid me from pursuing.

29. EVERYBODY INCLUDING HERNANDEZ

My apartment on Ma'Urth was as fresh as a can of peas and just as lively. I piled the books on the built–in wall shelf and chose music to blast through my speakers, grateful to be in a Frame where my sound system worked. Mournful was what I needed, so only real country would do, Hank and Patsy and George and murder ballads. The last thing I heard before the speakers began their soothing blast was the click of claws on the wood floor. The cats were here now, too.

Leon jumped onto the kitchen windowsill and stared outside. I went over to share his view. On the fire escape was the sentient lawn chair and on the chair with eyes closed was—Hernandez, strong and still as though sculpted there. Hot damn! He looked like he was sleeping but he wouldn't be, exposed in an unfamiliar place. Sure enough, as I watched, his shoulders clenched and he clutched the chair like it was a roller coaster. I hoped the chair wasn't making him re–live Jay's traumatic death, which Hernandez had witnessed.

"Hey, bud, thanks for letting me know. If that's what you did." I scritched Leon's head and reached past him to raise the window. Hernandez opened his eyes when my nail ticked on the glass. "Yo."

He broke into a huge smile: white teeth flashing, black eyes crinkling. I'd experienced his laugh a faint few times but this might have been the first smile.

"You match the cat." He rubbed his close–cropped pate. "And me."

I rubbed Leon's fresh fuzz, then my own. I had shaved us again last night, to kill time waiting for the Framekeeps visit. As Leon's fur grew out, it became clear he was a slob and his fur matted quickly. I kept fur over his scars, though.

Hernandez unfolded himself from the low–slung chair and rotated at the waist to unkink. "This chair a Traveler?"

"Sentient, anyway." I jogged to the bathroom to unlatch the window bars. He tossed his duffel bag in ahead of him. Once he had climbed inside the bathroom, there wasn't room to turn around so I backed out to the hall.

"I am so glad you finally got here. Are you?"

"Yeah. I think I am."

"May I hug you?"

"Asking permission?"

We held each other a long time, until we had to make a choice. Kiss or dance. We let go simultaneously. My skin tingled wherever we had contact, and the more layers of clothes between us, the more enthused I felt. I couldn't tell you what my time limit is to go without sex but apparently I'd exceeded it.

I led Hernandez out to the front room. He gave my abode a cursory glance, by which he picked up on more than most folks would know after snooping in every drawer.

"The chair indicated you had some bad news in this alley. That flash mob."

"The flash mob came down the alley?" Suddenly it was that night again, two ayem and Leon still wouldn't settle and I paced with him from room to room. "Have they been back since? Did the chair say?"

"Couple times. Is that why you've been away so much?"

"No. Mebbe. Dunno. Nobody tells me nothin' but I was supposed to stay out of Frame for a while." The Entourage had come back. Not the answer I wanted. My shoulders tightened for the umpteenth time of late. Could stress build muscle tone?

Hernandez reached to pet Leon, who squashed flat and scurried away.

I shrugged. "He's a cat. He has issues. How'd you know I've been gone?"

"Ben's worried. You never answer your phone." Hernandez sat on the couch like a carving of someone sitting on a couch.

"Ben's worried about me?" Any heavier irony and we'd sink through the floor.

"I figured you must be out of Frame but I couldn't tell him that because I didn't know what he knows about the Frames."

"Have you talked to him recently? How does he sound?"

"Find out for yourself. He wants you to call him. It's 'Jerry' on speed dial." He pulled a cheapo phone from an inner pocket of his windbreaker and tossed it to me.

"In a sec." I set it on the couch arm and continued into the kitchen, trying to remember the last time I ate.

"Get you anything? There's beer." I checked the fridge. "And... tomatoes. And goat cheese yogurt. With real peach bits." With Ben gone, there was no one to care for my pantry.

"I'm good. I stopped at a food truck."

"How long have you been in town, anyway? You missed a great scene with the Framekeeps this morning."

"So I hear from Miles. Got in last night, hotel in Times Square. Kind of place I don't even leave my toothbrush." He hefted the duffel bag, which he'd planted beside the couch.

Twinge. He'd heard about the Framekeep coup already. "You're welcome to crash here, of course."

"Thanks, I'll take you up on that, at least for tonight. Not sure where Anwyl needs me after that. Mind if I?" He twirled his finger in front of his eye, his symbol for taking a look around. I gave him a *be my guest* wave but my voice was petulant. "Anwyl knew you were coming? Why didn't he tell me?"

Hernandez went from window to window, checking locks and testing how wide each window opened. "You're asking me to explain Anwyl? What's wrong?"

"I'm just. It's been." I gave him a run down of the last couple days: the training, the Travel, the coup, and the revelation that my leaky brain would keep me sidelined from the action everybody else was in. Everybody including Hernandez.

""To each being a talent, to each talent a fate'," he mused. "Anya said that to me last night, it makes some sense now. I'm the opposite of you. My thoughts are airtight, Anwyl said I've got the soul of a spy."

"Sad to say, from him that's praise."

Hernandez had finished with the windows and was now examining the front door. "But I can't Travel on my own. After you left L.A., Anya then Monk then finally Anwyl tried everything to teach me. 'You give us no hope,' is how Anwyl left it. I'll never learn to Travel on my own. But it's easy for you." He sounded wistful.

"Trade'ya talents," I sniffed.

"I wish we could. Hold up." He timed how long it took to run from the front door to the bathroom window. Hernandez always knows his getaways. "Eight seconds. That's slow. It's getting around these corners. Lock the bathroom door to buy time." He joined me on the couch.

"Never mind, you're right, I don't want to trade talents. Being able to Travel is better than keeping my thoughts to myself. Crap. You made me feel better. I wanted to have a big sulk later."

He mimed opening the fliptop phone. "Call Ben now." Leon scurried into the room, this time with Dizzy sauntering alongside. "I didn't know you moved Dizzy with you."

"I didn't. She showed up on her own."

"That cat is something," Hernandez said. "She's got powers we can't even imagine."

"True dat."

Ben picked up on the second ring. "You mixed the red and white sauce before you put it on the chicken, like I told you, right?"

"Now I get it. You sent Hernandez to dinner at the Halal Guys truck. No wonder he's not hungry."

"Neeks," Ben purred, "at last. Hernandez said people told him you were fine, but when you didn't answer your phone for so long I thought you must have gotten an emergency laryngectomy."

"Makes sense that would be your conclusion. You sound good again."

"Know what this sound is?" The phone emitted a dull rattle. "My latest collection of newcomer chips."

My Ben worry knots loosened. "That's a good sound." I reached out to him through the satellite relay. He felt my touch through the ether and sighed.

"That's not what I needed to tell you, though. This is. Watch your back. Those cops found me in Philly."

"Mathead and Scabman? Those ex–cops you mean."

"They've still got badges and they found out my new name and they know you left L. A. They mostly asked about you."

"You talked to them?"

"No, this guy. I've been crashing on his couch. Now I'm exploring a new sector of the country and I'm living on cash. At some point I'll have to use a card or a bank and they can find me again, so I guess I'm on the move until further notice."

"I'm sorry. I've got friends who can help get rid of them, but probably not just now."

"More new friends. When can you tell me what your case is about?"

"Not yet. Not on the phone. It's too—don't let them find you, Benny."

"That part I figured out on my own. Hey, gotta get to a meeting."

If I had a star for every time he'd used that excuse to end a conversation, I'd be a galaxy. "Love you bro."

"Love you sis. 'She's my sister *and* my daughter. Understand?'"

"Nice delivery, Faye!"

When I hung up, Hernandez was scratching Leon's jaw but watching me, unsurprised by the conversation.

"Mathead and Scabman found Ben." I told him something he already knew.

"We won't let them get him," he assured me. "Or you."

30. I'VE GOT YOUR SECRET ANSWER

I needed food so we went out. Downstairs, Hernandez examined the foyer until he knew all its exits and we chatted about his daughters, their adventures in Spain, and their growing bond with their mother. His ego was solid enough that he could feel glad for them, even though he missed them like both his lungs.

"Nica! Over here, bitch."

The voice calling to me was so familiar yet so disorienting to hear in New York. I followed Hernandez' gaze down and over, saw the woman on the sidewalk from his first–timer's point of view. She had luxurious burgundy hair, luminescent skin, a compact streamlined frame, and—Hernandez would soon discover—a vocabulary that could melt steel. Even back in third grade she had been gorgeous and shocking. My Jenn was here in New York, paying a taxi. And leaning on a cane.

"Jenn?" I failed to keep the *WTF* out of my voice. Her cane snagged a sidewalk bump and made her stumble. She recovered like a ballerina, raised the cane, stood a moment considering it, then chucked it, like a spear, into the bed of a passing flatbed truck.

"Motherfucking M.S. is breaking my balls," she greeted me. Without the cane she wavered, but kept her feet planted and let us come to her. "I'm Jenn." She held out a hand to Hernandez and checked him out as she said to me, "No wonder you've been ignoring your phone."

Holy rollers, was Hernandez blushing?

"We were going out for a prowl but let's go back upstairs, we'll get dinner delivered," I said.

"No. I want to go out with you, help me get this shit upstairs first." Jenn hefted her purse. For her it was a modest bag, smaller than a cargo hold.

A few steps away, Hernandez watched her and waited for us to decide a plan. Jenn waved the purse at him and said sweetly, "Standing there like you've got jizz in your ears. Take this upstairs. Please?"

The *please* released him from staring. Somehow her words never offended, though from anyone else's mouth, they would end friendships and sink ships. Hernandez ran the purse upstairs and then we headed out, Jenn leading the way. She set a fast pace, but she kept light fingers on my forearm.

"Why are we stopping?" Jenn looked from me to Hernandez to the construction site at which we stared. I got out my phone and made note of the address.

"It's—for a case." At mention of *case*, Jenn made a noise that sounded confrontational. "C'mon, I'm done. What do you want for dinner?"

Jenn wanted Indian and I wanted Middle Eastern. Hernandez was still full from his lunch. In New York you can find good food of any persuasion within blocks, so we got takeout and took it to a bench at the far edge of Riverside Park. It always feels right to put Jenn in the middle so that is how we sat, facing the Hudson River—although we couldn't see it through the scrawny trees. The Hudson Parkway was just below us so all we could hear was traffic flow—which carries its own sort of peace. Still, the feel of the river was in the air, that sense of righteous movement.

"Doesn't your cousin live over there?" I peered across the river to New Jersey.

Jenn replied, "She does. That's where I crashed the last three days, waiting for you to show up or answer your fucking phone. I've got to get out of there, she's obsessed with taking care of me, makes me want to crawl inside my own asshole."

"Then you'll be glad to move in with me. As you know, I'm a lousy hostess. Anyway, I'll be out a lot working my case." Jenn made another confrontational noise. I was sorry she hadn't warmed up to the idea of the Frames. "How long can you stay? And what are you doing here? Why'd you ditch your retreat?" I tossed a falafel from hand to hand, to cool it faster. I was eager to eat it. The mushed fried garbanzos looked like a golf ball wrapped in moldy toast—a proof that looks deceive.

Jenn had decades of practice responding to my strings of questions. "I'm here until you kick me out, I get sick of being here, or my next retreat starts. If I go to it. I came because I needed to be somewhere where people would ignore me. The retreat was fine but I couldn't get into it."

"I'm surprised." I added a second falafel to my toss.

Hernandez stopped gnawing the giant street pretzel he'd bought to keep us company while we ate. "Describe the retreat," he injected. He wasn't going to let us leave him out of the conversation; I liked that about him. So did Jenn. The way she looked at him, she liked everything about him.

Jenn explained, "I'm always going to shit and doing shit to try to connect with G–O–D."

Hernandez rested the gnawed pretzel on his knee. "I understand. The connecting didn't happen this time?"

She slammed the lid on her takeout box, denting the Styrofoam. "The connecting doesn't happen any time, I just don't usually admit it."

"Since when is that true?" The times I'd talked with her after retreats, her enthusiasm had been genuine.

"Since forever. I'm still agnostic as fuck. I convinced myself for a while that I was having all these *spiritual* experiences," her emphasis was scornful, "but that was because I needed to have them. You know?" She tugged on her hair, pulled it perpendicular to her head—indicating utmost frustration.

"I don't buy that," I said. "You found something real at those retreats." I watched Hernandez over the top of Jenn's head. He nodded thoughtfully at the anger in her reply.

"I found something? Like what?"

I didn't react. It wasn't me she was mad at. "Maybe you hoped you'd find a cure at a retreat."

"Fuck no, that wasn't the point, I know I'm dying young. Change the subject, I started it so I choose when to end it. What kind of shitheel loser brings metaphysics to a picnic dinner, anyway." She threw a sideways glance at Hernandez, who looked out toward the river.

"Times I've faced off with death always left me wondering, what else is there?" Hernandez said, with a take it/leave it directness that kept his sympathy from overpowering.

"Well, honey, I've been sucking a whole lot of mystical cock to find that out and I've got your secret answer. It's nothing. There's nothing."

"Must make it hard to face what you're facing." Hernandez replied evenly. Which helped my understanding to coalesce. Jenn's retreats were her way to make the void less deep and empty. I'd figured that out a while ago, but I'd missed the key take–home message: her effort was backfiring; making her feel worse.

She started to cry. Jenn. Crying.

She clutched her elbows and buckled forward. Hernandez and I exchanged a look behind her back. Any effort to comfort could backfire.

"She's usually very chill," I told him. "Try not to judge her."

"Up yours, cunt." She sat up but her hair curtained her from view.

"Death is such a bummer." I delivered it stoopid sincere.

Which triggered a snort and then fury. Jenn hurled her food container across the path and it splattered, staining the bushes with yellow curry. She chucked my food, falafel by falafel. Hernandez handed his pretzel to her, and as she hurled it he fetched her some pebbles to throw. She threw everything while spouting a white–noise stream of obscenities. Finally she paused and looked at my falafels, strewn across the path. "Shit. Were you done with those?"

"I am in awe," I replied. "You sounded like Donald Duck."

She snorted again.

"Only good thing about the war," Hernandez mused, "was, sometimes when we felt like that we got to throw grenades."

We considered the falafels that littered the path. They continued to not explode.

"Next time order a side of grenades," Jenn instructed.

The sun was low enough to blast my eyes through the skimpy trees. I stared until I no longer had to squint and tree shadows touched our feet. The flow of the Hudson Parkway grew louder; rush hour. Jenn stood and looked around like she'd just arrived. She proffered elbows to us and said, "Come on, girlfriends, show me my new neighborhood."

We set off, sharing arms with Jenn.

31. NEW YORK RAT STORIES

It happened so fast, the life–or–death consequences didn't register until it was over. We were out of the park and crossing Riverside Drive. We had the green light but a kamikaze bike messenger zoomed into the intersection as his light turned red, pounding his bell instead of braking. I shouted a warning but Jenn was already in harm's way. She had jumped in the bike's path to hurl herself at a taxi door. The taxi had stopped a few feet from the curb, and the passenger door opened into the path of the bike messenger, while a shaky old gent propped his cane against the door and prepared to emerge.

Before Jenn acted, the bike messenger had two terrible choices—smash into the old gent and his door, or swerve into a crush of pedestrians. Jenn shoved the old gent's door closed and flattened herself against it. The bike whizzed past, just behind her, and the messenger pounded the bell in what I hoped but doubted was a *thank you.* Jenn retrieved the gent's cane from the asphalt, opened the door for him, kissed his bewildered forehead. "C'mon, we'll miss the light," she told us and we scooted across the street.

This wasn't the first time I'd seen sudden heroism from Jenn and I knew she wouldn't want to discuss it. *Like I had a choice,* was the most she would say.

Hernandez noted, "Excellent situational reflexes."

"Thank you," Jenn replied. And from then on, mutual regard bound them close no matter what their physical distance.

Body–slamming taxis takes a physical toll and by the time we got back to the Julian, Jenn needed to lay down. Hernandez and I left her on the couch and went to her cousin's in Fort Lee to fetch her stuff.

What had I been thinking, inviting Jenn to join me in a small abode with a single mirror in a lone bathroom? I'd shared an apartment with her once before, briefly. Every morning, she'd try on more outfits than I've ever owned, and strew the rejects for mortals to pick up. I never understood. To me, clothes exist to protect us from sunburn and indecent exposure charges. To Jenn, the union of garments is an art, practiced multiple times each day. For this visit to New York, Jenn had enough clothes to fill the Met.

Her suitcase was the size of a double–wide refrigerator and was packed with gold ingots. Hernandez and I wrestled the suitcase into my apartment and collapsed on either side of it. Jenn slept through our commotion, emitting precious wee snores. She looked worn out, a princess who'd fought too many dragons. I watched Hernandez watch her. He was curious, amused, and completely smitten. And he wasn't the only one. Leon stretched alongside Jenn, and Dizzy perched on her thighs.

When Jenn woke up, she and Hernandez went out to buy snacks for our slumber party that night, and I climbed out to the fire escape to catch up with the sentient lawn chair. As soon as I sat down, sensations washed through me and I experienced the world as the chair perceived it—dim shadowy views that changed from blue during day to charcoal at night; the chair couldn't see much but its senses of hearing and smell were acute. The chair showed me a chain of days and nights that seemed to be in chronological order, innocent at first. Ben in the chair... Kelly Joe... the upstairs kids... Leon... Synchronized steps goose-stepped down the alley and paused directly below this fire escape... Enormous rats followed. One bold fellow came to the bathroom window repeatedly and each visit grew more bold... The rat poised on the bathroom windowsill, headed inside, then suddenly Leon was there. When that huge cat pounced he was formidable. The rat got away but hadn't returned since...

The Entourage... The enormous rats... The Entourage... The rat at the window... The chair replayed those visits. I took this to mean they were related and important. "Tell me more about the window rat," I requested.

"'More about the window rat,'" Jenn quoted as she climbed out the bathroom window, tossing an observation to Hernandez, who stood behind her, "Nica has always talked to herself but she used to make sense."

"Maybe you had to hear the rest of the conversation," Hernandez said as he followed her onto the fire escape.

"Let's sit out here. You've got a view if you get the right angle." Jenn drooped over the side railing and peered in the direction of the Hudson.

"Rats on the fire escape might be a problem." I tried to alert Hernandez without mentioning 'my case' and pissing Jenn off. Assuming Jenn heard anyone who wasn't Hernandez. There was such spark between those two. Maybe I should stay in Frivolous Bedlam tonight and let them start a fire.

"Rats, New York, that's redundant," Jenn flopped next to my chair.

Around Jenn, Hernandez had a laugh that sounded surprised. He lowered himself to the fire escape below the bathroom window. "How many rats have you seen since you got here?" he asked, and we all started talking at once. New York rat stories. Everybody's got 'em. The light from the bathroom served as our campfire as we exchanged horror stories.

Our slumber party plans changed abruptly when our campfire light dimmed and Anwyl's shadow filled the space at the bathroom window. He reached outside to clap a hand on Hernandez' shoulder, ignoring Jenn and me.

"Well met. Come. We have much to attend." Just as abruptly, Anwyl was gone from the window and his voice carried back to us from deep in my apartment. "We must away."

Hernandez stood. His silhouette nodded in my direction then said to Jenn, "To be continued." He climbed inside the bathroom, his stance all soldier. He disappeared after his commander and in another moment we heard my front door slam.

"Who the fuck was that?" Jenn asked.

"That was Anwyl. My client. I told you about him."

"There really is an Anwyl," she said, like that made everything worse—if I was going to fabricate farfetched stories about Frames, apparently I should populate them with imaginary people. I swallowed a Gandhi pill and let it go.

"Do you think he'll be back tonight?" She wasn't asking about Anwyl.

"No real clue, but I doubt it."

"Shrug. For the best, maybe. We need to catch up, bitch."

With *shrug* Jenn referenced seventh grade, when we found it important to hide all emotions and developed two strategies to communicate with one another. In public, we narrated reactions instead of performing or feeling them; only during the privacy of our sleepovers, awake in the dark, would we spill the real beans about who we cared for and how we felt.

"Smile and nod. I'll get the bed ready."

We climbed inside the bathroom window and I locked the bars behind us, then shut and locked the window. Now that I knew about the snooping rats, the window would stay closed until further notice. Leon and Dizzy seemed to prefer entry via Frame Travel, anyway.

I shoved furniture around to make room for the Murphy bed. Jenn went into the bathroom to complete the extended convoluted processes that take her forever to prep for bed. She was fast tonight. By the time I lowered the Murphy bed, converted my desk chair to a nightstand for her, and set out fresh water for us, she was making late–in–process noises. I barely had time to read the last week of the *New York Times* and grow my hair a quarter inch before she emerged.

I switched out the lights and climbed into bed beside her.

"Tell me everything about Hernandez," she instructed.

"He's a vet, he mentioned that. He's been working cases with me since I started as a detective. He's also a custodian because he's a great dad who makes sure that –" Her adorable little whisper of a snore cut me off. I lay there for a long time, listening to her breathing, which was irregular and ratcheted with gritty sighs.

I lay very still so as to not disturb her. My breathing achieved an opposite sync, and with each exhale I sent strength into her next inhale. I don't know how I kept still. Every ratcheted sigh jolted me, made me want to shriek and throw grenades. Eventually and mercifully, the cats showed up. Dizzy walked across my stomach to curl up on Jenn's thighs. Leon stretched out on my pillow. With my ear pressed against him, I could hear nothing but his megapurr and with that, I fell asleep.

Come the morning, I was up, showered, dressed, caffeinated, and watching Jenn still sleep. Her head was collapsed into her pillow, her hands sunk into the comforter. She had always carried her sixty three inches like a six footer, but now she looked tiny. She would never be weak but she looked frail. I blew her a kiss, left her a note and a key, and went out to hunt me some Lobotomists.

32. SOMETHING TICKLED MY MEMORY

I intended to infiltrate one or more Lobotomist training pods, which seemed the most likely way to find the elusive managers. I had to practice leak–resistant thinking first, because managers and some handlers could read leaky thoughts. I could hide real thoughts beneath a stream of superficial ones. To blend with Lobotomists, I needed a stream of corrosive prejudices. I worked on my hating as I walked along Amsterdam toward the subway.

I hated these streets, I hated these people—wankers and losers and grabbers. It was time for a purge and from what I'd heard I'd find like minds at the meeting house on Keap Street in Brooklyn.

I nurtured a guilty secret, too. *I hoped the handlers didn't find out that I had tried to join a pod on Ma'Urth but they told me not to come back. I deserved another chance. They thought I couldn't measure up but I would show them they were wrong. I would prove it to them and then I would get the status and approval I craved and deserved.*

Coming up with these thoughts was spirit–quenching. By the time I rehearsed enough to join a meeting, I would be in a dark dark place indeed.

I knew my musician was gone but nonetheless I got off the train at Columbus Circle subway station and sat on the bench where he used to play and maybe breathed air that had once carried his music. I so needed it now, as I faced unfaceable loss. I've had way too much practice dealing with death. My mother, my high school buddy Joey, my cousin, my father, my favorite prof, two cats in a house fire, my uncle. Ick. All those losses had one thing in common. Jenn helped me through them. Losing Jenn was impossible yet spitting in my eye. Everything about her was special, so it figured that her M.S. would be advancing so much faster than the norm.

My stop at Columbus Circle didn't help so I went up to the street and headed east. City noise can be a tonic and inspiration to me but today I needed music. I inserted my earbuds and lost myself in the saddest tunes I knew. Within a couple blocks I was bawling so loudly I had to up the volume. In New York, nobody hears you cry, so I was surprised when a hand grabbed my shoulder. Maybe I was about to step into oncoming traffic and a fellow pedestrian didn't want to get splattered.

The hand belonged to a gangly, acne–laden pre–teen who was mouthing to me intently. I popped one earbud out and realized the loud tinny backwash from my earbuds carried several feet away. The kid was singing along with my current tune.

"'Leave ah–lone, you don't buh–long here'," the kid sang to my musical backwash. Every inflection was perfect, although he hadn't been conceived when Elliott Smith recorded *No Name #1*. The kid sang with relish and he carried the tune about as well as I'd carried Jenn's suitcase. The kid made me smile, which reminded me that self–pity sucks. I offered him an earbud and we crossed the street, singing together. "'Got ner–vous, started whistling, every thought a rih–coh–chet.'" We finished the song this way, our sing–along incomparably poor and loud.

"Thanks, that gave me a good morning." He flashed a mouth full of black and puce. Kids these days get to choose the colors of their braces.

"Same here and likewise." I pocketed the earbuds and set off solo again, a big smile stretching my skin and etching deeper laugh lines.

The smile eroded as I rehearsed. *I hated these streets, I hated these people, wankers and losers and grabbers. It was time for a purge and from what I'd heard I'd find like minds at this meeting house.*

I Traveled to Frivolous Bedlam, where the silly building chatter compromised my sour perspective, which gave it good exercise. When I could stay pissed off and resentful in Bedlam, I'd be ready for a Lobotomist meeting.

Three steps onto Brooklyn Bridge, he said, "Good morning, Nica, I welcome the return of your steps." Before I could reply he continued, "Many need my counsel today so I cannot undertake casual conversation. Do you also need assistance on my span?" When Brooklyn Bridge spoke today, there were so many background voices it was like all Ma'Urth's cell phone conversations were broadcasting through a cosmic loudspeaker. Around me were beings who seemed to be talking to themselves and it hit me that these might be some of the simultaneous conversations that Brooklyn Bridge was holding. I stifled my awe. Lobotomists don't feel awe.

"I'm good, thanks." It was a disappointment but for the best. Talking with Brooklyn Bridge even briefly unsoured my attitude. And I needed to focus on precision Frame shifts.

Expletive Deleted was in an ugly state, as though a riot had just concluded. Around me, the buildings whispered and whimpered. Their windows were shattered, their walls smeared with garbage and maybe blood. While I walked, I prepared. *I hated the streets of New York, the wankers and losers and grabbers. I deserved better, I deserved to join a pod and I'd prove it to them.*

Half a block ahead, male models headed inside the meeting house on Keap Street. A meeting must be about to start. I slowed. Was I ready for this?

If not now, when?

Upstairs were a crowd of male models and a smattering of miscellaneous beings. We the miscellaneous exchanged grim nods. I was glad the room was packed, it created a jumble of thoughts to—*It was time for a purge and from what I'd heard I'd find like minds at this meeting house.*

The meeting was long and unpleas–*inspiring*, providing reason to hate anything and everybody. I hovered on the edge of small group conversations, shyly yearning for inclusion. After the break, the handlers slapped certain shoulders. "Stand." Slap. "Stand."

My shoulder stung from the slap. I jumped to my feet and looked around. All the male models were seated. All the miscellaneous humanoids were on their feet. The handler who had done the slapping gave a compassionate sneer. "This meeting is for natives of this Frame. You who stand, leave now."

Another handler waved us out with impatient boredom. *I took heart in the fact that the handlers were also non–natives. I could belong, I only needed a chance to —*

"Stop puling and move along," the door handler snarled as though I had spoken aloud. I trotted down the stairs, *regretting I had offended.*

Outside, I went across the street then hung around. *I hoped I didn't offend by sticking around, but it was so hard to walk away when at last I knew where I belonged.*

In lieu of letting my thoughts wander, I admired the building. *People could be awful but they did make nice buildings sometimes.* This one boasted a façade that was distinctive black granite with ruddy pink flecks. Every time I looked at it, something tickled my memory but this wasn't a time to sneeze.

The meeting must be over; male models exited the building noisily. The handlers exited last. *I hated the streets at home. It was time for a purge and I could help make it happen.* I crossed the street to be closer to the action. A handler glanced at me like you would glance at an overflowing trash can. I watched them walk away. I was the only one left on the block. I patted the building goodbye. *I'd be back, and soon!*

I made it back to Frivolous Bedlam, where I dropped my vile impersonation and released my thoughts. It wasn't Frame Travel that had made me nauseous this time. I leaned over, gasping, and shook like a swimsuit model on Neptune.

"Cat Shaver, are you okay?" A line of food carts tilted my way.

"I'm just fine. Thanks for being concerned!" They popped a few wheelies then took turns giving me rides across town. Lounging on the carts gave me a chance to ponder what I'd just experienced.

Attending the meeting was easier than I had anticipated, although even more repellent. That the miscellaneous humanoids like me were second class at the meeting, was—like most of life's developments—good news and bad news. Being of lowly status, I could attend without attracting attention; but what if they excluded the miscellaneous humanoids when the managers visited? I needed to revise my strategy. My gradual infiltration plan was too slow. The way they talked at that meeting, they'd soon be trained and going away. If that happened, I'd never get to the managers.

A new strategy coalesced as the carts wheeled me onto Julian's block.

"Stop please, I need to hop off. Thanks for the lifts!" The air filled with the food carts' disappointed goodbyes as I Traveled to Ma'Urth. I needed to make a phone call.

"Nica? Have you found Sam?" Lilah greeted me. Based on the yearning in her voice, she had not.

"No, but I need your help. Can we meet to discuss it? When do you get lunch? I could stop by."

"I've got an investor lunch I can't postpone. I'm off work at five."

We arranged to meet outside Columbus Circle subway station at 515p, then I headed for the Lexington subway and a visit to Woodlawn Cemetery. I needed to check something there.

33. AND IT'S DANGEROUS

Rosie, the snip–of–a–girl guard, sat inside the cemetery gate's kiosk, still reading about celebrities. Today her frizzy hair was red.

She remembered me. "Tell your friends thanks. I haven't seen those hoodies since."

"They'll be glad to know that." It sounded like the illegal Connector remained disconnected, which meant my chances of a Lobotomist run–in today were low. As I headed into the cemetery grounds, the sun was warm and the breeze refreshing, but the trees' fall colors were gaudy. Funny thing about a cemetery. On a bright fall day this one felt more forlorn than it had at twilight. Or maybe the difference was in me.

The Connector had been behind a granite mausoleum. Today a grounds crew worked there, cleaning what looked like sooty grease. The mausoleum was made of a distinctive stone, black with ruddy pink flecks. Yup, I had remembered correctly. It looked just like the stone on the building that housed the Lobotomist meetings.

Back at the gate kiosk, I opened one of Rosie's visitor maps and pointed to that mausoleum. "The stone on this building intrigues me. How can I find out more about it?"

She picked up her walkie–talkie. "I'll get Rudyard over here, he's a cemetery historian."

Sure enough, Rudyard knew the facts and the lore. The stone on the mausoleum was a rhodonite granite with a B–movie history. It came from a renowned but short–lived, 19th century quarry called Witch Hollow, near Salem, Massachusetts. An unusual incidence of quarry worker fatalities and deaths of building inhabitants—plus the name and location of the quarry—spread rumors that the stone was cursed. The man who designed that mausoleum for himself was a tycoon with weak superstition and strong ability to spot a great bargain—the high–quality stone was grossly discounted as the quarry folded.

Of course, it could be a coincidence that the same stone showed up at an illegal Connector and a Lobotomist training facility. Or there could be a tie between that rock and Warty Sebaceous Cysts. I intended to find out which.

Granite, rhodonite, cursed, quarry, Witch Hollow. Waiting for a train to take me back to the city, I played with internet search keywords until I found the magic combo that yielded information. Around New York and New England were six additional buildings with the rhodonite granite. The two closest were in Queens— in fact, both were in Flushing—and before my rendezvous with Lilah I had time to check out those buildings.

The first building felt bad from half a block away so I Traveled to Frivolous Bedlam before I approached it. In Bedlam, the building was silent and its neighbors whispered as though on a sick ward. I returned to Ma'Urth and stood across the street from the building, which was surrounded by the green webbing of construction site fencing. There was no activity at the site but a big sign with artist's renderings showed the ambitious remodel planned by Lantana Ltd. Most of the structure was being razed, leaving only the first floor with its black stone facade. Rhodonite granite and Lantana Ltd. construction. Double whammy. Kelly Joe's demolition talents would be well applied here.

The second building had never been repainted, much less remodeled. Like other nineteenth century houses on the block, it was converted to stores and flats in a neighborhood that fell somewhere between down-to-earth and downtrodden. Varied ethnic restaurants made the air smell like a spice market. I got only a vague uneasiness about the building, but a steady stream of frowning people departed it, suggesting a meeting had just concluded.

I fell into step with a straggler. "There's a meeting tomorrow, right? At two?" The straggler's head jerked in what might have been a nod and she gave me the look you'd give somebody who spit at your mother. Had to be a Lobotomist in training; when fully trained she'd have more control over aberrant impulses like polite response to a question.

My gut told me that if I wanted to infiltrate a Lobotomist pod quickly, the distraught twin of Sam Strongfellow—feeling excluded from her brother's life for the first time—was a more likely potential recruit than my outsider who was determined to join the club.

Lilah's stilettos tapped their way east on 57th Street, rhythmic enough to mark time as she approached.

"What do you know about Sam?" she called to me as soon as I was within hearing range.

Maybe I confused *controlling the conversation* with *controlling the outcome.* I saved my reply until she arrived where I stood. "I'll tell you down here." I led her to the southbound subway platform at Columbus Station and we sat on the bench in silence. I assumed that she, too, was reliving our times hearing Kelly Joe's music. Her eyes glinted but she didn't cry.

I warned, "What I'm going to tell you won't make you feel better, except for that faint hope we get when we have action we can take. My story will sound nuts. Actually what happened to Sam is nuts. There's only one way to help him and even that might not work. And it's dangerous. Either or both of us could die."

Her response was, "Tell me all."

I told her as *all* as I dared. I had my words planned, or I thought I did. "Sam is part of a cult now. This cult attracts people who crave something—success, attention, sex, money—and who blame others for what they lack. The cult distorts such thoughts, controls through them. Sam's brainwashing is so complete that the only hope to snap him out of it is to identify the cult leaders—which are called managers—and show them up as frauds. First we need to learn their identities."

Her tears were back.

"My plan is for us to crash one of the cult's training sites. We have to act fast. The training will be done soon and they'll leave the meeting halls. So. Maybe you can't handle life without Sam. Maybe whatever your twin is doing, you want to do, too. And maybe you bring along the detective you hired to find your brother. I was the one who learned about the meetings and what I found out intrigued me. Maybe I like the way that cult thinks." I caught myself in a sneer.

"Which gives you a personal interest now, beyond my hiring you." Lilah was all business.

"Precisely. Now I need you to believe something farfetched. Some of the meeting organizers—called handlers—are crazy good at reading people. They read our body language, whatever, I can't say how they do it. But if we don't completely believe our stories, they'll know, and we're screwed. Big time. So when I walk near those meeting rooms I hate just about everybody."

"And I am so obsessed with my brother that if he thinks this is right then it must be. And I want to prove to him how important I can be to his new cause." Lilah's eyes looked at me but all she saw was Sam.

"That's perfect. Now. I have to stress. These people—and what I am proposing—terrify me. If you're not scared, it's because you haven't met them yet."

"I believe you. I can see you're serious."

"I couldn't be more serious. We could die." My voice scraped like rusted nails. Were there really no other options?

"When's the next meeting? Am I okay dressed the way I am now?"

I knew she would downplay danger to herself so I played my trump. "With us meddling, Sam could die."

A subway train came and went.

"But otherwise there's no chance of his breaking free of all this?"

"None, according to my sources, who could not be more credible."

"Then how can I refuse?" Her voice was garbled like an underwater train wreck.

We made plans to meet the next day and go to the training session in Flushing.

"Queens." was the last thing she said to me.

Back at the apartment, Jenn was elbow deep in her suitcase and naked except for gypsy hoop earrings. She had lost weight recently so was now a bony Madonna; but still worship–worthy.

"Good thing Hernandez isn't here. Or would that be too bad he isn't?"

"Not for me to say." She pawed fabrics pensively.

"Let me guess, you haven't a thing to wear."

"Shove it, princess, we both know you're the one with the clothes problem. When was the last time you got any? Clothes, I mean."

It takes two to rattle a cage. "I'm about ready for dinner. You?"

Jenn has a short attention span when it comes to conflict. "Definitely. Just need to take a quick shower first. I'll be out in a jiff."

"I'll be here."

Jenn's *jiff* meant it might still be autumn when she emerged. But that was just as well, because I had business in Frivolous Bedlam. I could go there, do that, and be back before she discovered I was gone. I grabbed all my copies of *Lose Twenty Pounds* and took us to Bedlam.

34. T–E–X–T–C–O–M–E–S–B–A–C–K

I sat on my couch in Bedlam and my seven copies of *Lose Twenty Pounds of Worry in Twenty Days* hovered before me. I had brought these books to Bedlam because I needed to understand book interactions.

"We came to this place before," I told my first copy of *Lose Twenty Pounds.* "Please train these books like you did the others."

I observed the flying lesson from the couch. The books didn't seem to share a collective consciousness like the healers or the grannies. When one book squawked, the others had to listen. Or not. The books displayed a pecking order—when certain books squawked, they got ignored or interrupted; and all the books, including the book I'd appointed as trainer, showed deference to a particular volume, a hardback with a cover that was plainer than the others, lacking the bold bright *#1 Bestseller* banner.

"Hey, everybody, land for a minute." They complied, some more quickly than others, and I looked at each book's copyright page. The book that earned deference was the earliest edition. I held it up before I released it. "This book was printed before any of you others. Did you know that?"

They all nodded and the trainer shed text: o–f–c–o–u–r–s–e.

"How did you know?"

W–e–j–u–s–t–k–n–o–w.

?–?–?

Y–o–u–n–g–e–r–s–m–e–l–l–s–g–r–e–e–n–e–r.

They used a lot of text to give me little usable information. "From now on I'll stick to yes–no questions. I don't want to waste your text, you could need it."

T–e–x–t–c–o–m–e–s–b–a–c–k. And the oldest ruffled its pages until I saw faint gray bumps where shed text was regenerating.

Wowza. I had even more questions now, but I needed to be home before Jenn finished in the bathroom.

"I'd better get us back to Ma'Urth. Please stack yourselves."

Several books did a quick flying loop before a squawk from the earliest edition got them to comply. They weren't uncooperative, they simply enjoyed being free.

I picked up the stack of books and opened my front door. I'd Traveled from the hall to ensure that Jenn wouldn't see me materialize in the front room. That might get her to believe in the Frames but it would launch an all–night discussion and I needed rest. Lilah and I had a big day tomorrow.

As soon as I stepped into Ma'Urth, I heard my name. "Nica," came a raspy genteel voice like a butler with a pack–a–day habit.

"Julian, how goes it?"

"I am well, thank you," the building replied. "I couldn't help but overhear your conversation with your tomes. I regret any intrusion."

"No need to ever apologize about that. You can't help but listen and I appreciate your discretion."

"I thank you a second time. From your questions, I thought you would like to know about the existence of the Frame Monasterium, where scribes have recorded the long history of the Frames, including the history of books. These reside in the Halls of Shared Knowledge. If you wish to visit, I can guide your Travels to Monasterium."

"Fantastic! I'll be back soon for your help with that! You're a peach!"

"I do enjoy fruitwood wainscoting on my upper floors. That is one of my most handsome features."

Jenn sat at the kitchen counter with damp hair and what I assumed was another perfect outfit. She was writing on a paper towel and humming bits of songs, which meant she was concentrating. She glanced up. "How many copies of that book do you have?"

"Seven. I want to give them to a few people."

"Isn't it such a good book? I can't believe you finally read a book I gave you!" Usually savvy and cynical, Jenn had an inexplicable soft blind spot when it came to self–help books.

"It—they are good books." I set them on the shelf and patted their spines fondly. "What are you writing?"

"My epitaph."

At first I felt nothing, like the day I grabbed the wrong edge of a razor blade and as the blood gushed I had time to think, *that's going to hurt.* "You're planning to have a tombstone now? A grave? I thought you wanted your ashes scattered into the world's most explosive volcanoes?"

"That hasn't changed and I just emailed you the list of volcanoes. You're going to post my epitaph on my blog. I emailed you the log–in."

A puff of a laugh got past the lump that filled my throat. "Okay. I'll be sure to save those emails. What kind of food are you in the mood for tonight?"

"I don't want to talk about this shit either, sweetie, but we can't put it off." She gave me a look. She was stuck in a pit and wanted help to climb out but feared she'd pull me in with her. "Not that any of it matters, worms don't read blogs."

"You know how it is. You have to tailor for the audience you want to reach. You have to gear your blog content to interest worms."

"Composting dos and don'ts?"

"Break–in tips for presswood coffins?"

She crumpled and tossed the paper towel. "The next time I talk about dying just fucking shoot me."

"Okay but hold off for a while. I'll need to borrow a gun first."

We looked at each other.

"I'm in the mood for Chinese tonight," she announced.

I spoke with pride. "I know a great *dim sum* truck."

"Now tell me everything about Hernandez."

We had so much fun that evening, and enough laughs to strain my stomach muscles, even though we were home and in bed by eight. Jenn feel asleep immediately. I lay there, considering how to resume our conversation about the Frames. Maybe I should get Hernandez involved in the discussion. That could boost my credibility.

As soon as Jenn's breathing kind of smoothed, I slipped out of bed and got back to work. First I went out on the fire escape to sit on the sentient lawn chair. Nothing new, I was relieved to learn. Then I went into the hall outside my door, Traveled to Frivolous Bedlam, and called out to Julian.

35. ANY KNOWLEDGE WILL HELP MY QUEST

My earliest memory is the first time I saw the ocean. I was three. I stopped with my feet in the surf, stared, patted the water, stared, stared until my parents feared a sudden brain disorder. Ever since and still today, when I'm at the ocean it sweeps me away.

The Frame Monasterium rivaled my discovery of the ocean, with a similar sense of power and beauty that would perpetually stretch beyond my imagination.

In sum, it was totally rad there.

At Julian's suggestion, I did my Traveling from his roof, where it was easy to see when I'd arrived. In Monasterium, the island of Manhattan was covered in brown sand, with an occasional building rising up. Only sentient buildings persisted there.

Edging the island like a great wall was a broad structure with shiny brown sides and a supple white roof that trembled in the breeze. On the New Jersey side of the Hudson River was a similar structure. Between the walls, the Hudson flowed with tremendous force—I could hear the rush of water from this roof, long blocks inland. According to Julian, my destination was that wall, the Halls of Shared Knowledge.

The deep smooth sand was slippery and soon I was carrying my shoes and walking with a forward tilt. Each time I sank into the sand, it replenished me like a foot massage. What was this stuff? I scooped a handful of sand and saw rounded polished bits of permineralized wood. Most folks would call it petrified wood but I dated a geologist once and he geeked me forever about some things. Each grain had dazzling bright spots like frozen sunlight and I felt good to hold it but somehow knew that I shouldn't keep any. I let the handful sift through my fingers.

The Halls of Shared Knowledge had walls made of stacked boulders. Same stuff as the sand, as polished as Cat's Eye agate and glowing with internal light. Each boulder reflected dozens of tiny Nicas. I touched one and found it warm. When my hand was in contact, I was filled with assurance about all that I knew (like the time I'd really studied, and left an exam certain I'd aced it) and humility about how little I understood (like the day I'd learned Ben was an addict). The boulders were stacked without support, a stone country wall built to gravity–defying height of twenty feet.

Now that I was close to the Halls, I spotted arched entryways every few hundred feet. I took the next arch. Inside the Hall, the floor shone with the same sand and the roof was parchment that diffused sunlight into every cranny. The walls were lined with stacked bookshelves like I'd seen in lawyers' offices, but these had parchment instead of glass fronts, and wood grain that pulsed and flowed. These bookcases were alive.

In the center of the room was a table covered by parchment that curled off the sides into thick rolls. This parchment glowed like light in a pitcher of cream. As far as I could see, tables with glowing parchment scrolls lined the center of the hall. Way down yonder, what might be two cacti were bent over a scroll.

"Welcome, seeker." Warm tones greeted me from many directions and I understood that the bookcases had spoken.

"Hello. I'm looking for information about how books became soldiers and killers." I expected to be shown to a 'history' wing.

The air vibrated with tones like a pipe organ, which must have been the bookcases discussing my request. Silence followed and a warm condescending voice said, "What is your interest in that tragic and terrible time?"

"My interest must remain my business, that is, I cannot divulge it. Frankly, I'm surprised you asked. I wouldn't expect the Halls of Shared Knowledge to question information gathering."

The air vibrated with tones that were less resonant, more shrill. "We seek your intent, not to restrict, but to protect. All knowledge is available but not all beings can adapt to all truth." My greeter had the smug arrogance of an academic. That always pushes my buttons.

"Thanks for caring. Please direct me to the info and we can all get on with our days." Now the tones of the pipe organ could accompany a slasher movie. "I am so sorry," I yelled, which won silence. "My need for haste has made me rude. I am allied with Anwyl, son of Rayn, a framewalker, and Anya, daughter of Niav, an exalted seer." Based on the tones of their reactions, my apology pleased them but Anwyl's name distressed them but Anya's name excited them. Maybe that left me operating in the black.

"I regret that I cannot confide in you but I am on a mission that must remain secret. I will be able to withstand what I learn. Anya would never give me an assignment that would be more than I could bear."

"Do you mean that Anya sent you here?"

"Everything I do must be for Anya and Anwyl's cause. All else is irrelevant should their efforts fail," I hedged.

Their tones became Wagnerian, as though they understood the conflict and the stakes. They conversed and I pretended to wait patiently.

Damn, close but no cigar. The reply sounded sympathetic, but held firm. "We must put no seeker at risk. Perhaps if Anya accompanied you."

"I don't know when I can get her here."

No response. I couldn't leave things like this. I needed a *yes* from them or future encounters would all be based on *no*.

"Is there anything you can show me about the history of books? Any knowledge will help my quest."

This led to discordant discussion, an *avant garde* student film soundtrack. When a Mozartian melody emerged, I knew I had my *yes*.

"Step to the viewer, seeker."

I had to assume this meant one of the tables with glowing parchment. "Which one?"

"Any. Knowledge shares equally from all."

Unless you restrict it, I didn't say. Snarky, yes; foolish, no.

Up close, the parchment glowed like albino abalone shell. It had a nape like peach fuzz and the direction of grain continuously shifted as pattern flowed. I watched the flow of pattern long enough to feel duped. A viewer with nothing to view. Perhaps this was their way of saying uck–fay off–fay.

"I don't speak parchment pattern," I said finally.

This generated a rom–com soundtrack, over which a mellifluous voice told me something I already knew, then something I didn't.

"You lack in patience, seeker. We assemble knowledge from a vast archive and that takes time."

Words appeared on the parchment, soon joined by holographic pictures and videos that were so lifelike they seemed to exist in a tiny reality within the viewer. Some images looked professional, as though from a news report; others reminded me of the first Framekeeps hearing that I had attended, when we watched memories from the minds of diverse witnesses.

The tiny reality included Frames and beings beyond my wildest imaginings, so alien that I couldn't describe what I was watching, but I understood that I was seeing the Frames long ago, before Maelstrom and before his mentor, Pandemonium. Back in that time, books were special, reading was ubiquitous, and in many Frames, communities were built around public gathering places called reading circles.

I wasn't permitted to view Pandemonium's rise to power nor her subjugation of books. In the scenes I viewed, books were beloved objects, then, out of view, Pandemonium converted them into beings and somehow made them sentient, animate—and deadly.

Of all the terrible images I viewed that day, the one that most haunts me featured a family of blue–furred humanoids with three young children. The children finished a rowdy play session then rested, paging through well–thumbed books. Suddenly they gasped—the books flew from their hands! The books collided in mid–air then flapped in wobbly arcs that reminded me of the first time my books flew. The children cheered and called for their parents.

The parents came running when the cheers turned to screams. During a collision, books shed volumes of text and the text sliced the youngest child into bits. As the surviving children wailed and pointed, the parents couldn't comprehend what the mound of pulp and blue fur could mean. The surviving children pointed to a corner near the ceiling, where the three books hovered, shedding text with each nervous flap of their covers. Below the books, each shower of text sliced a pile of stuffed animals into tinier bits. The parents pulled the children out of the room and slammed the door. One of the books flapped over to the remains of the dead child, studied it from various angles, then smashed itself into a wall, shedding all of its text at once.

A quartet of blue–furred beings in uniforms entered the room, carrying flaming torches and a glittering metal net. The book that had smashed itself into the wall hurled itself at a torch and was incinerated. The other books flew into the net without any resistance to capture.

In Frame after Frame, books could suddenly fly and shed text that caused unwitting destruction. As with the blue–furred family's books, in these early days, books seemed confused and sought imprisonment willingly. More than one book incinerated itself.

Bonfires raged. Beings dragged nets, bulging with books, toward the flames and few of the books tried to escape. As the books burned, the beings sobbed. The bookcase had described it truly: a tragic and terrible time.

Remaining books disappeared from all the Frames, and rumors spread that Pandemonium and her apprentice Maelstrom trained the books in hidden camps. Time elapsed, and then began the War for the Free Frames. Books reappeared in the first battle, flying in precision squadrons, shedding text on command, shedding text to kill.

I'd heard about that war from Anya and Anwyl. The side of wrong had seemed invincible, until Maelstrom made a power grab that broke Pandemonium's concentration and led to Pandemonium's capture in a collapsed Frame. Maelstrom continued waging war and producing killer books, with three disciples, Warty Sebaceous Cysts. Eventually, Maelstrom was caught in a collapsed Frame all his own. The Cysts went to prison for a stretch of years and as soon as they got out, they set in motion their plan to free Maelstrom.

That was about the time that Anya and Anwyl showed up in my office and took me to the Watts Towers...

The parchment pattern flowed and shifted. No more material to view. What I had viewed was helpful but not sufficient. I needed to see the in–between. I knew the *after* and had just learned the *before*. How did it happen? How did Pandemonium and later Maelstrom convert books to killers?

I wiped my tears from the parchment and as I headed for the entryway, the bookcases said, "Safe Travels, seeker." The tones were gentle supportive trills. Were the keepers of the Halls of Shared Knowledge also book sympathizers? Maybe that was the lever that would let me pry more information out of them. I would make no more demands now but I could lay groundwork for my next visit.

"'Thank you for sharing that knowledge. I come from a Neutral Frame." This provoked a chase scene soundtrack. When it subsided, I continued, "In my Frame, books remain inanimate to this day and we appreciate their many fine qualities. I wish that other Frames could know books as they once were and truly are."

Silence. I'd made an impression—but what kind?

"Farewell, seeker. Before you depart this Frame, you will find it informative and uplifting to observe activities at the river, where the Trees of Knowledge are harvested."

That was downright friendly. "Thanks, I appreciate the suggestion." I was at the entryway before I released the question that kept beating its wings inside my skull. "Does any Frame have a cure for multiple sclerosis?"

"Multiple sclerosis? That is a condition of Neutrals." The tone was disdainful.

"I see. Never mind and thanks anyway." I didn't point out that half the Frames are Neutral. The tone made clear that, to the bookcases, Neutrals were like worms. I mean worms as we see them back home, lowly and disgusting, because we don't see worms truly—few of us have had the privilege of meeting worms as the powerful healers they really are.

Lining the Hudson River banks were trees I didn't recognize, solid and broad like oaks, twisted over the water like Monterey cypress. These were the Trees of Knowledge, and I would eventually learn that they absorb and store information from the ground, water, and air.

A tree limb hit the river with an echoing crash. The river rushed it forward until the limb caught in netting that stretched across the river. Netting crossed the river every few hundred feet. Other nets held other branches. Water churned through the netting and the branches disintegrated into the glowing pieces that made up the Halls of Shared Knowledge.

On both river banks, what seemed to be picnickers were work crews, with beings of all kinds. They carried tree stones from the river banks to big wheeled carts. Some of the pieces were fetched by dog–like creatures which bounded on three, four, or six legs. When I'd touched the wall at the Halls of Shared Knowledge, I'd had a rush of awareness—what must the workers feel as they gathered those pieces?

As I watched, a decision formed itself and a plan coalesced. I was full of grand plans lately. If only I had foreseen what they would take from me.

36. I DON'T HAVE TO BELIEVE YOU

I pounded on my bathroom door. "Five minutes to show time." Always wanted to say that.

"What's the rush?" Jenn's voice was muffled through the door.

"Surprise you. Can't explain. Must show."

"Whatever it is, it took your nouns." She emerged naked except for her necklace and lipstick, rummaged in her suitcase, and was dressed the fastest I'd ever witnessed. Jenn likes surprises.

We were out the door before she gave in to her curiosity. "Give me some clues. Animal, veggie, or mineral?"

"All three. You know that case I told you about?"

"The aliens from other dimensions." Hers was a voice most often heard by dentists, discussing that old filling. She stopped in my apartment doorway. "That's my surprise, bitch?"

"Hernandez is working the same case, with Anwyl. I don't want you excluded from our conversations."

"You played the H card. That's manipulative." She locked my door behind her. "Why is this so important to you?"

"Come and find out." I held out my hand. "I'm not being girlfriend, you have to hold my hand or I can't take you. Also, I can't talk for a while—I need to concentrate."

She shot me a look full of ice daggers, but she took my hand.

We arrived in the hallway in Frivolous Bedlam and, as the first part of our grand tour of the Frames, I stumbled us back into my apartment, to collapse, panting, on the couch. Traveling with a living being was still a horrendous energy drain, although Jenn was much easier to transport than Kelly Joe.

"Is my surprise over yet?" Jenn's voice was so weak that her question transmitted as attitude more than words. She looked around like the room was part of a bad magic show. "Your furniture looks different."

"We're in another Frame now. My apartments are similar in both Frames. Outside, things are wa–a–a–ay different here. Let me know when you're ready to explore."

"Let's go," she said, in a get–it–over–with voice.

As we strolled my neighborhood in Frivolous Bedlam, I re–lived the marvels of my first visit. The engulfing noise. The chattering buildings with doors that slammed for emphasis. The streets filled with grazing vehicles and playful food carts. Jenn took it all in, without visible reaction.

A pretzel cart popped a wheelie at the head of a gang of food carts. "Hey! Cat Shaver! I've still got your pretzel with the bite marks! Can I get a bite from your friend?"

I thought this would charm Jenn. Instead, robotically, she followed my instructions to imprint her teeth on a fresh soft pretzel. I dangled her pretzel next to mine on the cart's umbrella awning. The gang of food carts cheered, then trailed us as we set out again. Jenn walked backwards, here and there, to watch the food carts. But mostly as we proceeded she stared at me, like this was a movie and I was its screen.

"What did we take and how are we sharing a trip?" she whispered.

"As impossible as it seems, this is a real place, my favorite place, a Frame called Frivolous Bedlam."

"Can we visit Saturn next? I've always wanted to see Saturn."

"I don't know how to get to Saturn. That would be cool though, huh?"

Behind us, laughter spread through the blocks as the buildings shared a joke. "Hernandez has Traveled to other Frames, too. Ask him if I'm making this up."

"Sweetie, I love this. I don't have to believe you."

"Yes! You do! How can you not believe this when all your senses are –" I cut off before I made her as angry as I was.

Jenn's voice was cold. "None of this is possible so it's a trick. I don't have to understand the trick to know that. I want to stop, please."

We stared each other down, then broke at the same moment and hugged.

"Soon. First there's something I need you to see." I led her to the A–B–C–D subway station on 125th Street. The station housed a holographic 3D map of the Connector system.

I popped open the map alcove and the Connector map hovered above us. Jenn's quick intake of breath told me she was suitably dazzled. I spun the map and tried to keep my voice from sounding like a planetarium narrator. "This is a map of all the Connectors in this part of the universe. Beings Travel from Frame to Frame by walking through Connectors. There are other ways to Travel, too—we got here today using another method I learned recently. But walking by Connector is the most basic method." I zoomed in, flew along one Connector. "Every place you see a break, a gap in the Connector, that's a Frame."

I zoomed in and out, awestruck by the countless number of gaps, the boggling infinity of the Frames. "You can look from any angle." I reoriented the view, became transfixed by the swirling knotted patterns of Connectors, a mandala of Celtic knots.

"Let me try." Jenn swirled and spun around the Connectors like a tobogganist. "This is fucking fuckable! You are something!" She was adoring but not believing.

"If you go this far," I pointed to the outskirts of the map, "you get to the far Frames and if you go far enough, you engage a fourth dimension of time. I don't understand that too well yet. My point is that there's more than our little piece of reality, Jenn. So so much much more. When a being dies in the Frames, they say, 'he went beyond the far Frames'. Maybe even death has a Connector. In the Frames, anything is possible, somewhere, so maybe –"

She interrupted me with a hug. "I love you, Nica. Thanks for taking me on your trip." It's what she used to say when we were teens and somebody gave her a psychedelic.

I set aside my latest effort to convince Jenn of the Frames' reality and hugged her back. I took her hand and got us back to Ma'Urth, where we sank into the back seat of a cab and rode home to the Julian in weary comfortable silence. At the least, my stories about the Frames no longer provoked anger. This might be progress. Maybe I had planted a seed and maybe it would grow to shelter her.

Back home, Jenn sprawled on the couch with Dizzy and worked on her breathing. "It's like missionary position and I'm fucking Godzilla." She breathed some more. "When we come down, how hard will I crash?" She stumbled toward the kitchen. "I need water. Do you want anything?"

Grab me a bottle of credibility tonic. "Since you're up, unlatch the bathroom window. I think Hernandez is on the fire escape."

"Now you have ESP, too?"

"No, but last time Leon stared out the kitchen window like that, Hernandez was outside."

She looked out the window, clucked praise to Leon, and headed for the bathroom.

The bathroom window latch clicked, fabric rustled, a male then a female voice murmured. I couldn't hear the words but the subtext made me blush.

Jenn, followed by Hernandez, came into the front room. They sat on the couch, Dizzy between them, and each rested a hand on the cat.

Hernandez looked worn. "You look beat," I greeted him.

"I am. I'm back for a few because Anwyl says I'll recoup faster at home."

At the mention of Anwyl, Jenn shoved away from Dizzy and Hernandez, into her corner of the couch. "Nica took me to another Frame that was louder than a raccoon orgy and showed me a 3D map of the universe." She sounded confrontational.

"Did she." Hernandez looked at me. I blinked at him.

"She says you've been to other dimen—Frames, too. And seen that map, too."

He spoke with measured syllables. "I think you're talking about a Connector map. I've seen that map once. I'd like to get more time with one. Lot to learn there." The warmth of his trust filled me. He couldn't see why I had done this, but he assumed that I'd had a good reason.

"Motherfucking horseshit." Jenn stomped over to my desk, snapped my laptop open, pounded the keyboard, announced accusingly, "Tomorrow's the last day for that found art exhibit on east 22nd. Will you come with me or are you too busy saving the universe?"

"Tomorrow I'm meeting with another client and don't know how long we'll need." I avoided apology; that would really piss Jenn off.

Hernandez said, "I could go later in the day. Got a few things in the morning. I could use a lookout for those things. You available?"

"A lookout. That's so horseshit." Jenn waited for reaction from Hernandez, got none. "Cops and robbers." No reaction. "Pirates and Indians. A lookout. Is that really what you said?"

"It is." Hernandez would be the last fish in any pond. He never rises to any bait.

Unfed, Jenn's anger shrank. "I won't get filthy on your stakeout thing?"

"Lookout thing. Only if you want to."

"Okay, I'll be your lookout, you'll be my art snob."

"Deal." Hernandez gave a big smile.

Jenn made his smile grow. "Date."

That night, we had a slumber party, *sensu stricto*: the three of us conked out where we sprawled and slumbered in the same room.

In the wee dark hours, I forced myself awake. I'd just had a nightmare—one I'd had before, back in Los Angeles. In the dream, the sky looked like bruises and I was menaced by large scary versions of Mathead and Scabman, edged in red like burning coals. I hate dreams that linger with irrational bad feeling. In life, Mathead and Scabman weren't menacing. Just mean, gross, and persistent.

Slumber parties are good tonic for nightmares. I listened to my pals breathe and soon returned to sleep.

The next morning, I awoke to the smell of Hernandez brewing coffee and I went to sit in the lawn chair on the fire escape, where I was pleased to learn that nothing was still new. When Jenn finished with the bathroom, the three of us went out for wakeup chow. We talked about nothing and joked about everything. It was a lovely dose of normal, the last the three of us would enjoy together.

37. THE IMPULSES OF THEIR MASTERS

I arrived at Grand Central just in time for the riot. Or my presence incited the riot. I was at Grand Central because I intended to go to Flushing, to become more familiar with the neighborhood around the Lobotomist meeting house before I took Lilah out there.

Grand Central was crowded as always but no longer crushed with morning commuters. I love Grand Central Terminal, the lofty ceilings that echo with decades of conversation. But I hate that netherworld passage to the subway, squashed between indifferent tile floors and fluorescent ceilings as low as a Neanderthal's brow.

I was in the Neanderthal passage when my lanyard began to stab me and shouts echoed in the terminal behind me. The cries got louder, closer, and more numerous. I backed away from the subway turnstile entrance—whatever was coming, I didn't want it to trap me by the tracks—and I pressed myself on the far side of a squat pillar. People filled the passage, gushed around the pillars—fleeing the terminal, it seemed. I waited, every muscle tensed, ready to jump in any direction.

Nothing followed in pursuit. Gradually, the panicked mob thinned and the space filled with groans from people who had been slammed against walls, pillars, turnstiles. I left my pillar and went from one to another of the groaners. No one near me were seriously hurt, but from the subway tracks came terrible shrieks.

The lanyard stopped stabbing me and tinny radio emissions indicated that security guards were converging at the subway trains. I headed back to the terminal, which was full of cops and news crews, plus scattered clumps of spectators uncertain whether it was safer to stay or go. The news crews surprised me—the crisis had evolved so quickly. Had the media been tipped that something would happen?

A cop tried to keep me from leaving. Soon the whole place would be locked down. I pretended to follow orders and stood against a wall with other bystanders, but kept inching toward the door as though trying to see more. My lanyard still prickled and I needed to be elsewhere. In the confusion of paramedic arrival, I slipped outside, where it was easy to run across 41st Street because cops held traffic at the corners.

I loitered beside a news truck to catch some of the feed from the live coverage, saw enough to give me the creeps, the shakes, and then warp speed away from there.

I no longer had time to go to Flushing before I met Lilah, so I found a bar with television and watched the story evolve from its initial disjointed confusion.

The anchors spoke with the breathiness of vicarious adrenaline rush. "Simultaneous protests erupted in Times Square Station and Grand Central Terminal this morning. Reports are sketchy but it appears as though protesters clashed with commuters, something caused a panic, and people ran. Authorities report at least three dozen injuries in the two locations. Four people are hospitalized in serious condition. At Grand Central there was one fatality, when an elderly woman went off the platform of the southbound 6 train and broke her neck in her fall."

A reporter on the scene interviewed a disheveled teen who was so eager to talk that she sprayed spit with each syllable. "I saw a guy push her. A short fat guy covered with zits or boils." The teen shuddered and so did I.

The teen's companion interjected, "He startled her on purpose then clapped his hands when she fell." I knew three beings who fit that description and behavior—any of the Warty Sebaceous Cysts.

When the news shows ran out of information they turned to talking head experts, who agreed that this was a tragically perfect example of mob psychology. None of the participants could say why they had run, no one knew why others were running.

Well, almost no one knew. I knew—or could surmise—because in news footage of the protesters, and cell phone videos from the mob, I saw the instigators. The protestors were the same group that had danced outside my apartment in a flash mob—the Entourage, acting out the impulses of their masters, Warty Sebaceous Cysts. It wasn't much of a jump to conclude that the Entourage had provoked panic that created the mob reaction.

Other talking head experts tried to understand the protest and speculate about the inexplicable phrases the protestors repeatedly shouted: *Go Kelly Joe!* ... *We're here, Neaks* ... *We see you, Neaks.* Or perhaps it was "nekes"—a play on "nukes"? Or possibly N.E.E.K.S. Was the message in code? Had a new terrorist group left a calling card today?

Well, kind of and maybe. It wasn't unreasonable to think of Warty Sebaceous Cysts and their Entourage as terrorists. I pondered as I walked to my rendezvous with Lilah. All I could figure was that the Cysts were muscle flexing, letting the allies know they were here and watching us. The Entourage could have abducted or hurt me today, had the Cysts wanted that.

I texted Lilah to adjust our meeting plans. The closures at Times Square and Grand Central meant we could no longer take the subway to Flushing in time for the Lobotomist meeting. A thought halted me, mid–step, until fellow pedestrians ploughed into my back and pushed me forward.

The Cysts and Entourage had obstructed my direct route to the meeting house. That had to be a coincidence, right, because how could they know what Lilah and I had planned? One possible answer chilled and energized me. Maybe I was about to do something that Warty Sebaceous Cysts had just tried to prevent.

38. A BEGINNERS' RECRUITMENT MEETING

"Yes, yes, we could die. You've mentioned that many times." Lilah rolled her eyes a lot when she was exasperated.

Lilah and I were traipsing the streets near the Lobotomist meeting house to let me get a better sense of the neighborhood and its escape routes. I wasn't convincing her to reconsider our mission and if I kept trying I'd drive a wedge between us. "We could die or worse. Did I mention the 'or worse'?"

She matched my neutral tone. "You ask for my help then try to talk me out of helping while leading the way to the place where I'll help."

"Mixed messages, you're thinking?" I let it go. If only I'd followed my instinct to flee.

Lilah sighed. "You've made it clear that we can fail, but I can't lose Sam without spending all the fight I've got in me. He would do the same for me. He would find a way to give more than his all."

"Not everyone has such high opinion of their siblings."

"They don't have Sam for a brother. He always wants everybody to have a chance. Thanks to him, Gary—my Sig O—and I are together. Gary isn't handsome and will never be rich, so I dismissed his attentions, until Sam showed me what a shallow fool I was."

Sam did sound like a good guy. Not for the first time, I wondered what deep yearnings had hooked him into the Lobotomists. "I hope we can get your Sam back."

"As do I, of course."

"Across the street there, the old building with the pink and black stone facade. That's our destination. It's okay for us to stare, we're wondering if we've arrived at the right address. From this step forward, we need to stay in character. No more talking or thinking like ourselves. And we stay in character no matter what happens."

"Understood."

"Let's walk to the far corner and circle back on the other side. That should give me enough time to feel disdain for my fellows."

"That was an idiotic thing to say but of course it would be. I tolerate you because you were the least stupid of the detectives I interviewed."

"You're a natural. But then you would be, your kind is born and bred for unearned arrogance."

We high–fived and resumed walking.

Getting in the mood for a Lobotomist meeting required a kind of meditation, with focus on a resentful life–denying mantra. But I suck at meditation. I have more thoughts than a street dog has fleas and I couldn't stick to my script. The best I could do was make the prescribed thoughts louder and clearer than the rest. When a real thought broke through, I adlibbed a rewrite of my thought script to try to incorporate it.

... wankers and losers and grabbers. Hernandez should check construction sites in Queens... How long until that freeloader found a job that got him off my couch, anyway?

It seemed to be a beginners' recruitment meeting. The recruits ranged from teen to mid life. There were more men than women, and most were white, but I heard many accents. Each attendee got a couple minutes to share their envies and resentments. Bosses, coworkers, boyfriends, ex–wives, children, parents, neighbors, strangers on the train. They'd done wrong. Soon they would pay.

Near the end of the meeting, newcomers were invited to speak and Lilah's hand shot up. She'd spent her whole life putting up with fools and lowlifes. Her brother had told her about the solution he'd found in another pod. She wanted that for herself, too—a pod of her own.

I winced. Nobody said *pod* here, they said *group* or *team*. When the word left her lips, the meeting handler looked at her intently. When I winced, he noticed me.

I winced because I hadn't told Lilah the full story about how we came to be here. I wasn't only here for her. When Lilah hired me to find her brother and I discovered this wonderful program, I tried to join Sam's pod, but they rejected me. Some b.s. about being done with training. People always said no to me. I would show them.

When the meeting handler noticed me, I worried that he would make me leave. *I just needed a chance, I would do whatever it took to prove my worth.*

I wanted to linger after the meeting but Lilah split right away, as always with a hint of sneer on her lips. I caught up with her halfway up the block. She tapped her wristwatch in greeting and I trotted behind her toward the subway station, falling into *the subservient mutt role that somehow I always found*. We went another block before she stopped to smooth her hair in a window reflection. Her body language changed and she no longer seemed pissed.

"This is far enough, isn't it? Can we drop these personas?"

"I think so but keep walking like you're in a hurry."

She did, and threw over her shoulder, "That was so awful."

"Agreed. A lot of sick puppies who think it's their time for a bone."

We pushed through the turnstiles to the Manhattan–bound 7 train.

"Do you truly believe that Sam has joined this group of sociopathic losers?"

"All my evidence says yes, sorry to say."

"Oh, Sam," she whispered, and then to me, "What time do you want to meet tomorrow?"

"I'm not sure. I'm reconsidering. It's so dangerous."

She followed me onto the train. "I didn't pick up on danger. What did I miss?"

"The handlers paid too much attention to us." The train took off with a bigger jerk than usual, jolting me into Lilah into the guy behind her.

I grabbed a rail and she smoothed herself out. "Perhaps I should go by myself from now on."

"No way will I let you do that."

I leaned closer to say more, but she ducked around me and took a solo seat between two strangers. "I didn't realize you could stop me."

That's the problem with strong–willed people. They're not good with obedience.

Of course, my own handlers could be saying worse about me.

39. PERSONALIZED TRANCES

As I headed up my block toward the Julian, Leon shot around the corner, chased by the devil's vacuum cleaner. He waited on the Julian's stoop until I reached to pet him, then shot away. I puzzled about what this might indicate until I reached my apartment door. Then I puzzled about why my apartment sounded like it had a house concert in progress.

The reason was that my apartment had a house concert in progress.

Kelly Joe sat at the far end of the front room, playing slide guitar. Dizzy sprawled on the floor near his feet but out of range of his stomping twisting leg. Anya was in the chair; she opened her eyes, shot me a smile like tropical moonlight, closed her eyes. Anwyl, prowling the kitchen, snapped the back of his hand in my direction: shut the door and come in.

I moved to the couch where I sat next to Hernandez. On his other side was—Jenn.

Now this was an interesting gathering.

Jenn leaned forward to see me across Hernandez, squeezed her eyes shut tight and long, a signal we had developed in high school. *Honey, do we ever need to talk.* Then she rested her head on the back of the couch and closed her eyes, too, looking carefree enough to levitate.

I felt an instant's twinge that Lilah was missing this. That day, Kelly Joe's music filled holes I didn't know I had. I looked around and felt so connected to everyone in the room. They each made me smile for such different reasons.

In a tremendous display of emotion, more intense than any I'd ever witnessed from Hernandez, he reached over and took Jenn's hand. She squeezed back.

Anya's face flickered, her expression inscrutable. Would I ever know her?

Anwyl's absent–minded prowling must be his equivalent of standing still. It reassured me to know a kindred restless nature.

Dizzy groomed herself as though no humans existed; as always, she was the ultimate in cool customers.

Then there was Kelly Joe. My teacher. My musician. That bleakness at his core. Didn't his own music affect him?

When Anya stood, I realized that Kelly Joe had stopped playing, and everyone was coming round from personalized trances. "Thank you, Kelly Joe," Anya said, and he looked up with the empty stare he had after playing. "In harsh times, it is important to keep our hearts open. Now that Nica has arrived, we will talk, all but Nica's friend Jenn, who must leave us for the non."

With Jenn, anything that smacks of direct order triggers rebellion. But she flashed a grin that on anyone else I would have labeled as shy. "I need to do some hand laundry. Is the bathroom far enough away?"

"Yes, that will suffice," Anya smiled, then resumed sitting like the Sphinx.

Anwyl helped Kelly Joe pack equipment, then clasped Kelly Joe's arm until the musician met his gaze. Anwyl studied Kelly Joe's eyes, then released his arm with a kindly pat. I so wanted to know what provoked this uncharacteristic empathy.

As soon as bathtub water rumbled behind the closed bathroom door, I said, "The Cysts caused a riot in the subway today. And they taunted me—us—on television." I thought my announcement would be big news but only Hernandez reacted, with a frown toward the bathroom door.

Anwyl nodded. "Expect such occurrences to continue. Warty Sebaceous Cysts seek to demoralize and intimidate."

"Why haven't they attacked me more directly? Or is that coming next?"

"Your death, like your actions, could hasten fulfillment of your prophecy. To kill all of us is their eventual goal, but for the non, they strive instead to dissuade you from taking action."

"They don't know me very well if they think that will work."

Anwyl chuckled and looked to Anya.

Anya said, "Time is short before Maelstrom's release. Warty Sebaceous Cysts attack our allies in many Frames." She turned to Hernandez. "In the days that crowd after this one, you and Kelly Joe must liberate buildings from the construction machinations of Warty Sebaceous Cysts. Such construction will aid in Maelstrom's release." She went into a long explanation about channeling energy to destabilize Maelstrom's prison. She concluded, "When we destroy construction sites we delay that inevitable, and we weaken their hold on this island. The allies need to control New York City on Ma'Urth."

"What time do we get started?" I asked.

Anya shook her head and told me, "This is not a night for you to join, as their actions require utmost stealth."

I flopped back onto the couch. "I get it, no leaky thoughts allowed." I pretended to be disappointed but I preferred to be excluded. I needed to be on my own and unsupervised for my secret projects. "If you don't have a job for me just now, I'd like to spend time with Jenn while she's here, and also I took a case before you got here. I'd like to finish my work for that client."

I sensed Hernandez' scrutiny. My story had tripped his bogus detector. The others didn't seem to think enough of my abilities to suspect me. They'd say my projects were too much for a Neutral. The only way I could persuade them that they were wrong was by showing them. Anya and Anwyl had never treated me like an equal so I don't know why I bothered to crave their respect. But I did.

"If you can't spare me the time, I understand," I added. "I just thought, maybe." Offering up what you want is sometimes the best way to keep it.

"Until next we meet, spend your time as you see fit," Anya ruled.

Anwyl added, "Our dangers grow when our numbers shrink. Stay together when possible."

The way things went down, I wasn't wrong, exactly. My projects were important. And a Neutral sort of, kind of, did handle them. Except for the unforeseen consequences.

As soon as fearless leaders departed, Hernandez tapped on the bathroom door. He and Jenn returned to the couch eventually. They kept stopping to smooch, as though their lips had to touch a certain number of times per minute. Dizzy rubbed around their legs, which reminded me that Leon had not showed up. I went out to the fire escape. Maybe the lawn chair knew why Leon was acting freaked when I saw him out front.

The lawn chair was gone. Its lock was gone, too. There was no sign of struggle—no scraped paint or broken pieces. Chair and lock were gone as though never there.

Had the Cysts taken the chair? Did they want to eliminate my watcher in the alley or did they want to spook me? Sorry guys, you only spooked my cat. Maybe they thought they could intimidate me. Instead, they compelled me to hurry with my projects.

Hernandez appeared at the bathroom window. "What happened to the chair?"

"I was going to ask you the same thing."

After I climbed back inside the bathroom, Hernandez made sure the bars were fastened and the window locked. I think we agreed, without words, to discuss the chair when Jenn was not around.

She waited outside the apartment door. I sat down at my desk. "I'm going to skip dinner. I need to meet with the client whose case I want to wrap up."

"Text us when you're done and we'll reconnect," Hernandez instructed.

When I replied with a shrug–nod, he frowned. Before he could lecture me about safety in numbers, I said, "Yes. We'll reconnect. I heard Anwyl and I hear you. I won't wander off on my own."

As soon as Hernandez and Jenn left, I grabbed my books and headed for the Halls of Shared Knowledge.

40. AFFINITY WITH BOOKS

"Nica, I do not presume to guess your intentions but please reconsider your upcoming actions," Julian said.

I was standing on the building's front stoop in Monasterium and I had just removed the strap that bound my stack of books. I watched maternally as each book rose and flapped in the air before me, casting jagged shadows on the gleaming sands of knowledge.

"I always appreciate your advice, Julian, and will keep it in mind. Rest assured I have considered this course of action carefully. Books, follow me."

As I led the books toward the Halls of Shared Knowledge, I continued to give them instructions. I left them fluttering just downslope from the Halls and climbed to the entrance alone.

"Welcome back, seeker," the even tones of the bookcases greeted me. "What new knowledge quest spurs your return?"

"Same old, actually. I still need to know how Maelstrom enslaved books, before he gets free and does it again. What you showed me last time was important and helpful and I am grateful for that. But I need to know how he did it. Nuts and bolts. Details."

The bookcase chorus grew silent. The lead bookcase spoke with the patience of someone who has all the time in the world. "It seems you have forgotten that we cannot fulfill that request. Moreover, not all that you request do we possess as shared knowledge."

"Then show me the parts you've got. And please put a rush on it."

I was wrong. I'd thought the voice couldn't get more patronizing. "Much harm can come from the sharing of knowledge about Maelstrom."

"What would you do with this knowledge, seeker?" asked another of the warm condescending gatekeepers, with emphasis on little old *you*.

I made my voice big and rich, suitable for pronouncement. "I will learn how to undo what has been done and restore to all books their true nature."

A moment of probably stunned silence was followed by vibrating tones that sounded like pushpins in a flushing toilet. They were laughing at me. Finally the lead bookcase got enough of a grip to say, gently, "That is a noble goal, seeker. Would that it were possible. The Halls of Shared Knowledge document the blood spilled in four attempts."

"Then show me those attempts. I can learn from those mistakes."

"Seeker, we will do nothing that sends you to a headstrong death."

Headstrong. It wasn't the first time someone had called me that. If you squint at it right, it's a compliment.

"It is my destiny to try," I said formally and maybe truthfully. The bookcase soundtrack evoked a family drama. I got the sense that the bookcases liked me, despite what they considered my wrong–way pigheadedness.

I raised my voice and made clear I was calling over my shoulder. "Books. To me."

The approach of my books was more fearful and impressive than I could have hoped. Shadows swelled on both sides of me as a dozen books in formation ascended the slope, then swooped to hover behind me, awaiting my next command.

The lead bookcase's voice was shrill, super–imposing authority onto fear. "No librarian may Travel with books unless war has been explicitly declared. Leave here—at once. Take your books." The conviction cracked during the final command. I sympathized with that sense of helplessness: until and unless they could corral my books, they couldn't make me do a frigging thing.

I replied, "No war has been declared although war is imminent. P.S., Maelstrom will not bother to declare war, he will simply attack as soon as he becomes free. I am not a librarian. Nor am I an ordinary Neutral. I have affinity with books, as you can see. With or without your help, I will try to free books from Maelstrom's enslavement. With your help, I have a better chance of success."

The soundtrack went Bollywood slasher movie. They didn't know what to think or do. I couldn't blame them.

"Excuse me," I interrupted their WTF–ing. "I have sensed that you do not hate books because you remember them as they once were. I believe you would welcome my success, however unlikely you think it. So for a moment, imagine— what if I did succeed?" The discussion resumed at lower frequencies that I could feel more than hear. It paused abruptly when I set down my book strap and called behind me, "Books. Stack yourselves."

This was a parlor trick but nonetheless impressive. My books shifted to hover in a line. The closest book folded its cover and sank onto the strap on the ground, the second book sank onto the first, the third book sank onto the second, and so forth, until I had a stack of twelve books. I tightened my strap around the stack to symbolize my control, and leaned the stack against the entry.

"How did Maelstrom enslave books? Please show me what knowledge you have."

I hadn't noticed that there was always a low hum of discussion among the gatekeepers, until now when it was absent. In the distance, I could hear the rush of the Hudson and the voices of beings working at the river.

At last, the lead bookcase said, "Step to a viewer, seeker."

I had convinced them—and confirmed that these bookcases might be powerful supporters of my quest. I mostly kept the strut out of my walk but came this close to doing a celebratory handstand.

The first articles taught me about book loyalty. Each volume shares a collective allegiance with other copies of the same book. Later editions inherit the loyalty of earlier editions. Before enslavement, loyalty was to the book's author and most fervent readers.

Maelstrom's mentor, Pandemonium, started the process of enslavement by stealing that collective loyalty. She abducted early editions of popular books. Converting the allegiance of those books controlled the allegiance of all later–published copies. When Maelstrom took over, the process accelerated. Maelstrom brought mass production to enslavement. He confiscated printing presses to print new, subservient editions of books he already controlled.

Some books fled and hid; other books actively resisted—they ambushed and killed Maelstrom's early editions, to restore free will to later copies.

This rebellion was brave but doomed. Maelstrom did not simply steal the loyalty of the books; he also trained them to kill. His trained books went after the rebel books and book genocide swept the Frames. The details of this period were sketchy because those who witnessed book battles rarely survived; but when it was over, only Maelstrom's books remained. Free books returned after Maelstrom was captured in Frame collapse. Whenever a new book got printed in a Neutral Frame, its loyalty belonged to author and readers, as before. This implied that Maelstrom lost the ability to enslave books in the Frame collapse. Or he lost access to books.

But how did Maelstrom control those first editions? Of this, the Halls of Shared Knowledge had no record. Rumors said he had stolen from Pandemonium a contraption that tortured the books and bent them to his desires.

I mused aloud. "This was a big operation. Maelstrom couldn't do it alone. What can you show me about accomplices?"

The viewer streamed with scattered reports. Maelstrom was secretive, but in a large enterprise, information leaks. Primarily, engineers and artists collaborated with Maelstrom. A few volunteered. Most were kidnapped and forced to assist. Nearly all were murdered when their roles were done. The Halls had knowledge of sixteen collaborators but records of the murders of only thirteen. Could any of those three still live? Maelstrom was trapped in Frame collapse long ago, well beyond the span of a human life. So no human accomplice could still survive. But the accomplices were probably not human. I needed to find out what happened to those other three collaborators whose deaths were not definitely known. Perhaps one of them could tell me what Maelstrom's contraption was, and where it was.

The viewer kept scrolling. Beings in the free Frames did not sit quietly while Maelstrom enslaved their books. Early on, activists who wanted to free the books engaged in protests and rallied for battle. But then Maelstrom's baby farm got discovered, and all attention turned to that. Book enslavement and the baby farm were key parts of Maelstrom's push to develop overwhelming power. They happened at about the same time. Perhaps they also happened in the same location, or with the same collaborators.

Even the name *baby farm* made me feel bad and told me I would be sorry to know more. But. *You're dozing on a jet and the cabin lurches. Your world spins and dives. People scream. Do you put your head between your legs, like they tell you, and stare at the floor? Or do you look out the window to see what happened to the wing?* I'd look out the window.

"I need to see everything about the beginnings of Maelstrom's baby farm," I said to the bookcases. They murmured heavily but soon the viewer flowed with new images. What I saw was not for the faint of heart. In fact, it ripped the bottom out of mine.

41. HERE'S THE WORST PART

The War for the free Frames paused abruptly, not long after the book rebellion. This caught the allies by surprise—they expected Maelstrom to continue battling. Instead, he disappeared.

The Framekeeps of that day convened a hearing, where Anya and Anwyl presented the case against Warty Sebaceous Cysts, who were on trial for collaboration with Maelstrom. At that hearing, Anya looked less grounded than she did nowadays, Anwyl looked less worn—and the Cysts looked as smug and sly as ever. During the hearing, the Cysts must have ducked variants of the same question a hundred times, in exchanges that went like this one:

"You had two masters. Now the lesser hides, as befits his cowardice, yet you lengthen your prison sentence each time you refuse to answer. Where is Maelstrom?" a Framekeep demanded.

"Would that we could say. He has left us confused and bereft," a Cyst snickered. The three Cysts were shackled, yet in the position of power, and seemed to gloat when they were taken away to serve their sentence of 1,000 cycles.

Holy frijoles, a thousand cycles? A cycle was kind of a year. How old were these enemies? Or my allies? "How long ago was this hearing you're showing me?" I called out to the bookcases.

The room buzzed with bookcase vibrations. I fought the urge to lift a bookcase door, to see what lay behind the parchment. Eventually one answered, "Long enough for the offspring of your progeny to enjoy visits from their grown children."

Which was a long winding road to *several generations*. Yet in this footage, the Cysts, Anwyl, and Anya looked only slightly younger. I set aside my amazement for another day and returned to the viewer.

After the Cysts were dragged to prison, Anya and Anwyl left the hearing room looking solemn. The free Frames waited to see what Maelstrom would do next, but he remained in hiding and, with his primary henchmen in prison, the War for the free Frames did indeed seem to be over. The Alliance declared victory and the Frames developed a festive air like Spain after Franco. Gradually, Frame Travel became routine again, for fun as well as necessity.

I learned this by watching footage that seemed to be a documentary. It featured interviews, most requiring subtitles—the interview subjects were hard to understand, what with all the sobbing.

A green–tinged humanoid wailed, "We finally saved enough to take our holidays and went to the place everyone was talking about, a vacation Frame for the whole family, with games, activities, wonderful food, and fantastic entertainers."

A being that resembled a plush pterodactyl moaned, "Big crowds. Always big crowds. New vacationlands to ease the crowding. They split us into camps all over the vacation Frame. The locations were supposed to cater to our interests but they isolated us."

A construction crane spoke without inflection, as though on heavy meds. "We wanted to go home but they said the Connector was busy with more vacationers arriving. We had to wait our turn and in the meantime they wanted us to take a train to another location. Our neighbors went but we held back. That night we escaped. We moved backwards through the Connector—we pretended we were new arrivals with children who dropped something and we had to go back into the Connector to look for it. We made it out. We never saw our neighbors again."

After that point, the documentary used a narrator to report the facts, which were pieced together from testimonies too hysterical to show on screen.

One day, the Connector shut down and trapped vacationers found out why their families had been lured to that Frame. Maelstrom feeds on negative emotions. He gets nourishment and pleasure from them. The more innocent the emoter, the better the feeding. The vacation Frame came to be known as Maelstrom's baby farm because he grew and harvested feasts for himself there. As soon as he closed the Connector, he began to torture children, and for an extra kick, made the parents watch. Parents began to kill their children and themselves; this was the only way to protect their loved ones.

Rescue came when Anwyl brought a vanguard of troops.

Maelstrom's baby farm was in a Frame that could only be reached by a single Connector, now closed. Anwyl's engineers worked to reopen the Connector, and he waited, so angry he glowed. As soon as the Connector opened, Anwyl stormed through it, heading a squad of powerful beings. Their powers held the Connector open while troops spread out to rescue surviving families. Anwyl's troops brought hundreds to safety. That was probably half of those who remained alive in the Frame. Then Anwyl's forces ran out of time. Maelstrom had been feasting at a distant enclave, but he now headed their way, preceded by guards with an army of books.

The documentary next featured military experts who debated Anwyl's options and choices. Stay and fight, or flee and collapse the Frame? Anwyl had no books to counter Maelstrom's book army and Maelstrom had surely devised many traps for enemies. So, to remain and fight, Anwyl most likely condemned his troops to death. Over generations, Maelstrom had been responsible for millions of deaths, and that day was the closest anyone had ever been to stopping him. If Maelstrom escaped that day, countless more might perish before someone got another chance to stop him. The only way to stop a being like Maelstrom was through Frame collapse.

No one who analyzed that famous day expressed surprise when Anwyl made the only choice a commander could sensibly make. He withdrew his troops and collapsed the Frame to capture Maelstrom. And so, Maelstrom was caged—along with hundreds of surviving vacationers, plus Maelstrom's guards. More than one in Anwyl's vanguard went mad with the thought of what might be happening to those trapped with Maelstrom.

Something like that, you can't say *here's the worst part*. It is all terrible beyond imagining. Bur my personal worst was how Anwyl learned about the baby farm. Anwyl may have heard rumors of mysterious bad doings in the family vacation Frame, but that wasn't why he arrived with troops. He came because he had learned the truth about the baby farm from one of Maelstrom's insiders, someone involved with the operation, who escaped and went to Anwyl.

That insider was Kelly Joe.

I guess I fainted. I came to, prone, on the glowing sands of knowledge. Above me, the parchment roof fluttered in the gentle breeze. I dragged myself back to the viewer, which was blank. "Show me what happened next."

"On another day, when you recover– " the head bookcase began.

"Now. This is the day. No delay." I gripped the sides of the viewer to make sure I stayed upright. "Guess you don't know much about Neutrals like me. We lie down suddenly when we need to think."

The bookcases conversed as though I had left the room.

"Please. I have to understand Kelly Joe's part in this. He's my musician."

The bookcases reverberated like a washing machine during an uneven spin cycle. I was about to give up and collapse again when the viewer resumed scrolling.

The Framekeeps heard the case against Kelly Joe. Prosecution sought death, and the trial debated Kelly Joe's role at the baby farm.

He was a young ambitious musician with growing popularity for his music, which back then was upbeat. Promoters would hire Kelly Joe to perform at sales events. His fame accelerated when he became the exclusive performer for the new family vacation Frame. Kelly Joe Traveled from Frame to Frame, luring more vacationers. Everyone agreed that without him, the vacation Frame would not have become a runaway success.

Eventually, the promoters brought him back to the vacation Frame to distract families who were upset about Connector malfunctions and tried to decline transport to the new theme camps in other parts of the vacation Frame.

At the Framekeeps hearing, against the wishes of his legal counsel, Kelly Joe took the stand to describe what happened next. He sounded as clinical as a coroner. "I focused on my success and I ignored signs that something was wrong in that Frame. No one can count how many souls I lost to my ignorance and denial." He stared into the past. The Framekeeps shifted and typed on their tablets. The silence lengthened, yet none of the functionaries ordered him to resume talking.

Kelly Joe returned his attention to the hearing room with a sneer, an expression I'd never seen on him. "They told me to perform near the Connector but I pretended I misunderstood and boarded an outbound train that was packed with vacationers. When the train stopped at a camp, I felt Maelstrom's presence. Some vacationers must have felt it, too, because they didn't want to leave the train. I let the guards remove them and send me back to the employee quarters and I asked no questions. I knew about the Alliance. I knew they had captured Pandemonium and hunted Maelstrom. I told myself that was politics—who could say if the Alliance would be better for the Frames than Maelstrom? I was a musician. It was my job to play music. To be adored."

Half a cycle—several months—after Kelly Joe took that train, his denial ended, when a mother snuck into his quarters. She and her family were among the earliest vacationers and they'd become friendly with Kelly Joe. She told Kelly Joe about the repeated torture of her two children, now succumbed to their pain; about Maelstrom's laugh.

Kelly Joe went out into the Frames, supposedly to do recruiting. He escaped the road crew—who lately acted like his guards—and found Annyl. His precise information about camp locations enabled Annyl's troops to rescue so many before Maelstrom sensed their presence in his Frame.

The mother was a reluctant witness for the prosecution at Kelly Joe's trial, and flustered everyone with a final revelation. Kelly Joe had engaged in witness tampering: he tried to convince her to change her testimony—to make him sound worse. "He said I owed it to the memory of my children to condemn him. He said when he went beyond the far Frames he would find them. He would—play for them." She could speak no further.

Kelly Joe stood to utter his last words of the trial. "I've earned no mercy."

The Framekeeps couldn't decide what to do with him—after all, if they sentenced him to die he'd be glad—so they kicked the case up a level to the moral authority of the Frames, a mysterious quartet called the Four. This caused a stir because not everyone believes that the Four exist. Legend has it that the Four steer the moral progress of the Frames and will never let evil consume the universe. Arguments against their existence usually start by pointing out what a crappy job they seem to be doing.

And so a possibly imaginary tribunal decided Kelly Joe's fate, which brought no closure in the only case to seek punishment for the baby farm. Many wanted the Framekeeps to sentence Kelly Joe to death and riots broke out through the Frames when the Framekeeps invoked the Four. The Four, if they existed, gave no sign that they would consider the case. The Framekeeps may as well have concluded with a séance.

Kelly Joe's life was scrutinized for many cycles, for signs that the Four had exacted punishment. Legend held that the Four did take action and Kelly Joe was cursed to live an extraordinarily long life, with ever–fresh memories of the baby farm and his contribution to it. His wrist was branded with the mark of the probably damned, and he was given two ways to atone. One was to share his music with anyone who needed it; the other was to follow his messages, which directed him onto paths where he might help others. His tattoos, then, came from the Four. Legend had it that the Four were also musicians, so I got stuck picturing the Four as a cosmic version of the Beatles. John would have set the punishment.

I lowered myself to the sands of knowledge. Or I fell. I crawled to a doorway of the Halls of Shared Knowledge and dragged myself upright there. I believe the bookcases spoke in farewell. "We wish you continued courage on your quest, seeker."

I don't know what or whether I replied.

I was on Julian's front stoop when I realized I'd left my books in a strapped stack outside the Halls. I stumbled back for the books, grabbed the strap, stumbled back to Julian, stumbled home to Ma'Urth, fell onto my couch.

Couch bad. I was looking at where Kelly Joe had played.

I found myself huddled in the stall of my shower, my shirt soaked with tears. When I came to, I was kicking the tile walls and pounding the glass shower door, which sagged where I had busted its hinge.

No wonder Kelly Joe had a death wish. No wonder he was so reckless. He couldn't die, unless he found a loophole in his sentence. He would live with his memories forever. I caught myself feeling sympathy for Kelly Joe, which made me kick the shower door one more time.

42. I SENSE WHAT IS ACTUAL

I texted Hernandez and Jenn.

::Problems w apt bathroom. Best stay elsewhere. Meet up in morn?

I needed to see nobody, which meant I should go back to Frivolous Bedlam. I took my strapped books with me because the books might not be safe if the chair thieves returned.

When I got to Frivolous Bedlam, I went for a run. Food carts rattled at my heels. "Cat Shaver, what are you doing?"

"Getting exercise to clear my head."

"Clear her head." The carts played with this for blocks.

I ran south along the Hudson, then I sprinted across town, faster and longer than I've ever sprinted before. I stumbled to a pause at Madison Avenue, arms behind head, gasping.

"Cat Shaver, are you okay? Do you want us to carry you?"

I wanted the carts to leave me alone but I couldn't snub their concern. "It's just—part—of the—exercise."

They experimented with gasping noises. The buildings joined in and spread gasps in all directions. In spite of my mood, I laughed.

I hobbled east and the carts stayed close, which was a comfort now that I could hear the crazoid babbling of the East River. I was in a face–your–fears showdown with my psyche and kept walking until I reached the parkland beside the East River. The carts held back on the other side of First Avenue.

The East River sounded harsh and angry, which didn't match its gentle ripples. Now and again it would shriek and this corresponded to times when a pelican dived under its surface. It couldn't be healthy for the pelican to go in that water. Ha, maybe immersion in East River water was how the bird had mutated to be so very large. Was that the same pelican that had intimidated my books when they were flying free?

Every time the pelican emerged from the East River, it skewed its head and flew erratically. Each time its flying got back to normal, it shuddered then made another dive into the water. This reminded me of parties with Ben's druggie pals. No way. Could the pelican be using the East River to get high?

The River howled like there was such a thing as *were*water, which convinced me that I had sufficiently tested my bravery. I headed west and so did the pelican— its shadow crossed me about the time the food carts resumed tailing me.

I maintained a light jog, punctuated with half block sprints, and reached home stinking and exhausted, just the way I needed to be. I sweat more on runs during bad times, as though my whole body sheds tears.

I might have pushed a titch too hard on my final sprint and had to cling to the bannister to drag myself upstairs. What kept me moving were thoughts of a shower with a working door. Some fool with the impulse control of a feral Chihuahua had busted my shower back home on Ma'Urth. Too bad I had not anticipated wanting a shower—I had no towels in Bedlam. Maybe I could run naked to breeze–dry. The food carts would love me no matter where I might jiggle.

I can never remember cheezoid lyrics and I can't sing to save a whale, so I substituted volume for accuracy as I climbed the stairs. "Born free, as free as the zum zoom, as free as—ow!" I pulled my top over my head as I entered my apartment, which caused me to collide with the door jamb. I kept humming and moving forward, though my top was so wet it stuck on my head. I yanked the top off with a "Ha!" but stopped singing. "Seriously?"

Anwyl stood in my kitchen, bemused or amused.

I wasn't embarrassed—hang with me long enough, you'll hear bad singing and you'll see me in a sports bra. Worse, I was instantly miserable again. Last time I'd seen Anwyl in my kitchen, Kelly Joe had been playing in my living room, albeit in another Frame.

Kelly Joe. I so wanted to question Anwyl about Kelly Joe's role in the baby farm, but I couldn't because I was pretty sure Anwyl would disapprove my visits to the Halls of Shared Knowledge, and I was certain he would forbid my efforts to free the books. With more time, I might devise a plausible alternate story about how I learned the truth about Kelly Joe. But today I could only fish the edges of that pond.

"Hey. You. Here. Welcome. I was going to shower but. That can wait." I'd forgotten to bring a change of clothes and my top was too wet to put on again without becoming a comedy act, so I tossed my top toward a corner and flopped onto the couch. Anwyl—what else—paced the perimeter. It was easy to imagine him prowling a forest, impossible to picture him in a supermarket.

"Trying to remember whether I've ever seen you relax," I grinned.

"Very well," he bared teeth in what must also be a grin, and strode over to take the other end of the couch. Huh.

I stood, slowly in case the couch might tip. "I need water. You?"

"As you please."

The water at the kitchen sink was so cool and refreshing I slid each forearm through the flow. Leaning over the sink, I guzzled a gallon of water, then brought two full glasses to the front room. When I settled back onto the couch, I manufactured a sigh and nodded toward the corner where Kelly Joe had set up his equipment on Ma'Urth. "That was such an amazing concert that Kelly Joe gave us."

"Kelly Joe played his music," Anwyl agreed.

"I can't imagine what it would be like to be so talented. I always get the sense that he's not happy, though. Do you get that sense?"

"I sense what is actual," Anwyl said.

"Not sure if that was a yea or nay. Anyway, do you know why he's unhappy?"

"That is a tale only one man should tell and that man is not here."

"How come you like him so much? I mean, I do too, but I like a lot of people."

"Each in our way, we seek justice for anguish," Anwyl replied. He was remarkably forthcoming today. Not saying he made more sense than usual, but I didn't have to pry the obscurities out of him. He even added a comment without prodding. "His gifts can win many a battle."

Anwyl always measures value in terms of uses. He sipped his water like he didn't want it but didn't want to waste it. Anwyl never just happens by so I was going to ask him what was new, why he was here. Then he looked at me and I knew. I took a mental gulp. He was here for me.

I stared at him for a good long while, savoring the moment. Never again would I be about to have Anwyl for the first time. I knew why he was here and he knew I knew and every molecule in me wanted to leap on him, but I held back and the pain of waiting was exquisite and thrilling.

He reached for me and I responded with all the passion and romance for which I am renowned. That is, I put a hand up between us and said, "Warning. I'm covered in sweat. I need a shower."

He shrugged. "If you did not now, you would soon enough."

43. MARZIPAN STANDS AGAINST EVIL

Wow. That's all. My Anwyl fantasies had been strength speed motion. The reality that night was slow caresses and a master showman's understanding of the right moment. In an instant's lucidity, I wondered whether he had broken his own rule and was reading my thoughts. But if he did that he would discover the things I was hiding from him and then he'd be angry with me. And he definitely wasn't angry with me. Although I wouldn't blame him if he was. Fortunately, my guilt attack was fleeting because thoughts had no place in my mind then. I was conscious of little except the intensity of the experience.

I woke up to the never–polluted sunlight of Frivolous Bedlam and Anwyl's hand on my hip. Mmmm. Good morning so far. Yet something was amiss and another moment awake made me conscious enough to know how I knew.

The lanyard was prickling, and maybe had been for a while, based on vague dreams about bee stings. I was concerned but not afraid. If I wasn't safe in Frivolous Bedlam with Anwyl right here then I was doomed, so no point fretting. I slipped out from under his hand, which dropped with the weight of deep sleep. I limped—marvelously sore!—to look out the kitchen window. Maybe I'd see a Cyst on the fire escape, gloating in my stolen lawn chair. By the time I reached the window, though, the lanyard prickling had ceased. Had it really been prickling, or had it taken me a few minutes to shake a dream?

Anwyl sat up. "Didn't mean to wake you," I greeted him.

He gestured for me to join him, and I was more than happy to comply. Some time later, he nibbled my nose and whispered, "I must away."

"Mmmm. Thanks for stopping by."

The instant he was gone I showered, then donned a sheet and went back to Ma'Urth to change. It was still early morning there and my apartment was empty. When I got back to cellular service, my phone buzzed away half its battery life. Jenn and Hernandez had sent many texts overnight. I replied with just one.

::Am fine but mostly out of service range.

I had two hours, by Ma'Urth time, before I should head out to meet Lilah, so I had time to pursue book enslavement leads. As I'd learned at the Halls of Shared Knowledge, three Maelstrom accomplices might have survived with knowledge of the baby farm and book enslavement operations. One of the beings was from Next Vast, which was Miles and Monk's Frame. I'd save that for third—I didn't want word getting back to the Watts Towers that I was investigating in their Frame. One of the beings was a male model from Expletive Deleted. I was in no hurry to return there. That left one choice, a humanoid from a Frame [that sounded like] Marzipan.

Traveling to a particular Frame for the first time can be tricky. Fortunately, Kelly Joe had done some of my early training in Marzipan. I focused on its most distinctive feature, its glowing yellow sky, and Traveled to reach that sky.

I arrived on a street that was empty except for a woman with a Modigliani neck. She was covered in dark blue fur like Christmas velvet and stood beside a food cart that was stacked with items that appeared to be pretzels covered in fuzzy blue mold.

"Excuse me," I greeted her. "Is this the Frame called Marzipan?"

Her voice had a 78 r.p.m. warble. "No, this is Marzipan."

I smiled to hide my groan. At least she hadn't laughed at my pronunciation. "That's what I meant."

"Then welcome, friend. Would thee like a proustel?" She proffered a pretzel. "They are renowned in many Frames for their digestive and nostalgic properties."

I had never eaten food from another Frame but no one had ever warned me against doing so. When I bit down on the pretzel, the fuzzy mold squeaked against my teeth. I fought my gag reflex and forced a smile, which turned genuine. The blue–furred woman laughed. The pretzel tasted –

– like a pretzel. But every bite of fuzzy mold evoked a wonderful memory... My most recent pretzel was in Frivolous Bedlam when a food cart requested bite marks in one... My worst pretzel was at a street festival where Ick and I played horseshoes with inedible fare. His pretzel was the horseshoe and my churro was the stake. No one was more surprised than Ick when the pretzel caught on the churro. That explosion of a *Ha!* when Ick was surprised—I heard it now as if he were beside me... My dad would pretend surprise when we played hide–'n'–seek. I'd hide in a closet and *boo!* out at him...

I didn't want to stop remembering but I was running low on proustel. My bites became nibbles but the smaller the bite, the less powerful the memory. I couldn't cheat the effect or extend it. I finished the blue mold treat with regret.

The vendor could tell I wanted more. "Thou art welcome to take a second proustel, but thou should not eat another right away, lest thou build an immunity."

A pair of humanoids approached, their outlines faint at first, becoming more solid: Travelers entering the Frame. They purchased proustels, bit immediately, and said, "Double the usual. We cannot return for a fortnight." The vendor filled a large bag with proustels. I fought a bizarre urge to grab the bag and run. Must. Have. Proustels.

The customers paid with thin gray coins and headed down the street, gradually shifting out of Frame again. The vendor called after them, "You are ever more blue. Slow thy pace to maintain thy hue." At this, one of them snatched a proustel from his mouth, the other yanked a hand out of the bag.

Memories can be wonderful but addiction isn't my thing. I took a step away from the proustel cart and its irresistible fuzzy mold but I forced a smile for this dealer in memory crack. I needed intel from her.

"I'm surprised you're alone. I'd expect long lines at your cart to buy these amazing things."

"I sell here where I do least harm. Here in the ruined city, no one comes without intention so I tempt no passersby." She closed the lid as she talked, making me wonder if she struggled against sampling her own wares.

"How did the city become ruined?"

"It was destroyed during the pogrom." I must have looked surprised, because she added, "A pogrom by a being called Maelstrom." She looked pleased when I reacted to his name. I got the sense that not everyone knew who he was anymore.

"Why did Maelstrom target this Frame for a pogrom?"

"No decent soul can ken such a being, but Marzipan stands against evil so mayhaps Maelstrom saw us as the fierce foes we shall always be. When he ravaged the Frames we did not cower in corners to avoid his attention."

I wished I had time to get to know her a little. This was my first encounter with a dealer who persuaded customers to go easy using her wares, or who boasted of fighting evil. "I heard that someone from this Frame helped Maelstrom establish the baby farm. Any truth to that?"

The vendor watched me closely during her reply. "It is good and right that thou knows about the baby farm. Too few do. When evil is held secret, more evil grows. A son of Marzipan was tricked to assist with that foul enterprise. Maelstrom tricked many, to savor the flavor of despair when a good being learned what they had assisted."

"What happened to that helper afterwards? Did he or she return here? Maelstrom wanted his accomplices dead. Is that why he staged a pogrom here?"

The vendor opened the cart lid, releasing a smell like hot chocolate by a campfire. "For a stranger, thou asks many questions. But who shall the answers serve?"

I stepped closer, forcing myself to concentrate on our conversation. Now the smell of the fuzzy mold was like grass on a summer morning and I so wanted another proustel. "You seem like a being of some power. Can you read thoughts?"

"Of course." Her eyes were the same plum blue as her fur.

"Then read mine. See that we fight on the same side."

"But should thou be a being of great power, thou could trick me."

I snorted. "Unless of course *you* are a spy for Maelstrom, in which case I risk my life by revealing myself to you. But I have to take risks, time is so short before Maelstrom escapes." And I had to get back to Ma'Urth to get to the Lobotomist recruitment meeting with Lilah.

A white–furred couple strolled up with arms linked. The vendor served them proustels and pleasantries but she kept staring at me and her hand shook while she served. As soon as the couple had strolled out of hearing range, the vendor whispered, "Did thou speak what I heard? Did thou speak with certainty of Maelstrom's escape?"

"Correct. Maelstrom will be free soon. I don't understand the details, and if I did there'd be no time to share them. We can't stop him from escaping. He will move to rule the Frames and we will fight to resist him. I am part of the resistance, along with Anya, daughter of Niav, and Anwyl, son of Reyn."

"Anwyl. I know that Framewalker," she said.

The way she smiled gave me a flare of jealousy, then shame—I didn't own Anwyl.

The vendor tugged the cart's awning to lower it, yanked a lever to release the wheel brake, and shoved the cart up the street, calling back to me, "I must alert my people. We have opposed Maelstrom many times. He will seek vengeance. We thank thee for this warning. I must away."

I caught up to jog alongside her. "I need information about the baby farm."

"Then walk with me and I will tell thee what little I know."

So I did, and she did, but she knew less than I did. When I left the vendor, I was no closer to understanding book enslavement or to finding out what had happened to Maelstrom's accomplice, but at least my news about Maelstrom's upcoming escape was important to her.

44. YOU BROUGHT HER HERE

I was five minutes late to rendezvous with Lilah and then we just missed a train and then we caught a train that sat in a tunnel waiting for traffic ahead to clear and by then we were frazzling.

Lilah smoothed nonexistent wrinkles from her skirt. "We don't need to be tense. Yesterday people trickled in for quite some time after the meeting started."

I dangled from a strap in front of her. "Let's take all this as a sign that we should try a different meeting. The handler showed too much interest in us yesterday. Let's get off at the next stop." The train jerked into motion again.

Lilah said, "I hate to lose our momentum. Let's just poke our heads in at the back of the meeting room and if it still doesn't feel right to you, we'll leave."

That was too reasonable a position to merit debate. The train picked up speed and made up time, getting us to Flushing just before the meeting started. I dropped my fretting and worked on my resenting.

As we walked up the block to the meeting house, practicing our negative attitudes, Lilah gasped. "Oh my—I—that's Sam!" And there he was, outside the meeting house.

Why would he be at this newcomer meeting? I wasn't expecting him, I hadn't prepared my sociopath thought spiel to accommodate him, and I didn't like surprises where Lobotomists were concerned. Now I was certain we should leave—but now there was no chance of diverting Lilah. As soon as she saw Sam, she doubled her pace and between phrases of her hate mantra she muttered, *oh Sam I found you.*

"Remember, you want to join him not save him," I warned her.

"I know. I've got this." Her heels tapped the pavement like the metronome in a military marching band.

"We're still just poking our heads in at the back of the room," I reminded her. Sam had entered the building and she crossed the street to follow him. Now we were too close to continue a conversation in our actual personalities.

The door into the building had been open yesterday but was closed today, and when it clicked shut behind us I jumped. Easy, Nica. I tested the door handle. Unlocked. I trailed Lilah up the stairs. With each step, I squeezed then released the muscles in my arms and shoulders, but my tension remained.

The room was packed today. Lilah was so fixed on finding Sam that I had to guide her to an open spot along the back wall. Based on body language, almost all the attendees seemed to be newbies. That was good for us. Even better, I didn't see the handler who had watched us yesterday. I squeezed–released my muscles again and this time lost a bit of tension.

Suddenly Sam was in front of us, with three other Lobotomists looking over his shoulders, smirking. He grabbed Lilah's arms and shook her. "I don't want you here. Get your spoiled, selfish ass out of here." He wasn't convincing, though. He struggled to be mean to Lilah. I felt a glimmer of hope for him.

Lilah shook herself free of his grip and grabbed his arms instead. "Sam. I'm not horning in, if you want this for yourself I respect that. But let us talk to you first."

At *us* he noticed me. He seemed to remember me. "You. You brought her here." He looked scared, and I wanted to believe it was because he recalled the way the allies trounced his group of Lobotomist bullies at Woodlawn Cemetery. But then he added, "Get away. *Please.*" The words were trivial. But the cold pale way he whispered, that spoke volumes. *You brought her here.* That whisper still haunts me.

A handler tapped the microphone on the front dais. "Places please." Sam disappeared in whirlpools of people shifting positions. I tried to steer Lilah toward the door but she wouldn't steer. I hissed into her ear, "Your presence is causing problems for Sam. Let's wait for him outside." That made her willing to leave, but the crowd was too thick for us to get to the door.

The handler continued, "I bring exciting news! The wait is over and our managers are here to meet each and every one of you!"

First reaction: *oh, yes, in spite of everything I'm glad we're here today!*

The cluster of people at the front had been surrounding the managers. Now the cluster dispersed and the managers stepped to the dais. Second reaction: *oh, no, this can't be happening!* I knew those roadkill dreads; I'd tried but failed to forget that bald scalp with all those scabs. Mathead and Scabman were here. Those low–rent cops were the Lobotomist managers, the warriors whose mind–controlled troops could decide battles in Maelstrom's favor? Mathead and Scabman? Kidding me?

On the one hand, discovering they were the managers was a relief, because they had always seemed threatening but stoopid. On the other hand, a deeper wiser part of my brain howled advice in my inner ear. I yanked Lilah's sleeve and repeated the advice. "Get out of here. Now."

She saw my expression and pushed toward the door. Too late.

Sam and other seasoned Lobotomists now blocked the exits, standing like bouncers expecting a rumble. Behind them, the missing handler—the one who had stared at us yesterday—locked the doors and pocketed the key. No one would leave through those doors.

Fortunately, we wouldn't need doors to escape. I grabbed Lilah's hand to Travel us to a new Frame, but the handler with the key shoved between us, breaking my grip on Lilah's hand. Sam pushed in front of the handler, said, "Allow me," took our arms, and propelled us up the aisle toward the front.

The handler at the dais said, "We'll start with a demonstration of what we do with spies."

Mathead leaned into the mike and smiled, her teeth yellower and sharper than I remembered. "Nica, come on up. Introduce us to your friend."

Scabman piped up, "We won't get another chance to meet her!"

As Sam dragged us frontward, other hands clutched my arms and held me in that room. To get out of Frame, I would need to bring them all with me. Maybe my adrenaline surge would let me take two or three people with me today, in much the way that people lift cars off of children. But I had five beings holding me—and I wasn't touching Lilah. No way would I leave without Lilah. Only Sam held Lilah, but she was way over there on his other side.

The newbies rumbled with anger at the mention of spies, but then grew quiet as the menace of the managers filled the room.

Scabman's voice was oilier than his skin. "Sam, we understand that one is your twin sister."

Sam jerked our arms. "I had no control over my birth or my sister." His hand shook where it gripped me.

Mathead jeered and prompted, "What have you got against your sister, Sam?"

Sam spieled about his arrogant egocentric twin. It was typical Lobotomist rant, polished by frequent repetition. Lilah gasped and sobbed as though Sam's words cut her to the soul. I'd worry about that later. I focused on the hands that held me.

After a few steps, it seemed like we were frozen in place while Mathead and Scabman slid closer to us. Meanwhile, Mathead licked her lips, which made her pointy teeth shine.

Sam got really worked up. He shook our arms as he ranted, wildly enough to cause whiplash. Each shake briefly broke the grips of some hands on me. He concluded, "She's spent her whole life admiring herself and ignoring me."

Lilah kept her voice cool. "Sam, don't you see that —"

"Shut your stupid trap," Sam sneered, and shook Lilah extra hard. She stumbled then limped—she must have snapped a heel.

Mathead applauded. "At last she's doing something for you, Sam. Now that she's here, you can prove your loyalty! By the way, which one do you want to off first?"

Sam looked from Lilah to me. "Could I do them together? Stop moaning, you stupid slut. Here's a secret you can take with you to your grave." He said this with such venom, the newbies cheered.

During the cheer, he dragged Lilah so her ear shoved against his mouth; he said something only she could hear.

Whatever he said got her sobbing and she reached to touch his face. "No, Sam, stay together!"

He called his twin terrible names and he shoved her, hard. Lilah stumbled into me, dislodging two of those who gripped me, then landed hard on her tailbone. Sam lunged over her, to shove and pull at the remaining Lobotomists who held me.

"What the hell!" one of them shouted.

I understood. Sam was buying me half a second of freedom to get us out of there. Thanks to Sam, my arms were mostly free. I kicked somebody's balls and for an instant, no one clutched me. I grabbed Lilah and I was already changing Frames before she was standing again. Sam blocked the others from grabbing me anew.

Mathead was slobbering, "Stop him! Hold them! Kill him! After them!"

"Run! Lilaaahhhh!" Sam's death wail was the last thing we heard.

45. WE WEREN'T IN BEDLAM

Every couple of steps I took us to a different Frame. The more Frames and the shorter the time in each, the harder it would be for them to follow. I tried to get us outside but the building had different dimensions in each Frame and I couldn't find an exit. It didn't help that I had to drag Lilah, who seemed to be in shock, with great heaving breaths that all sounded like "Sam."

With my latest Frame change, we were stuck in a deadend room with no exits. I'd been in a room like that once before. The only way we could get out would be to position ourselves exactly where we had arrived, and from there return to the previous Frame. Dragging Lilah made it impossible to move with the needed precision. I slapped my hand over her mouth. "Lilah! Help me if you want to live!"

"Is Sammy dead now?" She spoke like a toddler.

"Yes and we will be too if I don't get us out of here. Sam died to save you. Don't waste that!"

Lilah looked me in the eye, unblinking, then reached down to yank off her shoes; I'd forgotten about the broken heel. "You're right, Nica. I'm with you." And after that she was. I got us out of the deadend room and she helped me figure out how to exit the building. I showed her the kind of zigzag path that helped mask our trail, and after that she chose our path so that I could concentrate on the Frame shifts.

Lilah let nothing distract her, including her woozy retching, which got stronger and more frequent as the effects of first–time Frame Travel hit her. I took us to a Frame that had a neon blue prairie with grasshoppers as large as kangaroos. When I made an amazed noise, she barely looked up from her effort to create an unpredictable trail.

We ran for countless blocks, but then I Traveled us to a Frame with buildings similar to those on Ma'Urth and we discovered that our zigzagging had backfired. We were still on the same block as the meeting house. Seeing the building with its black and pink stone would have terrified me, but I no longer had the energy for terror; and anyway, it was quiet and empty on the streets of this Frame. Okay. Maybe staying near our starting point was a good thing, maybe those who pursued us would not expect to find us close by. Someone with a working brain would have to reason that one out.

I didn't know how much more two–person Travel I could manage. I proved I was losing it when I began singing *the hurt gets hurter and the pain gets painer* to the tune of "the rich get richer ..."

An idea had been trying to get my attention for some time. Get to Frivolous Bedlam. That was a great idea. Actually, I may have had that idea already.

"Someone." Lilah waved toward the corner. It's hard to whisper and retch simultaneously.

As I shifted us out of Frame, I saw what she meant—a flash of motion at the corner.

Our next Frame was also quiet, with no beings or chatting buildings, but we were too exposed standing in the street. "Back door!" Lilah whispered and led us through the closest building. We ran in the front door, across the foyer, and out the back. I think she was hoping for an alley but we reached a long walled enclosure with an incinerator and a dumpster. Doors from several buildings opened onto the same enclosure.

The instant our feet stepped into the enclosure, a shrill voice reverberated, "Behind me, they're behind me." The meeting house building was finking on us.

We crouched between the incinerator and the dumpster, which hid us from most of the doors. My burst of fear converted to energy and I took us to a Frame that was a lot closer to Frivolous Bedlam, because the buildings were loud and chatty. Maybe I imagined it, or maybe I heard a weak voice call, "Behind me, they're still behind me."

I shot us to what had to be a far Frame, because the Travel made us so dizzy we toppled over from our crouches. We lay on bare red dirt under a chartreuse sky with fast spiraling crimson clouds. This Frame change bought us some time—there were no buildings or beings in the vicinity. Visualization helps, they say. I visualized sucking energy from the cells in my body, to muster enough to take us to Bedlam.

Among our many problems was the fact that I never Traveled to Bedlam on first try. It usually took three tries. I would over– then under–shoot, then finally reach the Frame where the building chatter was absolute loudest. All the Frames near Bedlam were fun to visit, and I'd had no reason to refine my technique and get there on first try. No reason until now. Did I have three more Travel laps in me? Somehow I'd have to.

I got myself standing by pretending I was lying down in a different way; then I got Lilah standing so I'd having something to hold on to. I wanted us to walk—I wanted us away from this enclosure before I took us back to a Frame with buildings. I didn't know how persistent the fink building might be through the Frames.

Lilah clung to me. "How are you doing this? Changing things?"

"Later," I replied. "Help me get to where the street would be if we had buildings around us."

She re–lived our run. "Seventeen steps, running pace, that way."

Clinging to each other, we had enough support to make the trip. When we got back to where the street must be, I Traveled us toward the safety of Frivolous Bedlam. And I thought I got us there. The next Frame we reached, every building on the block was crazy loud, laughing and singing. The meeting house was silent. Clinging to each other, we limped up the street, blissfully barraged with building noise.

Behind us, my paranoia heard an emphysemic's whisper. "They went out to the street."

A door slammed behind us. We swiveled to see Mathead and Scabman, jogging down the steps from the meeting house.

We weren't in Bedlam.

They were looking down the street in the other direction. Lilah and I lunged behind a stoop and I changed Frames as we fell. The buildings were even louder here. Please let this be Bedlam. Lilah and I stared at each other, twisted but not moving, lest we make a sound that could be heard despite the building chatter. I didn't hear footsteps, but suddenly the back of a bald, scabby head loomed on the sidewalk just outside our hiding place. A dreadlocked scalp joined the scabs. Scabman and Mathead stood beside our stoop as though they didn't know we were nearby. But they had to know. They'd followed us here.

We were so close to Frivolous Bedlam. My whole body shook with the effort to tweak the Frames just enough, to get us to Bedlam. Mathead and Scabman wouldn't be able to follow because they definitely were not invited.

I managed one more Frame change. The building noise grew even louder. "Noooo." Lilah moaned.

Mathead and Scabman filled the open space beside the stoop. They no longer resembled the loser meth addicts I'd known in Los Angeles. Their eyes were pure red and they moved with their hands out like they sensed us through their skin.

Mathead's hands hovered over Lilah then yanked her to her feet. Mathead was splattered with dried blood, probably Sam's. I tried to move but was too weak, opened my mouth but no sound came out. Mathead chuckled. Scabman moved toward me, but stopped when Mathead said, "Forget her for now. She can't Travel, she can't move. Finish this one first."

With one hand, she held Lilah upright. Scabman took Lilah's other arm and they each yanked an arm, casually, using a small amount of their strength. They ripped Lilah's arms from her body and Lilah collapsed between them, somehow still conscious and screaming.

Mathead cackled, "Lung power! We've got an opera singer here." At Mathead's nod, she and Scabman each grabbed one of Lilah's ankles. Before they finished their second yanks, Lilah stopped screaming.

Or I stopped hearing her. Mathead was wrong. I could muster the energy to Travel one more time.

Now. Fucking *now* I Traveled to Bedlam.

"Hey, it's Cat Shaver!" a food cart yelled, and the buildings took up the chant.

First thought, I was safe.

Second thought, if only I had got us here sooner. "I killed them both," I whispered with the last of my strength.

Third thought.

I had no third thought.

46. I KNOW ABOUT YOU NOW

I came to alongside the Hudson River. I shuffled snapshot memories to understand how I came to be here, watching broken sunlight on choppy water.

When I got to Bedlam I tried to walk but collapsed and lay where I fell, nose pressing pavement, next to the stoop where Lilah had died a brutal death in a Frame unknown. Food carts worked together to drape me across a low cart, a freezer on wheels. The little freezer cart couldn't move with my added weight so other carts pushed it. They pushed me inside a parking garage to a service area where they washed me clean of blood and bits of Lilah, then they pushed me outside to dry in the sun.

If I hadn't brought Lilah to the meeting. If Sam hadn't been there.

I kept moving my lips.

"What did she say?" one cart asked. A long line of carts tended to me and this cart was near the end of the line.

"'I killed them both,'" the little freezer cart quoted me. The carts passed this down the line; the buildings picked it up and spread it, having fun with the syncopation.

"I killed!"

"Them both!"

I screamed myself unconscious again.

Now here I was at the Hudson, draped over the freezer cart, chest up. My feet dragged the pavement on one side, my head brushed the pavement on the other side, and in the middle was a backache worthy of a body inverted on a freezer cart. Because I was alive I could feel pain.

"Is this okay for you, Cat Shaver?"

I ratcheted my neck to look away from the river and find the source of the worried voice, the cart that dangled pretzels with bite marks. Its metal pieces rattled as though it were shaking. "Sure. Thank you for helping me."

Its shaking lessened. "Can you see the river? You keep yelling about the river."

"You have been very kind. I would like to go home soon."

"Moving out!" the pretzel cart called to the other carts and they shoved my freezer transport up river, toward Julian. When we were underway, the pretzel cart called loudly to the buildings on Eleventh Avenue, "She's going home." The buildings spread the word inland.

"Why did you tell the buildings?" I wondered.

"For Kelly Joe to meet us. You keep yelling about him so we found him for you. He's on his way."

"Oh." Dog knows what, in my delirium, I had been yelling, but Kelly Joe's name had not come up because I wanted to see him. *Never again* was when I wanted to do that.

"We're really sorry, Cat Shaver. You yelled the most for Lilah and Sam, but none of the buildings can find them in any Frame."

Tears were my only reply.

"Cat Shaver, if you keep leaking like that you're going to rust."

I hated myself for laughing, but enjoyed the way the freezer cart's corners dug into my back when I did so.

"She can sit now," said a familiar low drawl, and then Kelly Joe's arms were righting me. I pulled away from his touch. His help infuriated me.

I shoved his jacket sleeve above his elbow to see his current tattoos. Books with vivid dust jackets flew above a black rain of text. As though I had not been rude, he slid his other sleeve up to show me the tattoos on his other arm. The green hummingbird, chest arched in fighting pose, rested tiny talons on the spine of a book flying through blood–red air.

"Blood and violence," I muttered.

"War begins soon," he agreed. "From this –"

I slapped my hand up in a *stop*. I didn't need his wisdom. "I know about you now."

"I see that you do." He met my glare with a cool simple gaze, steady until the cart hit a dip and I had an excuse to look away.

One difference between us was that my murders had meaning. Lilah and Sam were dead but now I knew the identities of the Lobotomist managers. Stopping the managers would stop the Lobotomists. Anwyl needed my information.

"I need to see Anwyl. Do you know where he is?"

"Yes, I was with him until the buildings said you needed me."

"The buildings were wrong. Take me to Anwyl." I hated Kelly Joe almost as much as I hated myself. He seemed unfazed by my attitude, which really pissed me off.

"Anwyl can't talk just now."

"Then I'll be there when he can. I have information that can't wait."

"You'll need to be able to walk first."

I got off the cart, walked two steps—okay, one and a half—and was no longer sure which way was up. I dropped my butt onto the cart again.

Kelly Joe waited until I stopped wobbling. "I'm headed back where Anwyl needs me. The buildings can fetch me when you're ready."

"Don't! Give me a block, okay? If I can't walk by then you can go."

"One block." He walked a couple steps behind the cart, pulled out his harmonica and began bending notes in that melody–less way he had.

"Can you not?" I snarled, but he kept playing. "Please stop playing."

He paused. "I heard your first request." He resumed playing.

"What, like that joke? 'God did hear your prayer, the answer was no'?"

"That's a good one." He bent notes and hummed in between. The sounds began to sooth me, making me hate him more.

Inland, we passed between buildings who were playing with a syncopated rhyme. *I killed. Them. Both I. Killed. Them—both.*

Against all my will, I began to cry. Fortunately, Kelly Joe was far enough behind me that he couldn't see. But the pretzel cart was so damn sensitive to my moods. It rolled ahead and yelled, "Stop that, you're making Cat Shaver sad."

For a moment, quiet spread. Then random conversations resumed.

Kelly Joe took it all in. "Can you tell me what's happened to you?"

"No."

He resumed playing, a familiar yet unknown riff that broke me. I shrieked with an anger that came from so deep inside me that only my anguish ran deeper. Kelly Joe kept playing. I became empty of all feeling—except my resolve to make Lilah and Sam's deaths matter.

I made another attempt to walk, wavered, and grabbed Kelly Joe's arm, which knocked the harmonica to the ground. He picked it up while maintaining our balance. In another half block I was steady enough to say, "Take me to Anwyl."

About that time, the buildings spread rapid chatter that sounded distressed. By the time I could understand *fire* and *burning*, Kelly Joe was saying, "Come along, we'd best hurry."

47. WHAT LESSON CAN YOU LEARN FROM THIS?

We Traveled into flames and smoke and screaming buildings. We were in this Frame's equivalent to midtown Manhattan so the buildings were tall, and many of the bottom floors were on fire. Ahead of us were human shapes, black shadows against the yellow fire.

Kelly Joe pulled me into an alcove. "Those are not our fighters," he murmured, his lips against my ear.

There were nine of them and they worked in trios. *One* swung a sledge hammer into a display window, *two* kicked glass out of the smashed window, *three* tossed a jar that exploded in sooty flames. The trios moved up the street, attacking buildings as they advanced. One of the trios moved more slowly and got left behind. They ran into the street and almost immediately, one of them fell to pieces in a brief rain of text. A survivor yelled up the street, "Our own books killed one of us!"

From up the street a wide shadow stomped this way, yelling to the sky, "You're leaking. Save your text for the enemy! And don't fly so close to the flames!" The wide shadow kicked the new corpse and yelled to remaining members of that trio, "Can you help this one? No! What lesson can you learn from this?"

"Always know where your books are."

"Yes. Now catch up and work as a team of two."

Firelight caught their faces and I saw the distinctive inert expressions—like too many cheap facelifts— of Lobotomists. Maybe the managers were here, too!

I converted my fear to revenge–lust but before I could inform Kelly Joe that Lobotomist managers might be nearby, he said, "Stay close," and brandished a long–nosed metal tube, something like a barbecue grill lighter. He flicked a switch and it shot flame for two stories above his head. Pieces of incinerated books fell in the street.

The wide shadow, who must be a handler, had his back to us until Kelly Joe shot a lick of flame that ignited the handler's hair. The handler shouted "Attack!" to his other trios, while spinning and leaping to find his foe. Kelly Joe sprinted forward and kicked the handler in the chest, then fell on him briefly. When Kelly Joe resumed standing, the handler lay in a position that said he wouldn't be getting up again.

Kelly Joe studied the sky, then shot a long stream of flame far overhead. Eventually, book pieces fell—from books that must have been flying much higher than the previous ones.

By now the remaining Lobotomists were almost on top of us. Seven to two. Kelly Joe strode forward to meet them, showing no concern for their numbers, which bolstered my confidence until I remembered his death wish. However, our foes' snarls were superficial. When they realized their handler was dead, their attack lost conviction and before they rallied, Kelly Joe had killed two more, with a brute–force martial arts style I couldn't identify.

"Books behind us three stories up," I called. In one fluid motion, Kelly Joe reached the flamethrower tube over his shoulder, charcoaled more books, then turned to face the remaining five Lobotomists, who ran toward us in an inverted V formation. One of the Lobotomists held a bomb jar. Kelly Joe aimed his flamethrower at the hand that held the jar, which dropped, shattered, and blasted sooty flames.

Two Lobotomists were still alive and apparently meant to keep it that way. They ran south at the next intersection.

Kelly Joe checked the sky then slipped the flamethrower inside his jacket. He had us walk single file along the base of the buildings, skirting flames as necessary. Meanwhile, he instructed, "Books have poor aim when they cannot fly free, so they don't fly close to buildings, so that's where we should stay. Thank you for your warning, I didn't see those books," he concluded with the warm tone I'd savored during our training days.

I couldn't bring myself to reply and instead gestured south, the direction the surviving Lobotomists had fled. "Are they meeting up with more Lobotomists downtown?"

"Perhaps, or they may be headed for a Connector. We can't know, so we'll expect ambush from above, beside, and below."

"Where is Anwyl?"

"Wherever our foes are thickest."

I spotted Anwyl's silhouette two intersections later, directing activities in conflagration. He led about thirty allies. Closest to us, a few allies blazed flamethrowers into the sky, back forth high low, which kept the air space clear of books and full of smoke.

There were dark lumps all along the street—bodies. Down the block, the allies had a cluster of Lobotomists surrounded and after the allies closed in, there were additional lumps on the street. I was soon to learn that we never took Lobotomists prisoner—they killed one another in captivity, starting with the weakest, that is, those whose brainwashing might be reversible. Like Sam.

Some allies had a shelf's worth of books trapped with flamethrowers and tried to capture them, alive and unburned, in metal nets. I had seen Anwyl try this before—that time, when the book leader squawked a command, all the books flew into flames, destroying themselves to avoid capture. Today, when the leader squawked not all the books responded immediately, and a few were netted.

I stumbled as we stepped around the nets. "Why do we capture books?"

"Sometimes their allegiance can be switched. We'll need all the books we can get."

How could we switch book allegiance? I didn't get a chance to ask.

Allies ran out of the nearest burning building with humanoids in brightly colored robes. Anwyl shouted orders about moving them west, and pointed in our direction. He spotted us and suddenly was beside me.

"Nica," he said, as though we were alone in my bedroom. "These are not dangers you must share." He prised something from my arm: a curled singed clump of book, with characters of text poking out. Stuck to the text was a piece of my shirt and glistening on it was my blood. Now that Anwyl had removed the book shard, my arm stung and blood soaked my sleeve. He pressed his hand against my arm to staunch the flow.

"That you brought her here tells me this visit has grave urgency." He spoke to Kelly Joe but he continued to look at me, with a proprietary tenderness I filed to enjoy later. Even I couldn't think about Topic A just now.

"Nica said it couldn't wait," Kelly Joe replied.

"We can stop the Lobotomists before they kill more. I found out the identity of the managers."

Anwyl looked surprised and skeptical.

I talked fast, before the rush of memories could grind me down with guilt: I told him about scouting then infiltrating Lobotomist meetings, I told him about Mathead and Scabman, I told him about everything. Except Lilah and Sam. Kelly Joe matched Anwyl's skepticism with sympathy, which made me talk faster. "I don't know where the managers are this instant but we'll get them!" How eagerly I planned that bloodshed.

I had thought Anwyl would be proud of me. Okay, also pissed about my ignoring direct orders, but when it came to stopping the Lobotomists, the end had to justify the means. Instead, Anwyl reacted as though I'd just given a weather report. He took his hand from my arm, checked that the blood flow had stopped, and barked an order to the allies with the book nets. "Take those to a Neutral Frame and once there, bind and lock them."

He turned back to me. "You have risked much for little. You know not their identities, but only their Neutral disguise, which tells us nothing. Come, give safe transport to these allies." This last he said to Kelly Joe, who nodded and followed Anwyl to the group with the bright robes.

I was catatonic on the outside while I raved on the inside. I had learned nothing of value. I had gotten Sam and Lilah killed for no reason. No reason. No reason.

Anwyl's face loomed. He touched his forehead to mine and called my name a few times, bringing me back from the Hiroshima in my skull. He touched my face like he was making a promise, then shouted an order to someone and strode away.

I caught up with the bright robes as Kelly Joe led the group down the stairs to the E M line station at 53rd Street. The leader spoke to Kelly Joe with a voice that was far from trustful. She shrilled, "Anwyl son of Reyn arrives without invitation, then offers alliance. Yet, before we can evaluate his offer, Lobotomists attack and Anwyl rescues us, demonstrating why we need his alliance." When Kelly Joe said nothing, she demanded, "Do you take us for fools who would call that coincidence?"

Kelly Joe didn't answer until everyone was through the turnstile and on the platform. "I take you for lucky. Warty Sebaceous Cysts are attacking Frames that have opposed Maelstrom. Anwyl and Anya have been visiting the same Frames to recruit allies. Sometimes they find a Frame destroyed. You got attacked while Anwyl was here."

The leader stepped from her group to stand beside Kelly Joe. "You must see why our trust is difficult to bestow."

"I've known your people through the cycles. You are honest and courageous. Your trust is hard to win, but worth the effort."

The leader's shoulders dropped. Assuming this was a universal body language, Kelly Joe had reassured her.

The train arrived and we filled an otherwise empty car. Kelly Joe had mad powers. He Traveled the subway car and all of us inside it through several Frames without breaking a sweat. When we left the subway, Kelly Joe led the robes to a Connector in the building that—on Ma'Urth—housed the Museum of Modern Art. The leader went into the Connector first to check its safety, then gestured her group forward. As the last of her people passed out of Frame, she told Kelly Joe, "We accept Anwyl's offer. Safe Travels."

"Happy to bear that news," Kelly Joe replied. "Safe Travels."

Kelly Joe grabbed my wrist and Traveled me back to Ma'Urth. After so much stress and Frame Travel, I wasn't entirely upright, so he leaned me against the plate glass outside MOMA. "Anwyl needs me," was all he said, and then he was gone.

I had so much to think about that I didn't know where to start, so I didn't, which gave me some minutes of peace.

48. YOU DON'T WANT TO BE SEEN WITH ME

Jenn and Hernandez were making out on my couch until I walked in on them and started bawling. Like a cartoon baby. *Waaa waaa waaa.* They smothered me with concern and put me on the couch between them.

Jenn stroked my scalp fuzz and cooed, "They're motherfucking losers, whoever they are, whatever they did." However wrong I might be, she was always on my side.

Hernandez studied my face and got the idea. "Life during wartime. All worries. It's all bad." He twisted the clichés with a sarcasm that refreshed me.

Jenn clapped and added, "It'll get worse before it gets worser."

"Every cloud has a lead lining," Hernandez offered.

"Damn, you're good at this. After every dawn comes more dark." Jenn thought for a bit. "Does that one work?"

They went on to blacken and corrupt every earnest hopeful saying any of us could remember. Jenn and Hernandez were soon laughing hard. I snorted sporadically. The session ended when Jenn racewalked to the bathroom. "No more belly laughs until I take a whizz! Hello, kitties."

Dizzy and Leon strolled from the bathroom to the front room and by the time Jenn returned, Leon was purring behind my head and Dizzy was in my lap. Jenn noted, "Unsolicited cat sympathy. You must have had a butt fuck of a day."

I slammed my head against the back of the couch, which inspired Leon to groom my scalp. Even that couldn't cheer me much. Reality was back. "I hate me."

Hernandez squatted in front of me. "We're at war. Whatever you did, it was what you had to do. You'll doubt yourself but you're strong enough to keep doing what you need to do." He crouched there until I nodded.

"Question?" Jenn raised her hand as Hernandez took his seat again. "With whom are we at war?"

"It's what I explained back in L.A.," I said. "We are among a small but mighty alliance that spans many dimensions to fight Maelstrom and his evil minions, Warty Sebaceous Cysts."

"It was a serious question, bitch."

As I let that go, an unbaked plan came to me. "I note you both smell discreetly of gasoline," I began.

Jenn looked toward Hernandez like he was a saint and she was a believer. "We've been doing so much illegal shit, the crack whores are jealous."

"Then you're just the ones to help me. I've got a building that needs torching." I pretended I had something to do in the kitchen, to give them a chance to think about it. But they didn't.

Hernandez said, "Check it out while we've got daylight," and Jenn didn't even change clothes before we left the Julian. These are two people I love and respect enormously. That they trusted me on this, without details or explanation, made me think a little better of myself, until I remembered how Lilah had trusted me.

Hernandez and Jenn had a rental car they used to transport demolition materials and we drove to Flushing just before sunset. While Hernandez drove past the meeting house, I hid on the backseat floor and explained, "You don't want to be seen with me. It's the building with the black and pink stone." I didn't think the building could see in this Frame, but there might be a Lobotomist around.

Hernandez parked around a corner in a loading zone. "There's no construction site at that building."

"It's a building that intentionally helps the Cysts." I pulled myself up to lay on the back seat but kept below window level.

"It looks occupied."

"No one lives there. The downstairs pastry shop is out of business. There's a meeting room upstairs but the meeting is earlier in the day."

"There could still be someone around." Hernandez wasn't budging.

"Anyone in that meeting room might as well be dead. They've done terrible things and are training to do worse."

"Holy shit. When did this become Judgment Day and who made you the grim reaper?" Jenn demanded.

"Not to mix metaphors." I failed to lighten her tone. "It'll be dark soon. If no lights go on we can assume the building's empty, right?"

"Whatever these people did to you —"

"They're not people and we shouldn't linger here, it's more dangerous than you can imagine." That was for effect. Hernandez could imagine plenty of dangerous.

"Too risky," he said. "Torching Cyst construction sites has limited risk— Lantana and Digby cover up what we do, claim the fires are workplace accidents, because they want no cops involved."

"This building tried to get me killed. It told Mathead and Scabman where I was hiding."

"Mathead and Scabman," Hernandez stated, as though I'd swapped pieces on a puzzle he was trying to solve.

"You're talking like you believe her," Jenn would use that voice if she caught Hernandez spiking a baby's bottle with gin.

"They were here," I answered Hernandez. "They've probably left this Frame because I saw them. They turn out to be important to the Cysts. And to Maelstrom."

Jenn grew very still, in that way she does when she struggles to understand.

"No casualties," Hernandez decreed and he was slamming the door behind him.

"What's happening?" I demanded.

Jenn narrated, "He's talking to a delivery guy who doubleparked behind us. Hernandez has his wallet out and now they climbed in back of the delivery truck. I need you to dish, baby doll. Why is he listening to you when you're talking crazier than a—Hernandez is wearing the delivery guy's clothes. They're tight and they accent that adorable butt. He's carrying a clipboard and a box. I'm watching him in the side mirror now, he's walking into the building."

"No! He's going to see whether anybody's inside. We've got to stop him."

"But you said no one was in there."

"I know but maybe I'm wrong and anyway the building."

"Oh, right, the building," Jenn said in a voice like a padded room.

Hernandez could take care of himself, he wasn't Lilah. Or me. I kept telling myself that.

"What the fuck. It sounds like you're _praying_." Jenn's face appeared over the top of her seat.

"Don't look back here at me!"

"Oh, for fuck's sake." Her face disappeared.

In a way I was praying. I'd been trying to beam my thoughts through the Frames. _Annyl or Anya or Miles or Monk, man do I need you here. Kelly Joe, do you read me?_

"He's back in the delivery truck," Jenn reported. After a moment, "He's a fast dresser."

The driver's door opened and our car started before Hernandez was fully seated. He circled the block, parked in front of the building. "Jenn, be ready to drive. Lock the car doors as soon as I'm out. Unlock them when I exit the building."

He popped the trunk, rummaged behind us. Jenn climbed over the gear shift to take the wheel. What followed was the longest 193 seconds of my life. Then the car doors unlocked like gunshots and the passenger door opened and slammed.

Jenn drove us around the far corner and pulled over with the car idling. Their faces appeared over the seat, looking out the back window, behind us, comfortable in these roles; this must be their getaway procedure after they sabotaged a Lantana construction site.

I stopped holding my breath and sat up to look out the back window, too. Behind us, the second floor meeting room window began to glow. When it became too bright to watch in the twilight gloom, Jenn pulled into traffic and headed west to Manhattan.

I felt good. Hurting that building in one Neutral Frame hardly mattered—and yet it did.

Hernandez said to Jenn, "I had no time so arson will be obvious. We need to put the real plates back on this car and put some miles on it."

Jenn nodded. "Let's use our alibi." She said for my benefit, "It was my idea. We asked the rental car guy to help us plan a trip north to look at autumn leaves. I didn't understand what he drew on the map so I got him to start over. It took forever. We tipped him. He'll still remember that, don't you think?" she concluded to Hernandez.

Hernandez said, "He'll remember you."

When we got back to the Julian, Hernandez and Jenn came inside long enough to pack for a couple days, then left me to do alibi building in Vermont. As it turned out, they needn't have bothered. No cop was going to investigate arson in an empty building, given the chaos of that night.

49. DON'T FEED MAELSTROM

That night, Maelstrom got free.

The first explosion boomed from the northwest, way behind me, maybe back on the Columbia campus. I didn't remember jumping at the noise, but here I was jogging atop the seats of benches. I was already skittish before the blast startled me—I knew I had no business crossing Central Park alone after sunset, but I desperately needed a run and I had persuaded myself I could outpace trouble. I hopped back to the path, sheepish but unobserved: all attention was on the park's perimeters.

Another explosion bleached the sky, this time east of the park. Then north. Then south. Then west. Then west again. People called the blasts simultaneous, but actually they spanned about fifteen minutes. Simultaneous would have been easier to handle.

As I curved back toward the city, to the southwest edge of Central Park, more blasts echoed, near and distant, all over the island. With each boom, the air grew further pressurized, as though thunder was building a storm. With each boom, the demented cackling of the East River became more noticeable, except I couldn't— shouldn't—be hearing the river, because I was home on Ma'Urth, where the river was silent.

Already I wasn't thinking clearly—my first impulse was to head southwest to the Columbus Circle subway station. I couldn't get down the stairs, around the press of people streaming up and outside. Suddenly all the people looked like Lilah and I backed away, stunned that I could think—even for an instant—that I was back in those days when Lilah and I hung out at Columbus Circle station to hear Kelly Joe play.

Directly overhead, the air pulsed in a series of rapid blasts, punctuated with the deep screams of grown men. Suddenly the building's top floor, under reconstruction, was in flames—and from the sounds of it, several workers were caught on the burning floor. I swerved to get out of the way of men, clinging and swinging on the scaffolding, becoming acrobats to reach the ground faster than was safe to move. But of course safe is relative. By the time the last of them were down, the flames were out.

My next impulse was to find somewhere quiet so that I could focus on shifting Frames. But when something this big happens you want to be with your own kind. No one had to tell me. These construction site explosions were helping to free Maelstrom.

As if on cue, Hernandez texted me.

:: Digby bldgs on fire all over LA. On the news.

:: Same here with Lantana. You and Jenn ok?

:: Safe in motel upstate. Back at dawn. Wait on orders fr A n A.

Hernandez knew what this meant, too. Anya had explained how the altered construction would contribute to Maelstrom's release. When detonated in this Frame, each of the buildings directed energy to other Frames, where the energy was gathered and focused to Halcyon, a Frame the Cysts had stolen via genocide for this purpose. On Halcyon, the energy was further focused to shoot a narrow beam into the shield of collapsed Frames that imprisoned Maelstrom. It takes a lot more energy to cause an explosion in a Neutral Frame than elsewhere, so the net energy flow was enormous. Simultaneously, other altered buildings in other Neutral Frames fed energy to other stolen Frames in key locations. These directed their own energy beams into the Frame collapse, which created instabilities. A Frame collapse prison requires a balance of forces and the instabilities built an escalating imbalance. Anya understood the physics of it; all I knew was the result. Maelstrom's imprisonment was past tense.

I knew the exact moment when he got free. The air pressure built and built, then with one more explosion, *pffft*, the pressure was gone. I was surprised when my next breath drew oxygen, because the air felt so empty. The explosions had made the ground rumble but now it settled with a groan just below detectible hearing, like the planet had expired.

By then, traffic had stopped and the sidewalks were empty. People milled in the streets. It wasn't clear where might be safe. It seemed like no one wanted to be inside or exposed, so they stuck close to cars and buses, gaping skywards, darting fast glances while stepping in absent shuffles that kept them central to—away from the edges of—the pack. Every taxi was full of strangers who pressed together, eyes flicking from rooftop to rooftop, watching for the next explosion. *The explosions are over*, I didn't explain. Their work here was done.

My run became a sprint. I moved without destination. I discovered I was heading east. Why could I hear the East River in a Neutral Frame? At especially loud cackles, people would look around for the source of the sound. I looped and ran west. By now, people were returning to sidewalks. With the sidewalks filled, I had to run in gutters. The streets were still blocked with vehicles helter skelter at every intersection.

Near Rockefeller Center, I hurdled a Zip bike rack to avoid running into a woman who was collapsed, sobbing, "Not again. Why won't they leave us alone?" Her reaction was unfortunate—hysteria was a Maelstrom delicacy. *Don't feed Maelstrom*, I didn't say.

She had jumped to the obvious conclusion, a jump taken by millions all over the world. This had to be a terrorist attack. That was a reasonable guess, and the media ran with it. Bars and restaurants and hotel lobbies blasted television news that night. The explosions must be due to terrorists, the thinking went, in an incredibly polished, global attack. Near simultaneously, thousands of explosions hit hundreds of cities across six continents.

As the hours and the news broadcasts evolved, the reasoning grew less clear. No one stepped up to claim responsibility for the explosions and no additional attacks occurred. At each of the thousands of locations, damage had been relatively light, considering; and there were surprisingly few casualties. All of which left a puzzle, not a threat, and attention faded quickly. You know how it is for us. We need stories: villains and heroes and tragic bystanders. We got zip here—no motive, few consequences, zero explanation. But of course, by then no one was thinking clearly. Maelstrom was loose in the world.

When the explosions first occurred, I felt a bond with every person on the streets of Manhattan, but as my running exhausted me and the night wore on, those other people seemed stupid, foolish, menacing. Fortunately, it got easier to avoid them because the streets grew emptier. Maybe my reactions were shared. Maybe that was because Maelstrom was affecting us. That was my last moment of lucidity before I succumbed to Maelsthink, a distinctive hopelessness.

At some point I Traveled to Frivolous Bedlam. It took me a long time to get there because I calibrate my arrival based on noise level and the buildings were not their boisterous selves. They were alert and silent as though listening. I only knew I was in Bedlam when a food cart called out, "Cat Shaver is here and she is fine."

Did that mean others weren't fine? What were the chances I could pose questions to the buildings or carts and get answers I could understand? Should I go looking for the allies? The only thing I knew for sure was that here in Bedlam, the East River sounded more demented than usual—and frightened. With the buildings so quiet, the river's gibbering filled the air.

My indecision was profound. Now that zero people were around, I wanted to be near people, so I Traveled back to Ma'Urth. While I had been away, the atmosphere had grown more tense, and whenever I jogged past an open doorway, I'd hear a burst of argument or sharp words. Maybe I should go back to Bedlam, but I didn't think I could bear hearing the East River. On the other hand, my lanyard was prickling like poison ivy on a bee sting, and that was likewise growing unbearable.

I had so many fearful, half–finished thoughts that my head felt like my left calf, which had a humdinger of a cramp. I stopped to stretch and the cramp got worse. I set out again at a fast limp. I wanted to be home. Although what was the point, we were all screwed, maybe I should go for a swim in the East River.

"Nica." Anya's voice was alchemical—it turned my hysteria to hope. She walked toward me, more beautiful than ever I'd seen her; the darkness vibrated with her passage. She took my hands and her touch was more restorative than the warmth in her tone as she repeated, "Nica. Recognize these feelings as the mark of Maelstrom. He batters our minds and we must fortify. Let us walk and I will teach you."

We headed northwest toward the Julian. "The first step is to recognize his influence. The second step is to permit it to continue. The third step is to dismiss its power with a mantra. Each of us has a unique mantra and it may change over time. My mantra is 'these are not my thoughts, these are not my feelings, they shall not linger'. When Maelstrom is strong in my vicinity, I repeat this without pause."

A mantra sounded too simple to work, and when I tried hers, it did zip for me. As the blocks slid past us, I tried slogans and catch phrases and wise thoughts. Nothing helped. I wanted to give up, but Anya held my hand and, connected to her, I kept trying. The breakthrough came when I sang a reworked Talking Heads chorus. *This is not my beautiful thought. This is not my beautiful mind.* That reminded me of another lyric, which reminded me of another. Singing—anything—made me feel better. I let song phrases wander out of my mouth and eventually, one snagged. *Leave alone, you don't belong here.* If Maelsthink was a tick's butt, then that Elliott Smith lyric was a flame. I remembered the gangly kid who sang that song with me, and hoped he would find a mantra, too, and soon.

The instant I found my mantra, Anya knew. She squeezed and released my hand.

We passed a row of brownstones. It was well past midnight but most of the windows glared with lights and few had drawn curtains or blinds. I imagined occupants huddled in hallways, wondering why they felt so bad. From an open window came two adult voices yelling over each other in a fight where both were spewing, neither listening; deeper inside was the sound of a baby wailing, hoarsely, as though long ignored.

"So this is what it's like with Maelstrom free."

"The effect will change. Maelstrom is near so the effect is acute. Yet Maelstrom is weak so the effect is muted. His influence will wax and wane with his strength, attention, and proximity. Now that he is free he has many to feed him, and I believe he will make feeding his first priority. He will likely disappear for some time, while he grows stronger. When he is strong, all beings in all Frames will know pain and confusion."

"The suicide rate is going to skyrocket." And the O.D. rate. I had to reach Ben. Somehow I had to convince him to find and use a mantra. Didn't I?

"Yes. Maelstrom is free. Go home, Nica, and dwell on all you love."

She intended to ditch me again. "When can I be around you again?"

"Not for the non. My effort lies in Frames where a Neutral would incite mistrust. But believe this: you can resist Maelstrom without me. When Hernandez returns, continue as you have been."

Interesting that she knew Hernandez had left town. "What's the point? The construction sites already freed Maelstrom and burned in the process. We thought we got them all but we didn't."

"Mantra," Anya replied.

I sang one round of it and I realized that we had destroyed most of the construction sites, as evidenced by news reports—there were a couple dozen explosions in Manhattan, but hundreds in every other explosion center. I continued to hum my mantra while Anya spoke, which kept the glass half full.

"You identified sites under current construction, but some have their work long completed, and hidden in them is equipment which gathers negative emotion, to strengthen Maelstrom all the faster. Destroy those. Goodbye for now, Nica."

She clasped my hands in hers and then she was gone. By the time she had walked out of Frame, I was planning my next moves. I'd let Hernandez and Jenn know that Anya wanted the sabotage to continue. Anya hadn't expressly told me to assist, which was good, because I needed to devote maximum time to my book enslavement investigation.

50. I THOUGHT I HATED THEM BEFORE

It was hard to fight Maelsthink in those last blocks as I stumbled home, exhausted and alone. Luckily, I gave up trying to plan my next day's investigation and my only thought was how it would feel to stretch out on my couch. The lanyard's prickling was giving me a whole–body toothache. I revved my mantra but couldn't get it started anymore. I wanted to run but was walking ever more slowly.

The lanyard jolted me and I noticed my surroundings. I had just overshot my door. But the lanyard wouldn't warn me about that. Something was wrong, very close to home. I knew what it was when I felt a distinctive rustling inside my skull, like a rat nibbling there. I'd felt that before, when Warty Sebaceous Cysts read my outermost thoughts.

"Neeks," smarmed a greasy voice I was so sorry to hear again. It came from a short, dumpy, deadly Warty Sebaceous Cyst. The three Cysts were now beside and behind me. I ran up the steps of the Julian's front stoop, knowing I wouldn't be fast enough.

One of the Cysts tripped me and I went down. Another Cyst said, "Whoops."

I hit the steps hard with my shins and hands. My keys dug a hole in one palm. I found the energy to swivel and face them. I struggled to remember my mantra and as soon as I thought about it, they snatched it.

"*Leave alone*—Ouch! These steps are hard!" One of the Cysts faked a fall.

"*You don't*—take that, villain!" One Cyst slapped at the other two.

"*Belong here*. Oh, what a song! It makes me want to surrender to Anya."

"Not Anya, Anwyl!" the tall central Cyst wiggled his eyebrows obscenely, and laughed until his skin boils popped and oozed, which stained his chartreuse shirt.

They must have dressed to mock me, and to make clear they had been watching me. One wore a Lobotomist hoodie. One walked with the runway strut of a male model from Expletive Deleted. And one.

I thought I hated them before.

One wore a blond wig, stylish heels and a business suit in a Halloween rendering of Lilah.

"She wants to kill us, isn't that adorable?"

They were more absurd and more dangerous than I'd ever encountered them. Fortunately, their Entourage wasn't with them, I thought. The Cysts snickered and waved their arms. "Come forward, lads." Legs in sweat pants filled the street behind them. The legs belonged to a dozen Entourage, their silky platinum hair confined by runners' sweat bands.

Center Cyst said, "Get a good sniff, lads, this is the one," and the Entourage filed past me. Each leaned close to inhale, exhale; each was more intimidating and invasive than the previous.

Left Cyst advised, "Now, lads, don't hurt her too quickly because we want the fun to last and —"

Right Cyst interrupted, "That's enough for now."

"And off we go, lads in front."

"Farewell, Neeks, so wonderful to see you again!"

Abruptly the Cysts waddled away, trailing their Entourage.

Something behind me at the top of the stoop had hastened them away. I grabbed the railing to steady myself as I turned, half expecting to see the Julian had grown an enormous face. Instead, tall and stern on the top step with tail swishing, was —

Leon?

Leon's arrival had compelled the retreat of three Cysts and twelve Entourage? It was one impossibility too many. My mind went on standby as I dragged myself up the steps. I dropped my keys and when I reached for them, I brushed against Leon, who broke into one of his giant purrs. He leaned toward my hand to get petted and lost his balance. The world's unlikeliest superhero scampered into the building ahead of me and rubbed my legs, purring, as we headed upstairs. I clutched the railing to make sure he didn't trip me.

In my apartment, Leon sprawled with me on the couch. His purrs rumbled me while I sang my mantra, which jump—started my brain and dissipated my exhaustion.

Maybe not tonight, but Warty Sebaceous Cysts would be back; and when they were nearby, they would snoop inside my head. Thus it was only a matter of time before they discovered my plan to free the books. I didn't yet know whether my plan was possible. But if it was possible now, it would not be so after the Cysts learned my intentions.

I lay there and I rested and I revived; and as soon as I could manage it, I slid my lap out from under Leon and headed for the Halls of Shared Knowledge.

51. THE TIME OF THE TRAITOR

The Halls of Shared Knowledge were enchanting at night. The tree stones glowed, illuminating the walls from within. The whorls of each stone pulsed and shifted, mesmerizing me. Briefly, I forgot Maelstrom and the Cysts and only felt grateful to enjoy the wonder of the Frames.

"Welcome, seeker," came the bookcase greeting when I stepped into the Halls. "Your visit is late but no less welcome."

"You know what happened tonight, right?"

"Of course."

"Sleep is not as important as knowledge tonight. The races of Expletive Deleted. What are the ones who look like grandmothers called?"

"They are called grandmaters."

"The race they evolve from, the really handsome guys, what is that?"

"Those are called seeders."

"I need to find a particular seeder, or someone he may have confided in. He lived many years ago, so now he is a grandmater or dead. Show me everything that might help me find a particular seeder. For example, I probably need to know the government and social structure of Expletive Deleted—are records kept of births, deaths, or seeder transformations to grandmaters?"

"What is the name of the seeder you seek?"

"I don't know. He was an accomplice at the baby farm, one of the three who Maelstrom did not kill. As far as you know."

There followed a pause that was ten months pregnant, then the voice said, "Step to a viewer."

It took a couple hours to become an expert on Expletive Deleted culture and social hierarchy. The bottom lines were that if only a seeder had the information, it was buried in a mass grave. However, if the seeder evolved into a grandmater, all information survived, because the grandmaters share consciousness, like the earthworm healers— and many other beings through the Frames, as I was learning. The grandmaters lived unless somebody killed them, which rarely happened because they were sacred.

"Hey, Julian," I called to my building as I opened his front door upon my return from the Halls.

"Good evening, Nica. I speak without reference to this particular evening."

"Yeah, it sucks that Maelstrom is free."

I regretted exposing Julian to such language, until he replied, "As a former tenant in 4G was fond of uttering, it bites the big one."

Hearing that—in Julian's refined tones—I had to laugh. His windows rattled in a way that I took to be a polite titter.

"Is it safe for me to go back to Ma'Urth?" I hadn't felt any risk coming here; the Halls of Shared Knowledge felt so isolated from daily life. But I was nervous about going home.

"No Frame can be called safe now, as you know. May I assume you question the proximity of Warty Sebaceous Cysts?"

"Or their minions and colleagues."

"None are present in my sensory sphere. It would be unwise to inquire about their whereabouts—the buildings could mistake my inquiry for a request and summon them. If you will pardon my boldness, I offer two suggestions. Firstly, when you must Travel, do as you have done here and inquire of a sentient structure to ascertain conditions. I for one will not permit entry unless I deem it safe."

"That is terrific advice. What's the second suggestion?"

"Carry your books with you."

I should have thought of that. "I see what you mean! Thank you!"

As soon as I got home to Ma'Urth, I wanted to leave. It was a dismal morning. The sun had presumably risen but the sky was thick. Gray and damp.

I stuffed my books in my backpack, then I Traveled with them to my apartment in Frivolous Bedlam and trained them to stay inside the backpack, but fly out, fast, whenever I said, "Books, to me." From then on, I kept the backpack unzipped to allow them egress.

Leon was beside me the moment I returned to Ma'Urth and stayed with me when I went to Bedlam. He sat like an Egyptian cat statue as I trained the books, then followed me outside. Food carts surrounded us and followed with extra enthusiasm. *Huzzah! Cat Shaver and the cat she shaved.*

In Bedlam, the sky was clear but the wind was biting. I tried to go back to Ma'Urth to grab a warmer jacket but whenever I attempted to Travel to Ma'Urth, Leon did figure eights around my legs, tripping and delaying me. When I stayed in Bedlam, he moved a few feet away. I took this to mean that I should stay in Bedlam, so I renamed the cold wind as *bracing*.

My destination was Expletive Deleted, to search for information from the seeder who had been an unwitting baby farm accomplice. I only knew one way to get to Expletive Deleted and that was across Brooklyn Bridge. I would be well and fully *braced* by the time I got there.

Considering the dangers in Expletive Deleted, a Maelstrom stronghold, Leon might not let me Travel there so I worked on a Plan B. However, somewhere midtown, Dizzy appeared to strut alongside us, tail in the air. She allowed me to pet her once, then she ran off. When she returned, then ran off again, Leon followed.

Sans cats, the remaining trek to Brooklyn Bridge seemed longer and colder. My legs were stiff yet rubbery and I didn't know what lay ahead so I needed to preserve my ability to run. I turned to the food carts. "Can you give me a lift to Brooklyn Bridge?"

"Of course but no!"

"Hmm. I'm not sure what that means."

A push cart shoved forward. "We want to take you but we don't know that Brook–lenn. What you said."

"I'll direct you," I promised as I settled onto the push cart. The other food carts zoomed, raced, and popped wheelies as we continued southeast. Maelstrom's release didn't seem to have affected them. The only time they'd dropped their party attitude was when they transported me after Lilah's murder.

Lilah. My mood turned dark and I hummed my mantra, which didn't help. How could it? The dark about Lilah came from me, not Maelstrom. To get out of my head, I struck up conversation with the carts. "I'm glad but surprised you're so cheerful. You know about Maelstrom, right?"

The carts performed stunts and answered in between. "Maelstrom is free... It's terrible... Until Maelstrom comes here... We can do nothing... Except enjoy this morning..."

"Which of you has the zen pills? I need some too." They stopped doing tricks. Not giving Cat Shaver what she needed was serious. "That was just a joke."

Oh Cat Shaver! She told a joke with us in it! The carts cavorted with such enthusiasm that their wheels squeaked. On them it sounded cute.

A couple blocks from Brooklyn Bridge, the East River started screaming and the carts braked. I jumped off my transport, patted it to say thanks. No conversation was possible with the river that loud.

I sprinted to the center of Brooklyn Bridge. There, as hoped, the river's noise was muted by the Bridge's concrete and steel.

"Hello, Nica, your step remains hearty," Brooklyn Bridge said.

"I'm glad you think so," I replied, searching the outer struts for the spot Kelly Joe had showed me, the place to begin my Travel to Expletive Deleted.

The Bridge seemed to sense my intended destination and advised, "Shift Frames after my midpoint. Before that I have no room, while the seeders make their exodus."

So the seeders were leaving Expletive Deleted. It was an odd juxtaposition: I envisioned the Bridge packed with their sexy struts as they fled for their lives. "I only know one way to get to their Frame so I'd better wait. Let me know as soon as the way is open." I leaned against the nearest pillar. "What can you tell me about that exodus?"

"The rulers of Expletive Deleted currently celebrate the return of Maelstrom. The seeders must flee before the celebration concludes and their servitude turns to slavery."

I paced from one side of the Bridge to the other, willing the seeders to safety. Sometimes the wind carried giddy laughter from Manhattan's buildings. Their innocence was overpowering. "Why am I the only visitor? Bedlam is such a great place. I know that coming here is by invitation only but I can't be the only invite."

"You are not. However, 'all evil and many good shall excluded be, until the time of the traitor.'"

"Sounds like you are quoting a prophecy."

"Rather, that is a ward to protect Frivolous Bedlam. It was put in place during the last war for the Free Frames."

"When does the time of the traitor come?"

"Many have posed that question, without answer."

I gazed at the skyline. "Frivolous Bedlam is as safe as anywhere can be for now. But it does get lonely."

"Yes, the ward has had unintended consequences. Most seriously, the buildings have fallen into confusion, with none but themselves for conversation. There is room for your steps in Expletive Deleted now."

"Then here I go."

I wanted to know more about the ward—it seemed important—but I couldn't risk delay.

"Take much care. In the steps that depart Expletive Deleted there is great fear. Moreover —"

I reached Expletive Deleted and could no longer hear the Bridge for the tromping of the well–turned feet of the seeders. With each minute, the crowd thinned as seeders brandished inhalers that allowed them to change Frames and disappear. Their inhalers looked new, as did their knapsacks, and I got the sense these were *go bags* set aside for this emergency.

It was still night here. A symptom of this Frame's affinity for Maelstrom? Seeders dashed to the Bridge from the shadows of side streets and avoided the thoroughfare where a street party raged. There, under bright spotlights, Cobra people staggered. They plunged arms into enormous urns, pulled them out soaked in a thick ooze. They rubbed ooze on their necks then lurched to the next urn.

Up the boulevard on a stage, platinum–maned dancers moved with disturbing precision. That had to be an Entourage troop. If I allowed myself to react I would run back across the Bridge, so I cut myself off from my reactions and dashed to the shadows of a side street. It was surprisingly dark everywhere except the main thoroughfare. Had the buildings gone dark to support the exodus?

Roaring, a group of Cobra people threw an urn to break the plate glass of a shop front and lunged inside, leaving blood slicks on the broken glass. They dragged a seeder out of hiding, pinned him against the brick wall, and formed a semi–circle that looked like the birth of a gang rape.

I had books in my backpack. Together we might be able to save that victim and flee across the Bridge... Unless the Cobra people also had books nearby... But the rescue would show the enemy that I could control books... Maybe if I went back to the Bridge and released the books from there... As I groped for a viable rescue method, my inner survivor yelled, *Get out of this Frame. Now.* The Cobras terminated my ethical dilemma when they dragged the seeder toward the Entourage. That group was too large to fight.

The Bridge had indicated things would get worse when this celebration was over. If I was going to find a grandmater it would have to be now. I pushed deeper into the dark of Expletive Deleted.

52. YES, DEARIE

A hand grabbed my arm, a hand with scaly skin and a lead–pipe grip. The hand of a Cobra person. As fast as instinct, I Traveled us to an unknown Frame.

"Nica!" The voice was so sibilant it made my name sound like a hiss. "This is an insubstantial Frame!" It was Hari!–Ya.

I had transported us to a Frame with bottomless drops between discontinuous shards of sidewalk and street. We flattened ourselves against an ornate brick building and inched toward a sidewalk without gaps. I had a scraped cheek and ten broken nails by the time we got to solid ground.

"Sorry. I thought you attacked me so I took us someplace where you'd have no backup. Are your people really celebrating Maelstrom's freedom?"

She used her tunic to dab blood from my cheek. "Most do so, while the rest of us help the seeders and grandmaters to escape. Stay away from Expletive Deleted! You face more danger than any seeder."

I grabbed her arm. "I can't. I've got to talk with a grandmater. Can you take me to one?"

She stared like she was a psychic and I was her crystal ball. *Future cloudy, ask again later.*

"There is no time to explain. Please."

"If I tell you to leave, you must do so instantly."

"Agreed."

She took my hand and we Traveled back to Expletive Deleted, where the celebration had grown louder and wilder. Hari!–Ya murmured, "They will lose consciousness soon, but for too brief a time. Hurry."

She wound us through dark streets to a lit street with a scruffy park at the center of an intersection. Shouts and roars echoed from the dark as we approached the park, where a handful of grannies played in the dirt.

The grannies were arranging flower petals in a construct that resembled a Buddhist sand mandala. The design swirled and jumped like the Connector map seen in a kaleidoscope. It was explosively beautiful. A sudden breeze scattered petals and erased what must have been hours of work. The grannies continued the design into new territory, making no effort to repair the wind disruptions. Watching them place petals was so soothing.

An absence of celebration noise roused me. If the celebration noise had stopped, that must mean the celebrants had fallen into the brief stupor that was our last brush with safety.

"There is still time for you to escape if we hurry," Hari!–Ya said to the grandmaters.

"Save yourself, precious," a grannie replied, as though offering a fresh cookie. Another added, as though reciting a nursery rhyme, "Maelstrom will kill us."

"The Frames are vast, we can hide you," I said. It was so quiet that I lowered my voice mid-way.

"That is not our destiny," murmured another grannie, as though declining a foot rub.

"Ask your questions," Hari!-Ya told me, peering into the dark quiet streets behind us.

I squatted beside the grannies. "I need information about the seeder who helped Maelstrom create his baby farm."

"He did not intend to help with the baby farm."

"So you know of him? Did he die or did he transform to one of you?"

"Yes, dearie."

OMFSG, as Jenn might text. Already, there were scattered, groggy yells from the celebration area. Some celebrants were stirring. Hari!-Ya touched my shoulder. Time to scram.

"Go if you need to, I'll catch up," I said, although I knew Hari!-Ya wouldn't agree and I wasn't sure I could find my way back to the Bridge without false turns in the dark. She gripped my bicep and listened intently to noise from the celebration area.

I tried not to talk fast; that might make the grannies slower. "At the Halls of Shared Knowledge I learned that a seeder did help with the baby farm."

"No, he was there to enslave the books."

"How?!" My shout scattered petals. "I'm so sorry that I startled you. How did that happen? How did he enslave the books?"

Hari!-Ya pulled me to standing then—firmly and steadily—away. She guided me so I could walk backwards and continue to throw futile questions at the grannies.

"How did the seeder help with book enslavement? Please! It's important that I know."

A grannie looked up, and even at distance her eyes twinkled. "It certainly is, dear child."

The small kneeling figures looked like discarded bundles of clothes. "Should we carry some of them to force them to come with us?" I muttered to Hari!-Ya.

"No, they would resist and we would all die."

Sadness swept me.

A grannie stood briefly and volunteered, "He used the device."

It was hard to hear over the noise from the roused celebrants. "Did you say 'device'? What device?"

"The device that eats books. Maelstrom feeds good books to it and that makes bad books."

Hari!-Ya yelled in my ear. "Time to run or time to die."

From one of the dark side streets came a mob roar and brief terrified screams. It was easy to imagine that the celebrants, headed this way, had discovered a seeder.

I let Hari!-Ya grab my hand and Travel us out of Frame. We ran southwest and returned to Expletive Deleted when we reached the boulevard beside the

Bridge. "Hold. Some come this way," she whispered, and hold I did, for a few long seconds. Alone.

Hari!–Ya staggered out of the shadows toward her fellow Cobra people.

"Have you found prey?" Somebody called to her, and multiple sets of feet ran our way.

She slurred her reply like her tongue was thick with brew from the urns. "Not here! Across there, don't you see?"

The feet paused. "I see him!" someone yelled, and multiple sets of feet sprinted away from the Bridge, with roars that chilled my marrow. Meanwhile, Hari!–Ya was back to clutch my arm and we ran for the Bridge. She looked grim.

Amid the roars behind us came terrified screams. Intentionally or no, she had sacrificed another to guarantee my escape.

In the dash to the Bridge, our Frame Travel included rapid shifts yet the celebrant roars persisted as we changed Frames. "They're following us!" I gasped.

"They hunt seeders. Save your air for running."

When Hari!–Ya delivered me to Ma'Urth, I didn't recognize my home Frame at first: late morning, yet Brooklyn Bridge was well nigh empty. We were a few steps onto Manhattan's streets when she said, "Here shall I leave you. I must join the hunt for seeders or my loyalties will be questioned."

We clasped arms and she turned back to cross the Bridge.

"You saved my life," I said.

"If you wish to thank me, protect yourself."

And she was gone.

53. LEAVE ALONE

I trudged west and north. No sun penetrated Ma'Urth's damp fog or warmed the drizzle that soaked my clothes. Sporadic taxi drivers and occasional pedestrians shot unfriendly glances my way, as though checking my threat potential. I shot similar glances their way.

On the one hand, I could feel despondent, because the awful events in Expletive Deleted were likely occurring in other Frames, too. On the other hand, even in that Maelstrom stronghold, beings risked their lives in resistance, which made me hopeful and proud.

I had to believe that some seeders and grandmaters would survive, just as I had to believe that we would get Mathead and Scabman, that I would free the books, that Anya and Anwyl would prevail. Without such beliefs, forward motion became impossible.

My lanyard maintained steady prickling, which made me want to peel my skin off and gave me the wherewithal to Travel to Frivolous Bedlam. Marginally better: the sky was glacial but the wind had softened to a chilly breeze.

Food carts surrounded me. I was glad for the company but not their enthusiasm. "We waited at the Bridge for you," a pretzel cart said matter–of–factly. "You're walking funny. Do you need a ride?"

"I'd love one." When a churro cart came forward, I spread my jacket over warm soft pastries and climbed aboard. I nibbled a churro and stopped shivering. Deep fried dough rolled in sugar—Maelstrom can't take that away from me! Well, he can, but not just then. I took a bigger bite. "Hey, how come you guys have fresh food? No one is ever here to eat it."

"Cat Shaver asks big questions. We never wonder about that."

As soon as I said *no one*, a trio of humanoids walked by, grabbed pretzels from a cart, and continued down the street. By the time I got to mid–town, I saw at least a dozen sets of Travelers, the first beings I had ever happened upon in Frivolous Bedlam. All moved quickly and all grabbed food from carts. I wanted to know their business but didn't ask. This wasn't a time to trust strangers.

A soft voice asked, "May we?" and a blue–furred being from Marzipan stood before me. I scooped churros from deep under my jacket and handed them to his white–furred children. The kids squeaked thanks as the grown–up bustled them away.

Marzipan. In Marzipan could be more information that I needed. I was near the block where I'd Traveled to Marzipan and talked with the proustel vendor. She had ended our conversation abruptly, to warn her people about Maelstrom's release. Maybe now she'd have time to talk. Maybe I'd get lucky and find her in the same location. I jumped from my churro cart and hugged my jacket, which was warm like it came right out of a dryer. For that treat, I could ignore the sugar and grease stains.

I Traveled to Marzipan and I was indeed lucky, by about twenty feet. That distance kept me alive.

In an intersection twenty feet away, a squadron of books flew, shedding text as they headed toward a battle in progress.

Blue– and white–furred Marzipani were surrounded by Entourage. The furred beings fought ferociously. Some Marzipani got behind the enemy, to attack them from two sides. The Entourage had a peculiar battle style that seemed to be all offense. They did little to protect themselves. Perhaps they had been programmed for a certain kind of fight. When the Marzipani got behind them, the Entourage fell quickly. For a brief time, the Marzipani had the advantage.

Then the books joined the fray. The fighting paused and both sides seemed to acknowledge that everything had changed. The Marzipani resumed fighting even more ferociously and killed quite a few Entourage before thick rains of text sliced the furred beings into mounds. Blue fur turned purple, white fur turned pink.

I got out of Marzipan without drawing attention.

Back in Bedlam, I wasn't cold but I was shaking and to climb back on the churro cart I needed a boost from a hot dog stand with hydraulics. I kept seeing oozing masses of pink and purple fur.

For years, the Cysts had prepped armies for Maelstrom's return. Even without books they would be hard to beat. With books they were invincible.

The warmth of the churros no longer comforted me. *Leave alone.* My mantra didn't help much, either.

Those books showed no emotion when they pulverized the furred beings. Were they capable of knowing right from wrong? Were mine?

Maelstrom fed good books to a device. I'd better figure out what that meant, pronto.

My apartment in Bedlam usually felt like an oasis. Today it felt cut off. I yearned to know what was happening at home. When I get stressed I lose the ability to sit still. As Jenn would say, *You're ricocheting, Nica.* And now I was ricocheting between Frames.

I Traveled from my couch in Bedlam to my couch on Ma'Urth. My apartment on Ma'Urth felt more hollow than a sinkhole, which made me regret changing Frames in that way. Julian would protect me from walking through a door into trouble—but I wasn't sure he could keep the inside of my apartment safe. I deadbolted my door, checked that the bathroom window and bars were latched. Of course, anybody with any real power could—

That wasn't a thought I should finish. I peeked out the kitchen window at the fire escape and hoped the stolen lawn chair was okay. I looked around for more things to lock.

Back in the front room, Leon was on the couch, which made everything seem manageable again. I crooned sweet nothings, "Heyyyy, my bodyguard, want your head scratched? Oh, yeah, that's the spot..." I grabbed my laptop to watch news while I scratched Leon.

The internet worked fine, which disturbed me. With Maelstrom's escape, everything normal felt wrong. In the on–line news streams, the media professionals were more composed than they had been last night and commercials interrupted the special programming. Goodness, there were a lot of talking heads—no two alike but all the same. A few bottom lines emerged. American television programming is resilient, there had been no additional attacks, and no one had a clue what had happened. I closed the laptop and let Leon's purr rumble through me.

I must have fallen asleep because suddenly Leon was gone and the laptop was leaving my hands.

54. MUST BE SO IMPORTANT

Anwyl joined me on the couch. He had mud and blood on his tunic, scrapes on all visible skin. "I'd hate to be the other guy, huh?"

He rested his head on the back of the couch and his legs stretched into the room, one long lean line with a hint of bend at the middle. He stared at the floor, his eyes in shadow.

"Where did Maelstrom go when he escaped? Do we know?" Were his eyes closed? I whispered, "Are you awake?"

"I am," he whispered back.

"I saw other beings in Bedlam today. Why haven't I seen any before?"

"During war, Travel grows."

"Has the war started now? Where's Anya? What's our next move? I know you said for me to help Jenn and Hernandez but for what they're doing a duo is perfect so what are some other moves for me?"

He sighed, stood. "I am not here for your incessant questions."

"Don't go, I'll shut up."

"Yes." He pulled me into his arms.

Now this was the kind of wham–bam session I'd originally fantasized about Anwyl. It left me on the floor, gasping; Anwyl breathed deeply beside me. "There is –" I lacked the air to finish. Another dozen inhales and I tried again. "I need to ask you about one thing."

"Need? Or want?" He gazed at the ceiling.

"Yes." He regarded me peripherally. "How's that for an inscrutable non–answer? Now I feel like a real daughter of the Frames." I touched the edge of his mouth, which twitched. "You're not about to—smile, are you?"

He bared some teeth and pulled me on top of him.

Some time later, I said, "This is what I wanted to ask you about." I showed him news videos from Chicago. As in New York, the explosions that freed Maelstrom had sent people into the streets. For Chicago, last night's weather had been decent—clear with temps in the low 40s—but then, out of nowhere, tornadoes sprouted, causing scores of injuries and several deaths.

While Anwyl watched the Chicago coverage, he continued to sprawl ungarmented and I enjoyed the view. He had scratches on the skin that anybody could see, anytime. I got to see the rest. I wasn't callous. Uncaring. Unaffected by the violence I'd seen—or caused. Quite the opposite—especially because Maelstrom and the Cysts were just getting started. To remain functioning, my best defense was to unleash my inner Blanche DuBois, the younger Blanche who fought oblivion with desire.

My therapy, *aka* Anwyl, tapped the laptop screen. Why did I show him that news clip?

"Did those tornadoes have to do with our resistance to Maelstrom? You sent Kelly Joe to Chicago with some new allies."

"Well reasoned, Nica." He fiddled with my computer. "Here began the tornadoes."

A laptop window gave a bird's eye view of the beings in bright robes, stepping through a Chicago that had water where the streets should be. Jets of whirling water covered the robed allies with what looked like giant ants. These swarmed over the bodies then slipped back to the watery street, leaving stripped skeletons behind.

I leaned against Anwyl; I needed that support. "What are those water spout things?"

"Piranha ants, beings manufactured by Warty Sebaceous Cysts."

"Manufactured. Like their clockwork dogs and the flying chainsaws?"

"No. Those beings are primarily for show. The piranha ants are living weapons, akin to the dangerous beings like the gila chickens."

"Chickens? That's not even fair." I dragged myself up to sitting.

"The laughter ceases on first encounter." Anwyl touched my cheek in that intimate way that gave me flaming goosebumps. "Think anew of your involvement with this fight. Each day will bring new horrors. Anya will not compel you to take such risks. Nor, ever, shall I."

"So long as you and Anya believe I can help the cause, it'll take more than killer chickens to get rid of me."

"More will come." He did stuff on my laptop and steered the view along spotlit streets in Expletive Deleted, empty but for scattered naked remains. Seeders. He turned a corner and I recognized the grungy park. Some of the flower petal mandala was still in place. A heap of grannies lay nearby, dead but not defiled. Cobra people covered the heap in black bits, then set the bits on fire. As fire consumed the grandmaters, the flames turned the color of rose hips and chirped like silver birds.

I made a sorrowful noise that I tried to disguise as surprise. "Is that Expletive Deleted? What is happening there?"

"Many would rally against Maelstrom, should the grandmaters request it, so their murders are now on his hands. Warty Sebaceous Cysts seek to annihilate all seeders so that no new grandmaters will evolve. Seeders hide in safety for the non, and from their safe haven we will distribute them through many Frames, so that a few may survive. Hari!–Ya leads this important effort. You will assist her in moving seeders."

"Okay," I gulped. Did Anwyl know I'd gone back to Expletive Deleted? Was he trying to catch me in a lie?

Paranoia? Where?

Nope, Anwyl wasn't sneaky and deceitful like that. That would describe me, not him.

To get to the seeders' safe haven, Anwyl led me south on Amsterdam Avenue, then Traveled us to a Frame that must be very near Bedlam, based on the level of building noise. We entered a narrow featureless building that was a hole—

in—wall hotel on Ma'Urth. In a hall on the second floor, the building whispered, "Lobotomists have passed my door three times. They search my neighbors and they ask for you. The buildings now spread the question in their distorted way."

Anwyl pressed a hand against the paisley wallpaper of the hall. "Thank you for your vigilance. Before I depart this Frame, I will let many buildings see me in many places, so that they may spread the word that I have been seen often and elsewhere."

Anwyl led me into an apartment's shower stall. He turned the water lever— like this then like that—and led us into a room where the wall was sliding open with a faint buzz. Behind this secret entry was a suite of rooms with no windows and no other door. The suite was crowded with seeders and empty pizza boxes.

"There's pizza in this Frame?"

"Pizza is a universal food in all the Frames that I have known. Step inside. These are the souls you will scatter through the Frames."

The room pulsed with the same calm acceptance the grannies had shown as they arranged flower petals while their deaths approached. Many of the seeders were shorter and smaller than the gorgeous hunks I'd seen before. Their muscle— hugging clothes hung loose, exposing wizened skin.

"Are the seeders turning into grandmaters? I thought that only happened rarely."

"The greater the danger to the Frames, the more—and more rapidly— grandmaters evolve."

"Wow." My spine grew extra steel. The grannies must be so important to the fight against Maelstrom.

In one corner, a group of them hunched over another mandala, this one made of olives, string cheese, and other pizza components.

"Each day, Hari!–Ya will move these grandmaters, pair by pair, to Frames near and far, until her energy is spent. She will enlist your help. If a day passes without her visit, she is dead and you must get word to me." Anwyl touched my cheek in that bedroom way. "I shall not see you for an armful of days. Tread carefully. Treachery paves every road."

We parted ways in the building's second—floor hallway. His warning didn't faze me much because I was so proud that he trusted me with insider information.

I ran down the stairs like a gazelle. The new grannies had wiped Maelstrom's slime from my thinking but outside my thoughts began to glisten again. *Leave alone, you don't belong here.* I belted my mantra like I was Christina Aguilera. No room for gloom. This diva had a busy day of insurgence ahead.

55. LIKE THERE WAS A WIND, EXCEPT THERE WASN'T

Leon did his cockroach scurry beside me on the way home. The gray drizzle made us damp and he licked a paw while I held my hand on Julian's front doorknob. No resistance, the door opened easily. Safe to go inside. Leon scurried indoors between my feet.

I had time for a shower and granola before Hernandez and Jenn arrived and sank onto the couch. He looked like someone ran over his dog. She looked like the dog.

"How was your trip? Any problems getting back?"

Hernandez shook his head. "Smooth going—no sign that anything untoward happened last night."

"Do you know something about those terrorist attacks?" Jenn's tone straddled the fence between accusing and suspicious.

"They're not what you think –"

"You know more than me, I got that message already." Her cheekbones were sharper than usual and her eyes were puffy.

"Did you sleep at all last night?"

"I've already had a mother, Nica."

Hernandez stood. "Let's grab a bite. We need to scout some construction sites."

Jenn remained seated. "What's the point." She didn't say it like a question.

Hernandez returned to the couch like he might hurt the air if he moved too fast.

I got what was happening. "Maelstrom is affecting you. That's why you feel like giving up and don't know how to behave. You have to block the effect. Anya showed me how."

"Will you just." Jenn shoved herself to standing. "I need a shower and a nap."

"After we do this. Jenn, please. Last night something—a being of terrible force—was released into the world. I know you don't believe all this Frames shit but act as if you do. This being is cruel—evil—and he feeds on our negative emotions, so he makes us feel as bad as possible, then feasts. I can train you to block the effects."

"What, now you're a Padawan? Please stop. I'm not up for this."

Hernandez grimaced like her words cut him.

"Jenn. If you ever loved me, you need to do this."

I don't say that kind of stuff. It loosened her funk.

So I trained them. We kept at it until they found mantras that restored peace of mind. Jenn's was an elaborate chain of cuss words and Hernandez's was something about his daughters that he kept to himself.

I went out with Hernandez and Jenn on their next scout–and–prep mission. They had a few more current Lantana construction sites to damage, and then they'd go after already–completed remodels.

With each hour that passed, Manhattan's street congestion seemed closer to normal, but it wasn't life as usual. Few chatted into cell phones, the food trucks had short lines. People moved with a clench to the jaw and a stomp to the step, clutching their coats like there was a wind, except there wasn't. I worried about the ones still huddled at home.

Jenn and Hernandez could teach me about sneaky. At each construction site, Jenn would locate the most discreet exit and text its location to Hernandez. Meanwhile he'd be inside, pretending to look for work, but actually deciding where fire could do the best damage. He'd leave by the exit Jenn had selected. Sometimes, somebody would redirect him. Other times, he'd open that door and Jenn would be on the other side, ready to foul the lock with gum and paper. That would be their way in, when they returned tonight as arsonists.

Jenn and I were in an alcove off a street when a quartet of hardhats filled the alcove. Jenn converted her door grab to a lunge to retrieve a pack of gum that she dropped on purpose. Now, Jenn is sexy. It's her nature. Blowing her nose on the third day of a cold, she's down to a level of sexy that few of us ever rise to. All four construction workers helped her retrieve the gum then acted embarrassed about it.

These four young guys worked for Warty Sebaceous Cysts but they weren't even obnoxious, much less evil.

The encounter tweaked me. And as we continued down the block, Jenn asked, "Which side are we on in this thing anyway? Are we the good guys?"

"Does Hernandez seem like someone who'd fight for the bad guys?"

"We're putting a lot of people out of work."

"I know."

We connected with Hernandez and he read our faces. "Something happen?"

Jenn said, "We got interrupted, I didn't get that last door. Our next stop's on West 36th."

I felt the weight of trust from the books in the pack on my back. Time to go. Jenn and Hernandez were using their mantras and acting more or less like themselves. I had an idea I needed to pursue before I lost my nerve. I said, "I need to shoo, things to do," and backed away then dashed. I didn't catch their reaction to my hasty departure.

As I hastened away, I spotted an orange streak across the street. Leon had been shadowing us.

56. FOUR BEINGS SURVIVED

I sat on Julian's front stoop in Frivolous Bedlam, waiting for the buildings to relay my message to Kelly Joe. *No emergency. Nica needs to see you.* That's the message I sent; I'd find out what message the buildings conveyed. Frivolous Bedlam's sky was still too pale to be called blue—but the sun was warm on these steps. Here where Maelstrom couldn't reach, it was a lovely fall day.

A blue–furred couple hurried by me. "What news of Marzipan?" I called. They flinched and increased their speed.

The door opened behind me and I smelled sweat. And blood.

"You're alive and unharmed," Kelly Joe's voice noted. He remained standing behind me, which was fine with me. My distaste for him had grown while away from him and I had to force myself to look in his direction. Being around him felt like being around Jenn's mom, who killed a child during the fourth of her six DUIs.

"I'm sorry if the buildings said otherwise. I did try to communicate urgent–but–not–emergency." He had blood stains on his jeans and jacket. "Will you be in battles all the time now?"

"I only know about today. If you wish, I can teach you to contact me when I'm in another Frame."

The way he said it, he knew that I found his presence distasteful. Which broke me through to the other side of it. I'd always hate the man whose ambition helped establish the baby farm. So would he. Kelly Joe was no longer that person— but he'd never regain his own regard. In the face of such intense self–hatred, my distaste felt petty.

"You're my musician. Teach me."

He jumped down to the sidewalk. "I'm going to Travel to another Frame and you're going to come after me. You'll see what direction I walk, which will make your task easier. You won't often know that information. Focus on my being with you, keep your thoughts on me. Walk behind me and find the Frame I go to. Mind you, don't guess. Follow the signature of my energy."

After enough tries to wear down the pavement, I got the hang of it. Finally we were back in Bedlam, sitting on Julian's front stoop, and Kelly Joe bent notes on his harmonica, which restored the strength I'd lost. It annoyed me that his music could so readily affect me.

I focused on the positive. "Thank you for showing me how to do that, now I don't feel so cut off."

"If someone intends to hide from you, he will. If someone is many Frames away, his trace will be faint and you won't have the skill to follow. A being with power can detect your search, so don't follow an enemy or you'll get ambushed."

"In other words, don't think I've learned much of anything. Got it."

"You had the buildings fetch me."

"Oh right." I watched my feet as I tapped my shoes together, feigning forgetfulness. Then I copped to my reluctance. "I don't know whether I can trust you."

He stood to leave. "Then I'll be getting back."

"Wait. I do trust you overall," I said, and realized it was true. "I want to confide in you about a plan of mine. It could help the allies—maybe a lot—but if you tell Anwyl or Anya, they'll say it's too dangerous and make me stop. Can I trust you not to fink on me?"

"They want you alive because you have a role to play."

"I want me alive, too! For that and other reasons!" My backpack full of books grew so heavy that my spine curved toward my heart.

"I have allegiance to Anya and Anwyl but I'm your musician."

I kept my mouth shut. Kelly Joe wasn't looking for response, he was reasoning it through. He pushed up his jacket sleeves. No change in his tattoos: the green hummingbird and the blood and the books.

He lowered his sleeves. "If you have a plan, it may be worth trying. I can't say which action will be more dangerous, or whether taking no action is safer. If Anya or Anwyl ask me about this plan, I won't lie to them. Until they ask, I won't volunteer what I know."

My backpack became so light it pulled me up to stand beside him. "I want to free the books. Or maybe change who they obey. I know that part's possible because I have books who obey me."

He was watching me almost as closely as I was watching him, but I couldn't read his reaction. "Do you think I have a chance?"

"Surely I don't know. Is there an answer that would change your plan?" He bent notes on his harmonica.

"No." I'd had a rush of jubilance because he would keep my secret; it had a sweet short life.

"What is worth trying and what will fail?" He bent more notes.

"Exactly! If only we could find those answers..." As I searched for a fitting conclusion, he finished for me.

"We would still proceed."

The sweet chatter of the buildings flowed around us. "Yes. We would. We have to try. I've been to the Halls of Shared Knowledge. I learned that three beings helped with the baby farm and survived. Somehow they are also tied up with the enslavement of books. I've figured out how to question two of them. I need your help getting to the third, if she still lives. Her name is Mavis and she is from Next Vast. That's all I know."

He sat on the top step of the stoop. "Four beings survived." He stared into the shadows across the street. The sun had moved along and being near him gave me a chill.

I kept shifting my position until he looked at me. I wanted remorse from the fourth being to survive the baby farm, but he gave me bleak defiance, which disgusted me all over again. Before I had asked the buildings to fetch him, I'd vowed to avoid confrontation. I kept the vow about as long as a New Year's resolution. "What the fuck were you thinking?"

"Thinking? I didn't earn that credit."

"That's your excuse for helping with the baby farm? You weren't thinking?"

"I offer no excuse." He didn't break eye contact but he wasn't seeing me.

"How about regret? Apology?"

"What debt would that discharge?"

Gunning myself into his wall of self–hatred would get us nowhere. I kicked the bottom step and my throbbing toe helped me change the subject. "Why were you four spared?"

"The three escaped and Frame collapse kept Maelstrom from going after them. I was spared because Maelstrom enjoyed my reaction when I learned the truth, and kept me close to stir those emotions." Kelly Joe stood and stepped toward Julian's front door. "Never pity me."

"You can't leave now. I need your help to find Mavis in a way that won't get back to Miles and Monk."

He watched the shadows advance across the street. "Luck favors you. Mavis is in the New Yorks."

57. AT FULL SPEED, HOLD ON

Back in Los Angeles, when I'd visited Miles and Monk in Next Vast their Frame looked very similar to mine; but here in the New Yorks, there was a dazzling difference. In Next Vast, the buildings, sidewalks, and streets were translucent. The sky was clear and pale as in Frivolous Bedlam, and the whole place shimmered, even down in the subway, which is where Kelly Joe led me.

The subway turnstile spun in greeting then leveled its bars so that Kelly Joe and I could vault over it. We trouped down the stairs and along the platform, but I paused on the platform edge when he jumped down to the track. The train tunnel glowed with infinitely diffused light. This must be the view from inside a cocoon. However, wet muck and garbage lined the track, just like at home.

"Unh!" I emitted when he stepped on the third rail to avoid the muck. The third rail must not be a power source here, because he continued, unfried. "No electricity in this Frame, I take it."

"None that the trains need."

From the tunnel ahead of us came a rhythmic scraping, made by a subway train that moved away at a speed (if you could call it that) of about one mile per hour. I'd seen a train like this once, back on Ma'Urth, hauling steel pipe. It was called a worker train and it inched forward, forcing the trains behind it to inch, too, their windows steamed by passenger distress.

This train was two cars long, a hundred years old, and mustard gas yellow. The connectors between its cars rattled and the wheels squealed, but the train was silent, its welded bolted iron cars moving as a single solid unit.

Kelly Joe and then I jumped aboard and clung to the back railing. He greeted the train and introduced me to her. You know you're in Next Vast when the name is seventeen syllables and all consonants.

I told the train, "It's a pleasure to meet you. The closest I can get to pronouncing your name is to call you Mavis."

"That's a lovely alternative." The iron train's voice was as tough as butterfly wings. I might have said *gossamer* but that has a contradictory definition. It can mean something delicate; but it also refers to a spider web, one of the toughest materials there is.

Thinking about gossamer, I missed what Kelly Joe said about the reason for our visit. Fortunately, this early in the conversation it was easy to bluff my way back in. "I'm trying to understand how Maelstrom enslaved books. The Halls of Shared Knowledge identify you as involved in that process, because you worked at the baby farm. I don't see the connection between book enslavement and baby farm. What am I missing?"

191

The train said, "You must love this one, Kelly Joe, that she may speak of this around you."

He stared behind us, perhaps at the receding tunnel entrance. "I'm her musician."

"Is that so? Come and sit, lucky girl, in case I bump around these curves." The back train car was open like a flatbed truck and filled with building supplies. I perched on a bag of cement as Mavis continued, "The books were also innocents, and Maelstrom savors the pain of innocents."

"Do you mean he hurt the books when he converted them?"

"Of course, violence is not in their nature."

"How did he perform the conversion?"

"That I didn't see, I only heard the cries. I delivered crates of books from many Frames. Warty Sebaceous Cysts opened every box in every crate and selected which books to take away. They took books that were sweet and calm, brought them back full of anger and deceit. The books sliced their crates to escape. My steel got rough with cuts from text. They began to cover the cargo in nets, specially made to hold books. They didn't do that to protect me, of course."

"How did they decide which books to take? Anything you heard could help."

"They would read names on the side of the boxes. My impression was that those were the names of the books inside. They grouped the boxes with the same names. Then they would open one box, remove a book, and check a number."

I frowned at her chassis, trying to understand. "The number of pages?" I looked at Kelly Joe. "Maybe they only wanted the longest books?"

Mavis sounded sad. "I am so sorry, I don't know. I do recall that they took the lowest numbers. For example, nineteen nineteen, not nineteen fifty–two."

"Copyright dates? Earlier editions?" I asked. That would fit the pecking order I had observed among my own books.

Kelly Joe shrugged but he didn't seem to be listening. His jaw had a tic and he flexed his wrists like he was making his tattoos jump, under his jacket sleeves.

Mavis said, "Edition! I remember that word. They got excited with first editions. 'These will rule the others', they would say and it sounded like they were bragging more than usual."

I tried an idea on for size. It fit the evidence so far. "Maybe earlier editions controlled later editions."

"I don't know that either, but I can tell you that the books in the other boxes, the ones left behind on my back? They changed and became mean, too; but the books that went away changed first. Please forgive me for noticing so little, I didn't understand it could be important someday."

"Are you kidding? This is fantastic, you are helping me so much."

"I am tickled to be of service," Mavis warbled. "More curves ahead, and now that I'm at full speed, hold on!"

Full speed. I could have somersaulted off and hit the ground without a jolt. Nonetheless, I clung to her railing as though she were supersonic. "Where did you deliver the crates of books and where did Warty Sebaceous Cysts take the ones they selected?"

"I always met them in Times Square. I don't know where they went from there."

Kelly Joe came back from wherever his thoughts had dragged him. "In those days, Times Square was a Connector hub in many Frames."

My questioning continued but I got no additional information from Mavis. At the next subway platform we debarked.

"I'm here when you need me," Mavis gave a gossamer farewell.

"We'll surely be together soon." Kelly Joe patted her goodbye.

As we emerged from the subway, I tried a guess about their relationship. "She makes a good confidante." I wouldn't call that nosy.

Kelly Joe led us across the street. "When the worst battles commence, Mavis will be there. She's one of the greatest warriors the Frames have seen."

Below us, under the translucent pavement, Mavis trundled away. "How is that possible? Anyone can outrun her and she's about as mean as a daisy. By the way, if there's a Frame where daisies are assassins, I don't want to know."

Kelly Joe chuckled, "I'll not say a word about them." He offered his hand and when I took it, he Travelled us to Ma'Urth, then led us northwest toward the Julian before he added, "Mavis moves slowly, but she never stops. She does tire easily, here in her ancient days, so we won't use her until we must."

I grabbed a pretzel as we passed a food cart. "Lady!" the vendor yelled after me.

Oh right. I wasn't in Bedlam. "Oops. Forgot I was supposed to pay here," I said, which did not soften the vendor's expression. I fished a bill from my pocket, waved my hand for him to keep the change. As we resumed walking, I offered Kelly Joe a piece of pretzel. Declined.

I shoved that piece in my mouth then regretted taking the time to chew. Much as I loved a fresh pretzel, the rest would have to wait until this conversation was concluded. "I wouldn't call Mavis ancient. I've been to the Transit Museum so I happen to know that her style of train was built about a hundred years ago. That's old but not ancient."

"Mavis is not her shape, she's her materials. Before she was made into subway cars, she lived, in one shape then another, for all the cycles of the moon and stars."

"Wow. So Mavis has seen a lot." I bookmarked that info for future investigations.

"Indeed she has."

Kelly Joe would speed up then slow down but never quite wait for me. I assured him, "If you need to take off, go ahead. I can get myself home from here."

"I do need to get back. Anya and I were in three kinds of trouble and —" He vanished out of Frame before the last of his words reached me.

Kelly Joe had so many opportunities to work on his death wish, these days.

58. EVERYONE I LOVE IS AT RISK

Within moments of Kelly Joe's departure, I caught peripheral glimpses of an orange feline cockroach. Leon kept pace during the rest of my walk home and waited under a mailbox when I did some shopping for the grannies. It was nice not being alone.

Now that I was back in a Frame with cell phone service, I called Ben to find out how Maelstrom was affecting him. In fact, every couple of blocks I called Ben. He never answers phones. Futilely, I texted him.

:: Answer your phone, enneth–Kay!

That referenced a joke from our dating days, to confirm it was my calls that he was ignoring.

In the front room of my apartment, Jenn watched news clips on my laptop and Hernandez was on his phone in Spanish. I stowed my two large shopping bags next to the couch. Jenn looked at the bags, which were tie–dyed with rainbows. Long live 1967.

"That looks like a buttload of acid."

"Long story. I'll tell you later." She sounded much more Jenn–like, today, and I attributed that to her barely audible mutter, every several exhales. Her mantra.

She waved me over to the couch. "Check this out. There was a riot at home and they attacked a news crew and it was Fatty and she's in the hospital."

She replayed a clip. Watching made me furious—fear always converts to anger in me. On the night Maelstrom got free, near downtown Los Angeles, blackouts followed the building explosions and, to share light, people congregated in MacArthur Park. The congregation was crowded but orderly, until a new group barged in, shoving and shouting.

Outrage predominated in the eyewitness interviews.

"They came here looking to rumble, totally unprovoked attacks," said an angry young dad.

"When they knocked somebody down, they laughed!" This teen was trying to stop crying.

"We didn't fight, we fought back," said a bruised middle–aged couple.

"They ignored other news crews all over the place. They chased down that one, like they knew each other, or something."

Or something. Other news crews got plenty of footage of the intruding group, which had two components: frozen–faced Lobotomists led by war–whooping handlers. The latter stopped in front of news cameras to display their t–shirts. *Hi Neeks.*

Their pushing and shoving grew into a riot that put ten people into hospitals, two in critical condition. The object of the attack, news reporter Fatima Jones, was in serious condition; her cameraman, Mikal Petrescu, sustained critical injury. No attackers were in custody but with so much video footage of them on the air, police were confident they would have arrests soon.

Hernandez joined us on Jenn's other side. Their fingers twined instantly. He looked over her head to ask me, "Attackers got to be out of Frame by now, right?"

Jenn made the disgusted noise that was her reaction when we mentioned the Frames. "Those t–shirts!" Jenn knew *Neeks* was Ben's nickname for me. "Do you know those guys?"

"I know what they are. Brainwashed soldiers that fight for Maelstrom. They attacked Fatty because she's important to me. Everyone I love is at risk," I realized.

"Fatty is still in danger?" Jenn exclaimed. She had her phone out, texting. Fatty, Jenn, and me. It had been the three of us since grade school days. Jenn and I didn't see Fatty much, now that she was the glam queen of local news, but we were still tight. "At some point she'll have her phone again, right? Then she'll see this."

She showed me the text.

::Nica says expect more danger. Watch your bony ass.

"Good. Did you hear what hospital they're in?"

Jenn's phone beeped. It made me grin. A quick reply from Fatty must mean she was doing well.

::Fatty conked on meds but okay. Mikal bad –Ben

Ben was in Los Angeles and in the hospital with Fatty? I yanked the phone from Jenn. Her WTF–ing cut off when she saw whatever expression was on my face.

"Hey Jenn," Ben answered Fatty's phone.

I had the voice I'd use to lure a stray off a highway. "Ben, it's me and you're in terrible danger. The people who went after Fatty would love to find you. What the hell are you doing back in L.A.?"

"This is where I stay sober. Don't worry about me. I'm crashing at your office in the Henrietta, no one would look for me there."

"How did –" I cut myself off. Learning how he got access to my office could wait for a safer time. "Ben. You can't stay anywhere associated with me. They want to hurt the people I love. You're in the most danger of all."

"Aw, shucks, I love you too."

"This could not be more serious." Was he high? Why was he acting loopy? Must be the hospital. One time he'd taken me to an Emergency Room—stitches, no biggie—and he acted loopy then, too.

Hernandez clamped fingertips onto the phone. "May I?" I released the phone to him. "Ben, Hernandez. Nica's understating the situation. ... ... Okay, I get that. Here's what. You ever spend time in Santa Ana? ... I agree. Reason I ask, I got cousins there, you can stay with them, they got extra cars, you can get to meetings but keep away from places people expect to find you. ... I'll call them next. Go back to Nica's office and I'll have them pick you up. Now get out of Fatty's hospital while you still can. ... Later."

Hernandez went into the kitchen and made a call in Spanish. Jenn had a hitch in her voice when she murmured, "He gets everything." The day was one milestone after another. Jenn was in love with Hernandez. No man had ever pulled her in for a landing, before now.

As Hernandez pocketed his phone he said, "My cousin is on his way. He'll let me know when they get home."

"Thanks." That single syllable jammed in my throat.

"Your girls were okay?" Jenn asked. That's right, when I first walked in he'd been on the phone making dad–like comments. My Spanish was good enough to recognize those.

"They are," he said to Jenn. To me, he added, "The explosions in Barcelona weren't near them, but the Cysts have a lot of buildings there."

"You're talking Frames again." Jenn's tone was bland with a splash of battery acid. "Shower time."

Hernandez smooched her goodbye but by the time she was standing, he and I were deep into discussion, trying to add it all up—the attack on Fatty, taunting me publicly, whether Barcelona was special to the Cysts.

Some time later, Jenn stuck her dripping head out the bathroom door and shouted, "Don't you hear that car horn? And somebody yelling your name?"

Now that she mentioned it. We went to the street–side window and tugged the blind. Parked out front of the Julian was a red pickup truck, mottled by more dents than there are in a golf ball factory. The truck had no driver and its passenger hung out the window to look up at the building. The passenger had a twist in her waist that I couldn't have copied unless I was made of rubber. Which she maybe was.

Tee and Zasu had arrived.

59. WHAT FRAME ARE YOU FROM?

Zasu. She had the charcoal hair and jet eyes of all the Gumby people. Perhaps that commonality made it easier to keep her memories of her people sharp, now that she was the only remaining Gumby, courtesy of genocide, committed by Warty Sebaceous Cysts. Zasu had lived a sheltered life until recently. The wail she'd made when she lost Ziti, her betrothed—no teen should be gouged with grief that deep. Only a few months had elapsed but she looked years older; and yet—as when I'd first met her, before all the killing started—she looked as trusting as tomorrow's sunrise.

"Zasu!" I pounded the glass of my front window.

Zasu looked for the source of my voice. She held her head steady but rotated and twisted at the shoulders. It was another twist no human could make. A dense high–pitched voice said something and she pulled back inside the truck cab.

I knew that voice. It belonged to Tee, the red pickup truck, a curious blend of adventurer and hypochondriac. I smiled at Hernandez. "I think Zasu forgot about not acting like a Gumby person in Neutral Frames. I think Tee just reminded her."

"My truck just talked to her?" Hernandez gaped at the pickup he'd left in L.A. Last summer, he had missed the chance to meet Tee in other Frames where she was permitted to display her sentience. That the truck was talking and driving on Ma'Urth, a Neutral Frame, was yet another indication that the Frames were in crisis.

Hernandez and I hoofed it downstairs. "Wait'll you meet your truck, she is a hoot and a half." I led him out the front door.

"Well met, Nica!" Hugging a Gumby was a special experience. Zasu's arms made dozens of small bends to encircle me. I watched Zasu hug Hernandez then I frowned at the curb. It was empty.

"Where did Tee go?" I asked Zasu.

"Here is her message, 'I have things to do and will catch you later.' Do you laugh at me?"

"Kinda. That was a perfect Tee impersonation."

"It is an honor to make a friend laugh." Zasu's effervescence emphasized how dampened other spirits were.

"Maelstrom doesn't affect you, does he?"

"By deeds, of course, but not by influence."

Entering my apartment terminated our ability to talk, what with all the yowling. Humanoids typically prompt Dizzy to clean her butt, but she and Zasu have a thing. The cat who has blasé in her bloodstream galloped across the room, meowing like a smoke detector.

197

"Queen Desdemona!" Zasu was the only one who used Dizzy's full name. She scooped the cat up and said into her fur, "What good fortune to hold you again."

Leon prowled around our feet, more restless than I'd ever seen him. Dizzy vaulted from Zasu's arms then she and Leon ran out of Frame. What put those two in that kind of hurry? Not for the first time, I yearned for a Frame where I could converse with those cats.

Zasu explored the kitchen, gasped when the refrigerator door opened. "How lovely!" She touched the bright spot inside the refrigerator, where the light made a sunburst pattern. Watching this, Hernandez had a soft unclenched expression. Zasu was a wrinkle–smoother. My own tensions eased, including the permanent knots like Ben, Lilah and Sam, the Gumbys. Zasu wandered into the front room and rolled her shoulders. "Such a long journey. May I stretch? Will it disturb you?"

"It's fine, especially if I can watch."

"Of course. For safety, remain in this area." She gestured Hernandez and me into the kitchen.

Zasu lay down on the floor beside the couch and began to extend. The motion was slow—second by second, I couldn't see anything happening except for the gentle rippling of her skin, but after several seconds, only a small part of her body occupied her clothes, which lay where she had started. Her torso stretched along the floor until she circled the front room. Meanwhile her legs and arms flattened and expanded up walls toward the ceiling.

The bathroom door clicked open. I'd forgotten that Jenn was in the shower. Hernandez called, "Stop, love, and stay there."

Stop, love. I replayed it and yup, it was Hernandez' voice talking like that.

Zasu inhaled and sighed, then snapped back to her daily shape, using the momentum to leap to her feet. Before my amazement could settle, she stood before us, arranging her tunic. "I feel much better now, thank you. Hello," Zasu spotted Jenn.

Jenn stared at Zasu as though she had—well, stretched herself around the room then snapped back to human form while jumping upright and sticking her landing.

"Zasu, this is my friend Jenn and Jenn, this is our colleague, Zasu. That's not her real name but it's as close as my pronunciation can get."

"I. Zasu. When." Jenn tugged Hernandez' arm to join her on the couch. She looked around him at Zasu. "What Frame are you from?"

Zasu didn't realize how momentous this question was, coming from Jenn. "I hail from Halcyon but now I am a nomad, a Framewalker." She sat on the chair and questioned Hernandez about Edith, a teenage friend Zasu had met through his daughters. While they chatted, I prepped snacks in the kitchen.

I was setting these on the overturned box that was my coffee table when Jenn swallowed a beensy noise and whispered to me, "He just Traveled here, right?"

She stared toward the bathroom door, through which Kelly Joe walked. He stopped in front of Zasu.

"I'll take you to Anya. Now," Kelly Joe announced to Zasu. His voice was frosted steel.

I'd never heard him so curt, nor Zasu so formal.

She stood. "Hello, Kelly Joe, we met many cycles ago. You were my brothers' musician." For Zasu, the delivery was cold, but she had so much innate warmth that even now some radiated. He was trying to place her or to stop placing her as she continued, "Never have I heard music more enticing than you played that day. My mother and my brothers, like so many in our village, Traveled eagerly to the vacation Frame to hear you play again. From that outing, they never returned."

"I'm sorry for your loss." Kelly Joe sounded like a homicide cop.

"Thank you." She spoke without animosity but she kept talking despite all the cues that he was refusing to listen. "I fell ill that day and my father stayed behind to care for me. He played his guitar, which you had autographed after the previous engagement. We laughed at how poorly he played compared to you." She gave a sad smile. "I was so young, I did not understand when my father burned that guitar." Kelly Joe met her gaze. "My father would have welcomed the news, as do I, that your music serves Anya now."

No one spoke or moved. I got blasted with a memory from left field. *I was eight when we moved to the Midwest for a year. I trashed a rose bush with a baseball bat and a basketball—long story—and only one spindly branch survived, with a single fragrant yellow rose. It bloomed for weeks, long into winter, stalk buried in snow. It bloomed and it bloomed.*

Kelly Joe turned to Hernandez and broke the silence. "Anya asks that you come along to help with protection for this one, while Anya completes a mission." *This one.* The other time I'd heard Kelly Joe rude, he'd been heckling Lobotomists.

Of course and immediately, Hernandez stood. His pocket must have buzzed because he fished out his phone. He showed me the new message.

::Got him, got home. All good, Cuz.

Ben was safe with Hernandez' cousin. Hernandez nodded at me, then at Kelly Joe, who extended hands to Hernandez and Zasu and Traveled them out of Frame. Faster than a person could slip on black ice, Jenn and I were alone on the couch.

"Holy shit," one of us said, between stretches of silence.

"The Frames are real," Jenn announced, sounding so satisfied I thought she might smack her lips. She settled back into a corner of the couch and pulled her legs under her: long talk ahead. What followed was a Frames Q–&–A ping–pong match. I'd send an answer, Jenn would lob her next question.

I barely listened to the questions and attended not at all to my answers. I was thinking about Lilah and Sam. I felt worse than ever about my role in their murders. But now I also had Kelly's Joe's encounter with Zasu to think about. Kelly Joe was where I would arrive if I didn't find a way to forgive myself for the twins' deaths—the emotional equivalent of being trapped in a car buried by a blizzard.

Jenn had her arms around me the instant I started sobbing. "The fuck's with you?" She said sweetly, then added mother bird coos until I was able to reply.

"I screwed up and people died. Good people. Awful deaths."

"Oh, sweetie." My sobs and the coos resumed. "That bites worse than a vampire blow job."

"Don't make me laugh. I shouldn't be laughing. I should be saying 'It's my fault so I wish I died instead.' But I don't. I can't. And that makes me hate myself even more."

"Because you're glad to be alive? Fuck that. Anyway, you promised Ick."

That I'd live enough for both of us.

And then Jenn held me, for as long as I needed.

"I can't believe you still call him by his last name." I washed our breakfast dishes while Jenn tossed clothes from her trunk, hunting Today's Outfit.

"Hernandez hates his first name. Obviously, what we call him should be up to him. Are you ducking my question, bitch? What Frame is Hernandez from?" Her abrasiveness was fully restored for the first time since Maelstrom's escape. Easier to resist something when you believe it exists.

"Hernandez is from our Frame—he's human, could you not tell that?" Maybe she couldn't. What if I'd met Anwyl in a bar, what would I have sensed about him?

"But he's so—so much better." About Hernandez, Jenn was as abrasive as a duckling.

I piled her reject garments next to her trunk, pocketed my ID and Metro card, shouldered my backpack.

Jenn continued to explore her blouse options. "You're abandoning me," she noted evenly.

"I'll check back before too long but yeah, I've got some—what is the deal with this –" I couldn't open my front door. I flipped the latch, jiggled the knob.

Duh. I couldn't open the door because Julian was telling me, *don't leave.* At least, *don't leave in this Frame.*

Sometimes I think about that immobilized door. Was it a turning point or simply the next step on the road we were following, all along?

Jenn had stopped dressing to watch my struggle with the front door. Her current top was a soft peach color that reminded me of the grannies' flower petals, scattered by a breeze.

At some point, Julian would release the door and I would leave and Jenn would have to fend for herself. Jenn was tough—tougher than I am—but did she know enough to keep herself safe? Maybe I could find Leon before I left and somehow communicate that he should watch out for Jenn.

Or I could keep her with me.

"Are you ready to go out? Good. Then take my hand and don't talk for a bit, I need to concentrate."

60. WITH BOOKS WE WIN

The Halls of Shared Knowledge are many Frames away from Ma'Urth and after I Travelled Jenn and I there, I exited my apartment only to drop to the hall rug. "This rug is softer than it looks."

Jenn copied my drop. "Why do I feel so fried?" she demanded.

"You just Traveled a lot of Frames from home."

We must have dozed because we woke up about the same time. When I stood I wobbled into the wall—I'd sat in one position long enough to cut off circulation to my extremities.

"Nica, are you in need of assistance?" The building's voice was even more solicitous than usual.

"I'm good, Julian, thanks. My leg went to sleep, is all."

"I believe your entire body slept." Now that was adorbs. My erudite building was unfamiliar with the expression, *leg went to sleep*.

Using my arm for leverage, Jenn joined me standing, staring from me to the wall where I directed my words.

Julian continued, "I am pleased that you understood my warning to remain inside your apartment on Ma'Urth, and relieved that we have found a means to communicate in your Neutral Frame."

Jenn looked around for the source of the voice. "Mr. Parsons," she murmured, and she was right. Julian sounded like our tenth–grade chemistry teacher, Mr. Parsons, who wore bow ties with his lab coats.

I answered Julian, "Me, too! What was wrong, anyway? Why couldn't I go outside back there?"

"There was a disturbance on the next block. It appears to have moved inland and away. Is this your friend, Jenn? Again, I apologize for all that I can't help but overhear."

"Yes, and Jenn, this is Julian. He's a sentient building."

Jenn touched her fingertips to the wall. "I'm very happy to know you. I. This." She gave me a new look. There really was a Santa Claus and he left world peace in her stocking. "Thank you," she said to me, then rubbed her eyes. "I don't suppose there's caffeine in this Frame."

"There is not, but partial immersion in the river can be quite restorative," Julian said.

Jenn was silent and gawking on the walk to the Hudson. She clung to my arm because Travel had weakened her. To let her rest, we stood at the river's bank, watching limbs fall from the trees, erode to tree stones in the rush of water, catch in nets, come to shore in the hands of beings or in the jaws and beaks of dog–like creatures.

"When do we try the partial immersion?" Jenn was out of her shoes and rolling up her leggings.

"How about now?" I agreed.

We stepped cautiously from the bank to the water. The current was strong and the river bottom was not visible in the swirling foam. Jenn shuffled into the water like a cartoon zombie, with arms out and feet planted on the bottom. I copied Jenn's technique. The water shoved at my shins and I stumbled. Jenn took my hand and we laughed. What an experience!

When I touched the water, I joined the flow. Of the river, of the Frames. It coursed through me, and I somehow knew that I shared the sensation with Jenn and all the stone gatherers, up river. As the water swirled around us, I tasted wind on leaves and Jenn's laugh was so bright it made me squint. Almost beyond my hearing were scuffs and taps that I somehow recognized as countless feet moving through endless Connectors. In the river, everywhere was near. Everything connected.

We stepped out of the water at the same time. Jenn asked, "Did that just happen?"

"Shazam," I said, being otherwise speechless.

"Hello, friends," hailed a being from the tree stone gatherers. "Might you assist? Maelstrom has our Frames under siege, so our crew is short today."

Jenn clapped like a toddler and called to the gatherers, "Yes! How do we get out there?"

I told her, "You go ahead, I've got library research to do," and I waved regrets to the gatherers and headed up the path.

The gatherers made a practiced throw with a sisal rope and it caught on a branch above Jenn's head. Two humanoid gatherers used the rope to do a sideways belay across the river to where she stood. They had Jenn in the center of the river by the time I climbed the bluff to the Halls of Shared Knowledge. I climbed with gusto, thanks to my ankle–dip in the river.

My goal at the Halls today was to find out how Maelstrom enslaved books. The grandmaters had mentioned a device. That implied –

"Welcome, book tamer." The bookcase hailed me with a new warmth.

Now that was a good nickname. "Hi there, it's good to be back. Don't spread that around though, about me and the books."

"Certainly not. These are not the Halls of Stupidity."

Another flare–up of my chronic condition, open–mouth–insert–foot disease. "Good line!" I forced a laugh and after a moment the bookcases joined me. "Joking aside, your support means the Frames to me and increases by a million times my chance of success." I ignored the cynical mathoid inside me who riffed on what you get when you multiply a million times zero.

"How may we help thee today?" The warm tones were back.

"I want to see everything about the beginning of the enslavement."

"Still exploring the beginning."

I'd like to think it was strategy and not ego that compelled me to pretend my investigation had progressed. "And. The latest. I'm here to see the oldest and the newest."

"An intriguing approach. Please step to a viewer."

The *newest* footage played immediately. The scene jumped across the viewer with black and gray gaps, piecemeal and patchwork. The viewer informed, "This scene has no ending, it is in progress."

I zoomed in. That was Anya! Wasn't it? And Kelly Joe? They appeared and then they were gone. Others appeared and vanished, too. The black and gray gaps shrank as events evolved. The action was taking place on Manhattan's Lower East Side—in the background was the entrance to Brooklyn Bridge—but in a Frame I'd never been, with sidewalk and street that flexed like trampolines, and buildings that shed glass with crashes like cymbals. The racket was mind–boggling and the Lobotomists who filled the streets looked ready to stampede.

There was nowhere safe for them to be. Anya, Kelly Joe, and other allies would burst in from another Frame, just long enough to shoot flamethrowers. Meanwhile, books rained text whenever the allies appeared, hitting nearby Lobotomists. Other Lobotomists tripped on the bouncing street and, when one fell, the others walked over them. Closer to the buildings, they were safe from text but got cut by falling glass. Through all this, the trainers kept calling, without inflection, "To the bridge. Continue or die."

The allies would vanish then appear somewhere new, blast flames and disappear again. A group of allies appeared with nets, netted a cluster of hovering books, then vanished with the captured books. The trainers screamed, "Fools. Preserve those books, they are fresh and can be retrained. With books we win."

The allies did not return.

"Zoom in on that crate," I instructed the viewer. Books that weren't flying sat in what looked like fireproof safes.

Yup and damn. That magenta dust cover with the pink script. It was a chick–lit bestseller. You know the kind, full of movie diseases and manipulation. When I'd bought my copies of *Lose Twenty Pounds*, that novel had the biggest display in the bookstore. I bring this up, not to disparage the reading tastes of the American public, but to note that this was a recently published book and the Lobotomist safe was full of them. Which meant that Maelstrom had resumed enslaving books. The allies diverted a trickle while Maelstrom readied a flood.

61. THE TROUBLE THAT HAPPENS

When I left the Halls, I still didn't know *how* Maelstrom enslaved books, yet I'd learned much that was important. During the time that Maelstrom was trapped by Frame collapse, the enslavement of additional books stopped. Many trained soldier books were loose in the Frames and a service subculture sprung up to exploit these powerful weapons. These books became mercenaries, killing for hire. Middlemen called librarians arose; the librarians recruited mercenaries and controlled them with special nets and flamethrowers.

A mercenary's allegiance could shift suddenly. My guess about those shifts was that Maelstrom, trapped in his Frame collapse, held early editions of some books and sometimes he'd put one in his device, to change the allegiance of later editions. Which meant that back then, he'd kept the device with him.

When I got back to the bluff overlooking the Hudson, Jenn was still riding somebody's back in the middle of the river and seemed to have turned tree stone gathering into a game. Jenn was doing fine; I had time to make another visit to Marzipan in hopes of finishing my conversation with the proustel vendor.

This time I Traveled to Marzipan from Julian's front stoop, one hand on the doorknob behind me. If I Traveled into trouble, I would open the door and fall inside Julian while changing Frames.

The trouble I'm ready for is never the trouble that happens. When I got to Marzipan, the streets were deserted as far as I could see, which was not very far in the icy fog. I strained to hear in the dense silence. The silence that punctuates your 'hello' when your phone rings at 3 a.m. The silence before the pain when you run your hand through the table saw.

There was no sense that life had ever existed in Marzipan. But there was a presence. Something. Waiting. The lanyard gave me no warning. The lanyard was so heavy I couldn't inhale.

If I went to the corner I might see something. I lifted one foot, couldn't get it to step away from Julian's front door. My body had decided: leaving Julian had a bad risk to reward ratio.

Something rushed up the steps and slammed my shins, knocking me backwards. As I fell into Julian's foyer, I took a kick at the something, then realized it was orange and furry. Meanwhile, I Traveled away from Marzipan, so fast I was back to the Halls of Shared Knowledge before I hit the parquet floor of Julian's foyer. A vertigo headache imploded my eyeballs and when I clutched my eye sockets, I was surprised to find them still packed with my eyes.

The orange furry collider had Traveled beside me, and now shook his head a couple times as though to clear it. "Leon! I kicked you! I'm so sorry!"

I petted him and he purred, briefly but forcefully, which I took as reassurance he was fine. Apparently he had wanted me out of Marzipan, pronto.

Time to get Jenn and go home. Leon did his cockroach scurry beside me as I returned to the bluff overlooking the Hudson River.

Jenn spotted me immediately as though she had been watching for me. A pair of quadrupeds sideways–belayed her to the river bank while the rest of the crew called farewells. From the river shallows, she called up to me, "I need help getting up this mountain."

I ran down the path to join her. Up close I could see the slack in her muscles: Jenn looked exhausted. She kept her feet in the river until I arrived and when she stepped onto land, she staggered. I ducked down to toss her over my shoulder. I could carry her, but only as a sack of taters.

I have bony shoulders. Jenn shifted to get comfortable and spotted Leon behind me on the path. "That's the same cat from back home. There really are juju cats? Fuckin' A."

I got her back to Ma'Urth and helped her stretch out on my couch, then sank to the floor beside her. Traveling for two was like running on the bottom of a pool.

I awoke in a chilly dark, remembering a hot summer day of long ago.

In fourth grade, Jenn and I had a thing for soap bubbles and my hands have never been cleaner than they were that summer. All day every day we waved bubble wands, sudsing our backyards. One day we tried to adorn ourselves with bubbles, but our clothes were too rough for the delicate skins of the bubbles. So we stripped. It was Jenn's turn to plant bubbles all over me when her mother shrieked at us to get dressed. According to Jenn's mother's tone, she'd lifted her pillow and found slugs on her sheet. I grabbed for my clothes, but Jenn stood still and talked back, softly. "It's just our skin, mom."

She never let anyone shame her.

The things we remember and the times we remember them.

Jenn still slept and her breathing had no more hitches than usual. She didn't stir when I scribbled a note, donned my backpack, and grabbed the bags from my shopping excursion.

Lying there, Jenn looked about as tough as one of our soap bubbles. I didn't see Leon anywhere, but fortunately, Dizzy snoozed beside Jenn. "Keep her safe, Dizz."

62. HIS MOTHER WAS A HERO

I needed to talk to a grandmater. They were connected beings so I only needed to talk to one to reach them all. I headed for West 48th Street, but when I got to the block with the grannies' safe house it felt wrong and my lanyard began to sting. I walked that block humming my mantra and poised to Travel to Frivolous Bedlam. I passed the safe house as though it were just another building, continued to Tenth Avenue, and glanced back. I might have seen Lobotomists exiting a building.

I hightailed it to Frivolous Bedlam, where the block was empty and vibe free and the lanyard had no warnings. I entered the safe house building and Traveled to the Frame where the grannies were hiding.

I fussed with the shower knobs for a lot longer than Anwyl had done, but eventually managed to open the secret panel. The hidden room was nearly empty, with no male models, and only eleven grandmaters still there. Didn't look like Hari!–Ya would need my help much, transporting grannies.

The grannies did not look up from their placement of food bits and napkin scraps. Their mandala had grown to occupy the back half of the room.

"I've got something for you," I announced. No one looked up. With an unappreciated flourish I upended my shopping bags. Long tubes and small jars rolled toward the grannies, flashing with millions of beads in a multitude of colors shapes sizes.

I had their attention. Rather, the beads did. They dropped the bits of napkins and food and from then on crafted the mandala with beads. They barely glanced at the containers as they worked, yet combined the colors and shapes in spectacular patterns, as though Kandinsky had designed time–lapse flowers.

Behind me, fabric rustled and I jumped. Hari!–Ya lowered her hands, which were above one shoulder and gripped a machete.

"When I saw that the panel was open –" She sounded apologetic as she sheathed the blade in a sling on her hip. "Welcome, friend. This mission is soon complete, well ahead of Anwyl's schedule."

"And not a minute too soon." I described the beings I'd seen, searching this block in other Frames.

"Yes, our foes approach. Grandmaters, pack what you would take. Very soon we must away." They ignored us, of course. She said to me, "Persuasion I deem one of your specialties."

"It's hard to persuade a being who doesn't want anything." We watched the grannies arrange beads. "I need to ask them some questions, but I can ask on the other end of our trip." Two grannies emptied containers to make a mountain of beads and the others took beads from that pile. This wasn't packing to go, it was settling in for a night of mandala–building.

My frustration must have showed. Hari!–Ya said, "They will cooperate when the moment so dictates, won't you, grandmaters?" No answer, of course. Hari!–Ya's leathery skin crackled when she smiled. "Ask questions as you can. In a thousand breaths we must away."

"Okay, but I can't count that high."

"I can." Her laugh was odd but great, like rain on a snare drum. She joined me kneeling beside the grannies. "Nica, I wish for you to know that mine is not an evil race. Misguided, rather. Our thoughts are easily poisoned."

"I believe you."

"I must show you something that not even Anwyl knows."

Of course I said yes—it seemed important to her and how could I resist knowing more than Anwyl? She took my hand and Traveled me to a Frame that was distant, given my nausea and headache. She jogged us upstairs to a third floor apartment where a Cobra woman nursed two infants. A Cobra man was in the kitchen, washing dishes.

"These are my comrades, Raff and Nada. Cobras who support the allies are hiding through the Frames. Nada holds her daughter," Hari!–Ya gestured to a leathery blob with a misshapen skull that could only be an infant Cobra person. Then she reached for the other baby, a perfect and adorable infant male model. Seeing him made me want to drop everything and become a mother. "And this is my son." Hari!–Ya stared at her baby as though to memorize him. She told the others, "Here is Nica. When I am killed or captured, she will come to you."

When not *if* Hari!–Ya was captured or killed. Her role in the conflict guaranteed a short life span.

I said my hellos to the others, then told Hari!–Ya, "You can count on me. I will let them know what befalls you and I will do whatever I can to keep them safe. And I will make sure your son knows that his mother was a hero."

Hari!–Ya returned focus to her son for nearly a minute, ignoring all else. He whimpered when she returned him to Nada. Raff set aside the dishes and took his daughter so that Nada could comfort the boy.

Ironically, only the babies weren't crying when we left.

As Hari!–Ya Traveled us back to the grannies, she boomeranged from doubt to anger to doubt. "My son might have been safe from persecution at home, because even though he is a seeder, my family has long birthed seeders that evolved to grandmaters. We are respected despite the shame of our babies. Yet in these days when hatreds burn so hot –" Her voice broke. "I know not whether I chose rightly."

"That's assuming there is a right choice."

She stopped down the hall from the grannies' hidden room. I got the sense she wanted a moment to compose herself and get back in warrior mode. "Tell of your Frame. Do you know prejudice there?"

"Oh, yeah, we got that. You know. If I were a mom I would have done like you. Got my kid the hell out."

Which left her needing more time to compose.

The beads had revolutionized the grannies' mandala construction. The floor was now as colorful as a field of wildflowers.

"Take up the belongings you wish to take, we must away, grandmaters," Hari!–Ya greeted them. For once, the grannies listened. They grabbed empty bead tubes and refilled them by scooping them into the mountains of unused beads. They returned filled tubes to the bag.

There's no feeling like it—the satisfaction of buying somebody the perfect gift.

I knelt beside a bead mountain. "Grandmaters, I have an important question." They scooped beads. "You told me that Maelstrom uses a device to enslave books." The air shifted; they might be listening. "Where is that device?"

They scooped beads. I shrugged and stood, disappointed but not surprised. Had they heard me? Understood me? Were they completely incorrigible? About the time I mentioned having a question, two of them had uncorked some tubes and resumed work on the mandala.

Hari!–Ya touched my arm as though I were about to step into a sinkhole. "Tread carefully in that quest. You are important to our fight."

"Shit," I responded. Outside the building, synchronized marching sounded way too much like the Entourage. Below us, the building door smashed opened. Hari!–Ya pulled on the panel to the secret room and it slid shut, closing us in and buying a bit more time.

"Grab hands and away," Hari!–Ya ordered. The grannies stuffed bead tubes in their bosoms then stood and cooperated, perhaps because I had confiscated the bags of beads. *If you want the beads, come with us.* Quick but calm, Hari!–Ya arranged us, holding hands, and before she Traveled us out of Frame, I spotted the newest mandala section, where the grannies had just added beads.

Their mandalas always reminded me of the Connector map and this section was a part of the Connector map that I recognized. It included the area of Frame collapse where Maelstrom had been imprisoned. They had just poured black beads on top of the Frame collapse area. Could this be their answer to my question about the location of Maelstrom's device? How? They had started pouring black beads before I asked them where the device was.

When we reached a Frame that Hari!–Ya deemed safe, she wanted to leave a pair of grandmaters in that Frame. They wanted to stay together as eleven musketeers. Finally, I snapped. "Your resistance delays us and risks all our lives." This had no effect on the grannies.

Frustrated, I shook the bag of beads. A tube flew out and I stepped on it, crushing the beads. "Too bad you won't cooperate, really a waste!"

I hate it when *outta control* is the solution. A pair of grannies dropped hands and stepped away from the others. They would stay in this Frame. I held open the bag and the departing grannies selected 2/11ths of the beads and dropped down to begin a mandala.

As Hari!–Ya Traveled the rest of us to yet another Frame, I called to the pair we were leaving behind, "Find shelter. Protect yourselves. I'll bring more beads."

We had just deposited the third pair of grannies in a third Frame when I felt a rat gnawing inside my skull, a sensation that meant someone nearby was snooping in my thoughts. I went blank and stayed that way, so I lost track of which or how many Frames we visited.

We were down to the final three grannies when Hari!–Ya said, "We must continue separately. We have hunters behind us but they follow my trace, not yours. Take these to Next Vast. They are expected."

"I'm so sorry. I'm not skilled enough to Travel with three other living beings."

"You will succeed. The grandmaters have a lightness of being."

Hari!–Ya called to me as she disappeared out of Frame, "Farewell, my friend. I thank you for your promise."

It twisted my gut, wondering whether I'd see her again.

63. PANDEMONIUM'S MECHANIC

Hari!—Ya was right about Travel with the grannies. Taking three grandmaters through many Frames to Next Vast was no more difficult than transporting a ladybug. I got back to my apartment on Ma'Urth feeling positively perky.

Hail hail, my gang was all there. Kelly Joe did not look up from his guitar, which he played from the same spot where he had played at the last house concert. Everyone else nodded, smiled, or *what—upped* me. On the couch, Jenn sat between Hernandez and Anya. In the hall outside the bathroom, Zasu danced like sunlight on surf. In the kitchen, Anwyl paced.

Next thing I knew, Kelly Joe was packing up and Anya was standing beside him. "Thank you, musician, for that insight and hope. Nica, welcome home."

I flashed the smile of the unburdened. For once, I didn't have to dissemble about where I'd been; relocating the grandmaters was an Anwyl—appointed job.

Anya continued, "Why sought you this meeting?"

Hernandez got to his feet. "Want to propose an adjustment to strategy. You're fighting battles, outnumbered, while I'm underutilized. I know war. I know sabotage, too, but how about if I scale back on torching buildings and join you more often when you're fighting?" It was as close to questioning an order as Hernandez could get.

Anya replied, "Our modest numbers do not threaten our victories. All your abilities will be well and fully tapped. For the non, we look to you to ready this island for the cataclysm to come."

Hernandez seemed to want to say more, but sank down to the couch with a look to Jenn.

Jenn spoke up. "Aren't we hurting the buildings when we sabotage the construction sites? They're alive, right?"

Anwyl waved his fingers like Jenn's questions were a pesky fly. "Your damage affects only this Neutral Frame, where the buildings feel little."

Anwyl had been dismissive, but Jenn isn't easily dismissed. "Will we have enough people when the time comes to fight Maelstrom?"

"Whatever our numbers, we will make those enough," Anwyl said.

Anya corrected gently, "But when war begins, it will be Warty Sebaceous Cysts that we fight, not Maelstrom."

Anwyl explained, "Warty Sebaceous Cysts lead the wars. Maelstrom devours the survivors." Which maybe added to our insight, but wasn't good for morale. "But mistake this not. We are not yet at war. These battles are but skirmishes."

Some of the battles I'd witnessed might call skirmishes, but the conflict in Marzipan seemed harsher. I blurted, "I'm worried about Marzipan, it felt empty last time I was there. And bad. Deserted in a really bad way." Anwyl and Anya stared at me until I regretted speaking. As far as they knew, I had no business in Marzipan. But they stared for a more basic reason.

"She means Marzipan," Kelly Joe said.

"Oh, Marzipan," Anya said.

Hand to heart, their pronunciations were the same as mine. My sigh crashed waves into Gibraltar.

Anya and Anwyl exchanged a look. Anwyl said, "You bear ill news about Marzipan. Show us. Warriors, follow Nica."

Zasu joined Jenn on the couch—they weren't warriors. I led the others down my street on Ma'Urth, to the intersection with Amsterdam Avenue, where the cold empty fog had been thickest in Marzipan. Anwyl fell into step beside me. He had restless eyes today, checking every cranny and shadow.

We waited outside the corner Starbucks for Anya, Kelly Joe, and Hernandez to catch up. Something inside a building foyer had caught their attention. I had time for a little praise–mongering. "I have good news. Hari!–Ya finished her mission to relocate the grandmaters. I helped a little."

"Yes, she told of this. You have a new mission. Tonight Hari!–Ya must rescue another of our allies among the Cobra people. Join Hari!–Ya on Brooklyn Bridge at dusk, so that you might assist with the rescue."

I couldn't decide what jazzed me more—Anwyl's trusting me with insider missions, or standing this close to him for this long. Ego, libido, when they join forces I'm doomed.

In Marzipan the fog was thicker and colder. If the Frame was sick before, now its maggots had cancer. We weren't too late because there had never been any hope of saving Marzipan. Or anywhere else. I dropped to my knees. Slime coated my throat, barbed wire bit my lungs. I heard screams in the distance—make that, inside my head.

Anwyl crouched with his back to us. Anya pulled me close, pressing one ear against her heart. Its slow pounding elevated my attitude to the level of despair.

"Take cover? Over there?" Hernandez' voice trembled until Anya set a hand on his head.

Meanwhile, Kelly Joe marched into the intersection where the worst vibe throbbed and vanished into the fog. I strained to hear his steps between Anya's heartbeats.

Anya released us Neutrals at the same time that Kelly Joe called, "He's gone," and stomped back out of the fog, sounding disgusted.

Before I could pose the question, Anya answered, "Maelstrom was here."

Anwyl gestured for us to follow him, his ear cocked as though he followed a sound. Anya held my hand and I knew my attitude was improving when I resumed feeling afraid—it takes hope to feel fear.

A block later, I heard what Anwyl had heard—howls and screams.

The anguish came from a clump of blue– and white–furred beings on a school playground. They had the weary kindness of grade school teachers. Another teacher exited a building, guiding a stumbling child whose white fur stuck out in all directions. The emerging teacher cried, "He alone survives!" and more wails erupted.

They spotted us and shouted over each other. "Anya daughter of Niav... Anwyl son of Rayn! We beg your aid! ... Maelstrom engulfed us ... While we were stunned with hopelessness, Lobotomists stole the children ... Please save these innocents."

Impressive, the way they sprang into action. Hernandez ushered the Marzipani to the side of the school building, where they were more shielded. Anya posed questions that reassured while extracting critical information like *how many, how long ago*. Kelly Joe played his harmonica until the child stopped ducking whenever anyone spoke.

Anwyl ran out to the street at a crouch, following a scent. He called to us, "Here lies their path away."

"We're faster than they are, let's catch up." Kelly Joe pocketed his harmonica.

Anya told me, "Remain here. If foes appear, take the child to your Frame of safety." She meant Frivolous Bedlam and now was not the time to ask why she wouldn't mention it by name. She clasped my arms. "You did well to bring us here. Remain vigilant."

And they were gone. The teachers, the child and I huddled on the edge of the big empty playground.

The teachers debated what they might have done differently, to stop the Lobotomists. The disagreement grew heated.

To get their attention, I waved then pointed like Townshend thrashing a guitar, and I used a voice I'd learned from Anya, which filled the air without yelling. "Look! What you're doing!" The boy knelt, cringing, with hands over his ears.

The teachers clammed up and looked like Mrs. Meacham, my childhood neighbor, the day she drowned her daughter's guinea pig in the wash. "Maelstrom's got everybody upset," I reassured them.

"How long must we wait to know their fate?" one teacher asked. The playground filled with ghosts of missing children.

"I wish I knew. But while we're waiting, you can help me stop Maelstrom. Answer some questions for me." Belief that they could fight Maelstrom brought them back from the cliff where they'd been sparring. Sometimes fake confidence is what it takes. *Be the bullshit.* "Maelstrom had a device to enslave books. Someone from Marzipan helped Maelstrom with it. What is it? How does it work?"

The teachers grew tall and stiff. One with dark–blue fur stepped forward to face me. "We thank thee for these questions. Through all the cycles we carry the shame of complicity and we welcome this chance to ease our burden. I am the seventeenth in my line. My forefather, the seventh in my line, was forced to serve as Pandemonium's mechanic to that dire machine. At first he refused, which brought war to Marzipan and many died. The mechanic briefly escaped his sorry fate after Pandemonium was captured in Frame collapse, but then Maelstrom's minions abducted him. In those days, Maelstrom was believed dead. It was we, the Marzipani, who sounded the alarm that Maelstrom still lived, had abducted the mechanic, and intended to enslave more tomes.

"All this is knowledge common to all Marzipani. However, one of us also possesses the personal memories of that mechanic. In this way we retained his experience but limited the distress of those memories. Until now. The Marzipani are Maelstrom's eternal foes. Now we will share those memories so that we may give them to thee."

As though they operated on a switch, all the furred grownups closed their eyes.

Seconds or minutes elapsed. At some point my foot shuffled. The eyes of all the furred grownups popped open. I faked a smile and froze. Their eyes drifted shut again. I lost count after 67 breaths, which was the longest I've ever stood still. I'm told that even in deep sleep I'm restless. Science says that smiling makes us happier, even if the smile is faked. Maybe my fake stillness would—gak!

Twelve pairs of eyes popped open. Dark–blue reported, "According to the memories of my forefather, the mechanic, Pandemonium took a printing press and converted it to become an imprinting press. With this press, she and later Maelstrom enslaved books."

My reaction zoomed back and forth along the disappointed–insulted continuum. I'd hoped for a plausible answer. But could I recognize one if I heard it? "An *im*printing press? What does that mean, did Pandemonium make a magic printing press?"

A teacher with bright–white fur replied, "If by magic you mean a machine with workings that are understood poorly and by few, then yes, call it magic. It does not hurt to think it so."

Dark–blue added, "Remember that books are manufactured beings and as such, can be controlled. Pandemonium developed a means to control them. Books, when sent through this press, became the operator's slaves, as did their offspring."

"By 'offspring' do you mean later editions?"

They closed their eyes and after a time, opened them to say, "Yes."

"What can you tell me about how this press works? How do I shut it down or reverse the process?"

"Before he took his own life, the mechanic told his granddaughter all that we have conveyed to you. It was she who shared the memories with us but she has no gift for machinery so his mechanic's knowledge of the imprinting press is lost. Thus —"

"Not all have perished!" The teachers ran past me, all but Bright–white, who stayed with the boy.

Across the playground, Kelly Joe strode into Frame with three tots perched on his shoulders and back. Six older munchkins clung to a rug that he dragged behind him. He called to us, "The Lobotomists split in three directions. In the direction I followed were seven dead and these survivors. They've seen too much."

At *seven dead*, the teachers began to carry on, which emphasized how absent of emotion the children were. They stared at the teachers, the school, each other.

Kelly Joe blew a harsh chord on his harmonica and in the startled silence, he gave orders. He deployed some teachers to care for the children, some to fetch the children's parents, some to stand guard until the other allies returned. Then he walked away without a goodbye.

I jogged after him. "I have to go to Maelstrom's Frame. Show me how to do it safely."

He kept walking. "There's no *safely* to that."

64. GO THERE, STOP IT

"Then show me *least unsafely*." I jogged to keep pace. "I have to go there. It's what I have to do." Kelly Joe hadn't looked surprised, I realized in retrospect. "I know you don't want to go back to that Frame."

He cast me the world's briefest glance.

I replied to its content. "You're right, I don't know a frigging thing about it." We walked a block in silence.

"We'll start from Frivolous Bedlam," he announced. "That's the least unsafe route."

"Thank you," I said. When words are inadequate, keep them simple.

As soon as we Traveled to Bedlam, I said, "I need to stop at my apartment. I'll be quick." Kelly Joe waited on Julian's front stoop while I ran upstairs. Inside my apartment, I unshouldered my backpack, removed *Lose Twenty Pounds*, gave a few instructions, and returned outside.

On Julian's front stoop, Kelly Joe twisted notes on his harp. I asked, "Do you ever break out into a tune on that thing?"

"They're tunes to me. You left your backpack inside."

"I did."

"A woman of plots and schemes," he said without judgment.

"Sometimes they turn out to be plans and strategies." I sat beside him.

"Will you be looking for something in Maelstrom's Frame?"

"His imprinting press—a special printing press he stole from Pandemonium. He uses it to enslave books. It used to be in that Frame with him, based on what I learned in the Halls of Shared Knowledge."

"You've been to the Halls," Kelly Joe bent some contemplative notes.

"You're basically the only one who knows that, too."

"A woman of schemes and strategies."

Around us, the buildings traded knock–knock jokes in the sun. Kelly Joe did finger twirls with his harmonica. He stopped twirling and said, "We'll try a place that's isolated but close to Party City."

"Party City. I'm guessing the Cysts named that one."

"No allies have seen Party City for many cycles. We could walk into— anything."

"Tell me more about the isolated place." I followed him up the street.

"It is—was—where Central Park lies. Maelstrom always reshaped the land and it could be something else now. Also, Maelstrom has machines that eavesdrop and listen for sounds that don't belong. We'll walk in a way that disguises our steps."

He taught me the special walk as we headed into the Upper East Side. The basic idea was to walk without pattern, with an erratic gait like we were on the sands of Dune hiding from the giant worms. Easy to explain, mind–scramblingly hard to do. But finally I got it—or close enough—and Kelly Joe said, "Good. That'll do."

My buddies the food carts followed at a distance but when we got to Museum Row, they spun around and raced each other back toward Midtown. I didn't blame them. In Bedlam, the Upper East Side is yawnsville: most of the buildings are sentient and they stand around like Ph.D.s at a cocktail party.

Just past the Metropolitan Museum, Kelly Joe said, "Here we go." He took my hand and he didn't Travel us all that far but I got a headache–nausea package worthy of a jump to the Far Frames. Might have been stress.

In Maelstrom's Frame, it had been gray and damp for so long that the fog had mold. The air was still, expectant, a twilight gloom that never changed to nightfall.

Our approach along Fifth Avenue put us at the lip of a crater. To the west, where Central Park should have been, was a blasted pit with steep trails winding through sharp rocks and black canyons. To the east, the Upper East Side was a rubble of broken concrete and asphalt with, here and there, a building foundation, crazed and cracked. Every few blocks a building still stood, dark and void.

Muffled but sharp, clanks and growls filled the air. I couldn't place their direction. Kelly Joe put his hand over my mouth before I could warn him that those were the sounds of clockwork dogs. He put finger to lips but I'd already got the message to be quiet.

Using our erratic gaits, we tiptoed down the steep incline of Central Park crater. The rock that lined our trail was shattered and gouged and as we went deeper, the ground seeped as though infected. Loose rock covered the slopes and cascaded in spontaneous avalanches that echoed and masked any noise we made. Nonetheless, I did my best to move as quietly as Kelly Joe did.

As we descended, the dogs sounded near yet far. Other noises also came from everywhere and nowhere: scrapes of machinery, bursts of flowing liquid, footfalls.

Half way down into the crater, all ambient noise ceased. Kelly Joe spoke in his usual soft tones which, in the quiet, startled me like Tchaikovsky's cymbals. "The crater blocks sound below this point. Before Maelstrom was imprisoned, he didn't know this crater was dead to sound. He's had time to make that discovery but perhaps he hasn't done so."

"Or he could be spying on us right now."

"We'll know soon enough."

I listened for indications that the clockwork dogs were coming to get us. But I could no longer hear them. The Frame was on mute here. Clockwork dogs could be at the lip of the crater and we wouldn't hear them. Kelly Joe led us deeper into the crater.

"We can't change Frames from down here, we have to go back to the surface, huh? Because in other Frames, there's no crater and this area is solid rock."

"That's correct. We'll return to the surface soon to find the imprinting press. Or have you changed your mind about looking for it?"

"No, but we'd better go before I lose my nerve completely." I'd never been anywhere that felt as bad as this Frame did. Pain and distress suffocated us like nuclear fallout. "How could you stand it here for so long?" The words slipped out—I was incapable of discussing his past without heavy doses of judgment and maybe that was justified but now was not the time.

Surprisingly, he answered as though it were any old question. "Back then, Maelstrom hid his nature. Now, listen up. You'll get tired and sore, but you must maintain that erratic walk. Clockwork dogs have a poor sense of smell and weak eyesight but they sense changes to air currents, as do books and chainsaws that may be on patrol. If our steps have pattern they'll change air currents."

As soon as I nodded, he led us up toward the surface of Central Park crater. He stopped one more time. "Stay within reach. If we're spotted, grab my hand no matter what else happens. From here on, we can't speak, and we'll only gesture when we have to."

"Because gestures can change air currents."

"They surely can."

I followed his instructions flawlessly. That wasn't just for my own safety but to make sure that no one and nothing noticed our visit. If Maelstrom found out his Frame had had visitors, he'd make sure it could never happen again.

The erratic walk used muscles in alien combinations. By the time we were out of Central Park crater, I had cramps in my buttocks and both calves. Which helped with erratic movements but not with keeping quiet.

We headed into Midtown. There, the rubble of concrete and asphalt was uneven but not loose, so I didn't slip much; we heard many clockwork dogs but encountered none; and only three of my cramps progressed to charley horses—so our trek was full of luck. Perhaps that depleted our future supply.

South of Central Park crater, clusters of buildings stood intact yet brittle—like the marrow was sucked from them—and no longer plumb. I wished them the relief of final collapse. The damp air smelled like dead possum soaked in vinegar and building ruins added dusty mildew to the bouquet. I shoved my face into Kelly Joe's chest to stifle a gagging cough. He stroked my back, which calmed the spasm, then tapped my head to get my attention and showed me how he breathed through his mouth behind his shirt. We resumed our trek south, deeper into Party City.

We passed sporadic heaps of tattered fabric. I looked too long at one—it was a pile of bones in decayed garments. The fabric was colorful and the bones were small. About the time the pattern–recognition part of my brain thought *children*, the analytic part of my brain noticed they had been clawing at, climbing over each other. The self–protective part of my brain focused on my erratic walk and a recurring noise, a rasping mechanical squeak.

The squeak was explained when we got to Times Square, where stood a black translucent tent and a marvelous Rube Goldberg set–up which in other circumstances would have enchanted me.

A conveyor belt ran along 46th Street, ending at the tent. On its eastern end, near Sixth Avenue, the conveyor belt emerged from a Connector. The conveyor belt carried a steady line of crates from the Connector—and whatever Frame was on the other end of the Connector—to the black tent. The crates must be heavy, because the conveyor belt sagged under each crate. At the other end of the conveyor belt, in front of the tent, was a shallow pit and when the crates reached the end of the conveyor belt they tipped off into the pit. Every time a crate fell off the conveyor belt, the belt flexed upward with that rasping squeak.

When a crate fell into the pit, it broke open and spilled its contents. Books. Three mechanical arms plucked books from the pit and arrayed them on narrow trays that delivered books into the tent, one after another. Inside the tent was a massive metal box, the mutant spawn of a wringer washer and a pizza oven. The front had a hinged flap that dropped open with a shriek as each book arrived. Dense red air gusted from inside the box to cover the nearest book, then, with a groan, the gust changed direction and the swirling air sucked the book inside the metal box. The flap slammed shut and the tray advanced, bringing the next book closer.

One at a time, books slid out the back of the metal box into a narrow channel under black netting like the allies used to catch books. From there, each book fluttered and wobbled its way into an enormous netted tent that stretched south along Broadway and teemed with flying books.

This had to be Maelstrom's imprinting press and briefly I sustained hope that it faced imminent demise. The press wheezed and shuddered. Its metal was pocked with decay cankers; carbuncles of rust stiffened its joints. Every movement sounded painful. Each ingestion might be its last! This hope died when a flake of orange–crusted rust shook loose to expose bright new steel beneath. As I continued to watch, the ancient skin refreshed itself in other spots, also.

We observed the operation for some time. I tried to memorize every detail of the press and conveyor system and thought about how simple my life had been four month–eternities prior, before Anya and Anwyl entered my office in Los Angeles.

Kelly Joe made minimalist gestures—hand shaded eyes, hand cupped ear, head shook—which I took to mean that he didn't see or hear any beings nearby. Indeed, no one seemed to be tending or guarding the facility. Then his arm made a jerky ratcheting motion, imitating the three mechanical arms that fed books to the press.

A crate of books failed to split apart when it fell from the conveyor belt. A mechanical arm grabbed the crate and broke it open against the side of the pit by tapping it like an egg shell against an omelet pan—except this egg weighed hundreds of pounds and spanned several feet. Kelly Joe squatted and, moving in slo'–mo', hefted a chunk of broken sidewalk. He flicked it to hit the ground on the other side of the conveyor belt. All three mechanical arms swiveled in that direction. When nothing else out of the ordinary happened, two of the arms resumed organizing books and cracking crates, while the third arm swung back and forth as though on guard.

I got Kelly Joe's message. The mechanical arms were strong and they were sentient. I watched them until I understood their range of motion, knew where they could—and couldn't—reach. Warty Sebaceous Cysts must have designed the mechanical arms because they were absurd. One had a paw that ended in a butterfly net, one had a hand with fat gloved cartoon fingers like Mickey Mouse's, one was a wire–frame hand with six digits—the sixth being an extra thumb—and digit tips decorated in hot pink lacquer paint.

The mechanical arms, like the press, were rusting but sturdy with no sign of weak spots. I'd need explosives. Maybe I could steal the press, that might be easier than destroying it. But. There must be a reason that beings of genuinely great power hadn't tried that. Or maybe they had.

The arms continued to feed books to the maw of the press and next I fantasized about simply finding an *off* switch. But then somebody could switch it back *on*. Maybe somebody at the other end of that Connector. Whoever was putting crates on the conveyor belt would come to investigate if crates piled up and jammed the belt.

Why were there no guards? Maelstrom didn't seem concerned about protecting this treasure and his confidence was harmful to my own.

Maybe my books could take out the press. Books freeing books. That was justice. But what if they ran out of text before they'd sliced the press to bits? And then there were the mechanical arms. Maybe those arms were the reason no guards were needed.

Well, I could fret until cows stampeded, but the bottom line had to be this: the machine had been created, therefore it could be destroyed. Now that I'd seen the press, I could develop a better plan for its demolition. Admittedly, any plan would be better than my current *go there, stop it.*

But why were there no guards? I'd been coasting on my belief that I would succeed because I had to succeed. What a ludicrous idea. But then those were the kinds of ideas one should expect from a fool like me.

Kelly Joe touched a finger to my arm. I copied his slightest hint of skyward gaze. Overhead flew a squadron of books. They circled twice then continued south on Broadway, stirring commotion in the tent of newly enslaved books. The squadron was intimidating and thus reassuring. The press did need protection. I missed the protective weight of my own books on my back, as if my mere backpack of books could protect me from a squadron. As if that squadron was the only source of menace in this Frame.

As if I knew enough about the press or explosives to make a plan.

The skies filled with howls, close far near distant and, on average, closing in. My pulse rate doubled but Kelly Joe's movements remained slow, erratic, and spare. He led us to a building northwest of the intersection, a two–story steel box with plate glass windows overlooking the press. The plate glass windows had jagged breaks that zigzagged out from the corners: the building's foundation had shifted more than once. An open doorway led to a long flight of stairs. We maintained our erratic pace up to the second floor. At a landing the stairs changed direction and on that second flight of stairs, the outside noises were muffled then faint then gone.

At the top of the stairs was a large empty room. Inside it, Kelly Joe resumed a normal walk and went to the window overlooking the press. The glass was double–paned and both panes were cracked, making the view disjointed like someone had carelessly glued ripped pieces of photos. Nonetheless, the window was a fantastic reconnaissance point with a view east along the conveyer belt to the Connector, south along Broadway and the book cage tent, and below to the back of the imprinting press.

"We'll make return trips to and from this room," Kelly Joe said.

I almost felt hope: this room made a good base of operations and Kelly Joe intended to keep helping.

65. THE BIPOLAR ROLLER COASTER

Kelly Joe Traveled us home to Ma'Urth, where our reconnaissance room was a store that sold candy novelties. The room was packed with tourists but only a small girl in a pink jumpsuit noticed our gradual fade–in to the aisle by the window. She was a little bitty kid so no one paid attention when she squawked and pointed at us.

Outside, the streets were crowded like normal but the vibe was anything but. Moods careened on a bipolar roller coaster. Maelstrom had initially celebrated his escape by cascading fear and anxiety through the Frames, but negative emotions deflate with time, so now he plumped the deflated with excitement, the better to drain them again later. Maybe he wouldn't have to win battles—he could destroy us by unbalancing us.

Thinking like that meant I was on a downward plunge of the bipolar coaster. In fact, around me everyone seemed to be on different loops and the effect was a city that pulsed—not with its usual energy, but with the hysteria you hide when you don't want to spook the mugger whose finger is on the trigger.

At first I didn't understand why Kelly Joe detoured us around the Upper East Side. He pushed the pace like he had to hurry yet insisted we walk back and forth, up and down, block after block; and he seemed surprisingly satisfied to find one more hinky construction site. Then we got back to my apartment, which was packed with allies: Anya, Anwyl, Jenn, Hernandez, and Zasu. Kelly Joe entered ahead of me and announced, "We've checked the East 80s and found two more altered buildings." He rattled off the addresses of two construction sites. One I'd noticed and one I hadn't. They added up to a good alibi for where we'd been since we left Marzipan.

Anya's voice was the usual sunlight on tropical sand, even though her news was mostly funnel clouds. "This night, we shall not rest until we have destroyed all construction abominations of Warty Sebaceous Cysts on Manhattan Island. Come the morrow they will dispatch guards to protect their sites, but they will be too late. Jenn has images of the leader among these guards."

Jenn was so proud her face was pink to the roots of her hair. "I showed Anya this, that's why we have our mission tonight." Jenn carried my laptop from person to person and played a news piece about N.Y.P.D. deployments that would protect construction sites against saboteurs.

When the reporter interviewed the leader of the deployment, Sergeant Guy Bermudez, my eyeballs dissolved with Lilah's last scream.

"Nica?" Jenn noticed my reaction to the interview.

I shook my head—*say nothing*—and stared at the laptop screen. There was Scabman, now called Bermudez and surrounded by N.Y.P.D. uniforms; he headed a special tactical force to stop the construction site attacks. Mathead wasn't in the news piece but she was likely part of the tactical force. Scabman and Mathead had only recently disgraced themselves in the L.A.P.D. but now here they were, transplanted to N.Y.P.D. , apparently without a hitch. For other–Framely denizens, they knew an awful lot about how to play Neutral systems to their advantage.

"We'll get you –" I told the screen, and at Hernandez' frown, I pretended I'd been talking to Jenn. "We'll get you back here to celebrate when you finish off those sites."

Jenn enthused, "I can't wait to see those douchbag faces after tonight."

Yeah. I could have warned her to stay away from Mathead and Scabman. But much as I like to hear myself talk, there was no point—she was climbing the manic slopes of the bipolar roller coaster, which meant she was prone to terrible impulsive decisions. Jenn wasn't the one to keep Jenn safe.

Based on the reactions as Jenn migrated the laptop news story from person to person, everyone but Jenn recognized Scabman from past encounters and none of those were pleasant—but they were probably less awful than my latest interaction.

Anwyl indicated the laptop screen, "Here stands a powerful minion of Warty Sebaceous –"

"He's the one I told you about!" I stopped shouting. "He's the Lobotomist manager. Do you still need his real name before you can do anything about him?"

Anya and Anwyl exchanged a look that made me notice how much I was shaking. Anya murmured, "Well learned, Nica. This is information of potential importance, should we catch him in a Frame where his appearance is similar and his form can be recognized."

Anwyl continued, "This being's presence in the New Yorks confirms the significance of this turf. Our efforts this night may tip an early balance in our favor." He donned what appeared to be a black windbreaker, but was actually a wearable weapon cabinet with many hidden compartments, which he demonstrated as he continued. "Each of you has a crucial role to play. Protect yourselves and one another. No mission is more important than your breath and your life."

At Anywl's gesture, Hernandez distributed similar windbreakers to the others. Anwyl instructed, "Nica has no need of this garment. She will pursue a separate mission tonight, a mission of rescue."

The gadget nerd in me wanted one of those windbreakers, chock full of death–inducing *tchotchkes*. But yes, tonight Hari!–Ya and I would facilitate the escape of another Cobra person. Seems like I always did stuff separate from my team. I wavered between arrogance and despondence about this.

Jenn sagged under the weight of her windbreaker and Anya swapped out weapons until Jenn could move freely again. Seeing them together warmed me from the inside out: how amazing to share Anya with Jenn. And vice versa. Suddenly, the bipolar roller coaster took me in a steep spiral and my love—my need—for them terrified me.

Absorbing Anya's lessons about the windbreaker, Jenn mimicked Anya's smallest movements, but she was still and always Jenn. When Jenn was ready to go, she readjusted nonexistent balls in an imaginary codpiece. At Anya's giggle, Jenn grinned at me and winked at Hernandez.

As the others prepared for departure, Anwyl touched my cheek in that *naked and alone* way he had. "When you complete your mission, come directly here and await my return."

"Your wish, my command."

He flashed some teeth. "Mocking is most effective when tinged with truth."

My smug turned sickly. I didn't know what that meant and suddenly this modest uncertainty was the worst feeling ever. Another twist on Maelstrom's roller coaster. Hernandez had a persistent frown that suggested he was in a shallow downdip, and Jenn was still climbing steeply.

I drew Hernandez aside. "We need our mantras a lot now. Jenn seems especially susceptible, so– " What? Like Hernandez could force Jenn to do her mantra.

Jenn finished converting her windbreaker into a fashion statement and linked elbows with Hernandez to pull him close. They squeezed through the door together as they exited.

Anya overheard or guessed my concerns. "When moods change with such speed, Maelstrom's attention is near. We can safeguard Jenn this eve but you will be far away. Be vigilant in mind and body."

I nodded because she waited for a reaction.

She held my arms and my gaze. "You are strong and can withstand Maelstrom."

I nodded with conviction. She left my apartment with Anwyl and Zasu, discussing strategy.

Kelly Joe was the last to go out. His eyes had a scary sheen—if he was this excited about tonight's mission, it must be ultra dangerous. He slammed the door behind him, then re–opened it and leaned on the doorknob, looking down. The explanation strolled in from the hall: Dizzy. Kelly Joe frowned at the cat as she headed my way and he seemed about to speak, but then Anwyl called him and he was gone.

"Hey Dizz, I'm headed out too." She rubbed against my legs repeatedly in an unusual show of affection. I stumbled against her more than once as I grabbed snacks and a jacket, but I appreciated her nearness. Now that my homies were gone, my apartment felt more empty than my refrigerator.

"Where's Leon?" I wondered as Dizzy trailed me down the block. "It's been a while since I've seen you alone, Dizz."

An orange streak blasted through my legs and behind me. It was Leon, running like hellhounds were on his heels. I turned to see a second blur of fur as Dizzy shot away, just ahead of Leon. The cats disappeared around a corner.

Weird.

"Since when are there stray cats in New York?" Beside me, a woman in the latest autumn trench coat interrogated the universe.

"Actually those aren't –"

"Binky, calm down, they're gone." Binky had to be the Chihuahua dachshund thing that cowered between the woman's ankles. The woman performed a three–step cha–cha that freed her from Binky's tangled leash, and said, "I don't know who to call about stray cats, do you?"

"Don't worry about those cats," I assured her. Binky's eyes strobed, watching for cats or worse. Rat dogs leave me cold, but compassion spiked now. Something about the dog's eyes. Maelstrom was getting to Binky, too.

I resumed my trek to Expletive Deleted, where I would soon yearn for events that were simply weird.

66. SEPARATE TO SURVIVE

With my first step onto Brooklyn Bridge, he greeted me, "This is an ill night for Travel. I will do what I can to keep your steps safe. Hold for a time." I stopped. I waited. Finally, "Proceed—quickly, then pause three Frames hence."

In Expletive Deleted, nothing went according to plan. Hari!–Ya was not waiting for me at the Bridge—at last I spotted her among marchers who filled the streets with angry chanting; many wore identical masks of a male model with bloody daggers protruding from the skull.

Near the area where I was supposed to meet her, I found a woven bag holding a cloak and one of those masks. I pulled them on and ran to catch up as the march stormed north toward the Williamsburg Bridge. The marchers howled for Maelstrom to deliver them from inferiors. Their collective breath smelled like fertilizer.

As I shoved my way forward, it was easy to find Hari!–Ya. The march had a festive, Rise–of–the–Third–Reich feel and all the marchers were really into it, with one exception. Her "hostile" gestures looked more like flinches. Like many of the marchers, she carried a placard with a cartoon depiction of a seeder getting lynched, but she waved hers like it smelled bad. I slammed into her from behind and shook her placard like I meant it.

Another female Cobra jostled us and spat on the placard in a companionable way. Hari!–Ya clapped a welcoming hand on the woman's shoulder and shouted in my ear, "She is ours to save. Mark her well."

The marchers stomped onto the Williamsburg Bridge then stomped in place, waiting their turns to go through the narrow Connector to the government complex suspended above the East River, where the Framekeep coup had occurred. Hari!–Ya kept us on the outskirts and I guess the plan was that we would slip away. But we got pushed forward and we had no choice but to walk the Connector.

The government complex was in ruins. Streetlights were broken and demolished buildings cast shadows like enormous broken teeth. The march pushed south and to stay unnoticed we moved with them. Hari!–Ya and the Cobra woman we were to rescue waved their placards. I held their elbows and steered us to the far west edge of the complex. We marched as slowly as we dared. The vibe of the march was nothing compared to the menace behind these ruined buildings. Jumping into the East River began to seem like a viable alternative to remaining in that complex.

The Framekeep meeting hall had a jagged cavity where the doors had been on the day of the coup. As the marchers cheered, beasts poured from the building openings. I braked. Those beasts, slobbering hot oil, were clockwork dogs.

The suspended streets shook with hundreds of synchronized stomping feet and the far end of the complex filled with goosestepping men. They wore orange plaid suits and had sequined sword scabbards slung over one shoulder. They moved with the precision of a single manufactured being distributed through hundreds of bodies, which is what they were. We'd been joined by a large contingent of the Entourage.

They brandished swords like a demented dance troop and the marchers screamed their enthusiasm. I screamed, too. In fear.

The East River had been babbling like it was overdue for its meds and now spirals of water shot up the bridge pillars. For the first time, I liked that river—because the shooting water made the Entourage hesitate. Any being that earned wary looks from the Entourage couldn't be all bad.

Spotlights snapped on, flooding the area in harsh light. The marchers blinked and the Entourage swiveled toward the Framekeep meeting hall. Three beings stepped outside, each more stubby and ugly than the previous, all wearing orange plaid caftans. *Please let this be a nightmare.* As soon as I thought this, the three beings—the Warty Sebaceous Cysts—turned to applaud in my direction, which meant they were close enough to read my leaky thoughts. It was the last complete thought I allowed myself.

At the sight of the Cysts, the marchers went berserk with joy then silent as Center Cyst raised his arms.

Left Cyst called out, "This concludes your final march."

"Such a shame you have to go," Right Cyst shouted over scraping noises. The Entourage had produced whetstones and sharpened their swords.

"What can we do?" Center Cyst complained rhetorically. "They leave us no choice. They've allowed traitors in their midst."

"Now we can't trust any of them."

The marchers may have worshipped the Cysts but apparently had little experience with them. Cluelessly, they cheered and shouted stuff like *lead us to Maelstrom.* I think that's what they said. I couldn't hear much, because I had plenty of experience with the Cysts and I had a roar in my ears from the adrenaline surge. I knew. We were all supposed to die.

From the moment I saw the Cysts, I'd backpedalled my Cobra women away from the marchers. This complex only existed in one Frame. In other words, if we changed Frames there'd be nothing around or below us until we fell 100 feet into the East River. I'd rather fall in the river than let the Entourage hack me to bits, but I was going for *c, neither of the above.*

"Run," I instructed, and we did.

From the ruins of the Framekeep meeting hall, a Cyst said, "Now, lads." The Entourage dropped their whetstones and moved among the marchers, swords slicing air. Confusion gave way to terror and the march became a stampede. Clockwork dogs bit and lunged to herd the marchers back toward the swords.

Spotlights followed us as we sprinted for the Connector. A Cyst called, "Nica, don't leave us! Fetch her, lads." Clockwork dogs yipped and their clanking gears grew louder way too fast as they galloped toward us.

The Cobra woman we were supposed to rescue yelled, "This area persists in other Frames."

"Then get us outta here!" We grabbed hands and Hari!–Ya ricocheted us to a far Frame.

Four clockwork dogs followed our trail to the new Frame and as they chased us, acrid hot oil sizzled in their overworked joints. Behind them, eight of the Entourage materialized, brandishing swords and shouting at the clockwork dogs like bettors at a cockfight.

Hari!–Ya lunged us through many Frames while the other Cobra Woman reported on our pursuers and I kept us sprinting toward the Williamsburg Bridge. We would have a Frame to ourselves for a few hundred steps. But then gears would grind and swords would flash, and there our pursuers would be, always closer than the last time we saw them.

"Separate to survive," the other Cobra woman shouted. She took off in a new direction and changed Frames without us. The dogs took the bait and chased her. Hari!–Ya and I enjoyed several minutes without pursuit. Then the Entourage reappeared, wiping gore from their eyes. I assumed they had killed the other Cobra woman. There was never opportunity to learn her name.

Hari!–Ya tried to release my other arm. "She spoke truly. In separate Travel one of us may survive."

I held on. "No. I have an idea." Whatever she saw in my eyes convinced her to let me lead.

It was at that moment that I evolved to a true creature of the Frames. In my leaky outer brain I put all my *confused frightened irrational* for the Entourage to enjoy, while my subconscious steered me. Perhaps most impressively, I did all this during dry heaves from rapid distant Frame Travel.

We changed Frames and lost our pursuers for a time. At next appearance the Entourage was farther back but had spread out, north and east, probably to get between us and the Connector to the Williamsburg Bridge. I took Hari!–Ya south and west.

Hari!–Ya yelled. "Nica! This way is –"

"I know!" I gestured with a hand cutting my throat. *Don't talk.* If she finished that sentence it might give me a readable thought.

Our pursuers were slow to realize that we had reversed direction, which increased our lead. My Frame changes were awkward and apparently easy to follow but it was the running that would save us now. I ran like a Kenyan on a switchback mountain road and pulled Hari!–Ya to keep up. We zigged and zagged then we ran straight and flat out. I climbed a pillar, shouted to Hari!–Ya, "Up! Now!" Twenty feet up, I grabbed her hand and changed our Frame.

We were in the part of the government complex that existed in no other Frame. We would only be here a moment and my hope was that by the time we fell twenty feet, we'd be back in the government complex and still above the streets.

The pursuing Entourage materialized, following our Travel trail effortlessly. They were close enough to smell—the stench of rotten teeth. As hoped, they entered a section of street that no longer existed. Miraculously, our pillar persisted in this Frame and I tightened my grip on it and tried to enjoy the vision of the Entourage running on non–existent ground. After a cartoon instant of treading air, one by one they fell the long fall toward the East River. They fell with an enraged surprise that I found very satisfying.

If only we had not stayed to watch their plummet toward the river.

One of the Entourage clung to a pillar. He waved one finger in a *naughty naughty* gesture then brandished a semi–automatic gun. Water from the East River shot up his pillar and dislodged him but as he fell, he sprayed bullets, chipping cement and steel from our pillar before he fell out of range.

We flattened into the pillar to make smaller targets. A chip of something speared my thumbnail and it burned like gasoline and I hoped it would keep burning because it confirmed I was alive.

At last it was quiet, except for the distant shrieking of the East River. "Well played, Nica. Mmh." Hari!–Ya tried to shift position and slipped. The pillar was slick and our toeholds were narrow, so my arms had to bear most of my weight. I couldn't take Hari!–Ya's hand without dislodging our grips.

"We need to Travel separately back to the government complex," I realized.

Hari!–Ya's reply was faint behind the River's cackling, which crescendoed as water spiraled up our pillar. Before I could clamp my mouth shut I swallowed a nasty gulp, suggestive of a corpse dissolved in battery acid. It made me hallucinate. The water bumped and jolted us as it retreated down the pillar. Hari!–Ya slipped again and lost one arm's grip.

"Grab hold," I shouted and jutted my elbow toward her, bracing to handle the extra weight. Water hit my eyes and stung like wasps. I blinked but couldn't soothe them. My eyes must be bleeding: red bloomed like time–lapse flowers on Hari!–Ya's torso. I blinked faster. She had bullet holes in her chest.

Hari!–Ya slipped again. "My son," were her last words.

"I promised," I assured her.

Another spiral of water swept us. When I blinked to clear the wasps, Hari!–Ya was gone.

67. SIMPLE PLEASURES

"Let go, Nica."

"Release your grip."

Two voices pestered me to fall in the river. If I did that, noxious water would burn me. Silver–lining–wise, the pain might dull my memories of Hari!–Ya, blooming red.

I couldn't see who was talking, the glare of sunrise on the East River was too bright. When did it get to be dawn?

"We can't protect you from falling until you fall."

Love and confusion jolted me. The statement made no sense, in a way that only one being made no sense. Monk. I reviewed recent memories. Yes, that voice did sound like Monk, and the other voice sounded like Miles.

I willed my neck to tilt toward the voices. The Watts Towers stood in the East River below me. I hoped that water wouldn't corrode their steel. How often does a person fear corrosion of a loved one?

I might be delirious.

"Let go. Drop. We'll catch you," Miles reminded.

I tried to let go of the pillar but, clinging overnight, my arm muscles must have spasmed for so long that they stopped processing signals from my brain. I grabbed my sleeve in my teeth and dislodged one arm from the pillar. This put extra weight on my other arm; it pulled free and I fell. I slipped a few feet, thunked into the pillar, bounced a couple feet, whacked the pillar again. It took four rounds of slip–thunk before I hit Miles and rebounded onto Monk. All of which certainly got my blood moving again. A pottery shard on Monk's girder stabbed my cheek. I welcomed the pain and the taste of blood.

"Your laugh holds tears," Monk noted.

"I can't believe I'm alive. And with you."

"We share your surprise and pleasure."

In this Frame, Brooklyn Bridge was the only bridge across the East River and that was where we headed. The river was full of boats that seemed to be playing a slow version of soccer with splashed water instead of a ball and tugboats in goal.

"The shots tipped us something was up over here," Miles said. "Guns aren't allowed to play with their ammo so we came to do a look–see. Figured we'd find young pistols, fooling off."

"That was not my expectation. Anya warned that Warty Sebaceous Cysts have enslaved firearms."

Even I could have told Monk that a schoolmaster tone would make Miles testy.

Miles replied, "Then take a bow for always knowing everything." He accelerated to get ahead of Monk, which brought him close to the boats' game. A spectator boat honked and flashed a searchlight at him. "Don't flash that unless you mean it, girl," Miles called to the boat.

The Towers bickering, flirting. Warm sun on my back. Maelstrom and the Cysts had taken simple pleasures like these from too many beings who shouldn't be so suddenly, terribly dead.

"Your soul shivers today," Monk noted.

And then I was telling them everything. About Hari!–Ya and the Cobra woman we were supposed to rescue. The murdered children of Marzipan. Lilah. Sam. Fatty and Mikal. Ben's susceptibility to kidnap—not to mention relapse and overdose. The stolen lawn chair. When I finished, I didn't feel better, exactly, but talking to concerned friends always helps.

The Towers had stopped moving while I spieled, hovering just north of our destination. When I finished, they resumed the last leg of the trip to Brooklyn Bridge.

"How come you're in the New Yorks? Who's protecting L.A.? I thought you went home after the Framekeeps coup."

"We did go home," Monk said with a sigh.

"Plenty of other cats got Ellay as their gig," Miles reassured. His fresh cement was now fully encrusted with pottery shards, completing the repairs to the damage sustained during his kidnapping. Fascinating: repair work done on Ma'Urth showed up in other Frames, just as injuries incurred in other Frames showed up as damage on Ma'Urth. I added that to my infinite list of *how–is–it–possible–that...* Frames questions, when this—when Maelstrom—was over. Assuming our side won, of course.

"When Anya summons we can but answer," Monk's new sigh was bigger than the last.

"My brother gets homesick, he's a stay–at–home dude." Miles' tone was sympathetic.

"I'm like that, too. And I had to leave home to find out," I realized.

"Home is where I never get lost," Monk said. "But Anya wanted us here."

The air vibrated around Miles. He sounded excited. "The first battle will be fought through the New Yorks before much longer."

"Yes, Anya and Anwyl have mentioned that strategy!"

"That is not strategy, it is prophecy."

"Won't the Cysts attack somewhere else then? To be unpredictable?"

If Monk had a nose, he would have sniffed. "Prophecy cannot be outsmarted."

"Or maybe this is one of the prophecies they don't believe in?"

"Their disbelief is matched only by their belief."

There might be a Frame where that made sense. "Damn I've missed you, Monk! And Miles! I thank every day that you're back safely."

My hair wafted in the static charge that was their spread of affection.

When we got to Brooklyn Bridge, Monk hoisted himself onto Miles and rose like a ladder extension. He tilted to hang over the Bridge and all I had to do was drop a few feet to the footpath.

When Monk touched Brooklyn Bridge, the Bridge said, "That tap on my balustrade—after all these cycles is it truly Monk?" The name he actually said was Monk's real name, seventeen syllables and all consonants. "Well met, old friend."

"The Frames spin and our hearts stretch," Monk recited, then listened a moment. "Miles stands below. He 'likes what you've done with your girders, you must catch a nice flock of pigeons that way.' I quote him there."

Which set us all laughing. No one sounds less like Miles than his brother!

Laughter made their leave–taking easier. And harder.

"Guide her safely home," Monk instructed Brooklyn Bridge.

"Like you always do but double," Miles called from below. And then they were gone and I headed west.

"You walk with a limp," Brooklyn Bridge observed. "Have you an injury?"

"I'm stiff but not hurt. Unlike too many others." It took effort to keep moving. When the Towers departed, grief took over. I wanted to drop to my knees and pound the pavement. You'd think I'd be used to death by now.

"I understand. I am grateful to feel your tread, one never knows when... " The Bridge sounded like he didn't want to finish that sentence.

"I've got lots of tread left," I vowed.

"Yes, I feel that determination in your steps."

68. ASSASSINATION ATTEMPT?

I'd been away from Ma'Urth long enough that the bipolar vibe walloped me. Still, I was relieved to be back in a familiar world. I couldn't wait to get inside the Julian but there was something I had to do first.

I entered Hari!–Ya's safe house on Ma'Urth then changed Frames once I got inside.

Raff and Nada, the Cobra couple who cared for Hari!–Ya's son, were still there but Raff was packing their things. Nada nursed the misshapen potato that was her infant Cobra daughter. But where was the other infant, Hari!–Ya's son?

Raff brought forward an adorable toddler who had been unpacking a bag nearly as fast as Raff packed it. "Here is Hari!–Ya's son, Dar–Yo." He saw my disbelief. "During times of threat to the grandmaters, the seeders grow and evolve rapidly."

"Rapidly is an understatement. Thank you." The toddler handed me a cloth, pilfered from the bag. He was cuter than a dozen boy bands. I squatted to match his eye level. "Dar–Yo, I'm Nica. It's okay if you forget my name. You'll keep seeing me as you grow up. And when you're ready, I'll have amazing stories for you, starring your mother."

Nada had begun to cry and now rubbed her tears like they were to blame. "Already she is gone."

I could only nod. I stood quickly so that Dar–Yo didn't have to witness my sadness, although he surely felt the vibe coming from all three adults. The baby girl began to mewl. Raff hoisted the boy to his shoulders and Dar–Yo smiled, but didn't laugh.

"How will I know where you've Traveled?" I asked.

"We will send word through Anwyl."

"Okay, that should work. May I help you pack?"

"Thank you, yes. The sooner we are away –"

There were too many dark endings for that sentence.

Back on Ma'Urth, walking home, I thought about nothing but Hari!–Ya. I had to lock down those memories—I couldn't lose a single second with her. I was just the caretaker, after all, until I could give the memories to her son.

The Julian's front stoop was bright with sun and Dizzy stretched the length of the top step, soaking it in. That's what I needed! I sat with her and partook of purr therapy. Once again, the cat was friendlier than usual; maybe that was her reaction to Maelstrom. One of her ears had a freshly shredded edge and a deep puncture but she showed no sign of discomfort when I explored the injury with a gentle rub. Here was proof that everyone was at risk—Dizzy was too smart to get into fights unless absolutely necessary. "Defending the Free Frames can be dangerous work, huh, Dizz," I cooed and she stretched, inviting me to pet her belly—a first.

I was about to notice something about her front paw when she sprang to a crouch, puffed and hissed, then climbed up my torso and tensed as though preparing to sprint over my shoulder and away. I clutched her to me as I stood. Her heartbeat rattled like a drum roll. The source of her fear—Leon—swaggered up the sidewalk with a menace I'd never seen in him.

"Leon! Did you do this to Dizzy's ear? Stop right there, I won't let you hurt her again."

He kept coming as though I were talking to a cat.

Perhaps the cats sensed that I intended to stop Leon and protect Dizzy. Leon puffed out and Dizzy flattened against me, front paws on my collarbones.

Only Leon's eyes flicked. He was a killer intent on his prey. How had I seen that cat as innocent? His look validated all of Anya's fear of cats. Dizzy was so fearless she ignored threat from Anwyl by cleaning her butt. Dizzy was always grooming. She washed her paws more often than a nurse with O.C.D.

Dizzy's paws. Deep down, I finished my earlier thought about her front paw. On the surface, my thoughts focused on how scary Leon had become, although I was unsure whether cats could read my leaky mind. "Leon, knock it off," I yelled.

The thought I buried: this cat was not Dizzy. This cat—one set of claws on either side of my jugular—was a stranger that Leon wanted to hurt. Dizzy had a funny front toe—one black pad among white pads. This cat had all white pads. Otherwise she looked identical to Dizzy. But now that I stroked her, pretending to want to comfort her, perhaps her fur was a different texture. I was holding a cat that was not Dizzy yet was nearly her twin. Coincidence? Or assassination attempt?

Leon hadn't been fooled by the fake Dizzy but for now I had to keep treating him as the bad guy.

I kissed the top of the fake Dizzy's head. "You're okay, Dizzy, I won't let him hurt you. Easy now, you're safe, let's go inside." I backed up and gently adjusted her position so I could hold her with one arm while I reached for the front doorknob. The adjustment got her paws away from my throat.

It was the fastest I've ever moved. I let go of the cat and jumped backward off the steps. I stumbled but I was happy with my performance. I escaped those talons: by the time the cat began to fall and clawed for purchase, I was mostly out of reach. She merely gouged my shoulder and ripped my shirt.

Leon was all over her. I'd never seen a real catfight before, only the feline versions of pro wrestling. Here, a cloud of fur obscured my view and the tussling was silent except for the occasional thud of body slam. Then they vanished, taking their fight into another Frame. Okay. Leon could take care of himself. I hoped that he would only hurt the other cat as needed to convince her to stay away.

The fake Dizzy didn't hurt me, so I had no proof she was evil—perhaps she was misguided about where her best interests lay. A moment's knife–twist of anxiety: where was the real Dizzy? No. I wouldn't worry about her until I had evidence that I should. Dizzy was more cunning than a cold war spy.

Up the stairs to my apartment, I buffed this shiny attitude but couldn't repair the dents in my trust. The fake Dizzy didn't hurt me but she could have. If not for Leon. Would there someday appear a fake Leon? Were cats the only ones who could be fakes?

I slammed and locked my apartment door behind me. Inside the Julian I had protection, but even so I could feel it: danger everywhere and closing in.

69. OUR SPIRITS SHALL NOT BE BROKEN

Anwyl was stretched out on the couch, doing stuff on my laptop in windows only he could open. "Your mission has concluded too soon," he greeted me, setting the laptop aside.

Following instructions can have an upside. Because Anwyl knew about my activities of last night, I didn't have to hide my horror about what had gone wrong. He kept his arms around me while I described Warty Sebaceous Cysts' appearance, the Entourage chasing us, Hari!–Ya's death.

After that he was less comfort. "Another betrayal."

"Are you saying a traitor brought the Cysts there?"

"It is the most probable explanation."

We lay there; I felt extra gratitude for the protection of the Julian. I had questions about the fake Dizzy but Anwyl wasn't the one to ask. His hatred of cats was already profound. What if he overreacted against other cats? For now, Leon was on top of the imposter cat problem. Maybe Zasu was the one to talk to about fake cats.

My seesawing thoughts compounded my exhaustion. I must have slept for a bit—the morning sun had moved and now shone behind a different column of blinds. Anwyl slept beside me, his nostrils flaring in a silent snore.

The lanyard prickled. Again. It was lanyard pain that pulled me back from sleep. Now what? I strained to hear sounds of approaching danger, but colliding air particles were making too much noise. A third lanyard pulse stopped when the Julian's front door slammed and the foyer echoed with voices: Jenn and Zasu, loud enough to awaken Anwyl—and any tenants who had tried to sleep in today.

Anwyl set the laptop on my desk and sounded angry as the saboteurs trooped inside my apartment. "Your arrival is tardy. Dawn is long past." He must have been quite concerned about them—especially after my tale of the government complex—but he had given no sign until now.

"We finished before dawn then walked back, a few miles," Kelly Joe replied. His placid sense of fulfillment told me that last night he did some knocking on death's door.

Anwyl grunted. He didn't need to inquire about the success of their mission. The enthusiasm level was too high for failure. Anya joined Anwyl at the laptop, beaming. Hernandez and Jenn dropped onto the couch beside me. They reeked of chemicals; the only odor I recognized was gasoline.

Hernandez was the only one who was still. Regarding his time in Iraq, he'd once told me, *I noticed too much. Too many ways to die. All my buddies were on adrenaline*

234

cruise. I couldn't stop thinking and thinking's not how you survive. Perhaps last night revealed more ways to die. For him. Or for Jenn.

Jenn's adrenaline cruise headed to port. "I'm exhausted but not sleepy," she nestled against Hernandez, then sat up to proclaim, "You should have seen Zasu!"

Zasu stood in the hall outside the bathroom, swaying as though dancing to internal music. "Destruction goes against the Gumby nature," she said, "but this Gumby will always happily serve Anya."

"If we had more Gumbys, Maelstrom would be fucked," Jenn said admiringly.

"Enough Gumbys have died." Kelly Joe looked up from cleaning his harmonica with a string that might have started life as a bootlace. He sounded like he took responsibility for the Gumby genocide. I was pretty sure he'd had no role in that terrible deed. Although: that I had to think about it showed how deep my doubts ran when it came to Kelly Joe.

Anya, on the other hand, seemed to trust Kelly Joe completely. She called him over to see whatever Anwyl had on my laptop.

Zasu watched Kelly Joe with eyes like a Buddha statue. She seemed to forgive Kelly Joe for his role in the deaths of her family. She seemed to have an attitude that was even harder to achieve than forgiveness—she accepted him *as is.*

Funny, I always expect a warranty.

Anya stepped away from the laptop to address us. "We have done well," she smiled. "We have secured this island against our foes."

Hernandez disagreed. "We didn't get every construction site. We kept finding more."

Anya smiled, then gestured for us to gather around my laptop. "With this you shall know our success." She queued up a news story.

Sergeant Guy Bermudez was giving a follow–up interview about his special tactical force to stop the construction site arson. Bermudez bragged, "Criminals aren't rocket scientists. We publicized that we'd start this morning, but then we deployed last night, and by midnight we had six suspects in custody." The eyes of Bermudez, aka Scabman, told a different story. They were angry and frightened. Yes, the tactical force was done. But not because they caught the arsonists.

I liked seeing Scabman frightened. He deserved worse, but it was a start.

Hernandez settled in to the couch, no longer looking troubled.

Anwyl instructed Kelly Joe, "We will avoid unnecessary risk. The building abominations that survived will have guards, so for the non, we will attack no others." He looked to Hernandez, "Building abominations are powerful when plentiful. By decimating their numbers, you rendered them insignificant." To all the saboteurs he added, "You have done well. Warty Sebaceous Cysts will exact revenge and we may measure our success by their severity. For this night's deeds, expect retaliation designed to break the spirit."

"But our spirits shall not be broken," Anya flashed a special smile to Hernandez, Jenn, and me, a smile more powerful than a thousand mantras. "When next this group convenes, our war will have begun in earnest. We must away," she ordered Anwyl, Kelly Joe, and Zasu, and they headed for the door.

Before he went out, Anwyl tossed an order to us Neutrals on the couch. "Fortify your bodies and hearts, gather sustenance now for the days to come."

Kelly Joe walked a few paces behind the others, maybe so he could tell me, "These could be your last days on your own." He bent notes on his harmonica as he strolled out the door. I got the message. Whatever I was going to accomplish with the books needed to happen soon.

70. WHAT MAKES YOU THINK I HAVE CATS?

By the time Kelly Joe shut the door, Jenn and Hernandez were stacking zzzz's. I had been awake all last night, too—if catatonic clinging to a pillar above the East River counted as awake—but my chance of slumber fell between zip and nil. I tightened the blinds until the room got as dark as it was going to get.

A light shimmered from Hernandez' phone, which was on the back of the couch with a call coming in. A call from the cousin where Ben was holed up. I took the phone into the bathroom, completed the call but said nothing.

"Hey," the caller said. "If you know my voice, make a noise."

"Mmwah," I replied, the smooch I used to blow to Ben when we were newlyweds sharing a bathroom mirror.

"Hey, sis," Ben recognized the smooch. "I might have to move again. Two women have been showing up at my meetings. They pay too much attention to me and one of them forgot her birthday." The date she got sober. Recovering addicts don't get their birthdays wrong.

I stared into the bathroom mirror, trying to see Ben on the other coast. "Go somewhere unpredictable. Keep moving. You're a prize catch for my enemies."

"You sound important."

"I know, it's weird. I'd apologize for getting you involved, but, sooner or later, everyone will be involved."

"Now you sound like a movie ad."

"I still owe you an explanation but get yourself safe first."

"I like the role reversal. Today, you're the drama queen. From now on I'll just borrow phones, so you'll get calls from numbers you don't know."

"Nothing new there. Unless you actually answer when I return the call."
Inside I was begging, *Call every day to let me know you're okay.*

"Oh, Neeks," he said. And then he was gone.

Feet pattered the length of my ceiling. The kid upstairs always ran, getting ready for school.

A run, that's what I needed. I changed to sweats and headed out. On the stairs, from somewhere above came an arrhythmic bleating. Someone was in pain. Check it out. I reversed direction. Two flights above my apartment sat a pre–teen in a plaid skirt and green sweater that could only be a school uniform. The bleating was her crying.

"Hi, can I help?" I began.

A woman stepped from the apartment across the landing, her mother's barometer having sensed that a stranger was near her girl.

"I live in 2C," I greeted the mother.

"Have you seen my cat?" the girl inhaled in hope; I shook my head and she exhaled in fear. "She disappeared before breakfast yesterday."

"What does she look like?"

The girl showed me photos of a charming calico. I promised to text with any news, day or night, and reversed direction on the stairs once more. I fought an inexplicable chill. Why did the fake Dizzy's appearance coincide with the neighbor cat's disappearance?

When I got to the foyer, I Traveled a quick trip to Frivolous Bedlam and called to Julian.

"Good morning," the building said. "You sound harried."

"Harried would be an improvement. How many cats live in you on Ma'Urth and how many of them have you seen in the last day?"

"What makes you think I have cats?"

"It's not an insult. I love cats myself. I know of three on your premises."

"Fascinating. I assumed cats were a metaphor, not real beings. The buildings speak of them—that is, the buildings who are not self–sentient—but they speak of so many things."

I allowed him the snob undertones. Much as I loved all the buildings, I could see how their eternal goofy chatter might get old.

"What about dogs. Do you have dogs?"

"Yes, of course. Dogs are beloved companions in many a Frame. I am interested to know that you believe in cats, some of my fellow sentients have speculated about the cat's role in belief systems."

"No sentient building can detect cats?"

"No. We know only their lore. Some of us do believe in cats—Henrietta falls in that category—but most of us are skeptics. I regret I can offer no assistance to you regarding—cats." The word amused him.

"I'm sorry you've never experienced a cat. Maybe someday I can help you meet one." Another item on my *to–do–if–we–beat–Maelstrom* list.

I Traveled back to Ma'Urth, determined to get a run before Hernandez and Jenn woke up. I hardly ever crossed paths with neighbors, but as I left the Julian here was another, a cute little hipster with a fuzz beard and the latest eyewear. He ascended his basement apartment stairs with a bag of trash and a folded lawn chair. A bizillion chairs have the same blue and white webbing, yet I knew that this was the sentient lawn chair stolen from my fire escape. "Hey! What are you doing with that chair?"

He ceased ascent.

"Sorry, didn't mean to sound accusing. I had one like that and somebody took it."

"It might be this one, somebody dumped it down my stairs. I was gonna leave it at the curb. Think I'm allergic. Headache every time I sit in it. There you go. See ya."

And with that I was holding the chair. He crossed the street mid–block without acknowledging the taxi that honked to a stop beside him.

My hand throbbed, holding the chair. Without further ado I unfolded the chair and sat in it, lopsided. The frame was bent now. I planted my forearms the length of the metal arms. Now I would find out who stole my chair from the fire escape.

And I did find out.

As the chair relived its abduction, *I felt a touch on each shoulder* and I cringed in expectation of being touched by Warty Sebaceous Cysts, the Entourage, or a Lobotomist.

The hands on my shoulders were quick, unexpectedly gentle, calloused and cool. I knew that touch. And with that knowledge came the realization that my life in the New Yorks was a house of cards in a tornado.

71. TRUST IS A TETHER

It made no sense.

The hands yanked me but the bicycle lock yanked back. My aluminum frame buckled. The hands dropped me. The fire escape shuddered, metal snapped near my feet. No lock protected me now. The hands grabbed me again and I bounced as my abductor jogged me out to the street. Faint harmonica notes grew louder. My thief cursed, and his voice confirmed his identity.

Anwyl stole the chair.

Another whispered curse and I flew, hit brick, scraped the unbent part of my frame. It was dark and damp where I landed this time.

Based on the chair's memories and info from the hipster neighbor, Anwyl took the chair then threw it down the stairs to the basement apartment because Kelly Joe approached. He hadn't wanted Kelly Joe to see him with the chair?

So. I knew *how* the chair was stolen. *Why* was not forthcoming.

On the morning when I had discovered the chair was missing from the fire escape, Anwyl had been asleep beside me. I'd awakened to my lanyard prickling, looked outside, saw no dangers, considered waking him but then the prickling stopped and he woke up.

Like this morning.

Or was it the other way around? He woke up—so the lanyard warning stopped?

Trust is a tether and when it breaks I'm lost in the stratosphere.

Maybe my lanyard was trying to warn me about Anwyl, a being of great power who can stifle lanyard alerts—except perhaps when sleeping. The two times that Anwyl was asleep in my presence were the two times the lanyard alerted me to danger that seemed to disappear when he awoke. Maybe, instead, the danger persisted but the alerts were silenced. By him when he awoke.

I wrapped the chair in a towel and hid it in the back of my closet. Hernandez and Jenn didn't stir from sleep. I paused to enjoy their synchronized breathing. I bet Ick and I breathed like that. The best of love in the worst of times. Jenn's exhales had a darling little gasp that fell just short of labored breathing. I ignored it, as I had ignored how frail she looked when she walked in this morning.

I took a long hard run to outpace my worries. I kept going until my only thoughts were of the scant few things I could influence, like what to bring home for breakfast. When I got back to my apartment, Hernandez was doing a smorgasbord of push–ups and Jenn was in the shower. Which meant I had time to talk to Hernandez.

"Hey. I need a sounding board."

He rolled into a sitting position on the floor. "What's up?"

I told him about finding the chair and learning that Anwyl took it. "Is there any point telling Anwyl that I know?"

"What's the advantage?"

"I want to know why he did it. Silly me. Why do I think he'll tell me the truth?"

Hernandez shrugged. "He does, when the truth helps the cause. No question it was a strange thing to do but he always has reasons."

Should I tell Hernandez about my lanyard and its warnings about Anwyl? Hernandez was trustworthiness incarnate, but Anya had said to tell no one about the lanyard. I needed time to brood about that. "Can you do those clap—your—hands—while—suspended—by—your—belly—muscles push—ups?"

He could.

"Should I confront Anwyl? What would you do?"

"What we've been doing. Go with their flow." He pulled up the bottom of his t—shirt to wipe his forehead.

"How come you don't need answers?" I didn't ogle the smooth taut skin on his stomach; only Jenn could do that now.

"I've learned to need what I can get." The push—ups segued to squats and lunges.

"Now I feel like I can't trust Anwyl."

"Maybe you can't."

"Stop zenning me!" But he was right. If I focused on uncertainties I'd lose the ability to proceed.

Jenn emerged from the bathroom, which helped me return to here and now. Hernandez and I flipped for the next shower and he won. When it was finally my turn to clean up, I stuck my head out the bathroom door and advised, "Don't go anywhere while I'm in here. I need your help on a special project."

"Turn the water off and tell us what the project is," Jenn demanded. "Don't you laugh at me, bitch."

I warned Hernandez, "She's not good with surprises. If you put her Christmas present out early, she'll peek. Every time. Except for one year."

She laughed, "Ben is such! An asshole!"

I explained to Hernandez, "Ben put her gift out way early, wrapped in duct tape. She needed a scalpel to open it."

Jenn took the high road with her subject change. "Today's museum closes soon. Hurry up or we'll go without you," she threatened, but I knew they wouldn't.

Later I had to wonder what might have ended differently, had we gone to museums that day.

72. WE'RE JUST A BUNCH OF NEUTRALS

Traveling with Hernandez is like dancing ballet in a suit of bricks. I took him to my apartment in Frivolous Bedlam and stumbled my way home for Jenn. I was weaker than a politician's backbone and, back on Ma'Urth, I collapsed on my couch, panting.

Jenn was stern. "What did you do with my guy?"

"Give me a sec and I'll show you."

I took so many slow deep breaths that Jenn got bored with being impatient and opened her suitcase. "Will we be indoors or out?"

"Mostly," I inhaled, "out," I exhaled.

I dragged myself into the kitchen to swig orange juice with a chaser of antique coffee then I held out my hand and took Jenn to her guy. It was much easier to Travel with Jenn; she was almost as light as a grannie.

In Frivolous Bedlam, Hernandez stood looking out my front window. Jenn threw herself into his arms; over her head he appraised our surroundings. "You have new skills."

"We're in a different Frame, right? Everything looks the same but different and Godzilla's fucking me again. I need air." Jenn opened the window, stumbled back in the blast of noise from a thousand buildings talking at once.

"Welcome to Frivolous Bedlam. Of all the Frames I've visited so far, this is my favorite," I said to them, and reminded Jenn, "I brought you here once before but you were too disbelieving to see it."

"I want to explore," Jenn said and headed for the door.

"You're such a Frame–hugger now." I followed her downstairs, and called back to Hernandez, "Leave the window open."

We stood on Julian's front stoop, acclimatizing to the decibels. A knock–knock joke made its way along the block. Jenn gaped at the buildings. Hernandez divided his attention among the surroundings, Jenn, and me.

I said, "I brought you here because I need your help with an investigation." I called above us, "Books. To me."

A dozen books flew out of my opened window, sunlight glinting on dust jackets. Hernandez had only seen books fly during the genocide of the Gumby people. He jumped Jenn to the sidewalk and threw himself on top of her. As if his flesh or bones could protect her, should these books be foes.

"These are my books. They won't hurt us."

I had to repeat to be heard through Jenn's spluttering: "What the fuck, get off me, I want to see."

Hernandez stood and gave Jenn a hand. I circled my finger above my head. *Lose Twenty Pounds* led the books to circle us. The covers flapped as though to metronomes, with smaller books flapping twice as often. "At ease," I said. The books hovered behind me.

"Fuckin' A, flying books." Jenn clapped her hands.

The buildings' jokes had turned to mutters. "Don't be afraid," I called to the buildings. "These are the books of Cat Shaver. I will never let them hurt you. They are trained to obey me."

And trained they were. I'd left *Lose Twenty Pounds* with instructions and now they moved like an award–winning dance troupe: graceful, swift, with mesmerizing control. We walked around the block with the books in a V formation flanking us. Jenn and Hernandez kept turning to watch the books.

I stepped into an intersection, pulled a carrot and a pebble from my pockets and tossed them as high as I could. "Books, stop these."

Summer made authoritative noises I recognized as orders in Refrencian. *The Blue–Eyed Shan* and *Farewell, My Lovely* shot skyward and rained narrow columns of text. The carrot hit the ground minced, the pebble became a hail of sand. The books had released text sparingly, leaving scattered characters impaled in the street.

Asphalt heals quickly from text cuts and neither harvested carrots nor eroded pebbles have sentience, so my demonstration caused no harm. Yet the buildings had gone silent. Jenn's "Did we just see that?" resounded in the quiet.

A shadow covered the minced carrot and pebble. Above the books a pelican circled, an enormous bird with a scarred beak. He showed up the last time I had the books outside in Frivolous Bedlam, too. His presence must have reassured the buildings because soon they chattered normally again.

Maybe I could find a Frame where I could converse with that pelican. Or maybe he could understand me here. I called up to the pelican, as much as I said to Jenn and Hernandez, "Books are not inherently evil. They have been enslaved by our enemy. However, these books do my bidding and I will someday free other books. I believe the information exists to tell us how to free them, and I am on a quest to obtain that information."

I don't know why I put it like that, like I'd yet to visit the Halls of Shared Knowledge or Party City; but, after all, I didn't know this pelican, even if the buildings seemed to trust him. Anyway, it never hurts to play close to the vest. I've confirmed that, all two or three times in my life that I played that way.

The buildings started a chant. *Can be FREED. Find out HOW!* and that morphed into *Knock–knock. Who's there? Free! Free who? Free the books.*

Maybe not the best way to keep a secret. Fortunately, within seconds the meaning was lost. *Free books. Book sale. Sailboat sale! Book boat!* Maybe all the nonsensical building chatter started as sensical conversation somewhere; maybe some of it was important. Could it be decoded? How many people and hours would that take?

"Nica, sometimes you suck! This is no time to take a thought vacation!" Jenn shouted, which brought me back to my street in Frivolous Bedlam, where my books cowered in the pelican's shadow. Hernandez's look said waiting–for–a–download–over–dialup.

I leaned my head back to address the pelican. "We need your help. We fight with the allies, and oppose those who would enslave the free Frames, just as they have enslaved books and subverted their nature."

I hadn't seen that level of admiration on Jenn's face since I convinced our moms that earning a certain detention should be rewarded—but if I inspired the pelican, he showed no sign. He resumed circling above my books.

"Books, shelve yourselves," I said softly, and they flew into my apartment through the open window.

As soon as the last book was inside, with a powerful flap of wings, the pelican headed west toward the Hudson River.

"Do you think he understood you?" Jenn asked.

I shrugged to hide my disappointment and channeled Kelly Joe. "Time will tell."

Back inside my apartment, Jenn asked, "Were the cats here before?"

I ran to the patch of sun on the front room floor, scooped one of the masses of fur that was lounging in the sun, and straightened with Dizzy in my arms. I checked her front paw to confirm it had Dizzy's markings, but I already knew this was the real Dizzy because Leon sprawled beside her, grooming her—an act of love.

Dizzy's coat had clumps, much like Leon's when I'd first met him. But unlike some other cats I could name or reach out to pet, Dizzy was fastidious and was already working out the kinks in her fur. Which was fortunate because I would never be stupid or drunk enough to try to shave Dizzy.

Leon broke into one of his mondo purrs. I exchanged cats, careful to bend my knees before I hefted Leon. The purr got louder. I set Leon on the couch for inspection—he was a mess of scratches, punctures, gouges, but they seemed to be healing. He must have caught up with the fake Dizzy.

I warned Jenn and Hernandez about the fake Dizzy incident, then said, "Now I need to explain why I brought you here." I shared a summary history of book enslavement. I talked fast because we needed daylight for our next endeavor. I concluded, "It's unusual, my affinity with books. I don't know how deep it goes or whether Maelstrom can steal their loyalty from me. But I think he can't. I think freeing the books is why I'm important to the allies, a role I'm meant to play."

The books flew around the kitchen, pivoting, diving—playing. We watched them like they had the future written on their covers. I hadn't asked Jenn and Hernandez for help in destroying the press, but the request was all around us.

"The imprinting press. It's important. It will have guards, whether you saw them or not," Hernandez said.

"Kelly Joe said the guards won't know what they're guarding. Maelstrom trusts no one. In the Frame on the other end of the conveyor belt, workers who load books onto the conveyor belt probably die at the end of each shift, supervisors every couple days."

"All procedures will change if Maelstrom finds out someone is after the press."

"Yes. Absolutely. We won't have much time. I say 'we' in case you agree to help me."

"We already agreed," Jenn replied.

Hernandez looked at her a long moment then grilled me. "What's your plan? In detail?"

"Er. Destroy the imprinting press. Use explosives, probably. My friend the war vet could help with that part or the plan."

My friend the war vet grunted.

"When Maelstrom took control, he made sure no one could make another press. He killed the twin geniuses who created it. By all report, the twins' understanding of physics made Einstein look dim so a replacement might happen but not tomorrow."

"Anyway we have to try to get rid of that fuckhead thing," Jenn said.

Hernandez shook his head. "Agree that somebody needs to try. What do Anya and Anwyl say about your plan?"

"I—they. Only Kelly Joe and you know."

"And that pelican," Jenn reminded. "And the Halls of Shared Knowledge."

"Why the secret?"

"At first, because I thought they'd stop me. Now," I caught myself rubbing my waist where the lanyard was hidden. "My gut tells me that as few people should know as possible. Anwyl is having problems with traitors."

"That's to be expected in a guerrilla war."

"We should be the ones to try this because we're more expendable." We reacted to Jenn's pragmatic blandness. "Listen, girlfriends, we're just a bunch of Neutrals."

"I can't buy in until I've had a recon look," Hernandez said.

"How about now?" I stood.

Jenn jumped up from the couch, wavered, gasped an inhale.

Hernandez reacted, "Nica and I got this. We'll do the recon, you stay here and rest up."

Jenn stopped wavering. "Rest won't help. I'm getting worse. But I'm part of this mission and I need to see what I'm getting into, too."

They stared each other down. Impasse, meet standoff.

I said, "The recon should be relatively safe. There's a building with windows that look out on the press and the conveyor belt. We can Travel inside the building, stay inside it."

Hernandez didn't say no.

"I'll take you one at a time." I held out a hand.

Hernandez held Jenn's arm so she couldn't take my hand, and his voice was frozen steel. "I'm first in, last out."

"We agree," Jenn hugged him.

"Alright, girlfriends. Let's take a look," Hernandez said.

73. WE PLOTTED DESTRUCTION

For me, it's the unhappiest place on Ma'Urth. Times Square. Remember the neutron bomb? Destroys life, ignores structures. In Times Square I feel that alone, the sole survivor of a neutron bomb blast. Yes, those streets teem with people. Something about the way they teem.

The candy store was packed with tourists. I led Hernandez and Jenn to the second floor, back aisle, where the reconnaissance windows were blocked by displays for chocolate colored confections. I took Hernandez' hand and, as we wound between shoppers, I Traveled us to Maelstrom's Frame. We left Jenn with the merchandise, scoffing at nutrition labels.

In Maelstrom's Frame, the room was quiet except for the rasping squeak from outside as the conveyor belt released a crate of books. The room was empty except for a heap of dusty tattered clothing in a corner. I hadn't noticed that last time.

Outside, crates appeared from the Connector and moved west along the conveyor belt toward the press. The crates appeared at a regular rate but then, for a time, the far end of the belt was empty. After the empty stretch, from out of the Connector came six lumpy bundles that leaked bright orange fluid. The fluid lost its glow as it spread over the conveyor belt. The bundles were corpses, the fluid must be the blood of crate loaders who had finished their shift.

Workers. Corpses. I communicated this to Hernandez in gestures. Kelly Joe had talked in this room without tripping eavesdropping devices but that didn't mean talking was safe now. On our way to Times Square, I'd given Hernandez and Jenn lessons in erratic walking and Hernandez had picked it up fast. Now he moved erratically from window to window, checking the Square from every angle the windows allowed. I leaned my forehead against the glass and rested my eyes. It hurt to blink. Travel with Hernandez was not getting easier.

I strung a quick line of barbed wire around my thoughts but some doubts jumped the fence. *Why didn't I wait for Kelly Joe to come with us?* I didn't know when he would be available and speed remained of the essence. *What if I have to Travel us all out of here pronto?* I had to assume that in an emergency, I would muster whatever reserves it would take to get my beloveds to safety.

Below us, the six corpses piled up at the near end of the conveyor belt. The mechanical hands swept the corpses aside like leaves from a drain. The corpses landed atop heaps of cloth that erupted in motion as a thousand rats and a million roaches ran from a feast of older corpses. The cloth heap on the other side of this room was more sunken and tattered than the heaps outside, so the feast was probably long over. My curiosity did not provoke me to poke the tattered pile.

I tapped Hernandez' arm, waved bye–bye, and went to fetch Jenn.

Jenn wasn't in Maelstrom's Frame half a second before she plugged her nose and pantomimed barfing. She was right, the smell was horrific. Brains are good at hiding bad news and mine had blocked the sour pungent stench of rot and torture. I could only nod in reply. I couldn't figure a gesture to convey *you think this is bad, wait'll you smell outdoors.*

Jenn struggled with the erratic walking, so Hernandez carried her from window to window for her look–see. She clung to his back like a koala.

We repeated the end–to–end viewing several times. I tried to see through their eyes, then pretended I was Anwyl, then Anya. I memorized the scene outside. Whatever we missed could kill defeat capture us.

Jenn pulled out her phone to take photos and I exchanged a look with Hernandez. Nope, neither of us had thought of that. Great idea, but she gave up in frustration. She showed us the phone screen—the image wouldn't save. It was like the whole Frame was a vampire. I took Jenn's hand and Traveled her away from that place where despair was the happiest sensation.

On Ma'Urth, none of the candy shoppers noticed when we returned to the store and made their aisles a bit more crowded. I left Jenn with a quick hug. Easy peasy return Travel. But not for long.

When I went back for Hernandez, I couldn't budge him out of Frame. I tried to go fetch Kelly Joe for help, but I couldn't Travel myself away, either. I was out of Travel oomph. We were stuck in Maelstrom's Frame. *Not here please not here.* I wouldn't have thought it possible to panic when so low on energy, yet hysteria broke, a stampede of lunatic horses. Against my will, I sank to my knees on the floor; it was layered in stains, caused by acts too dreadful to contemplate. I contemplated them, until Hernandez touched my shoulder and nodded. He trusted me to make it happen, to take us home.

I closed my eyes and I breathed. In out. In out. The hooves ceased to pound in my ears. My shoulders ached with the weight of my backpack straps. My backpack. Heavy with books. In my haze, I'd nearly forgotten an essential part of the plan. My books had their own mission to complete here.

I set my backpack on the least stained part of the floor and unzipped it. With erratic pulls on the zipper, unzipping the backpack seemed slower than smoking a cigarette, which I fantasized doing. I felt like I'd smoked half a pack at once. I stifled a snicker, imagining my mouth bristling with ten ignited cigarettes.

Delirious, maybe. And/or dreading what had to come next.

I reached inside my backpack, touched each book spine. Each book had its own feel. I slipped my books out, one by one. When we'd first arrived they were hyperactive, bumping and jiggling inside the backpack. Now they were as inert as if in a Neutral Frame. With a silent kiss to each cover, I placed each book around me on the floor.

I might never see them again. Or if I did, they might attack me, possessed by the other side. Nonetheless, I had to leave them here. They had a vital role to play.

Piecing together information from all my sources, I'd learned that book enslavement is a two–step process. Going through the imprinting press primes a book for takeover and control. But at that point allegiance is still fluid. Subsequent training finishes the imprinting, commits the book to a particular master. That training hadn't started for the books outside this room. In that long tent were thousands of books with fluid allegiance. Some of the books already belonged to Maelstrom because he controlled earlier editions. But most of them were winged pit bull puppies: how they turned out depended on their treatment.

Sure, my books could speak Refrencian, but they could also communicate with fellow books in ways that touched who the books really were. If my books didn't get detected and destroyed, maybe they could persuade those winged pit bull puppies to join the allies.

That was their mission. Like all parts of my plan it was as solid as an ice cube in a campfire. But dig. Throw one ice cube in a campfire, the ice cube melts. Throw enough cubes and their melting snuffs the fire.

I reached a hand up. Hernandez pulled me to standing.

When we returned to the candy store on Ma'Urth, one person noticed our appearance among the corn syrup aficionados. "Oh thank GOD!" Jenn shouted, startling a kid who knocked over a display of candy cell phones. Hernandez swept Jenn into his arms and I helped the kid right the display.

Back in my apartment, we plotted destruction.

"The press looks like iron and steel. There are bombs for that," Hernandez said. As the only one unphazed by our Travel, he served us apples and cheese, sliced ultra–thin so we wouldn't tax ourselves in chewing. "Unless the press is magic. We can't take out magic."

"My understanding is there is no magic, just different physics, subsets of the full range of possibilities."

"Does that mean our bombs will explode the press if they have similar physics to the press?" Jenn asked.

"Yes, as far as I've been able to determine." I couldn't eat but the crackers worked well for building 'card' houses. Construction steadied my nerves. Now that we were back, I could think of nothing but how flimsy my plan seemed, more wishful than purposeful. And how far beyond help my books were.

"Can we do a test explosion in the Frame where the press was made?" Jenn asked.

Hearing a good idea made me feel better. I ate a cracker house. "That's a great idea! Assuming the Halls of Shared Knowledge can tell me where to do that test."

"Finish our shopping before you go back to the Halls," Hernandez instructed. He was already headed back into the kitchen for more food. Jenn's appetite was its voracious self.

I said, "For what it's worth, Kelly Joe seems to think this is doable. Destroying the press."

Hernandez reacted to my anxious tone. "He'll be with us, right?"

"I believe so. Yes." Kelly Joe wouldn't help to this point then stop. He wouldn't keep my secret then fink at the last moment.

"And Zasu. We need Zasu," Jenn said.

"If bombs don't work where the press is, maybe we can take the press to a Frame where the bombs will work," Hernandez said. "Think it's transportable?"

"If anyone can move it, Kelly Joe can."

Hernandez stood at the kitchen counter, making lists on scraps of paper grocery bag. "Implosion, explosion, and fire. We'll rehearse the timing. We'll be making noise for no more than a minute." Hernandez added softly, "Grab her food."

Jenn had fallen asleep with a cheese and apple sandwich dangling from her lips. I took the food, stretched Jenn out on the couch. The only way we could share the space was if I stretched out, too.

That turned out to be our last sleep until the mission was over.

When I came to, Hernandez knelt beside the couch and showed me his scraps of paper. We each had a shopping list. And he'd ordered our actions, blow by blow. His organization and attention to detail converted activities to strategy.

Shopping came first. The substances on our shopping lists ranged from innocent to controlled. Each shopping list included coded notes about quantities we could buy in a single store without arousing suspicion or triggering a report. Jenn and I shopped together, all afternoon in a widening circle. We'd take a cab back to the apartment each time our arms got full of bags. The cab rides gave Jenn rest periods, too. Hernandez set out separately with his own, shorter list of items that couldn't be purchased legally. He knew some guys who could help with those purchases.

Jenn and I were on the Lower East Side when Warty Sebaceous Cysts retaliated for destruction of their construction sites, so we witnessed the devastation as it occurred. Maybe someday I'll stop reliving those scenes in my head; but the TV stations will still be playing that infamous footage, shot from the helicopter and the barge.

74. BRIDGES AREN'T MADE TO TWIST

It was our last purchase of the afternoon. Jenn and I were at a pharmacy on Chambers Street; after this we would split up. She would join Hernandez at home to assemble our purchases into explosives and incendiaries. I would head for the Halls of Shared Knowledge to find out where the imprinting press was constructed and what its weak points might be.

At first the crush of marchers seemed like a demonstration headed east for City Hall. They marched into City Hall Park—then kept going, out to the Brooklyn Bridge. They were eerily silent, a parade band without instruments or music. When Jenn and I exited the pharmacy, the marchers had attracted onlookers who debated the gimmick of the march.

"They're like the guards outside Buckingham Palace," a Swedish accent said to me, admiring. "So quiet and focused!" He pushed forward, craning for a better look.

I stuck my head between two shoulders to crib a view, then grabbed Jenn's arm. The marchers on Chambers had the hungry vacant eyes of Lobotomists. "Get away from here. Now!"

But we couldn't *get*. More marchers swarmed from north and south, funneling everyone onto the streets going east. The Swede got knocked down and no marcher paused or changed direction. Just before the Swede got trampled, he clawed himself upright but had to join the march toward the Brooklyn Bridge.

I pulled Jenn or she pulled me, back against the wall of the pharmacy, which had lowered its night gate for protection. I considered changing Frames but feared calling attention to us. The marchers coming in from the north and south had the platinum hair and glinting smiles of the Entourage, today dressed like 1950s tourists. They could detect Frame Travel in their vicinity.

Jenn and I got sucked into the flow toward the Bridge. To flow more slowly, we flattened against buildings until the crowd crushed us forward. At the waterfront, the march expanded into a park. Jenn and I had room to shove out the side of the marchers. We slipped into a hole between buildings where a tenement had been razed; we climbed scaffolding that shivered and creaked. We lay on the scaffolding to keep the lowest possible profile and we watched the rest unfold.

Entourage marchers reached the Bridge first, then Lobotomists poured in behind, then more Entourage, then more Lobotomists. Trapped among the squadrons were luckless pedestrians who bounced and pinged between the relentless marchers. The Entourage and Lobotomists kept an identical pace, an odd one, a beat slower than a normal gait. Meanwhile, another march swept toward the Bridge from the Brooklyn side.

In front of the Bridge, a knot of pedestrians stopped with arms linked in united resistance—they were done marching against their will. Without breaking stride, the marchers punched and pounded the pedestrians, then swarmed extra thick around the knot of resistance. When the swarm dissipated, the pedestrians were gone.

Jenn and I pressed low against the scaffold planks and clutched each other's hands. Yells screams shouts kept growing in volume. The honks of distant taxis became a barrage from all directions including the sky. It was as though the city were under a dome and every sound reverberated. Maybe, just maybe, those faint agonized moans were sirens. Approaching? I counted the seconds between moans as though they were lightning and thunder.

The march seemed to last forever but it must have moved quickly because as the last marchers reached the Bridge, N.Y.P.D. police only just arrived—in cars and bikes, on horseback and foot. The cops yelled for marchers to stop but marching continued. The cops dragged marchers from the back rows to force compliance. It took two cops to pin a single marcher, to stop the forward movement. One marcher, knocked to his back, continued to pump his legs like an overturned bug. A cop pounded with a nightstick to stop the wriggling.

Many cops followed marchers onto the Bridge to grab them. Suddenly the cops were turning and shouting to one another and running to land. From this distance the cops seemed prescient, but they must have felt the change before we could see it.

It all happened so fast. The Bridge began to quiver in time to the pace of the marchers. The quiver evolved to sway and the swaying motion grew exaggerated. But that was okay, because bridges are made to sway. The marchers persisted with their odd identical pace and the sway undulated along the spans. On both levels of the Bridge, the surface tilted, sagged, tilted; which added up to give the motion a twist. Bridges aren't made to twist. Suspension cables strained and a chunk of the pedestrian level broke free. It flapped against its cables, which snapped dozens of marchers into the air. The remaining marchers continued without pause.

On the lower level, the vehicle level, spans ruptured, separated, tilted. A tractor–trailer truck plunged off a tilted span. A couple seconds later, a spray of water marked its entry into the East River. There were so many cars on the tilted spans and although they sprouted brake lights, they slid down, lower, down. People jumped out of sliding cars and tried to scale the incline while dodging other sliding cars.

A broken piece of pedestrian walkway swung on its cables and hit adjoining pieces. The twisting and sway of the Bridge intensified and the motion got more complicated as the Bridge stopped moving as a single structure and different pieces took on different motions. A span from the lower level snapped and hit the upper deck. Still marching, marchers slid on unfathomably massive slabs as though on giant sleds. The air below the Bridge grew dark with falling marchers. The remaining marchers kept moving forward.

Metal shrieked like shopping carts in an enormous blender. At our distance, the sounds were muffled yet Jenn and I had to hold our ears. On the bridge, the decibel levels must have exceeded a hundred Who concerts.

The end came fastest of all. An invisible giant squeezed the Bridge together from its ends. The center buckled and slabs of concrete splayed away. After that it was hard to see what was happening. Dust clouds plumed then disintegrated in huge splashes of water. Within seconds, every surface for blocks held the same ashy beige powder. I licked my lips and tasted concrete.

Sounds continued to ricochet so I couldn't tell where the screams came from. Some were surely from me.

The Brooklyn Bridge had survived many swaying events during its years on Ma'Urth, most recently during a transit strike and a power outage, when many more pedestrians took to the Bridge than was typical. The rhythm of crowds' feet got the bridge swaying. But the swaying didn't escalate because those pedestrians weren't walking in sync to take out the Bridge. These marchers were.

We stood on the scaffolding to see if any survivors emerged. Jenn divided her time between what was happening and its news coverage on her phone. Somebody in a helicopter posted footage that showed the marchers from each side— Manhattan and Brooklyn—continue toward the middle of the Bridge, a suicide march with the spans buckling around them. Suicide for the Lobotomists, certainly. Murder for the trapped pedestrians. The Entourage may have saved themselves by Traveling out of Frame.

"Do they not know they're about to die or do they not care?" Jenn stopped the streaming video. "They've got so many more troops than we do. Look how many they just wasted."

"I expect Anwyl and Anya have resources we don't know about but—yeah. I think that's one of the Cysts' take–home messages here."

"One of them. What are the others?"

"This is what happens to those who help the allies. Brooklyn Bridge is supposed to be impartial but has helped us in small ways." Jenn had not yet had the pleasure of meeting Brooklyn Bridge or being recognized by her unique steps. "This could be a strategic move, too. By destroying the Brooklyn Bridge on Ma'Urth, Warty Sebaceous Cysts now control access to Expletive Deleted, a Frame which is important politically—and maybe symbolically."

Jenn got a text from Hernandez just before I did.

::R U safe?

::Something big going down.

I let Jenn text our reply.

Yes, Brooklyn Bridge still existed in other Frames, but would the Cysts attack other Frames also? The allies couldn't possibly protect the Bridge in all its Frames. I wanted to throw a fit but the scaffolding was too rickety. I tried to cry but my tears were dammed by concrete dust. I rubbed away Bridge remains to clear a path down my face.

Below hearing, I felt Brooklyn Bridge moaning and the East River berserking. It was like I was in multiple Frames simultaneously. I clung to Jenn's arm and the scaffold railing to hold myself in Ma'Urth.

Jenn showed me a text from Hernandez that made me feel a little less unsafe.

::Stay put. Tee is coming for you.

It was the wrong time, or maybe exactly the right time, for petty concerns: Phooey. Hernandez had finally had a conversation with his truck. I had wanted to be there when that happened.

75. WHEN MY SIDE KILLED IT WOULD BE NOBLE

So much brown dust filled the air it was like looking through a used bandage. Shadowy in the haze, the Brooklyn Bridge's gothic arches still stood, with a few slabs of roadway swinging on snapped cables.

The cops' body language shifted from arrest to rescue. We didn't know it then, but not a single body would ever be recovered of those who fell with the Bridge. The official speculation was that the bodies rested under tons of concrete, or had been swept distant by the chaotic currents that developed in the collapse. In reality, the Cysts moved them all out of Frame.

A horn honked on the street below our scaffolding. The horn belonged to a red truck with more dents than a golf ball. It was Hernandez' truck, Tee, with Zasu waving from the passenger window. "That's our ride," I didn't need to say. Jenn was already climbing down the scaffold ladder.

Jenn sat in the middle and I took the driver's seat but Tee continued to drive—until we hit gridlock at the next intersection, where cars alternated at right angles. Traffic by Mondrian. The streets grew translucent and the traffic dissolved. "Did we just change Frames?" Jenn asked. She'd been watching news on her phone and looked up when the connection failed.

"We did. I knew a shortcut," Tee said, gliding us through empty translucent streets. "But it won't help for long. Nothing is ever easy. I have to take you to Anya and all routes to Anya hold danger or gridlock." Air gusted from Tee's vents. "So sorry about that nasty odor. My air filter has never been this clogged. How much longer dare I defer maintenance? That is the question."

Zasu and I exchanged smiles, which cracked the dust on my cheeks. Tee was tough, especially for a hypochondriac. "It's good to ride in you again, Tee."

"Aren't you sweet. You are always welcome. My vinyl is your vinyl, since my Neutral wouldn't spring for leather."

"He had girls to raise," Jenn frowned at the dashboard.

"Of course he did," Tee said in a don't–poke–the–bear voice. "Here we are." Tee parked in a loading zone on Bleecker Street under a red sign with a red fish. *Le Poisson Rouge*. A nightclub for barely–of–age–ers. "I'll say when it's safe for you to leave. Until then, incognito." The windows tinted an opaque black. We couldn't see out so I assumed no one could see in.

As we waited, Zasu hummed a charming melody. Kelly Joe had played that tune for a couple kids at the subway station. That was back when I first knew him.

I had just met Lilah.

"Ow–ouch," Tee warned, and I loosened my grip on the steering wheel. The truck griped, "I'll be glad when this war's over and we can all relax. What I wouldn't give for fresh 30–weight. Say what you will about Hernandez, he understands regular oil changes. Go. Run. Now." Tee swung open her doors.

Zasu sprinted us across the sidewalk. The outside hit hard after the tinted soundproof truck cab. Concrete dust stung our eyes. Sirens echoed from every direction.

Inside the open door of the nightclub it was a *rouge* world. Red light thickened the air above red stairs between red walls. The stairs were steep and long. Zasu held us at the top of the stairs and apologized. "I know the way to Anya but I can only transport myself between Frames."

I hooked my arm through Jenn's. "Lead the way, we're right behind you."

Down we went and out of Frame. I'd figured the red decor was a gimmick in the Ma'Urth nightclub but it persisted. The stairwell stayed redder than a Communist lipstick factory. There was one giant improvement in the new Frame, though.

At the top of the stairs, Anya stood, and greeted us with smiles like we were headed for the beach together. "Brooklyn Bridge is under siege and our foes fill this area in many Frames. You will be safest here with me, until Kelly Joe can escort you home," she told us and turned back to the street.

Outside, a narrow line of Lobotomists marched east. Each Lobotomist pushed a wheeled contraption which had iron appendages affixed at intervals around each wheel. The contraptions seemed to have started life innocently, as lawn mowers, shopping carts. Baby strollers. As the wheels turned, iron appendages hit the ground with a rhythm that matched the steps of the Lobotomists. The iron magnified the step as though many walked where one did.

The sound of marching reverberated from all directions, so there must be other Lobotomists pushing more contraptions along other streets. With the contraptions, the Cysts would need far fewer feet to collapse Brooklyn Bridge in this Frame.

"Come closer, they cannot harm you. We observe from another Frame," Anya said. That explained why my view had a wavering aspect and none of the Lobotomists noticed us. We joined Anya outside and watched the grim advance of Lobotomists towards Brooklyn Bridge.

Again and again, Anya dissolved from view, became translucent, became solid again. During her translucent moments she'd say 'north flank, all, two beats,' or 'west center, half, six beats'. In this way she directed an attack on the Lobotomist marchers by jumping to other Frames to give orders to allies who waited, poised for attack.

Small teams of allies would appear in the Lobotomists' Frame, stab or garrote Lobotomists, grab the contraptions, and vanish out of Frame. Lobotomist bodies lay as they fell and the living marched over them. A big pileup occurred when living Lobotomists tripped over their dead. The next allies to attack kicked writhing bodies aside to grab contraptions, then tossed an explosive into the tangle.

Until then, I'd fantasized that when my side killed it would be noble.

Lobotomists fought without regard for their safety. This made them easy to kill and Anya won Bleecker Street quickly. She led us toward the East River, which whimpered like an injured dog in this Frame.

At the intersection of Bleecker and Bowery, Kelly Joe led a larger handful of allies in destroying Lobotomists as they exited from side streets. Similar fights were being waged at every intersection as far south as I could see, between here and Brooklyn Bridge. In every fight, the allies were outnumbered but it was Lobotomists who were dying.

"From the river!" Anya shouted, and vanished from our observation Frame. She materialized beside Kelly Joe in the attack Frame.

Over the East River, sunlight flashed on dust jackets as squadrons of soldier books flew toward us. Anya called to two clouds over the waterfront, "Swiftly, sound the retreat. Books arrive! Retreat!" The clouds scudded away in opposite directions and as they moved, they shredded into smaller slips of clouds that went to different intersections. The clouds repeated Anya's words and duplicated her voice, until it ricocheted, distorted, between buildings.

Allies looked up from their battles, confirmed the approach of books, and disappeared out of Frame, leaving the streets to the Lobotomists.

Except at Kelly Joe's intersection. He led his allies up into a building but, as soon as the books passed, they resumed attack on Lobotomists. The books began a slow circle–back. Anya aimed a flamethrower and shouted another order to retreat. Kelly Joe replied, "We can't stop now, we have them!" His jacket was soaked with gore and one sleeve was shredded. On his exposed arm, his tattoos were full of books.

"We cannot stay. We will lose too many."

After a long moment, Kelly Joe shouted orders for his allies to leave the Frame.

The clouds continued to spread Anya's voice and message into the distance. "Retreat! Books arrive!"

In every intersection, Lobotomists regrouped and resumed their march. They would soon destroy Brooklyn Bridge in another Frame.

Jenn looked at me.

"The books. I know. We have to."

76. WHAT I'M SUPPOSED TO DO

Tee did fancy Frame maneuvering to get us beyond gridlock, then returned to Ma'Urth and stayed there for the trip uptown. Kelly Joe rode back to the Julian with us. He sprawled in Tee's truck bed, since the cab was full with Jenn, Zasu, and me.

"Anya doesn't think I can get you home safely without—him." Tee sounded miffed. "I'm so relieved he stayed out of my cab," she stage–whispered. "You know who that is, right? The Pied Piper of –"

"We know who he was and who he is," Zasu replied. It was the first time I'd heard her interrupt anyone.

Faint harmonica notes. I opened Tee's back window and Kelly Joe's music filled the truck cab, bright and somber; sunshine on an avalanche. We listened in silence. Perhaps even Tee was moved.

Or not. When Tee pulled in front of the Julian, she snipped, "I wouldn't trust him."

As soon as Tee pulled away, Jenn muttered, "Hernandez needs to sell that bitch."

"Tee seemed unusually stressed today," I said.

My apartment smelled like trout simmered in paint thinner and neat stacks of handmade weapons lined the kitchen counter.

"Glad you're here," Hernandez greeted Kelly Joe and Zasu. "Five is a good number for this operation."

Everyone listened carefully as Hernandez explained his creations. He shook a steel tube with a rope wick; it sloshed and rattled. "These will burn hot, but take a few minutes to fully ignite. First thing we do is place these all around the perimeter, then... "

Everyone except me. He would fill me in later, after my visit to the Halls of Shared Knowledge.

I changed Frames inside Julian's foyer but I couldn't walk outside into Monasterium. Julian held his front door closed.

"Please stay inside, Nica, or depart this Frame. I hear war." His voice was tight.

"You are right, the war has begun, Julian. But we can't stop it by hiding indoors. My visits to the Halls may help us change the outcome." For emphasis, I shoved my shoulder into his door but it wouldn't budge. "Inside buildings won't be safe, either, if you prevent me from doing what I'm supposed to do."

He released the door.

I jogged half a block toward the Halls of Shared Knowledge before I understood that the tightness in Julian's voice had been terror.

Near the Halls, the air was so smoky that visibility was nil. My shoes stirred a gray ash that covered the sands. The ash was hot and I developed a high–stepped prance to minimize my feet's contact with it. Flecks of singed paper and scorched bark rained around me. My arm stung and I slapped an ember that ignited my arm hair.

As I approached the Hudson River, my lanyard jolted. I backed away, preparing to flee out of Frame. The pain level dropped when I headed up the incline to the Halls. This wasn't an urgent level of pain, so I continued on my mission.

Far away—probably across the river—were screams plus other noises I was sorry to recognize: the insistent revving of flying chainsaws and the mangled oily barks of clockwork dogs. What the hell? Were Warty Sebaceous Cysts attacking Monasterium? I tripled my pace. I had to finish my visit before they crossed the river.

Triple my pace was not very fast, though. The smoke was thicker here and my eyes got a sting that blinking didn't clear. I stripped off my tank top, turned it into a mask to cover my nose and mouth, and zipped my sweatshirt over my skin. Usually I'd enjoy the touch of the fuzzy innards but now it made my skin crawl. My body already understood what my conscious mind was refusing to acknowledge.

I couldn't see the Halls of Shared Knowledge but I should be close enough to touch them so I groped my way forward through raining embers. Damn, I must have taken a wrong turn. Ooof! I tripped in a pile of rocks. My movements got frantic as I scrambled to back away—the rocks were hot enough to scorch my clothes.

The air never cleared but my understanding did, after I stubbed my toe on a rock that crackled like lizard skin. The scorched hot outer layer peeled away and the rock beneath was infinitely smooth and refreshingly cool. This rubble wasn't rocks, it was a collapsed pile of tree stones, formerly the walls of the Halls of Shared Knowledge.

I couldn't find the Halls because they were no longer here. Or anyway this section was gone. How far did the destruction extend? I shuffled forward, fearful of tripping and losing what little sense of direction I could maintain in the opaque air. I monitored the lanyard's level of pain while blocking doubts like this one: if I had to run, how would I find Julian?

A few minutes of searching brought me to a short section of wall, uncollapsed; and an entranceway. I stepped through the arch and a bookcase whispered, "Welcome, seeker."

"Do you whisper because you are hurt, or because someone might hear us?"

"Listen well, then flee and do not return. Maelstrom's minions sought you here. They demanded to know what you had learned in your visit. We were forced to relinquish those records and those records were destroyed. Destroyed!"

"How bad is your damage?" Between words, I stuffed my tank top into my mouth. My need to cough was intense. But coughs can be heard much farther than whispers. How long would it take the flying chainsaws to cross the river?

"Our damage is modest yet unfathomable. Never before have the Halls been attacked. Never again will records be lost. Already we implement new procedures. Be reassured. Elsewhere the Halls survive and will be rebuilt here. But we remain a target so long as Maelstrom persists. We dare not assist you. And now you must flee."

"Okay," I gasped. It took all my will to keep from coughing.

The voice sounded smug. "The attackers knew of one visit. We were not forced to provide knowledge you gleaned on later visits."

That almost counted as good news. The Cysts knew I knew about the imprinting press, but not how much I knew.

I patted the stones in thanks, then swiveled so that my heels touched the remnant of wall. This faced me inland, toward Julian. I took off running with eyes closed, pictured myself running along a ruler. I kept the tank top stuffed in my mouth to muffle the coughs, which I could no longer control. Whenever I tripped, I sped up; that saved me from falling except twice.

Near the Halls, the hot ash deposits were so thick they singed my calves. I kept running and when my calves felt cool air, I opened my eyes. To the southeast was a tall dark lump that might be Julian. I adjusted direction and picked up my pace. The smoke was less thick here and it thinned with every block as I kept running.

One good thing about the muck in the air: it had made me less visible.

Maelstrom and the Cysts were on to me. How? Food for later thought. What mattered now was that Maelstrom cared. Sure, this destruction might be retribution because the Halls helped the allied cause. But my gut told me there was a different explanation: the Cysts destroyed the Halls to keep me from learning more about Maelstrom's press. Which meant there was something to learn. Something Maelstrom wanted to hide. Maybe I'd learned it already and maybe I hadn't. But he wouldn't bother if the press were indestructible.

77. ALMOST AND NEARLY

"Which tells me that the press can be destroyed."

Back in my apartment on Ma'Urth, I concluded my summary of my visit to the Halls of Shared Knowledge. My four accomplices donned carpenter's belts packed with weapons, while I added the obvious. "Because of this, Maelstrom will deploy forces to protect the press. If we ever had a window of opportunity, this is it."

Kelly Joe knew a Frame where we could carry our arsenals to Times Square without raising SWAT teams. He linked arms with Hernandez and Zasu and Traveled them there. I was supposed to bring Jenn but the weapons added a spiritual weight that exceeded my Travel powers. Kelly Joe came back for us, then we five walked through an empty Manhattan that was as bland as a pencil sketch left in the sun.

On our trek to Times Square, I had too much time to think about the weak points in our plan. If anything happened to Kelly Joe, we couldn't all change Frames together or quickly. If anything happened to Hernandez, we wouldn't know how to deploy the plastic explosives; he refused to share these because they took time and training to use safely. If anything happened to me, my books might stop cooperating.

My insides were in knots with every muscle kinked. We stood to win big, or lose most of the beings who mattered to me. Including me.

We reached our reconnaissance room and Traveled to Maelstrom's Frame without incident. The room was almost as we had left it. My backpack was on the floor but the room was empty of books. Would I ever see them again? Presumably they were out there, trying to convert newly turned books. Unless –

Now wasn't the time to finish that sentence.

We erratic–walked to the windows.

"Mmh!" The noise escaped me: the changes outside were startling.

Not everything had changed. Crates of books continued to move along the conveyer belt to the imprinting press, where the mechanical hands continued to feed books into the press. The enormous netted tent still ran south along Broadway and was even more packed with newly enslaved, untrained books.

Now, however, the conveyor belt and press were no longer accessible from the street. Around the book enslavement operation was a tall barricade, a lattice of razor wire. Outside the barricade, in all directions, were guards. Lobotomists with *machetes* and Entourage with three–barreled rifles prowled the streets. Soldier books patrolled every intersection and flying chainsaws buzzed between, with clockwork dogs gallumphing below.

Surely ours was now a suicide mission. Success was about as likely as Maelstrom being struck by conscience and destroying the press on his own. I looked to my *compadres* to begin our retreat. They continued to study the scene outside from every angle the windows allowed.

Maybe I was overreacting. No books or chainsaws flew over the conveyor belt or press—they patrolled outside the barricade. Almost all the guards were outside the barricade, which had no gate for easy egress. About a dozen Entourage were inside the barricade, but they were a block away, down where the conveyor belt exited the Connector. Their backs were to the press and they seemed to be watching for trouble that might come through the Connector with the crates of books, which now arrived lidless. All the safeguards were to prevent access to the conveyor belt and press, to protect what was inside the barricade.

But we were already inside.

If we were discovered, we'd have several seconds before the Entourage who were inside could get from the Connector to us; and at least half a minute before the full force of guards was upon us. That might be enough time to finish the job. And get away.

My biggest regret was that I still wore my lanyard. I didn't need its stabbing reminders that danger was near. Here. Everywhere.

The five of us stepped away from the window at the same moment. It was time and we knew our roles. Zasu wrapped her arms around us all, creating a quick group embrace. Then I stopped thinking and prepped my glue bundles, confident because Hernandez was a great military leader and I trusted this team to succeed despite the odds.

Hernandez tapped Jenn's watch. *Start timing.* He, Kelly Joe, and Zasu lit the slow—burning incendiary tubes and distributed them so we each carried some outside. I lugged my glue bundles, dangling from clothesline.

Jenn extended three fingers. We had three minutes to get the incendiary tubes in place. After that they would burn too hot to handle. The tubes made little noticeable smoke, especially compared to the diesel exhaust of the flying chainsaws.

Downstairs outside, we stood tight against the building and moved as little as possible. We had practiced noiseless moving and we held to that, although Maelstrom's guards made such a racket, our stealth was lost in the commotion outside the barricade.

Outside the barricade, commotion. Here by the press, hypnotic repetition. The squeaking of the conveyor belt, the scraping of the mechanical hands, the chunking of books into the press, the squawking of newly enslaved books. Every movement was predictable. This close to the press it smelled of greased steel, like Ben's street skating phase, an ordinary familiar smell which was comforting.

Kelly Joe and Zasu went first. Kelly Joe erratic—walked into the open area beyond the press and crouched. From there, he could see all three mechanical hands, the base of the press, and Zasu. He became scenery. I could barely spot him and I knew where to look.

He moved a finger to direct Zasu's arms. She stretched them out and around, to place incendiary tubes around the base of the press. On the far side, her arm didn't reach, so she stretched her torso until it did.

The press blocked my view of the enormous tent full of newly turned books, but their twittering swept us in waves. I convinced myself that some book voices sounded familiar, calling in the queer sharp tones of bookspeak and Refrencian. I envisioned my books carrying out their assignment, letting the new slaves know they had a choice about whom they served.

The incendiary wicks hissed like snakes on their deathbeds. How long would it take Maelstrom's eavesdroppers to locate that sound?

Jenn extended two fingers. Two minutes left. We were right on time. Zasu and Kelly Joe got a thumbs—up from Jenn as they returned to the building facade. Now Hernandez slipped behind the press and snaked under the netting that created its enclosure. Distorted by the netting, his movements looked jerky like a silent movie. That close to the press, if the mechanical hands detected his presence he had no protection. And he couldn't even Travel on his own. *He'll be fine. He'll be fine.*

The metal of the press had a top seam. Hernandez aligned plastic explosives along that seam then backed away and snaked out of the netting, all without turning his back on the mechanical hands. When he returned to the building, he gripped the detonator with one finger hovering above the switch that would detonate the explosives. The plastics would split the metal seam and get more air inside the press, to help the incendiaries burn hotter and faster.

Jenn raised one finger. In one minute, the incendiary wicks would flame and the heat in the tubes would rise rapidly. That would be our cue to run close, lob grenades toward the maw and under the feet of the press and run like hell to the stairs that led to our reconnaissance room. We had enough firepower to obliterate ten presses, if they were made of Ma'Urth—ly steel. If.

The concrete walls of our building might protect us from shrapnel. There should be just enough time for Kelly Joe to Travel us out of Frame before the guards arrived, drawn by the explosions.

But that grand *finale* was a long minute away. Before the incendiaries flamed, we had to eliminate the threat posed by the mechanical hands. Disabling the hands was my contribution, and like the rest it went flawlessly. At first.

Down the block, deep in the book tent, books squawked in tones that sounded taunting, like bar bullies. *Step outside and say that.* Other book voices replied and soon many books twittered at once. Outside the barricade, some guards headed down that way.

Not now. I couldn't think about what all that meant.

Zasu, Kelly Joe, and I dangled lengths of clothesline and erratic—walked to the conveyer belt. The clothesline ended in tubes of crazy—glue, sliced open then wrapped in thin foil so the glue wouldn't dry.

On my periphery, Jenn's fingers counted down the seconds. *Ten, nine, eight.* We set the bundles on the conveyor belt and erratic—walked toward our building. Still right on time.

Behind us, the distal end of the book tent erupted in screeches and rushes of movement. Were books fighting? A crush of books hit the net on this end, as though trying to get out of the way. I peeked over my shoulder. Outside the barricade, most of the guards ran away from us, toward the source of the disturbance inside the book tent. Nice to lose the guards. But. My neck muscles added nine knots, one for each of my books out there, somewhere, in danger.

Five, four. Kelly Joe, Zasu and I made it back to our building.

Damn! Our strategy, timing, and positioning were perfect. Jenn and I exchanged grins as the mechanical hands detected intruders on the conveyer belt. Each hand grabbed a crazy–glue bundle and squeezed. Glue extruded, clamping fingers to other fingers. The hands flailed, spreading glue that jammed their wrist joints.

Three, two. That's when things went south.

"Betty," Jenn whispered. Betty was Jenn's cat, long ago. Betty got a paw stuck to a wad of duct tape, and in the few seconds before I threw myself on the cat to suppress her, she flailed around the room so wildly that Jenn's snow dome collection was a total loss.

Trapped by crazy–glue, the mechanical hands whipped and snapped, pummeling book crates, the imprinting press, each other. They screeched like opera divas imitating sirens. The Entourage who were on our side of the barricade, down at the far end watching the Connector, spun in our direction, saw the flailing hands. Half of them ran our way.

One. Flames shot from the incendiaries, the best fireworks display of my life. The Entourage who had stayed at the Connector broke into a run and shouted for reinforcements. Outside the barricade, guards flowed.

I can't separate out the rest of the chronology, the events are simultaneous in my memories.

In its wild flailing, one of the mechanical hands swept the top of the press and came away with plastic explosives stuck to its gluey mitt. Another mechanical hand smashed the side of the press, which extinguished one incendiary tube and stuck another to its glue wad. As the hand flopped and waved, that incendiary also went out. The third hand whacked the netting of the book tent, which sliced a gash in it.

While the hands went berserk, the fight inside the book tent had spread. Frightened books found the gash and widened it in their rush to escape.

Good news, bad news. The near end of the conveyor belt and the press were protected under text–proof netting, but the far end of the conveyor belt was not. Many escaping books flew that way. Frightened, untrained, they shed most of their text unintentionally. The conveyor belt and the Entourage who were inside the barricade were sliced to tiny bits. This eliminated our most immediate threat. However, books continued to pour through the gash in the tent. Some lost control and tumbled into the side of the netting around the imprinting press. One book hit an incendiary tube and burst into flames. Two others hit incendiary tubes and snuffed the flames.

Escaping books and flailing mechanical hands had removed most of our carefully placed explosives. Sure, we still had the grenades but could we get them close enough to the press? The way the hands whipped and snapped, they could be in a Cat–5 hurricane. And with each second that elapsed without lobbed grenades, we came closer to the moment when Maelstrom's guards would join us inside the barricade.

Until the future day when Maelstrom destroyed the Halls of Shared Knowledge, they would carry the story of how these allies *almost* and *nearly* destroyed Maelstrom's imprinting press.

Jenn grabbed my arms and yelled above the crashes of the mechanical hands and the squawks of the terrified books, "Thank you for showing me the Frames." She stretched up to kiss me, swiveled to Hernandez, grabbed his chin to pull his attention from the press, and yelled, "I love you."

His reply was a gargoyle's frown. Somewhere below consciousness he understood her intentions.

Jenn lunged to push the switch on his detonator. The plastic explosives, still glued to one mechanical hand, blew that hand into the barricade and tore an enormous new gap in the book tent. Immediately, Lobotomists shoved through the hole in the barricade, mindless of the blood and flesh they left on the razor wire. I think someone shouted to put out those fires.

Jenn grabbed my grenade and suddenly she was an athlete. She sprinted to the press and as she ran she pulled the pin, stuffed that grenade in her belt, then pulled the pin from her own grenade. Hernandez dived for her but she did a quarterback two–step and got past him. She dodged the frenzied whipping of two mechanical hands, made it to the maw of the imprinting press, clamped hands on the sides, and vaulted herself inside. I think the press squealed.

I think books outside the book tent squawked bookspeak that began to calm the stampede inside.

But all I heard during those seconds was Hernandez' wail, "Noooooooooo!"

"Get inside!" Kelly Joe yelled at Zasu and me, as he dived to cover Hernandez.

We were on the stairs to our reconnaissance room when the ground lurched and a brief gale flattened me into the stairs. I have no memory of the sound of the explosion but I did notice a clink on the stairs. A circuit board with chipped edges spun on the step above me. I shoved it in my carpenter belt and Zasu helped me stand.

Oily metal the size of a rioter's brick smashed the wall beside her cheek. Projectiles that might have been oily bolts splintered the wood of the door, leaving pockmarks shaped like a smiley face with a bullet through its forehead. I began to shiver.

"We must away." Zasu put an arm through mine. But she couldn't Travel me and she wouldn't leave me there.

And I wasn't budging. "Jenn."

Zasu walked up a few stairs then dug in her heels, wrapped her arms around my waist, and said, "Go, then. Quickly." Her torso stretched outside with me to look, but her legs stayed planted inside, ready to yank me upstairs when need be.

Outside, nothing was as it had been. A wind from above marked the flapping of thousands of escaped books. The air was black with their unintentional text drops. Silvery mush lined the ground where the razor wire barricade had stood, cut to infinitely small pieces by text shed in panic. Beyond the barricade, pools of beige and red mush filled open areas—most of the guards had met the same fate as the barricade. The survivors among Maelstrom's minions pressed against building exteriors, trapped until the books calmed or flew on.

Text–proof protective netting still covered the area directly over the imprinting press but that netting had no job to do.

The imprinting press was gone. A shallow hole in the asphalt marked where it had stood. One gluey mechanical hand lay beyond the hole, prone but still flailing. A piece of metal the shape of a V stuck in the concrete wall outside our doorway and X–shaped cracks in the wall testified to the force of impact. The metal looked familiar. That rusted weld had been a corner at the maw of the press.

The squawks of the books, the shouts of Lobotomist handlers. The clunk thud whack as scraps of rusted metal hit the street. The foe regrouped and remnants of the imprinting press rained on the scene of its crimes.

Kelly Joe and Hernandez were gone. No beige and red mush oozed where they had been, so I could assume that Kelly Joe had Traveled them out of Frame before explosions shoved shards of press in all directions. Try saying that ten times fast.

I was glad to be in shock. Otherwise I'd have to face my last observation before Zasu tugged me back to the stairs.

The press was gone because Jenn was gone.

78. MORE JENN THROUGH THE WORLD

Hernandez or me—hard to say who was worse at mourning. I had opportunity to compare our mourning styles because we were alone with our grief in Frivolous Bedlam. Anya needed everyone for some battle but we got left because we were liabilities in our current states of mind.

I wallowed in dark thoughts. No doubt Maelstrom had books at Anya's latest battle. We'd destroyed the press so he couldn't enslave more books, but he already had a vast army—trained killers who enjoyed their work. He could probably win the war with existing book soldiers. Why hadn't I thought of that before?

I could use some purr therapy but I hadn't seen Leon or Dizzy for ages. Who knew what unfathomable dangers they'd encountered? They were tough but they weren't invincible. They could be dead.

Because of my effort to destroy the imprinting press, thousands of untrained, newly enslaved books fled in an aerial stampede that killed many. Maelstrom's books chased the survivors, so they might be dead now, too. My books would have perished with those other innocent tomes.

I couldn't wrap my head around any of that, but I tried, to protect myself from thinking about Jenn's last moments.

Which Hernandez couldn't stop thinking about. "I should've had a better plan. I should've been the one. I should've known. I could've stopped her. What she did. Inside that thing. I should've had a better plan." He'd run thoughts round a loop then pound a wall with hand or head. I tried to reason with him initially, but reason was not in his current repertoire. I tried to stop him when he punched holes in Julian's walls, until the building caught me in the foyer and said, "The damage is superficial, I repair while he sleeps. This process of destruction may help his healing, so I am happy to enable it."

Since then, during waking hours I let Hernandez have the apartment. I sat on the front stoop so that building chatter could stupefy me.

Inside, above and behind me, Hernandez' rants were punctuated with soothing murmurs. That meant Zasu had stopped by. Soon the rants—and wall pounding—would cease. That would mean that Zasu had gotten Hernandez to fall asleep and she would then come out to check on me.

I didn't want soothing so I considered going for a walk before Zasu got downstairs, but food carts were parked at both ends of the block, silent and watching. Their concern was harder to take than Zasu's.

I couldn't remember Jenn. I tried but no memories came—like I never knew her, she never existed, we didn't share most of our lives. This evil soul–freeze was always my first reaction when someone I love died. Once in it, I was aware that I needed to get out but I could never figure out how. Previously, the way I escaped was that Jenn would lead me out.

The sun was bright but not warm. My shadow wavered on the step below me. The door opened behind me and I felt trapped in the open.

Zasu said, "Good morning, Nica. Today's sky is so blue, we could be in Halcyon."

I feigned compassion. "Homesick must be especially hard when your home is gone."

She joined me on the stoop. "I have my memories and my knowledge that Halcyon persists, although empty. One day will come my time to return."

"I need my memories," I muttered. I stared at the pavement and tuned in to building chatter. They'd converted the song *London Bridge* into a knock–knock joke. Building nonsense often started as sense. Maybe this joke started as more bad news about Brooklyn Bridge.

Just when you think your back muscles can't clench any tighter.

Zasu hugged me, her arms molding to my body contours. I didn't hug back but couldn't deny the value. If you want comfort, get a Gumby to hug you. Or rather, *the* Gumby; the others were dead. If I had feelings, they'd be much improved from the hug. Each day Zasu visited, each day with infinite patience and cheer while I mostly ignored her. Saint Zasu. I said that ten times fast but my success didn't count because I only talked inside my head.

"And so here we are," Zasu released me from today's hug. "We did not survive to only grieve." She kissed my head and then she was gone.

The sun stretched my shadow down the steps.

She was right.

"Bite your mother's ass." Quoting Jenn, I replied, hours after Zasu left. And then I screamed, because I could hear Jenn saying it.

Inside my apartment, Hernandez slept on the couch. Once I forgot to put water in a pan and cooked it over a high flame. His forehead looked like that pan— pocked with welts, discolored by bruises. His knuckles were raw and pink. The plastered walls and the hardwood countertop showed signs of battering.

I kicked the couch below his head. I couldn't tell whether he opened his eyes because the circles around them had become so dark and the sockets so prominent. When his breathing changed, I said, "It was bad luck, not poor planning, dumbass. The mechanical hands went nuts and what Jenn did was the only way to save the mission and she moved fast to beat us to it. Only a shit–for–brains would blame himself." I lacked Jenn's flare for foul language and he winced at her name but held his position in the gloom.

"Are you talking to me or to yourself?" he replied.

"I don't know. But get the fuck up. We need to go home and spread more Jenn through the world."

He got up. I could barely budge Hernandez out of Frame. It was like he'd packed himself with dirt since the last time I transported him. Or maybe that was me.

When we arrived in my apartment on Ma'Urth, Hernandez pulled his modest collection of clothes out of his duffel bag and strewed pieces around the floor as he searched for tonight's perfect outfit.

"Which one do you like?" He held up two identical t–shirts. Without waiting for an answer, he dropped both t–shirts and grabbed a third.

I planted my phone in its speakers and attempted a musical homage to Jenn, but—not for the first time—I marveled that such abominable taste in music could coexist with so many remarkable qualities. My homage lasted for most of Jenn's favorite song, until death in hypothermic water became preferable. I removed my phone from the speakers when Celine started the heartbreaking soaring conclusion. Hernandez looked relieved.

"I need to take a shower," I said, "Back in a few." I took the longest shower I've ever taken, thirteen hours if timed in a Frame where their minutes equal our hours. Not long enough. Jenn only had a shower that short when the water heater went out. I left the water running while I dressed, brushed my teeth, and read all the labels in the bathroom. My toothpaste is 3 per cent baking soda. Seventeen minutes.

Hernandez and I staged a rolling wake that evening, Jenning around Manhattan.

I stopped to applaud the fuchsia jacket and red slacks of a woman waiting for a light to change. "Love that color combo."

On the subway, we sat across from an arguing couple. The young woman reminded me of Lilah, which threw me out of character and into a funk. Fortunately, as we debarked the train, Hernandez leaned in to the young woman's ear, to advise, "He's a dick. You can do better."

I got back in the game when we passed a food truck that sold smoothies and I patted the sign: *Add the face melter, $2*. "Fuckin' A, we've got to try that!" so we did.

A bus shut its doors as we ran up to it. I yanked my top to give the driver a quick flash of breast. The doors opened.

As we took our seats, Hernandez asked, "She did that?"

"Not since high school."

He shrugged, "High school counts."

On the bus, I struck up conversation with an elderly gentleman reading a pamphlet in another language. "Is that Greek?" and it was. Before he left the bus, I learned a few handy phrases.

By evening's end, I faced dueling overwhelms. I had lost Jenn and regained my memories of her. She came back to me when I tuned in to life around me. The evening seemed to help Hernandez, too. Traveling back to Frivolous Bedlam was much easier than when we'd left—we were no longer packed with dirt.

79. I CLUTCHED IT TO MY HEART

We slept better than we had since Jenn's death. We made it past dawn, then Julian woke us with repeated slams of my front door. I rubbed my face. "What's up, Julian?"

In reply, the building opened my street—facing window.

The window view was filled with cement columns studded with pottery shards. The Watts Towers were outside. "Monk and Miles are here!" I yelled to Hernandez and ran down the stairs so fast that I became airborne on the front stoop. I launched myself onto the nearer Tower, who turned out to be Miles.

"Our bird knows how to fly," he said and my skin buzzed with the static electricity that meant the Towers were laughing.

Hernandez stepped outside Julian's front door, his eyes black with misery.

"Go ahead and hit us if you need to," Miles offered.

Hernandez flexed his battered hands and said, "I'm good, thanks." He climbed Monk, hand over hand to the Tower's peak.

From below came a scrape and a squeak, "Oh! Sorry!" A food cart—no doubt popping wheelies—had run into Monk's base. The carts had kept their distance lately but my vibe had to be more welcoming this morning and anyway they seemed drawn to Monk and Miles. In fact, my entire block was now packed with food carts and trucks, tilted onto back wheels to see the tops of the Towers. When the cart hit Monk, the others gave a collective gasp and backed away like giant magnets had tugged them.

Monk replied, "Apology without wrong is a fruit without seed."

"My brother means, no harm done." But the carts seemed unconvinced, until Miles added, with a playful yell, "Watch this!"

Suddenly we were flying—somehow, the hundred foot sculpture that was Miles jumped to the far side of the carts. I shared their whirs of astonishment. A smoothie truck with pink and orange striped awning swiveled to keep Miles in view and he leaned over her.

"Love that awning, girlie, you are ready for sun and now you got me ready, too!"

Miles can make anyone giggle. Ice broken with the carts, he jumped back beside Monk. The food carts cheered and I laughed, which made me cough. My laughter was rusty.

A bit of wonder glimmered in Hernandez' eyes.

Miles turned serious. "Trashing Maelstrom's imprinting press, that's a game changer. Nica, Hernandez, you done good and you need to give yourselves credit."

Monk added gently, "Love may be gone but never departs."

"Maelstrom and the Cysts are barking mad now and that shows how hard you hit 'em," Miles continued.

"The proof is in the fury," Monk agreed.

My head iced over. Last time we upset our foes, we lost Brooklyn Bridge. What did they do for revenge this time? Did it affect Anya's current battle? "How did they retaliate? Is everyone okay?"

"We were ready for 'em and all's well. But you ringleaders need extra protection until we give them something new to be mad about. Nica, you've got protection but we're taking Hernandez with us, we got a set–up to keep him safe in Los Angeles." Miles said my hometown's name with flawless Spanish pronunciation.

Hand under hand, Hernandez descended from Monk as though in a hurry to reach the street. "I can't leave Nica. She's got to be in more danger than anybody. I'd better stay with her."

"Prophecy protects her," Monk said.

Huh? I reviewed the obscure phrase that was supposed to be my prophecy. *In the blackest of days, a seer, a walker, and a Neutral will lead the foes of darkness.* Where was the protection in that?

Monk recited, "'Only the master of slaves can destroy the champion of slaves.'"

I could dimly see why somebody thought that applied to Maelstrom and me, but Frames prophecies made horoscopes look precise. I'd never heard the slavemaster prophecy before and wished I still hadn't. I lost the strength in my legs and fumbled to sit on the stoop. "How many prophecies am I in?"

"That all depends on what new surprises you've got in store."

The admiration in Miles' voice offset some of the terror that this prophecy induced.

Hernandez joined me on the stoop as if to say, *where she goes, I go.* "Need to get something straight. The prophecy doesn't say Maelstrom *will* kill Nica, just that he's the only one who can?"

Monk made affirmative noises. I appreciated the distinction and ratcheted my terror down to dread.

Hernandez lobbied, "Let me stay here, Nica needs backup in the New Yorks."

Miles spoke patiently. "She's got protection, you're the one we can't guarantee as safe."

When Miles mentioned protection, something rubbed my back and made it rumble.

Leon! Now I could admit how frightened I'd been about his extended absence. He looked unharmed but ill–kept—he needed another shave. "You mean that Leon is my protection," I realized.

"Got that right." Miles said.

Hernandez wasn't giving up. "You told us not to trust cats."

"When a cat is near, that idea has purpose." Monk sounded frustrated, like Hernandez was being irrelevant.

"Are you saying Leon isn't a cat?"

"Only superficially," Miles replied, then cut us off. "No more questions or debate, we've got to move."

Leon squinted at me. I reached over to pet him and his megapurr started before I touched him.

"I need to be here with Nica!" Hernandez clung to Julian's front door knob. Suddenly I understood his refusal to leave the New Yorks: this was where he'd known Jenn.

"I need a favor," I told him. "Could you take Jenn's stuff back home to L.A. with you?"

He hunched like an anvil was falling toward him, but then he straightened. "What. Okay. Sure."

I told the Towers, "We need to pack."

Leon, Hernandez, and I Traveled back to Ma'Urth. Jenn's stuff was everywhere in my apartment. Removing it was brutal but leaving it would have been harder still.

While Hernandez shoved clothes into Jenn's U–Haul of a suitcase, I emptied the hall closet and found five cloth–bound books. Jenn's journals. She wrote daily, had done so for as long as I'd known her. I thumbed through the cloth books. She had filled four since her arrival in the New Yorks. The fifth journal was empty. I slid to the floor of the closet and clutched it to my heart.

At last I cried about Jenn.

Hernandez didn't question my absence and when I emerged from the closet, his eyes were more puffy than mine felt. I put three journals in the suitcase and set the other two on my bookshelf. Seeing those shelves empty gouged more holes in my heart, a hole for each of my lost books.

By the time we returned to Frivolous Bedlam, Hernandez and I looked like we'd caught a sudden cold. He strapped Jenn's suitcase onto Monk's base and I sat on Julian's front stoop, petting Leon ceaselessly as I prepared for my next goodbyes. I couldn't hear what the Towers said to Hernandez but he returned to me with wonder in his voice, the kind he'd had in the early days, like when we'd first heard Anya's voice come from a cloud. "The Towers have a special way of Traveling long distance. They'll get me home faster than a jet would."

Miles, Monk, and Hernandez took off to the west, Miles flirting with buildings as they went. I imagined them crossing the Hudson, which pleased me, but that reminded me of Jenn gathering tree stones. Which made me shut down thinking, which infuriated me. I just got my memories back and now I couldn't take them! If I avoided memories of Jenn they'd fade. And then she'd really be gone.

"I need a run. You with me?" I asked Leon. He was. We paced each other across town.

"Hey, Cat Shaver, race with us." A trio of food carts lined up along Madison. The request had pleading in it.

I lined up with them. "On your mark, get set—what the!" Everyone except me was already racing.

"Go go go," the carts yelled and the buildings took up the refrain. The carts were unscrupulous racers. Every time I tried to pull ahead, a cart darted across my path. Leon jumped out of the race and perched on a pretzel cart.

I stopped running and called fondly, "I'm out. Bunch of cheaters."

A cart replied, sounding puzzled, "Of course. Cheating is the funnest part."

I squawked like a parrot with a pack–a–day habit. I loved these guys. Jenn would have loved them, too, but she never got a chance to know them. The thought made me stumble but I kept moving.

I'll grieve for Jenn forever, but debilitating active mourning was done with me, again, for now. I needed to go home to Ma'Urth, get a decent night's sleep, and find my allies.

But first I had one stop to make in Bedlam.

80. I CAN'T GO BACK THERE

In Frivolous Bedlam, Brooklyn Bridge still stood but looked like he had stopped a meteorite swarm. He called out to me, "You'll want to stop there. As much as I would savor your steps across my span, I am not a safe structure."

"But they've only collapsed you in a few Frames."

"My health in some Frames defines it for all. Knowing this, they attacked those Frames first."

"Why are they trying to destroy you?"

"I never seek to understand a mind I do not wish to know. Be assured, they cannot destroy me until the dark day when they take Frivolous Bedlam. So long as I stand here, I stand."

"They won't get Frivolous Bedlam." The thought of Warty Sebaceous Cysts near these buildings gave me the conviction of Joan of Arc.

"None will avoid this war when—unnh."

The Bridge wobbled and the East River's cackling spiked.

"You okay?" I waited. I asked again. I waited.

"Time," Brooklyn Bridge whispered, then went silent. I had to conclude the Cysts had just collapsed Brooklyn Bridge in another Frame.

I took off running and returned to Ma'Urth at a jog; Leon stayed nearby. Lunchtime and the Manhattan crowds were heavy. It felt good to get jostled.

Shortly after Leon and I reached my apartment, Hernandez called, which meant he was in a Frame with phone service.

"Hey! How's the trip so far?"

"I'm home, been back for hours." Monk and Miles had taken Hernandez across the United States—more than three thousand miles—in a few hours, but Hernandez' voice held no *amazed*.

"What's wrong?"

"That day in Ben's apartment." He meant the day that Ben allowed us to hide a young man named Ziti in his apartment. Unbeknownst to Ben, Ziti was a witness to the Gumby genocide. The Cysts came to Ben's apartment, murdered Ziti, and buried Ben's memories beneath an indefinite fear that he'd be sorry if he excavated for them.

"That day," I confirmed.

"My cousin and his family, they're all like Ben was that day. Except for *la pequeña*. All she can say is, 'they stole the friend'. Ben is gone, Ben is nowhere."

"He thought he was being followed. He might have gotten out in time." Or.

"I'm checking his meetings. I warned Fatty and Mikal. They just got out of the hospital. Cysts could attack them again."

"Okay. Yeah. Thanks. Keep me posted."

"My guess? Ben's alive. They can mess with you more that way."

"Okay. Yeah."

I was out of words. The phone slipped from my hand, crunched on the floor. Ben had to be alive. I'll know when he's gone.

Maybe if I'd told him about the Frames.

I wanted to go find the allies, join a battle—any battle—but my previous plan was the wiser one. Get decent sleep and head out in the morning. Hernandez' news was not a sleep–inducer, however. I paced around my apartment. Leon paced with me, then stopped at his food bowl.

I needed a run. I was on the front stoop and the Julian's door had just clicked locked behind me when the lanyard blasted me with pain. I doubled over and grabbed my abdomen—not the best position to face imminent danger. As I straightened, time became fluid and I was aware of many things at once.

I'd come outside unexpectedly and Leon was still inside. I'd dropped my front door key and it glinted on the sidewalk, close but out of reach. Around my block, nothing seemed out of the ordinary. Parked cars lined the curbs. Taxis noodled around a delivery truck that was double–parked. Scattered pedestrians did not look my way.

The lanyard stabbed again. I pretended all was as usual and continued to the sidewalk to fetch my door key. My nerve endings jangled, which made my skin itch. A blur shot up the stairs from the basement apartment and stood a boot on my key. It was my old enemy, Scabman.

He wore the same cheap blue suit he'd worn during TV interviews about his N.Y.P.D. unit to stop construction site arson. His eyes glowed red, as they did in my nightmares and on the day that he ripped Lilah limb from limb.

A taxi skidded up the curb and the driver jumped out, dreadlocks swinging.

"Cabbie? Really?" I greeted the other Lobotomist manager.

Mathead flashed her pointy teeth and opened the cab's back door. "Get in."

I couldn't let them touch me, because then they could Travel me to a Frame where they could do what they pleased. Scabman tried to herd me toward Mathead and I tried to go anywhere but there. I made a sprint up the stoop but Scabman jumped higher. I launched for the street, screaming for help.

Daylight, busy streets. No help. Come on, people!

Did I recollect a story where Manhattanites stood around while a pedestrian got murdered?

My launch surprised my attackers and bought me a few seconds of escape. Then somehow Mathead was in front of me and right behind me were the cloying chemicals of Scabman's bubble gum breath.

Mathead dropped her hands. Scabman's boots scraped to a halt. The lanyard pain stopped. I spotted Dizzy behind Mathead's legs. The cat's fur was puffed like she was ready to fight. Seeing Dizzy is apparently what stopped Scabman. I ran to the far side Dizzy, dared a look behind me, and saw the view that had stopped Mathead: Leon, crouched and swishing his tail.

To recap. The cat who seems to understand English and the cat who might not be a cat had just saved me from the bogus cop and fake transportation professional who pretended to be human. Just another day in the Frames.

The Julian's front door unlocked as I reached the top of the stoop. Getting my shaking hand to the doorknob empowered me to turn around. The tableau remained unchanged but now Mathead glared at me, her eyes glowing crimson.

I promised her, "The Lobotomists will need new managers soon. You're going to pay for what you did to Lilah and Sam."

Mathead's expression said *whodat?* and I wanted instant vengeance. "Leon, Dizzy. Take –" Before I could finish the sentence, Mathead and Scabman had evaporated out of Frame.

My defenders followed me inside, tails in the air.

Now sleep was even less plausible so on to Plan B: fortify, then find the allies. I sat with Leon and Dizzy on the Julian's front stoop and forced myself to gnaw a healthful cardboard protein bar. I also forced myself to remain on the stoop, which now reminded me of Scabman and Mathead. I needed to reclaim it from those fears.

A tow truck pulled away, towing the taxi that Mathead had driven onto the sidewalk. Not long after, a shadow flapped across my legs. Overhead, an enormous pelican circled. His beak was scarred, his eyes were as black as the day after Armageddon. He seemed to return my stare. Surely this was the same pelican who intimidated my books in Bedlam.

The pelican flew east, away from the river, returned, circled overhead, flew off again.

He did this a few times. He must want me to follow him, because when I stepped in his direction, he flew further but when I stopped, he came back to me.

When I stood, Leon got up, too; Dizzy stretched to take our spots in the sun.

The pelican led Leon and I through Central Park and out the other side, close to the Met. As soon as we were out of Central Park, the pelican turned and led us back into the park. Ho–kay, guess he overshot.

Then things got screwy. The bird would fly into Central Park, I'd follow, he'd fly out again. It took six repetitions before I noticed that he dove steeply lower each time he entered the park's airspace, and flew steeply higher each time he exited.

At last I got it. He wanted me to go downhill when I entered the park. But Central Park was at the same level as the street. And nowhere did the elevation change as much as the pelican's flight path implied.

Except in Maelstrom's Frame, where Central Park was a crater.

"I can't go back there," I shouted to the sky. It being Manhattan, no passersby looked up. The pelican continued to dive into Central Park. I dropped to the curb and pressed my forehead into my knees. I couldn't go back to Maelstrom's Frame.

A horn blasted me to my feet. I'd blocked a bus stop. From a nearby bench, Leon played sphinx and watched the pelican's steep dives and climbs. I dropped onto Leon's bench. I was near the spot where Kelly Joe had first Traveled me to Maelstrom's Frame and we followed trails into the Central Park crater.

I wanted to assume that it was safe for me to go to Maelstrom's Frame because the pelican said to go. Of course, perhaps I misunderstood everything. Perhaps this was just a bird riding air currents.

I walked toward Central Park with Leon close beside me. Correction. On Ma'Urth, he was right there. But when I Traveled to Maelstrom's Frame, Leon did not follow, to my dismay.

In Maelstrom's version of the Upper East Side, the streets around me were empty but I wasn't alone. The air echoed with the grinding of clockwork dogs and militaristic shouts. I could not have been more exposed. The previous shells of buildings were collapsed in heaps of fresh rubble. My nose stung with an odor like sulfuric sauerkraut, giving me another reason to hurry. In three steps of erratic walk I was over the sharp lip and into the Central Park crater. I kept up the erratic walk as I descended, earning cramps in both legs.

The slope was steeper than I remembered it, the rock more rubbly, and the landscape barren of previous patches of feeble plant life. The rock edges were jagged as though recently blasted. I picked my way downslope without breaking my neck or raising a ruckus.

All these signs of fresh destruction. Were these what the pelican had sent me here to see?

Eerie, how silent the crater got when I reached the level where sound was blocked. With Kelly Joe, that silence had been reassuring. Today, it made me think I was missing something I shouldn't be missing. I headed back up toward the surface.

Those marching steps and shouted orders that echoed around me sounded like troops in training. Was that what the pelican wanted me to know?

Closer to the surface, I was more exposed yet no more enlightened. I looped north, descending into the crater once again. Here, below the sound barrier, the flatter surfaces had a peculiar sheen. I stopped and stared. What was shiny? Should I go closer or back away? My eyes glazed with strain as I tried to see more. Again, a surface glinted. As though the surface had moved. Over there, another glint. Way down below, another one.

Watching for glints was like watching fireflies—wherever I wasn't looking, a light flashed. I went deeper into the crater, sensing the reality before my thoughts articulated it. Finally, I had to stop. I could walk no farther. From here on down, the trails and slopes were blocked. They were covered in books.

Lose Twenty Pounds and *Summer* hovered by my shoulders. With a hushed squawk from *Lose Twenty Pounds*, books rose from their resting places and idled on all sides—as far as I could see—creating a breeze that hit me from all directions. *Summer* squawked and every book dipped, down then up, in the book gesture of respect. To me.

I grabbed my two books and pressed one to each cheek. "You're alive. I'm so proud and grateful. What—what of my other books? Did any survive?"

The Blue–Eyed Shan limped into view. Missing his back cover, he flew in floppy arcs. He, *Summer*, and *Lose Twenty Pounds* shed text on the trail above me. The light was dim so I had to examine each sentence from multiple angles. Gradually I read that five of my nine books had survived; and all these books in the crater were now allies. An arithmetic book had estimated that nearly ten thousand books were here.

"I'll need help to get you out of here. Stay hidden. I'll be back."

81. NICA'S ARMY

Kelly Joe's driver's license was issued in Kansas.

"Sir, this license expired eleven years ago." The truck rental clerk cemented her smile and I imagined her foot punching the *weirdo alert* button below the counter.

"Why so it has, so it has," Kelly Joe returned the license to his wallet.

"No biggie, I'll be the only driver anyway." I inserted myself between the clerk and Kelly Joe to sign the paperwork. The clerk's jowls twitched and she disappeared in the back room for so long that I expected her to return with the F.B.I. But she emerged with truck keys and an expression to sour honey.

We rented the biggest truck we could drive without a special license. Outside Central Park, we parked it behind a street jackhammer operation. I donated a collection of $20 bills to the workers and they let me redistribute their *Temporary No Parking* signs. At quick glance, our truck seemed to be part of their operation.

Zasu stayed with the truck on Ma'Urth while Kelly Joe and I went for the books. Travel to Maelstrom's Frame is disgusting as well as dangerous. Its air feels like a neglected outhouse smells. I lost count of the number of trips we made, perhaps through the numbing effect of continuous lanyard pain while in Maelstrom's Frame.

We'd get back to Ma'Urth, the pain would ease. We'd dump our packs and duffel bags full of books, grab empty bags, and head back for more while Zasu unpacked our bags and stacked towers of books in the truck. Books tend to organize and each time we returned to Central Park crater, the remaining books had rearranged themselves on the sides of our trail within easy reach.

On the latest trip back to Ma'Urth, when I unshouldered my stuffed backpacks, an orange streak flashed past my feet. "Leon is protecting me but he's staying on Ma'Urth. I guess he doesn't understand where I need the most protection. Or maybe he can't Travel to Maelstrom's Frame."

"He can, but his energy would draw attention to his presence." Kelly Joe grabbed empty duffel bags and we returned to the Park.

I spoke loudly, hoping Leon would take this as an apology for questioning his behavior. "Seems like Leon understands everything we are doing."

"Only he can say for sure."

Every time we returned to Maelstrom's Frame, marching steps sounded closer to our crater. In the distorted echoes of that place, sometimes they marched from one direction and sometimes from another. The howls and clanks of clockwork dogs punctuated the steps.

On the latest trip, as we shouldered our filled backpacks, the lanyard stabbed me so violently that I stumbled and grabbed Kelly Joe's arm. I was surprised to find my shirt dry—with a stab like that, I expected blood. Above us came panting from rusty snapping jaws. The clockwork dogs were so close. The pavement sizzled with the drops of hot oil that they spewed as they galloped.

Damn. Our bags were full but we still had about a hundred books waiting along the trail. We couldn't get them all on this trip. I stuffed a few extra in the waist of my jeans, which made me so stiff I had to tilt backwards to walk.

The edges of the crater erupted with falling rock. Clockwork dogs clattered over the edges and inside, dogs slipping on the steep rubble, which slowed them. They must not sense our location, because they continued down into the crater, below where we stood. Kelly Joe gestured that we should get uphill, pronto. I turned my back to the dogs, then strained to listen for noises that would mean they had changed direction and were headed our way.

A thousand marching steps filled my ears, shook the ground. Boot toes appeared at the lip of the crater and rock avalanches slid around us. Kelly Joe grabbed my arm, ran us to the surface, and Traveled us to one hell of a far Frame. Spinning vision, instant retching, feet sinking in ooze. Then my knees scraped sidewalk outside our truck and books scattered around me. We were back on Ma'Urth.

"That has to be our last trip, we can't go back again," I told Zasu as we helped her stack the latest books. I hated to leave dozens of books behind to face a nasty fate that might someday include coming against us in battle. Still, it was with great relish that I slammed and bolted the truck doors, with thousands of freed books inside. "We can drive this truck to Bedlam, right? That's the safest place for these darlings."

Kelly Joe said, "No. We can't trust their loyalties. Bringing these books might invite evil to Frivolous Bedlam."

I hate reality checks. Kelly Joe was right. We dare not bring these books to Bedlam. They weren't slaves anymore. They joined the allies because my books persuaded them to do so; and, sure, some of these books wanted to protect the free Frames, but many wanted revenge against the enslaver. It doesn't matter what Frame you're from. Revenge is not a stable motivator.

So now what? We needed to stow this treasure and a truck this big was tough to park, much less hide. Should we take it out of the city? Who might we bribe to ignore it? Now that the books were safely locked in one place, it seemed like a vulnerability to keep them in one place.

And was anywhere on Ma'Urth safe for these books? A large number of cops and taxi drivers seemed unusually interested in activities near Central Park, today. Maybe they patrolled for the enemy. Or maybe my imagination was on the fritz after so much time in Maelstrom's domain.

"I know," I said eventually. "Let's get in the cab and I'll explain."

When Zasu opened the rental truck's door, she said with surprise, "Dizzy, you are a welcome visitor!" She slid the curl of fur onto her lap and made room for

Kelly Joe, Leon, and me. As soon as we were settled, I told them my idea, tentatively at first, until Kelly Joe began to nod.

Step 1. Double–park the enormous rental truck in a quiet neighborhood like the deadend streets just north of the United Nations, on the bluff above the East River.

Step 2. Transfer some books to a van/car trunk.

Step 3. Park that van/car in an extended parking lot.

Step 4. Repeat steps 2 and 3 until the rental truck is emptied.

Zasu and Dizzy stayed in the rental truck. Kelly Joe led Leon and I on a swift walk. As we proceeded, I tried to figure how many vans we would need, and whether my savings account could cover so many rentals until we found a longer–term solution for book storage.

Kelly Joe walked on the street side of parked cars. Twice, we had to flatten against the cars to avoid becoming traffic statistics. "I assume there's a reason we're walking in the street?"

"Be mindful of open doors," he said. I thought he meant *look for cars that aren't locked*. Then a van door popped open as we drew near. No one was inside until Kelly Joe climbed behind the wheel and gestured for me to hurry. As soon as I got in the passenger side, he drove back to our rental truck. We crammed the volunteer van full of books then stored it in one of those multi–row stack–parking structures like vending machines for cars.

Does it count as theft if the vehicle is sentient and offers you a ride? When the vehicle alters its own license plates and paint color, does that make it an accessory?

I asked, "Is it your intent to steal all the vans we need?"

Kelly Joe replied, "We steal from thieves. I've requested help from cars that were previously stolen."

A sedan door popped open for us. We drove it back to the rental truck, loaded the trunk with books, stowed the sedan in a parking structure. And so it went, long past dusk.

As Kelly Joe and I packed a minivan, Zasu emerged from the rental truck cab, clutching Dizzy and silently sobbing. Whenever tears hit the cat's fur, Dizzy groomed herself furiously.

"Zasu, what's wrong?"

"I mourn my lost self. This Zasu is a bloodthirsty being who rejoices in the size of Nica's army."

"Don't call the books that. Let's call them our comrades in the fight to restore peace to the free Frames." This settled Zasu and unsettled me. Way too big a part of my ego liked the sound of that: *Nica's army.*

82. THE EVOLUTION OF MEANINGS

We distributed our arsenal of books in long–term parking across much of Manhattan and were down to our last loads of books when a horn tooted, a distinctive razz like a clown imitating a mockingbird. I knew that horn! Sure enough, up the hill roared Hernandez' battered red Toyota pickup.

"Tee has joined us!" This restored Zasu's spirits.

I had time to wonder what Hernandez was doing for transportation if he was back in L.A. but his truck was still in the New Yorks.

Tee triple–parked beside the van we were loading. "Yoo–hoo, Anya needs us. All hands on deck or should I say cab. Hop in." Kelly Joe and I exchanged looks. "Anya sent me, honestly, and it's serious."

"We believe you," I assured Tee. "But this van is parked less than legally and if it gets towed we'll lose irreplaceable cargo."

"I've got cargo space in back," Tee offered.

Yes. Her pickup bed might hold the remaining books. Soon, Tee's pickup bed, the latest volunteer van, Tee's cab, and our laps were full of books—not comfortable, but we managed to empty the giant rental truck.

Kelly Joe got in the van. "I'll catch up," he said, and drove that last cache of books to one final parking structure.

Tee revved her engine. "I can make up the time. Anya, here we come!" She peeled out—in reverse.

Inside Tee's cab, the floorboard books, Zasu, both cats, and I slid into a jumble as Tee accelerated backwards down the hill toward First Avenue. Fortunately, the red pickup changed Frames before she charged into the intersection. She raced us through a Frame without buildings, luminescent in moonlight. Fragrant silver meadows sloped to a shimmering East River that hummed melodically as it flowed. I'd never been anywhere where the East River could be called peaceful; and yet, this Frame felt familiar.

Zasu pressed hands against chest. "My heart swells," she cried, "Please stop this vehicle!"

"No can do. Anya said to hurry." Tee didn't slow down.

"We can take half a minute," I told Tee. Tee's brakes expressed her disapproval. I opened the door for Zasu.

Outside, Zasu stumbled in a circle, arms wide, embracing all: moon and sky as bright as faith, nightingale songs floating on a kiss of a breeze. We were in Halcyon, Zasu's home Frame. This was the first time she'd been home since genocide stranded her as the sole known survivor of the Gumby people.

Zasu dropped to her knees, plowed her arms through the rich soil, inhaled its perfume.

Tee snipped, "It's been ninety–five seconds and she's still playing in the dirt."

I gave Zasu another half a minute, then called, "Anya's waiting."

Zasu stood as though she would return to the pickup, but then spun to stare east, to the far side of the Williamsburg Bridge, which glowed in the moonlight. Zasu exhaled. "Others are here. I am not alone."

Could it be? She sensed the existence of other Gumby people, across the river.

"I must." And she was gone, running, a shooting star across the Williamsburg Bridge.

"That's not our direction. We can't follow her," Tee revved in the dirt. "Now what? Oh. Him."

Tee's shocks sagged as Kelly Joe climbed inside her cab. Tee peeled out, making both doors slam. I explained about Zasu and for the rest of our journey, Kelly Joe stared across the river.

Tee skidded us to a stop in an area of rolling hills just north of Brooklyn Bridge, which was still standing here in Halcyon—although perhaps not for long.

By moonlight, war is ghosts and shadows. A line of allies—mostly Marzipani whose fur gleamed silver tonight—stretched across the entrance to Brooklyn Bridge. Behind them was another line of allies. And another. They brandished metal mesh shields that reflected so much light I had to squint. The light came from headlamps, worn by lines of Lobotomists, marching toward the allies. Between each line of Lobotomists was an empty space and in that space, the light dimmed and flickered. Dimmed, in rains of text. Flickered, as light hit the razor edges of the falling text—a deadly confetti. Enemy soldier books flew between each line of Lobotomists.

The front line of allies threw spears that stopped the front line of Lobotomists, then ignited flamethrowers and raised their shields against the books. They survived the first line of books but their shields took heavy damage and only reflected light in patchwork now. Those damaged shields wouldn't survive a second rain of text, but here came a second line of Lobotomist headlamps. And behind them, a second line of enemy books.

Tee had parked behind a hill. At the top of the hill stood Anwyl and Anya, directing the defense of Brooklyn Bridge. Without warning, Dizzy leaped through Tee's window and raced uphill. She sprang onto Anya's neck and shoulders, biting and scratching. Anya fell down the hill, flailing, with the cat on top of her.

Anwyl reacted fastest. He drew a sword and ran toward Dizzy—who now sat next to Anya and watched the top of the hill, where Anya had stood before the cat attacked her.

In the air above the hill, one of the Entourage hovered in a foot–powered helicopter, just arrived from another Frame. His sunglasses and wide smile glinted in moonlight. He pedaled to rotate two sets of steel blades. The blades on top powered the 'copter. The blades at the base held books suspended by their spines. As the books spun, they dumped volumes of text on the spot where Anya had stood and the text churned the dirt to silver mud. Had Anya remained in position, she would now be shredded.

It seemed that Dizzy had attacked Anya to prevent her assassination.

Kelly Joe yelled, "Stop, Anwyl! The cat saved Anya! Behind you!"

Anwyl spun and threw his sword. It split the 'copter. Before the 'copter hit the ground, the Entourage pilot vanished out of Frame.

When the 'copter fell, its blades snapped, which freed a dozen books. All but one took off across the East River, ignoring squawks from the remaining book. Deserters? The remaining book extended its razor–edged cover and shot toward Anwyl. Anya whipped off her shawl and snapped it at the book, which hit the ground with such force that it spit silver sparks. Kelly Joe put a hard boot on the book and stomped, which snapped the book's spine.

From the Bridge defense came a wail. The first line of shields and then the allies they protected had disintegrated in a rain of text. Lobotomists, their gray hoodies spectral in the moonlight, marched across the remains of those allies toward the second line of defenders, who hurled spears and brandished intact shields, which would protect them—until books reached them. Once again, the enemy's books made all the difference in a battle.

But this time we could respond in kind.

I ran to Tee's truck bed, unzipping my backpack as I went. I dropped the backpack and yelled, "Books! To me." My original books rose from my backpack and hovered beside me as I gave them orders.

They circled the pickup and squawked commands. The books in the truck bed shot into the sky as though ejected by steam jets. The night got very dark as allied books flew to join the battle at Brooklyn Bridge.

On the bridge, the second line of allies were in trouble; their shields were so damaged they no longer glinted. The allies hunkered low and launched spears, preparing for death without surrender.

But it was not their night to die. The allied books flew high and fast to reach the front line of the battle. Briefly, a blanket of shadow blocked moonlight on Brooklyn Bridge and when the moon shadow thinned, the front–most line of Lobotomists was gone, leaving the terrible mush of flesh torn by text. One Lobotomist headlamp lay intact in the ooze, blazing light at an irrelevant angle.

Lobotomists continued to march forward and allies still hunkered beneath shields. Apparently both sides assumed the Lobotomist deaths had been collateral damage: that Maelstrom's books had shed text on the wrong line of fighters.

When a second line of Lobotomists fell, with no Marzipani injuries, the remaining Lobotomists faltered and the allied shields tilted up. The allies sought a better view of what was happening.

I couldn't translate the squawks of the enemy book leaders, yet the evolution of meanings was clear. *Fools, take more care, you killed fellow soldiers. ... More dead?! Are you deaf as well as blind?... We are under attack! Our enemy has books!*

The allies on Brooklyn Bridge were the last to realize that everything had changed. But once they understood, they charged, and attacked with ferocity. The Lobotomists stopped marching in sync. They pivoted, they turned, they ran into text from their own books.

Within minutes, the enemy books and troops were in pieces too small to identify.

The allies on Brooklyn Bridge clutched one another as though confirming they weren't dreaming in this surreal moonlight. Behind me, Tee's horn razzed victory toots. On the hill, Anya and Anwyl watched the allied books intently—yet without any sign of surprise. Beside me, Leon and Dizzy observed the cavorting of the two-legged beings.

I sent congrats to Jenn, wherever she was, beyond the Far Frames.

Kelly Joe shook my shoulders in a *way to go!* and sprinted to the top of the hill, where he clapped a hand on Anwyl's arm and spoke with more animation than I'd ever seen in him. When Anwyl responded, he turned in my direction. I stepped behind Tee. I wasn't ready to face Anwyl with my knowledge. That he stole the sentient lawn chair. That the lanyard warned against him.

The allies streamed from Brooklyn Bridge, cheering. They surrounded the hill, Tee, me. I think we all realized that we got lucky that night—our attack was a surprise and our books happened to outnumber the enemy's. Nonetheless, I added my cheers to the celebration.

We had books. We were ready for war.

#####
The End of Book 2.

ABOUT SUE PERRY

Concert stage, dark except for a deep blue spotlight. Singer drops to one knee and his narration evolves from murmur to rant. "This is the story of a man who got what he wanted but he lost what he had. He got what he wanted but he lost what he had. He –"

It goes on forever. It's mesmerizing. Uncomfortable. Confessional.

Pretty sure this memory is from the time I saw James Brown, decades ago, but the lost identity of the singer isn't the point.

I've spent my life gazing across some fence or other, admiring greener grass over yonder. I've acted on so many impulses to jump the fence. No complaints, but it sure has taken me a long time to appreciate where I'm standing right now. And nowadays that blue spotlight chant fills my head whenever I contemplate a new jump.

Sometimes I jump back.

I was a low–budget television producer until I wrote a psychological thriller, *Was It A Rat I Saw*, which Bantam–Doubleday–Dell published in hardcover in 1992. Soon after that I became the mother of twins, jumped into graduate school, and became a disaster scientist. I dabbled in academia, government research, and consulting.

I stopped writing fiction for nearly two decades, then noticed how much I missed it. I resumed writing novels with the literary fiction *Scar Jewelry*, then began the FRAMES quartet with *Nica of Los Angeles*. Also in the works is another series, a young adult paranormal horror romance, *DDsE*.

Funny. Back in the day, I had a single book idea at a time. Now I'm flooded with them, can't keep up with them, though I write every day.

I live in southern California. I had to leave for five years to confirm this is where I belong. I live with multiple cats, comfortably close to my twins and granddaughter. Like my life paths, my friends and family are all over the damn place. I like to visit them, spend time at the ocean, explore cities, and go out to hear live music.

We can stay connected via social media, where I engage in bursts punctuated with lulls. I'm most active on my blog, Required Writing (sueperryauthor.com), and on Goodreads. You can also find me on Substack, Facebook, Twitter. Hope to hear from you!

Made in the USA
Las Vegas, NV
05 January 2024

83786080R00173